PHARAOH

VALERIO MASSIMO MANFREDI

PHARAOH

Translated from the Italian by Christine Feddersen-Manfredi

MACMILLAN

First published 2008 by Macmillan
an imprint of Pan Macmillan Ltd
Pan Macmillan, 20 New Wharf Road, London NI 9RR
Basingstoke and Oxford
Associated companies throughout the world
www.panmacmillan.com

ISBN 978-0-230-53073-7 HB
ISBN 978-0-230-70401-5 TPB

1 3 5 7 9 8 6 4 2

A CIP catalogue record for this book is available from
the British Library.

Typeset by SetSystems Ltd, Saffron Walden, Essex
Printed and bound in Great Britain by
Mackays of Chatham plc, Chatham, Kent

Visit **www.panmacmillan.com** to read more about all our books
and to buy them. You will also find features, author interviews and
news of any author events, and you can sign up for e-newsletters
so that you're always first to hear about our new releases.

TO MARCELLO, MARZIA, VALERIA AND FLAVIA

This novel was first published in Italian in February 1998, three years before the attack on the Twin Towers of September 11th, 2001.

'And he said, Go forth, and stand upon the mount before the Lord. And, behold, the Lord passed by, and a great and strong wind rent the mountains, and brake in pieces the rocks before the Lord; but the Lord was not in the wind . . .'

I Kings 19:11

1

Jerusalem

*On the ninth day of the fourth month in the eighteenth year of
the reign of Nebuchadnezzar, King of Babylon*

In the eleventh year of the reign of Zedekiah, King of Judah

THE PROPHET TURNED TOWARDS the valley, overhung with the
smoke of countless fires, then raised his eyes to the empty sky
and sighed. Trenches surrounded Zion; battle rams and machines
of siege threatened its walls. In the ravaged houses children cried,
begging for bread, but there was no one left to break it for them.
Those who once looked after them had been driven out onto the
streets, consumed by hunger, only to collapse in the city squares.

'It's over,' said the prophet, turning to his companion, who
followed close behind him. 'It's over, Baruch. If the King doesn't
listen to me there will be no salvation for his House, nor for the
House of God. I know I must try to convince him, but I'm afraid
all hope has gone.'

As they made their way down deserted roads, the prophet
stopped to let by a group of dry-eyed people transporting a coffin
with a grim, quick step. The pale colour of the shroud that
wrapped the corpse shone in the darkness. He watched them for
a while as they scurried down the road leading to the cemetery
the King had opened along the city walls which could no longer

hold the cadavers that war and famine produced every day in such great numbers.

'Prophet, why has the Lord our God chosen to uphold Nebuchadnezzar of Babylon and allow all the nations to suffer under his iron yoke?' asked Baruch as they set forth again. 'Why does He stand behind one who is already so strong?'

They were close to the palace now, near the Tower of David. The prophet walked into the open square and then glanced back as the moon rent an opening in the clouds and illuminated the silent mass of Solomon's Temple. His sorrowful eyes beheld the moonlight touching the great columns, shining on the sea of bronze and on its golden pinnacles. He thought of the solemn rites which had been celebrated for so many centuries in that square, of the crowds that had thronged there on feast days, of the smoke of the sacrifices that had risen up to the Lord from its altars. He knew in his heart that it was all over, that the Temple was destined to lie abandoned and silent for many years or for many centuries, and he struggled to hold back his tears.

Baruch nudged him. 'Rabbi, we must go. It's late.'

THE KING was still awake, despite the late hour, and had called the heads of his army and his ministers to council. The prophet walked towards him and all turned at the sound of his cane striking the stone floor.

'You asked to see me,' said the King. 'What do you have to say?'

'Surrender,' said the prophet, coming to a stop directly in front of him. 'Dress in sackcloth, cover your head with ashes and leave the city barefoot. Prostrate yourself at your enemy's feet and beg his pardon. The Lord has spoken to me, and He said, "I deliver my country to the hands of Nebuchadnezzar, King of Babylon, my servant, I deliver unto him even the cattle from my fields." You have no choice, My King. Surrender to him and implore his clemency. Perhaps he will spare your family and perhaps he will spare the House of God.'

The King lowered his head and was silent. He was gaunt and pale, with dark, hollow circles under his eyes.

'He is the heart of his nation,' thought the prophet as he waited for Zedekiah's response, 'and he knows how numerous are the defences his people have raised to defend him: borders and garrisons, ramparts and forts. So when the enemy finally arrives at his door, his despair and his horror must know no bounds. His agony must be immense. Worse than that of the poorest and most humble of his subjects, who has always known he was naked.'

'I will not surrender,' said the King, raising his head. 'I cannot believe that the Lord our God has truly spoken with you and has truly told you to deliver His people into the hands of a foreign tyrant, an idol-worshipper. I am more inclined to believe that it was a servant of the King of Babylon or the tyrant himself who spoke to you, and corrupted your heart. You speak out in favour of the enemy invader and against your own king, anointed by the Lord.'

'You lie!' the prophet cried in disdain. 'Nebuchadnezzar put his trust in you. He made you the shepherd of his people in the land of Israel. It was you who betrayed him. You who plotted secretly with the Egyptians, who once held Israel in slavery!'

The King did not react to the prophet's words. He turned towards the window and seemed to be listening to a low rumble of thunder. The clouds had clamped down on the walls of Zion and the Great Temple was now just a shadow in the dark. He wiped his damp brow with his hand while thunder crashed over the desert of Judah.

Total silence fell again, because there were no longer dogs or birds or any other animals in Jerusalem. Famine had devoured them all. And the women had been forbidden to weep for their dead so that the city would not resound with their perpetual wailing.

The King suddenly spoke. 'We have always had to fight for the land the Lord has given us, crushed as we are between powerful enemies. A land continually torn from us and yet which we must perennially, desperately, reclaim as our own. And each time we must stain our hands with blood.'

The King's face was as pale as a corpse's, but his eyes seemed for a moment to burn with his dreams. 'If He had given us another place, remote and secure, laden with fruit and with cattle, protected by the mountains and unknown to the other nations of the earth, would I have had to plot with the Pharaoh? Would I have needed his help to free my people from the yoke of Babylon? Answer me!' he demanded. 'And be quick, because time has run out.'

The prophet looked at him and saw that all was lost. 'I have nothing more to say to you,' he replied. 'The task of a true prophet is to invoke peace. But you dare to challenge the will of the Lord. You pretend to tempt the Lord your God! Farewell, Zedekiah. You have refused to listen to me and thus darkness will henceforth mark your way.'

He turned to his companion and said, 'Let us go, Baruch. There are no ears here for my words.'

The King listened to the sound of the prophet's cane tapping away through the pillared atrium and dissolving into silence. He looked at his counsellors and saw the terror in their eyes, the exhaustion brought on by their long vigil.

'The time has come,' he said. 'We can wait no longer. Put into action the plan that we've prepared. Assemble the army in the utmost silence. Hand out the last rations, for the men will need all their energy.'

At that moment, an officer of the guard appeared. 'King,' he said, 'the breach is nearly open. A unit under Ethan's command is about to leave from the eastern gate to make a sally as planned and divert the enemy's attention. It's time.'

Zedekiah nodded. He took off his royal mantle and put on his armour, hanging his sword at his hip. 'We shall go now,' he said.

He was followed by the queen mother, Hamutal, his wives,

his eunuchs, his sons Eliel, Achis and Amasai, and the chiefs of his army.

They descended the stairs to the women's quarters and from there entered the palace garden. A group of stone-cutters had nearly finished opening a breach in the wall near the pool of Siloah and two men had been sent out to explore the area to make sure that their passage would be unhindered.

The King waited for the last stones to be removed and was the first to go through. From the valley rose a hot, dry wind that had crossed the desert and he leaned back for a moment against the stones of the wall, trying to overcome the anguish that was suffocating him. The officers hurriedly ushered out the others, directing them to sheltered positions behind the rocks.

In the distance a trumpet blast suddenly sounded, followed by the clash of battle. Ethan had attacked the Babylonian siege line and horns blared throughout the valley to call Nebuchadnezzar's men to the ranks. King Zedekiah felt encouraged: perhaps the sacrifice of his men would not be in vain, and he would be able to pass the enemy lines unharmed and reach the desert, where he would be safe. Shortly after, a light flashed down in the valley, swinging three times to the right and three times to the left.

'The signal, finally!' said the army commander. 'The way is clear. We can proceed.'

The password was relayed to the other officers, so they in turn could instruct their soldiers. The order for departure was given.

The King marched at the centre of the line and with him his oldest sons: Eliel, his firstborn, who was twelve, and Achis, who was nine. The youngest, Amasai, was only five, and the King's aide-de-camp carried him in his arms to keep him from crying and alerting any enemy spies in the vicinity to their flight.

They reached the bottom of the valley and the commander turned his ear towards the east. 'Ethan fights on,' he said. 'Perhaps we will be safe after all. May the Lord give him strength and give strength to the heroes fighting at his side. Onward now, quickly. We have to move as fast as we can.'

They turned south towards Hebron, with the intention of reaching Beersheba and from there escaping into Egypt. King Zedekiah was followed by about 1,500 men, all those who were still capable of bearing arms.

But Ethan's troops, exhausted and famished as they were, could not hold out for long under the counterattack of the Babylonians, so numerous, well fed and well armed; they were soon routed and massacred. Many of them were taken alive and tortured to death. One, his will broken by agonizing pain, revealed Zedekiah's plan, and Nebuchadnezzar was immediately informed.

He was sleeping in his pavilion on a scarlet-draped bed, surrounded by his concubines, when an officer sent by his commander, Nebuzaradan, awoke him.

The King got out of bed and called his eunuchs to dress him. The officer was instructed to bring his armour and prepare the war chariot.

'Call my guard,' he ordered. 'I shall not wait here for Nebu-zaradan's return. Tell him to go directly to the valley of Hebron. I shall wait for him in Riblah.'

The officer bowed and left to attend to the King's orders.

A short time later, Nebuchadnezzar left his pavilion and mounted his chariot. The charioteer cracked his whip and the entire squadron followed in a column, raising a dense cloud of dust.

Towards the west the clouds had dispersed and the pale light of dawn wavered in the sky. The song of the larks rose towards the sun as it slowly cleared the horizon. The Judaean prisoners were being impaled. Their commander, Ethan, in recognition of the great valour he had shown, was crucified.

WHEN KING ZEDEKIAH reached the plain of Hebron, the sun had already climbed high in the sky. He sat in the shade of a palm tree to drink a little water and eat some bread and salted olives together with his men. His officers had gone off to look for horses, mules and camels in the stables of the city, to enable them to cover ground more quickly.

When he had eaten, the king turned to the army commander. 'How long do you think it will take my servants to find enough animals to get us to Beersheba? My sons are exhausted and they cannot walk much longer.'

The commander began to answer, but suddenly fell still, listening to a distant sound like thunder.

'Do you hear it too, My King?'

'It's the storm that was approaching Jerusalem last night.'

'No, sire, those clouds are over the sea now. This is not the voice of the storm . . .'

While he pronounced these words his face filled with dismay and terror as he spied the war chariots of Babylon at the top of the high plain that rose above the city.

'My King,' he cried, 'all is lost. All we can do now is die like men with our swords in our hands.'

'I will not die,' said Zedekiah. 'I have to save the throne of Israel and my sons. Bring me some horses, immediately, and have the army drawn up. The Lord will fight at your side and tonight you will join me, victorious, at the oasis of Beersheba. The queen mother and my wives will wait here. They will travel much more comfortably with you on your journey to Beersheba.'

The commander did as he was ordered and drew up the army, but his men felt their knees buckle under as hundreds of chariots flew at them at great speed, as they saw the glittering blades protruding from the axles which would cut them to pieces. The ground trembled as if shaken by an earthquake and the air filled with the whinnies of thousands of horses and the din of bronze wheels.

Some of the soldiers looked back and caught sight of their King riding off, and shouted, 'The King is escaping! The King is abandoning us!'

7

The army instantly scattered and broke up, the men running in every direction. The Babylonian warriors gave chase in their chariots as if they were hunting wild animals in the desert. They ran them through with their lances or pierced them with their arrows as if they were gazelles or antelopes.

The Babylonian commander, Nebuzaradan, watched and waited. Without warning, he swiftly took off after Zedekiah as the King of Judah fled on horseback with his sons, holding the youngest one tightly against his chest. Nebuzaradan raised his standard high as he rode and a group of chariots enlarged into a semicircle in response to his signal, abandoning the hunt to go after the runaways on the plain.

Zedekiah was soon surrounded and forced to stop. The Babylonian warriors brought him before Nebuzaradan, who had him put in chains, along with his sons. They were given nothing to eat or drink, and were not allowed to rest. The King was dragged through the plain littered with the corpses of his soldiers; he was forced to march alongside those who had been captured and taken prisoner, and was made to face the scorn and hate they felt for him because he had abandoned them.

The column of chariots turned north towards Riblah, where King Nebuchadnezzar awaited them. Zedekiah was brought before the King with his sons. The oldest, Eliel, tried to console little Amasai, who was wailing desperately, his face smeared with snot, dust and tears.

Zedekiah prostrated himself with his face to the ground. 'I implore you, Great King. My inexperience and weakness made me fall prey to the promises and the threats of the King of Egypt and I betrayed your trust. Do with me what you will, but spare my sons. They are innocent children. Take them to Babylon with you. Allow them to grow in the light of your splendour and they will serve you faithfully.'

Prince Eliel cried out, 'Get up, Father! Rise, O King of Israel. Do not soil your forehead in the dust! We do not fear this tyrant's rage. Do not humiliate yourself for us.'

The King of Babylon sat in the shade of a sycamore on a cedar-wood throne, his feet resting on a silver stool. His beard, curled in ringlets, fell to his chest and on his head he wore a tiara set with precious stones.

It was hot, but the King was not sweating. Though a breeze arose from time to time his beard and his hair and even his clothing were as still as a statue's. The King of Jerusalem lay at his feet with his brow in the dust but Nebuchadnezzar's gaze was fixed on the horizon, as if he were sitting alone in the middle of the desert.

He said nothing, nor did he give any signal, but his servants moved as if he had spoken, as if he had given them precise orders.

Two of them grabbed Zedekiah by the arms and lifted him, and a third seized his hair from behind so that he could not hide his face. Another took Prince Eliel, dragged him in front of his father and forced the boy to his knees, pinning his arms behind him and planting a foot in the small of his back. Not a sigh escaped the young prince; he begged for no pity. He pressed his lips together as the executioner approached him, brandishing his sword, but he did not close his eyes. And his eyes were still open when his head, severed from his body, rolled to his father's feet.

Zedekiah, crushed in horror, was overcome by a convulsive shuddering, swamped in a bloody sweat which dripped from his forehead and his eyes and ran down his neck. A deranged, uncontrollable hiccuping rose from his gut and his eyes wheeled around in their sockets, as if trying to escape the sight of that motionless trunk pouring and pouring out blood and drenching the dust. The desperate howl of young Amasai tore through his soul and his flesh, as Nebuchadnezzar's servants took the second of his sons, Prince Achis.

He was little more than a child, but the sight of that abomination had tempered his soul like steel, or perhaps the Lord God of Israel Himself was holding His hand over that innocent head. The executioner's sabre swung down on his neck as well, and his body collapsed, his blood mixing with that of his brother.

Amasai was too small to be decapitated and so the king's servant slashed the boy's throat like a lamb's sacrificed on the altar on the first day of Pesach. The blade turned his wailing into a gurgle and his small lifeless limbs paled in the dust. His lips turned purple and his eyes, still full of tears, grew glassy and dull as life fled his body.

Zedekiah, drained of his voice and his strength, seemed to crumple to the ground, but then suddenly, with an abrupt burst of energy, he sprang from the hands of his guards and, grabbing a knife from one of their belts, rushed at Nebuchadnezzar. The sovereign did not move; he remained immobile on his cedarwood throne, with his hands resting on its arms, while his servants seized Zedekiah and tied him to the trunk of a palm tree. The executioner approached, grabbed his hair with one hand to pull his head fast against the tree and with the dagger in his other hand gouged out both of his eyes.

Zedekiah was engulfed in a red flame and then sank into endless darkness. As consciousness abandoned him, he remembered the words of the prophet. He realized that from then on, he would walk in a place infinitely more horrifying than death and that never again, as long as he lived, would he be able to feel tears running down his cheeks.

King Nebuchadnezzar – his will having been carried out – had Zedekiah put in chains and began the journey to Babylon.

THE PROPHET reached Riblah the next night. He travelled little-known paths to succeed in crossing enemy lines. As he journeyed through the night, he saw the maimed corpses of the soldiers of Israel impaled on sharp poles. Ethan's body was hanging from a cross, covered by a flock of crows and surrounded by starving dogs that had bared his bones up to his knees.

The prophet's soul was already filled to the brim with this horror when he reached Riblah, but when he saw the mangled and unburied bodies of the young princes, and when he learned that the king had been forced to witness their suffering before his eyes were put out, he sank into the dust and gave himself over to despair. In that atrocious moment he could think only of the endless affliction that his people had always had to suffer for having been chosen by God. He wondered how the Lord could have placed so intolerable a burden on the shoulders of Israel while other nations living in idolatry enjoyed infinite wealth, comfort and power. And these nations were the very instrument which God had chosen to punish the unfortunate descendants of Abraham.

And in that moment of profound discouragement the prophet was shaken by doubt. He thought that it would be better for his people to forget that they had ever existed, better to mix among the other peoples of the earth like a drop of water in the sea, to disappear rather than to suffer, generation after generation, the burning pain of the scourge of God.

He set off without having taken anything to eat or drink, his eyes filled with tears, his soul as dry as the desert stones.

NEBUZARADAN entered Jerusalem some days later with his troops and he settled into the royal palace with his officers, his eunuchs and his concubines. He had kept several of Zedekiah's concubines found at Hebron or left behind in the palace for himself; others he had distributed among his men. The rest were sent to Babylon to be used as prostitutes in the Temple of Astarte. The queen mother, Hamutal, was treated with the honour her rank deserved and was housed near the Damascus Gate.

For more than a month, nothing happened: Nebuzaradan's servants combed the city to hold a census of all the surviving inhabitants, taking special note of blacksmiths and farriers. The population began once again to hope, because the farmers were allowed to bring food into the city, which could be bought at high prices. No one, however, was allowed to leave, The gates were guarded day and night, and those few who had tried to escape by dropping ropes down the sides of the city walls were captured and crucified on the spot, so that they would serve as an example to the others.

The elders did not share in the people's hope; they were certain the worst was yet to come. Inevitable punishment loomed frighteningly, unknown and menacing.

One night Baruch was wakened by a Temple servant. 'Get up,' the man told him. 'The prophet wants you to meet him at the bean vendor's house.'

Baruch understood the meaning of the message. His master had used it on other occasions when they needed to meet in isolated surroundings, protected from watchful eyes.

He dressed, put on his belt and walked through the dark, deserted city. He took a secret route, going through the houses of trusted friends or walking on the rooftops or along underground tunnels to avoid the patrols of Babylonian soldiers making their rounds.

He reached the assigned meeting place, a house falling into ruins that had belonged to a bean vendor at the time of King Jehoiakim and had then been abandoned because the man had no heirs.

The prophet emerged from the darkness. 'May the Lord protect you, Baruch,' he said. 'Follow me. A long journey awaits us.'

'But Rabbi,' protested Baruch, 'let me go home to get a knapsack and some provisions. I didn't know we were leaving.'

The prophet said, 'There's no time, Baruch. We have to leave now. The ire of the King of Babylon is about to be unleashed on the city and on the Temple. Quickly, follow me.'

He swiftly crossed the street and started up a little road that led to the Temple. The immense building appeared in front of them as they turned into the square that flanked its western wall.

The prophet turned to make sure that Baruch was following, then set off down another little road which seemed to lead away from the square. He stopped at a doorstep and knocked. They heard scuttling within and then a man opened the door. The prophet greeted him and blessed him. The man took a lantern and led them down a hallway into the house.

At the end of the hallway were a number of stairs cut into the rock that led underground. At the bottom, their guide stopped. He scraped the ground with a shovel, uncovering an iron ring and a trapdoor. He inserted the shovel handle into the ring and pulled. The trapdoor lifted, revealing more stairs, even darker and narrower than the first. A puff of air arose from the opening, stirring the lantern's flame.

'Farewell, Rabbi,' said the man. 'May the Lord assist you.'

The prophet took the lamp from his hand and began to descend the stairs, but before long a distant cry was heard, and then another, and soon the underground passage rang with a chorus of shrieks, muffled by the thick walls of the ancient house.

Startled, Baruch turned around.

'Do not look back,' said the prophet. 'The Lord our God has turned away from our people. He has withdrawn His gaze from Zion and has given us over to His enemies.' His voice trembled and the lamplight transformed his features into a mask of suffering. 'Follow me. There is no more time.'

Baruch followed him and the trapdoor slammed behind them.

'How will that man find his way back?' he asked. 'We have his lantern.'

'He'll find the way,' answered the prophet. 'He's blind.'

The passageway was so narrow that sometimes they had to turn sideways, and so low that they often had to bend and stoop. Baruch felt suffocated as if he had been closed up alive in a tomb, and his heart beat wildly in his chest. The sense of oppression was intolerable, but he followed the even step of the prophet, who seemed to know every foot of that secret passage in the bowels of the earth.

Finally, the dimness began to ease and they soon found themselves in an underground chamber. Light flickered through an iron grille in the ceiling.

'We're inside the old cistern under the portico in the inner courtyard,' he said. 'Come now, we're almost there.'

He walked to the end of the large room and opened a small door that led to a passageway as dark and narrow as the first. Baruch tried to understand in what direction they were heading, and he suddenly realized that his master was leading him towards the heart of the Temple itself, sacred and forbidden, the resting place of the God of the Multitudes! They went up a rough staircase, at the top of which the prophet pushed aside a slab of stone then turned to him.

'Follow me now,' he said, 'and do what I tell you.'

Baruch looked around and his heart swelled with astonishment and awe. He was inside the Sanctuary, behind the linen veil that covered the Glory of the Lord! Before him was the Ark of the Covenant and on it were two kneeling golden cherubs whose wings held up the invisible throne of the Most High.

The cries of anguish from the city were much clearer and closer now, magnified by the echoes filling the deserted porticoes of those immense courtyards.

'Take all of the sacred vessels,' instructed the prophet. 'They must not be profaned. Put them into the basket you'll find in that cupboard. I'll do the same.'

They gathered up the vessels and, crossing the small space of the Sanctuary, brought them to another room, where the High Priest customarily lodged.

'Now we must return,' said the prophet. 'We will take the Ark with us.'

'The Ark?' exclaimed Baruch. 'But we'll never manage to carry it away!'

'Nothing is impossible for the Lord,' said the prophet. 'Come now, help me. When we return we'll find two pack animals waiting for us.'

They went back into the Sanctuary, put acacia wood poles into the rings of the Ark and lifted it, with considerable effort. By now the cries were filling the Temple's outer courtyards, and they had become the inebriated shouts of foreigners drunk on wine and on blood. The prophet walked with difficulty, because his limbs no longer had the vigour of youth and the sacred relic of the Exodus was heavy with wood and gold.

Baruch was not surprised when he saw, in the room where they had left the sacred vessels, two donkeys with pack saddles tied to a ring which hung from the wall.

The prophet goaded them with a stick and they began to pull with such strength that the ring was nearly jerked out of the wall. The two men heard a click and part of the wall turned around on itself, uncovering another dark passage that led underground. The prophet untied the two animals, put one in front of the other and linked the two pack saddles with the poles that supported the Ark. He fastened the Ark to this makeshift base and arranged the sacred vessels in the bags hanging from the saddles.

'You follow last,' he said to Baruch. 'Make sure we don't lose anything and close the passages which I'll have opened. We still have a long journey in the dark ahead of us, but at the end we will be safe. These animals will not betray us. They are used to walking underground.'

They started down the passage and began to descend a ramp dug into the rock and completely immersed in darkness. They proceeded very slowly and Baruch could hear his companion's cane tapping as he explored the ground in front of him at every step.

The air was perfectly still and reeked with the penetrating stench of bat excrement.

Time passed and the ramp became almost completely horizontal; the passage must have reached the level of the valley under the city.

They walked in silence for nearly the whole night until, as dawn was breaking, they found a stone wall in front of them filtering the first light of the new day. Baruch moved the stones one by one so that the little procession could cross to the other side, where they found themselves in a small cave.

'Where are we, Rabbi?' he asked.

'We're safe now,' answered the prophet. 'We've passed the Babylonian siege lines. The road for Hebron and Beersheba is not far away. Wait here and do not move. Put the stones back in place so no one will realize we've passed this way. I'll be back soon.'

He left and Baruch did as he had been ordered. When he finished he peered out of the cave's opening, hidden from sight by broom and tamarisk bushes, and saw his companion, who waved for him to come out. At the side of the path was a cart full of straw. Baruch emerged and hid the Temple vessels and the Ark under the straw, then yoked the donkeys. They then got onto the cart, two simple farmers setting off for their fields, and continued their journey.

They took out-of-the-way paths and overgrown mule tracks, avoiding roads and villages until they reached the desert.

The prophet seemed to be following a route well known to him, with a precise itinerary. He would stop at times to observe the countryside, or step off the cart and climb up the side of a hill or a mountain ridge to get an overview, only to clamber back down and continue on his way. Baruch watched as he covered barren hilltops with his quick step, as he climbed heaps of black flint scorched by the sun, as he trod fearlessly through the domain of scorpions and serpents.

They spent six days and six nights practically without speaking, their hearts oppressed by the thought of the destiny of Jerusalem and her people, until they reached a gorge carved by a wide torrent. Two completely barren mountain ridges rose to their right and left. Deep greyish-white furrows in the hillsides were dotted with spare, spindly desert thorn bushes.

Baruch suddenly noticed, on the left, a cliff with a strange pyramid-like shape, a shape so perfect and so cleanly carved that it seemed a man-made object.

'I'm afraid we'll find neither water nor food ahead, Rabbi,' he said. 'Are we still far from our destination?'

'No,' answered the prophet. 'We've nearly arrived.' He pulled the donkeys' reins.

'Arrived . . . where?' asked Baruch.

'At the sacred mountain. Mount Sinai.'

Baruch widened his eyes. 'Sinai . . . is here?'

'Yes, but you won't see it. Help me to load the Ark and the sacred vessels onto one of the donkeys. I'll walk him by the halter. You stay here with the other donkey. Wait one day and one night for me. If I haven't returned by then, you head back alone.'

'But Rabbi, if you don't return, the Ark will never be found again and our people will have lost it forever.'

The prophet lowered his head. The desert was immersed in the most complete silence. Not a single creature could be seen moving as far as the eye could see over the endless rocky plain. Only an eagle wheeled through the sky in wide circles, letting himself be carried by the wind.

'And if this were so? The Lord will make it arise from the depths of the earth when the moment comes to guide our people towards their last destiny. But now my task is to bring it back to its place of origin. Do not dare to follow me, Baruch. Since the time of the Exodus, the true location of the sacred mountain has been revealed only to one man in every generation, and only one man in every four generations has been allowed to return there. The last before me was Elijah. I alone, the first since the time of the Exodus, will be given access to the most secret place of the whole earth, where I will hide the Ark.

'If it is God's will, you will see me return after one day and one night. If you don't see me return, it means that my life is the price that the Lord our God has demanded for safeguarding the secret. Do not move from here, Baruch, for any reason, and do not attempt to follow me, because you are forbidden from treading this land. Help me, now.'

Baruch helped him to load up the donkey which seemed the stronger and covered the pack with his cloak.

'But Rabbi, how will you manage on your own? You are weak. You're no longer young enough to—'

'The Lord will give me strength. Farewell, my good friend.'

The prophet set off through the desolate expanse of stones between the two mountain ridges and Baruch stood motionless under the burning sun to watch him. As the prophet walked away, Baruch understood why he had wanted to take just one donkey with him and leave the cart behind. The prophet chose the stones on which he placed his feet so that no trace of his passage would remain. Baruch was afraid. The foremost symbol of the existence of Israel was travelling towards an unknown destination and would perhaps vanish forever. He watched with dismay as his master became smaller and smaller, until he completely disappeared from sight.

THE PROPHET walked alone through the desolate wasteland. He trod the realm of poisonous snakes and scorpions and he felt the burning eye of God delving into his innermost being. He reached a point at which the valley opened up and was dominated by a mountain on the right that looked like a crouching sphinx and by another on the left that looked like a pyramid. Suddenly a furious wind struck him, nearly knocking him over, and he had to grip the donkey's halter tightly to stop it from running off.

He struggled forward against the wind until fatigue and the pain tormenting his soul cast him into a kind of delirium. He felt the ground tremble beneath him as if shaken by an earthquake, then felt as if he were being enveloped in bursts of flame that were devouring him. He had known that this would happen, for it had once happened to Elijah.

As if in a dream, the prophet abruptly found himself at the mouth of a cave at the foot of a barren, sun-scorched mountain, and he began to climb to its peak. Midway up the mountain, he found a figure carved into the rock which represented a staff and a serpent. He turned to scan the valley and clearly found what he was looking for at the bottom, a line of stones tracing out a rectangular shape. That etching and those stones made him sure that he found himself in the most humble and secret place in Israel: the site where God had first chosen his dwelling place among men.

He made his way back down to the entrance of the cave, took a flint blade and began to dig inside the cave until he found a slab which covered a ramp buried under a fine white powder. With immense effort, he unloaded first the Ark, which he deposited in a niche carved into the stone, and then the sacred vessels. He was about to turn back when he slipped and bumped against the wall which closed off the underground tunnel. He heard an echo, as if there were an opening on the other side. Afraid that someone might find another way into this hiding place, he lit a pitch torch and secured it into a crack in the wall so he could have a little light. He took the flint blade he had been digging with and hit the wall repeatedly. He could hear the echo growing stronger and stronger. Suddenly he heard a sharp click and then a loud crash. The wall caved in and he was dragged downwards as if in a landslide, and he thought, blinded by the dust and half buried in the rubble, that his final hour had come.

When he opened his eyes and the dust had settled, his expression contracted into a grimace of horror, because he saw what he would not have wanted to see for anything in the world. He bellowed out in desperation and his voice emerged from the mouth of the underground chamber like the roar of a wild beast caught in a trap, resounding off the naked, solitary peaks of the Mountain of God.

BARUCH AWOKE with a start, certain that he had heard a cry: the voice of his master, broken with tears. And he remained awake to pray.

The next day, since his master had not returned, he turned back across the desert, heading towards Beersheba and then Hebron. He entered Jerusalem the same way he had left it.

The city was empty!

All of the inhabitants had been torn from their homes and taken away by the Babylonians. The Temple had been burned to the ground, the royal palace demolished, the mighty walls of the ancient Jebusite fortress dismantled stone by stone.

He waited, nonetheless, counting the days that the prophet had been missing and trying to calculate how long it might take him to find his way back, until one day he reappeared, thin and ragged, at the bean vendor's house.

Baruch approached him and grasped at his tattered robe. 'Rabbi,' he cried, 'we have seen the destruction of Zion! The city once so full of people is empty, its princes gone!'

The prophet turned to face him and Baruch was shocked. His face was scorched, his hands cut and wounded. He had a crazed look in his eyes, as though he had been hurled into the depths of Sheol alive. It was not the sight of the annihilation of Jerusalem – a consequence of the Lord's will, after all – that had plunged him into such grim desperation; it was something else, something that he had seen up there on the mountain. Something so terrible that the destruction of their entire nation, the uprooting and exile of its people, the slaughter of its princes, no longer mattered.

'Rabbi, what did you see in the desert? What has driven you into this state?'

The prophet turned towards the night advancing from the north. 'It all comes to ... nothing,' he muttered. 'I know now that we are alone. Complete solitude without beginning and without end, without place, without purpose or cause ...'

He tried to walk off, but Baruch was still holding him by his sleeve. 'Rabbi, I beg of you, tell me where you have hidden the

Ark of the Lord! I know that one day He will call his people from their exile in Babylon. I obeyed your orders, Rabbi, and I did not follow your steps, but tell me now where you've hidden it, I beg of you . . .'

The prophet's eyes were full of darkness and tears. 'It's all useless. But if one day the Lord shall call someone, he must walk beyond the pyramid and beyond the sphinx, he must cross wind, earthquake and fire until the Lord shows him where it is hidden. But it will not be you, Baruch. And perhaps no one. Ever. I have seen what no one was ever meant to see.'

The prophet pulled free of Baruch's grasp and walked off, soon disappearing behind a heap of rubble. Baruch watched him in the distance and noted his strange rolling gait. One of the prophet's feet was bare! He ran after him, but when he reached the other side of the ruin the prophet had vanished, and as long and as hard as he looked, Baruch could not find him.

He never saw him again.

2

Chicago

United States of America, 24 December 1998

WILLIAM BLAKE COULD barely get his eyes open. The acid taste
in his mouth was familiar, the result of another restless night of
tranquillizer-induced sleep and poor digestion. He dragged himself into the bathroom. The harsh neon light above the mirror
revealed a greenish complexion, sunken eyes and tousled hair.
He stuck out his tongue. It was coated with a white fur and he
closed his mouth with a grimace of disgust. He felt like crying.

A hot shower eased the cramps in his stomach and muscles,
but washed away his remaining energy. He slipped down to the
floor nearly unconscious, and lay under the steaming downpour
for long minutes. Then, with a supreme effort, he reached up
towards the tap and turned it to cold. The water spurted out in a
freezing stream and he was jerked to his feet as if he had been
whipped; he tried to bear it for long enough to regain a lucid
mind, an upright position and an awareness of the misery he had
been plunged into.

He dried himself vigorously with a bath towel, then turned
back to the mirror. He carefully lathered his face, shaved and
applied an expensive lotion, one of the few reminders of his past
lifestyle. Then, like a warrior putting on his armour, he chose a
jacket and trousers, a shirt and tie, socks and shoes, considering a

number of combinations before he settled on what he would wear.

He had nothing in his stomach when he poured a shot of bourbon into his boiling black coffee and gulped down a few mouthfuls. This potion would have to do instead of his usual Prozac this morning; he was determined to face the last stations of his own personal cross-carrying expedition, scheduled for today, on willpower alone: the session with the judge that would confirm his divorce from Judy O'Neil, then his afternoon appointment with the rector and dean of the Oriental Institute, who were expecting his resignation.

The telephone rang as he was about to leave and Blake lifted the receiver.

'Will,' said the voice on the other end. It was Bob Olsen, one of the few friends he had left since fate had turned her back on him.

'Hi, Bob. Nice of you to call.'

'I was just leaving, but I couldn't go without saying goodbye. I'm having lunch with my old man in Evanston to wish him a merry Christmas and then I'm off to Cairo.'

'Lucky you,' said Blake in a lifeless voice.

'Don't take it so hard. We'll let a few months go by, things will quieten down on their own and we'll talk about the whole thing again. The board will have to re-examine your case. They'll have to listen to your reasoning.'

'What reasoning? There are no reasons. I have no witnesses, nothing.'

'Listen, you have to get back on your feet again. You have to fight this. You can do it. You know, in Egypt I should be completely free to move around. I'll try to get some information. Whenever I'm not working I'll find out whatever I can. If I meet someone who can testify that it wasn't your doing, I'll bring him back here, even if I have to pay their fare myself.'

'Thanks, Bob, but I don't think there's much you can do. Still, thanks anyway. Have a good trip.'

'So – I can leave without worrying about you?'

'Oh, sure. You don't have to worry about me . . .' He hung up, took his cup of coffee and walked out onto the street.

A bell-ringing Santa Claus greeted him on the snowy pavement, along with a gust of bitterly cold wind that must have licked the entire icy surface of the lake from north to south. He reached his car, which was parked a couple of blocks down, still holding the steaming cup of coffee in his hand, got in and headed downtown. The shopping district was splendidly decked out for the holidays: the bare trees had been covered with thousands of tiny lights, looking like a miraculous out-of-season blossoming. He lit a cigarette and enjoyed the warmth as the car began to heat up, the music on the radio and the scent of tobacco, whisky and coffee.

These modest pleasures gave him a little courage; made him think that his luck would have to change. After all, once you hit bottom, there's nowhere to go but up. And somehow, doing things that his health-fanatic wife had prohibited all those years all at once – like drinking on an empty stomach and smoking in the car – made the terrible regret he felt at losing both the woman he still loved so intensely and the work he couldn't imagine living without seem just about bearable.

HIS WIFE, Judy, was looking very elegant, perfectly made up and coifed, just like when he used to take her out to dinner at Charlie Trotter's, her favourite restaurant, or to a concert at Orchestra Hall. In a sudden flush of anger, he thought that in just a week or two – or a couple of days, for hell's sake – she'd be using her wiles – her low necklines, her voice, that way she had of crossing her legs – to entice someone else, to get herself invited out to dinner and to bed.

And he couldn't help but imagine what she'd do in bed, with this someone else, and imagining it, thought that she'd be better than she had ever been with him. All this while the judge told them to be seated and asked whether there was any chance of reconciling the differences that had led to their separation.

He would have liked to say yes, that for him nothing had changed, that he loved her as much as the first time he'd seen her, that his life would be loathsome without her, that he missed her dreadfully, that he would have thrown himself at her feet and begged her not to leave him, that the night before he had found, forgotten at the back of a drawer, one of her slips and that he had gathered it to his face to breathe in her scent, that he couldn't give a shit about his dignity, that he would let her walk all over him if only she came back.

Instead he said, 'The terms of the separation have been duly considered and accepted by each one of us, Your Honour. Both of us agree in requesting this divorce.'

Judy nodded, and then each of them signed the divorce papers and the alimony agreement, which was completely unrealistic as he hadn't worked in months and his resignation would be officially accepted in a few hours' time.

They took the elevator together and descended for two unnerving minutes. Blake would have liked to say something fitting, something important. Something that she would never be able to forget. As the floor numbers followed each other relentlessly on the panel, he realized that he could not think of any memorable phrase and that, anyway, it wouldn't have made any difference. But when she left the elevator and walked into the lobby without even saying goodbye, he followed her and said, 'But . . . why, Judy? Bad things happen to everyone, you know, a string of negative coincidences, that can happen . . . Now that it's all over, at least tell me why.'

Judy looked at him for an instant without showing any emotion, not even indifference. 'There is no why, Bill.' He hated it when she called him Bill. 'The fall follows the summer and then comes winter. Without a why. Good luck.'

She left him standing in front of the building's glass doors, still as a toy soldier in the midst of the snow that was still falling in big flakes.

On the pavement, sitting on a piece of cardboard propped

against the wall, was a man bundled up in an army jacket, with a long beard and greasy hair, begging. 'Anything to spare for me, brother? I'm a Vietnam vet. Give me a few coins so I can put something warm in my stomach on Christmas Eve.'

'Well, I'm a Vietnam vet too,' he lied, 'so don't break my balls.' But when he looked at him briefly, he saw that there was more dignity in the eyes of even this poor devil than there was in his own. He found a dollar in his jacket pocket. 'Sorry, I didn't mean to be offensive,' he said, throwing the money into the hat in front of the man. 'It's been a really bad day.'

'Merry Christmas,' replied the man, but Blake didn't hear him, because he was already too far away and because he too, in that moment, was drifting through the freezing air like one snowflake among many, weightless and without a destination.

He walked on and on without being able to think of anywhere he'd like to be or anyone he'd like to be with, apart from his old friend Bob Olsen, who had supported and encouraged him through all these ups and downs. Bob might have been able to think up some merciful lie that would have helped him through today. But he was leaving for Egypt, warm sun and work. What luck.

Blake stopped when his legs refused to hold him up any more, when he realized that if he fell into the snowy slush that muddied the street, the cars would run right over him. He imagined that the judge was probably just then leaving the courtroom and the empty building to go back home, where he had a wife cooking, kids sitting in front of the TV, a dog, definitely a dog, and a Christmas tree covered with balls.

And yet, despite all this – the snow, the judge, his wife, the cars, the balls on the Christmas tree, the divorce and the whisky in his black coffee – despite all of it, his instinct had guided him – like an old horse returning to the stables – to the university. The Oriental Institute library was just a few blocks over on his right.

What time was it? Two thirty. He wasn't even late. All he had to do was go up those stairs to the second floor, knock on the door of the rector's office, say hello to the old mummy and the dean, and stand there like an imbecile and listen to their bullshit, then offer up his resignation, which they, given the circumstances, would have no choice but to accept. And then shoot himself in the balls, or the mouth, what difference did it make? No difference at all.

'WHAT ARE YOU doing here at this late hour, William Blake?'

It was all over. He'd lost his job, the only job on earth that had any meaning for him, and he would probably never get it back. And someone had the gall to ask him, 'What are you doing here at this late hour, William Blake?'

'Why, what time is it?'

'It's six in the evening. It's freezing cold and you're blue. You look like someone on the verge of death.'

'Leave me alone. Just forget you saw me, Professor Husseini.'

'No, sorry. Come on, get up. I live just a couple of blocks away. We'll have a cup of hot coffee.'

Blake tried to refuse, but the man insisted. 'If you'd rather, I'll call an ambulance and have them take you to Cook County, since you're out of insurance. Come on, don't be an idiot. Thank your lucky star that only a servant of Allah could be out at this hour instead of at home with his family around the Christmas tree.'

OMAR AL HUSSEINI'S apartment was warm and had a good, somehow familiar, smell.

'Take off your shoes,' Husseini said.

Blake did so, then dropped onto the cushions placed around the living room, while his host went into the kitchen.

Husseini mixed a handful of coffee beans with some cloves and a bit of cinnamon and the room filled with a penetrating fragrance. He began to crush the coffee in a mortar with a changing, drum-like beat, accompanying this musical pounding with the motion of his head.

'Do you know what this rhythm is? It's a call. When a Bedouin crushes coffee in his mortar, the sound that he makes travels for great distances and anyone who is passing, anyone wandering through the solitude and immensity of the desert, knows that a cup of coffee and a friendly word are waiting for him in this tent.'

'Nice.' Blake nodded, slowly beginning to recover. 'Moving. The noble servant of Allah sounds his wooden mortar in the urban desert and saves from certain death the stupid loser abandoned by the cynical and decadent Western civilization.'

'Don't be an idiot,' said Husseini. 'Some coffee will make you feel better and put a little blood in your veins. I swear you were about to die of exposure when I found you. You probably didn't even notice, but at least two of your old colleagues passed right in front of you without even condescending to saying hello. They saw you looking dazed and half dead from the cold, sitting on a slab of frozen stone, stiff as a piece of dried cod, and they didn't even ask you if you needed any help.'

'Well, maybe they were in a hurry. It is Christmas Eve. Maybe they hadn't finished their shopping – the presents for the kids, the cheesecake for dessert. You know how it is . . .'

'Yes,' said Husseini. 'It is Christmas Eve.'

He took the coffee that he had crushed in the mortar with the spices and poured it into the pot of water that was boiling on the stove. The aroma immediately became more intense, but softer and more penetrating. Blake realized that it was the smell of the spices and coffee that permeated the carpets on the floor, along with that of incense.

Husseini handed him a steaming cup and offered him a Turkish cigarette. He sat on his heels in front of Blake, smoking in silence and sipping the strong, aromatic coffee.

'Is this what it's like in your tent in the desert?' asked Blake.

'Oh, no. In my tent there are beautiful women and luscious dates. There's a wind from the east that carries the fragrance of flowers from the high plain and you can hear the bleating of lambs. And when I walk out I see the columns of Apamea in front of me, pale at dawn and red at dusk. When the wind picks up, they sound like the organ pipes in your churches.'

Blake nodded, then took another sip of coffee and a drag on his cigarette. 'So,' he said, 'why didn't you stay in your fucking tent in the desert? What are you here for if you hate it so much?'

'I didn't say that I hate it here. I said it's different. And I said so because you asked me. And if you want to know the truth, the only place I lived after the age of five was a refugee camp in southern Lebanon: a filthy, stinking sewer where we played among rats and garbage.'

'But . . . what about the columns of Apamea, pale at dawn and red at dusk, that chime in the wind like organ pipes?'

'Those I only dreamed about. That was how my grandfather – Abdallah al Husseini, may Allah preserve him – described them to me, but I've never seen them.'

They sat in silence for a long time.

'I don't understand why you were kicked out,' said Husseini eventually. 'I'd heard that you were one of the best in your field.'

'You can say that again,' answered Blake, holding out his cup for more coffee.

Husseini filled it, then said, 'There was nothing I could do about it, because I'm not a full professor, but what about your friend Olsen? He could have cast a vote in your favour.'

'Olsen had to leave for Egypt and so he couldn't be there, but he sent in a note protesting the decision. Only him. No one else stood up for me. Anyway, if you really want to know how it went, I'll tell you. But it's a long story.'

'It's Christmas Eve and we both have time on our hands, I'd say.'

Blake lowered his head into his hands, overcome by a sudden wave of memories and anxiety. Maybe it would help to talk about it; who knows, maybe he'd get a handle on how to extricate himself from the whole mess, regain credibility.

'It was about a year ago,' he began. 'I was examining some

microfilms with texts from the New Kingdom which had been transcribed by James Henry Breasted just before World War One broke out. Stuff from the period of Ramses II or Merenptah, and there was something about a possible connection with the biblical Exodus. On the edge of the sheet, next to the transcription, there was a note scribbled in the margin. I'm sure you've seen samples of Breasted's handwriting . . .'

Husseini nodded. 'Of course. Go on.'

'So you know how neat and regular it is. Well, that note, like I said, seemed really hurried, and it referred to another folder of his writings where he supposedly specified these connections to the Exodus. The note wasn't even that clear, but I was intrigued by the idea. It would have been the discovery of a lifetime. Actual historical proof of the Exodus! I looked for that phantom folder in all the cellars and back rooms of the Oriental Institute, searched through all the old records, but there was no sign of it anywhere.'

Husseini passed him another cigarette and lit up one himself: 'Yeah, you even came to ask me about it. I remember now . . .'

'That's right. Anyway, I turned up nothing. Nothing at all. And yet that note had to mean something. It became kind of an obsession for me. Then I got an idea. Maybe Breasted didn't leave all his writings to the Institute. Maybe there were private collections, even though they weren't mentioned anywhere.

'I started by looking for his heirs. Thank God, City Hall records were already on the Internet by then, so it wasn't as hard as I'd thought it might be. In the end I found Breasted's last descendant: a fifty-year-old lawyer who lived in one of those nice old houses on Longwood, on the city's south side. I introduced myself as a researcher and asked him about a folder that might have contained the transcriptions of hieroglyphic texts that I was interested in, without really letting him know what I was after.'

'How did he react?'

'Oh, he was very cordial. He said that I wasn't the first to come looking for that transcription and that I should give it up, because no trace had ever been found of any such folder, and his great-uncle's papers – what was left of them – had been sifted through at least a dozen times over the years, whenever someone like me chanced upon that note. He offered to let me examine his library if I wanted to try it again, but said that nothing had ever turned up. Courteous as he was, he made me feel like a real fool.

'If only as a matter of pride, though, I accepted his invitation and started to look through the papers in his private library, not really convinced that it would get me anywhere. I went back the day after and the day after that, because I'm stubborn and I just didn't want to give up. Well, I finally came upon a trail that I thought might help me to find the solution.'

'Feel like eating something?' interrupted Husseini. 'It is dinner time, after all. I don't have much in the house. How does desert-style sound?'

'Sounds fine to me,' said Blake.

Husseini put some pita bread in the oven and took a pot of spicy sauce out of the refrigerator, along with some hummus, hard-boiled eggs, cheese and beans.

'Do you have any beer?' asked Blake. 'Or are you observant?'

'Not exactly,' said Husseini, handing him a bottle from the refrigerator. 'My mother was Maronite.'

Blake continued his story as they ate. 'Breasted had a lover. Her name was Suzanne de Bligny, the widow of a French diplomat from the consulate who had settled down in Minneapolis, and there was correspondence between them. I also found out that Mrs Bligny's late husband had been stationed in Egypt, at Luxor.'

'I can imagine,' said Husseini. 'The golden age of Egyptology! The heyday of the Hôtel du Nil, of Auguste Mariette and Emil Brugsch . . .'

'Well, their letters suggested that they keenly shared these interests. I found out that Madame de Bligny had a daughter, Mary Thérèse, who married a certain James O'Donnell, an air force officer who was shot down in combat over England.'

'A dynasty of widows,' commented Husseini, placing the warmed sauce on the table.

Blake spread some on his pita bread and added some beans. 'It would seem so. In any case, it turned out that Mary Thérèse O'Donnell was still alive. She was eighty-five years old, and she had kept all the correspondence between Breasted and her mother. I asked her if I could consult it and I finally found the folder that I had been searching for all that time.'

'And I can imagine that in the meantime you neglected everything else: departmental meetings, academic parties, student visiting hours. And your wife, right?'

'Yeah, I guess so,' admitted Blake. 'I was so taken by this investigation that I didn't even realize time was passing, or what I was neglecting. I didn't stop to think that an unguarded trench is immediately occupied by the enemy.' His expression clouded over, as if all the distressing thoughts that had temporarily lifted, had suddenly renewed their grip.

'What did you find in that file?' asked Husseini.

Blake hesitated, as though he were reluctant to reveal a secret that he had kept to himself up until that moment.

Husseini lowered his gaze and helped himself from the platter. 'You don't have to answer me,' he added. 'We can talk about something else. Women, politics. With everything that's been happening out my way, there's plenty to keep us occupied.'

Blake ate quietly for a few more minutes. It was quiet outside too. No one was on the streets, and the snow, which had begun to fall heavily, muted even the tolling of the bell in the university tower. Blake stood up and walked to the window. He thought of the scorching sand of the Valley of the Kings and felt for a moment that he'd dreamed up the whole thing. Then he continued with his story.

'The file referred to the note that I had read in the Oriental Institute papers, and there was the beginning of the transcription of a hieroglyphic text that began with this phrase: *I followed the*

Habiru from Pi-Ramses through the Sea of Reeds and then into the desert . . .'

Husseini nodded. 'Impressive, no doubt about it. How it matches the beginning of the Book of the Exodus. But you know that the ethnic name *Habiru* has been interpreted very differently by the experts. Although it's commonly assumed to mean "Hebrews", there's no way that can be taken for granted. I hope you didn't go and shake up the whole Institute on this basis alone . . . They would obviously have put your ass on the line.'

'The style of the ideograms was extremely similar to the so-called "Israel Stele",' observed Blake, clearly offended.

Husseini seemed to reconsider. 'No, that's very impressive, I'd say. Sorry, I didn't mean to question your competence. It's just that certain things are very hard to believe. I'll make more coffee. Would you like some?'

'Sure, as long as you don't start playing that music with your mortar again.'

'American-style, filtered,' said Husseini, taking a pot from the coffee maker, 'otherwise we'll never sleep again.'

'That transcription, backed by Breasted's reputation as the foremost expert in the field, contained the most explicit evidence of the historical reliability of the Book of Exodus ever found in any source apart from the Bible. And so I was determined to get to the bottom of it. Breasted had diligently noted where the original could be found. He had seen the papyrus in the house of a certain Mustafa Mahmoud at El Qurna, and had tried to buy it for the Oriental Institute. He had only managed to read the first line and copy the ideograms before the papyrus was put away.'

'El Qurna is a tomb raider's paradise. Crawling with forgeries as well, my friend. My bet is that he fell for a trap.'

'Even so, I felt that the stakes were too high for me to drop my investigation there, and anyway Breasted was no dupe. If he was convinced that papyrus was authentic, I'd say there was a good chance that it was. Having weighed all the pros and cons, I thought it was worth the risk and I persuaded the department to allocate a considerable sum for field research that I would carry out personally. Olsen's vote was conclusive for the financing.'

'So you failed. And afterwards they were all there like vultures waiting to pick at your carcass. Right?'

'Just a minute, dear colleague. I'm not that stupid. The papyrus did exist. And probably still does.'

Husseini took a deep drag on his cigarette and shook his head. 'Nearly ninety years have passed—'

'I'm telling you that the papyrus existed . . . does exist.'

'If you can't prove it, it's as if it didn't, and you know that better than I do. Anyway, I'd like to know how you can be so sure. You're not going to tell me that at El Qurna you found the heirs of Mustafa Mahmoud—'

'I did, as a matter of fact. Even better than that.'

'Better?'

'Photographic evidence. Partial, dark, but extremely significant.'

Both men were quiet, the Arab scholar watching the thin line of smoke that rose from the butt of his cigarette, his guest turning the empty coffee cup over and over in his hands. The whine of a police siren echoed distantly between the glass walls of the skyscrapers, travelling through the curtain of snow all the way to the room where they were sitting, like a disturbing, alien wail.

'Continue,' said Husseini.

'I knew I was playing for high stakes. Looking for a document which may lie at the very basis of thousands of years of tradition means running enormous risks – a short circuit at best, but a catastrophe at the worst. I knew I had to move cautiously and I was careful not to expose myself directly. I took one of my students, Selim Kaddoumi, along.'

Husseini indicated with a nod that he knew him.

Blake went on, 'He's a smart kid, working on his PhD with me, on a grant from the Egyptian government. He's completely bilingual and he made all my contacts for me. He talked with the old fellahin of El Qurna, distributed a little money here and there where it counted, obviously keeping a small percentage for himself, until he really chanced upon some important information. An old collection dating back to the golden age had turned up and the underground antiquities smugglers were said to have a number of pieces ready to sell. So at this point I stepped in. Italian designer suit, drove up in a rented luxury car and made an appointment, passing myself off as a possible fence.'

'Why?' asked Husseini.

'Selim had seen a Polaroid of one of the pieces that was up for sale and he sketched it for me. I thought I recognized one of the finds described by Breasted in the folder that I'd seen in Minneapolis: a gilded bronze bracelet set with amber, hematite and carnelian. What's more, there were also papyri in the lot. It was reasonable to suppose that the papyrus I was looking for could have been one of them, since there'd been no word of it since Breasted's times. My gut feeling told me that I'd had a stroke of luck that I would never even have dreamed of. Anyway, it was worth a try.'

Husseini shook his head. 'I don't get it, Blake. A piece suddenly shows up after some eighty years just while you're looking for it. Didn't that make you suspicious?'

'Well, that's not exactly how it was. There was no way I could be sure that the papyrus I was looking for was in the lot. I wasn't even sure that the bracelet Selim had drawn from a photo was the same one that Breasted had described.'

Hussein looked at him, confused. 'But then—'

'The plot thickens, servant of Allah,' interrupted Blake, 'true to script. But to tell you the rest I need something stronger to drink. Too much to ask?'

'Afraid so. But I can give you another cigarette. A little nicotine will keep you going.'

So Blake took a deep drag on the cigarette and continued. 'I had met an official from our embassy in Cairo. Olsen had introduced us, in case I needed a hand in contacting the Egyptian authorities or the Minister of Antiquities. One evening he called me at the Oriental Institute's guest facilities to set up an appointment at the Cairo Marriot. It was his favourite hangout, because they serve hamburgers, steaks and French fries. Waiters in cowboy hats, you get the picture.

'He told me to watch out because he knew there were other people – powerful, dangerous people – trying to get their hands on that lot. He wouldn't say who they were, but he did say they were people who didn't take kindly to competition. He was warning me as a sort of a favour, like saying, "Watch it. That stuff's too hot, so stay away." But for me it was a fantastic confirmation of what I was hoping for. If there were other powerful people or institutions interested in those finds, it meant that there had to be something tremendously important there, like – for example – the Breasted papyrus.'

'Right,' agreed Husseini. 'So how did you imagine you could slip it out from under their noses?'

'Well, I may have been presumptuous, but I was also well organized. If the game had been fair I would have won.'

'Sure, tell me about it. They alerted the Egyptian police to you, and you were found with compromising material on you, or in your room or your car.'

'Yeah, more or less. But it went well to start with. The dealer knew his stuff. He showed me the pieces one by one, and described them in the correct historical terms, but he was really interested in getting rid of the jewellery, especially the bracelet, a necklace and a ring, all from the Nineteenth Dynasty. He had also brought objects which were less important but from the same time period: two more bracelets and a pendant, along with scarabs, ankhs and ushtabi figures.

'When I brought up the papyri he started asking questions. He must have been aware of the interest this find had stirred up. When I managed to convince him that there wasn't anyone behind me, he softened a little and showed me the photograph. I swear that I nearly had a heart attack. It was my papyrus, no question about it. I knew the sequence and the style of the ideograms in the first line by heart and I'd read the description in Breasted's papers time after time. I had no doubts.

'I tried as hard as I could to disguise my excitement and I asked him if he could give me the photograph. That would have been a victory in itself. I would have been able to read the whole text.'

'Did he agree?'

'No. He hesitated and then put it back in the inside pocket of his jacket. He said something like, "I'd better not. If it were found on you or in your house it might cause trouble." He said that he'd have to discuss my offer with the person he was working for, and that he would call me. That was the last I saw of him. Because that was when the police rushed in. He disappeared in the confusion and I was trapped there with all that stuff on the table in front of me. The rest is history.'

Husseini seemed to be reflecting on the story in silence. He turned to look at Blake: 'Was it dark when the police burst in?' he asked.

'Well, the place was a big underground warehouse at Khan el Khalili, packed with all kinds of goods and poorly lit by a couple of light bulbs. Anyone who knew his way around would have been able to get away, but I didn't know where to turn and, anyway, I had no intention of running.'

'Who do you think informed the Egyptian police?'

Blake shrugged. 'My mysterious competitors?'

'Yes, that's likely. Especially if they thought they'd find that papyrus. Most likely they'd bribed the police commander and he was acting on their instructions.'

'I was arrested, listed as *persona non grata* and expelled from the country.'

'And you were lucky. Any idea what an Egyptian prison is like?'

'Yeah, I got a good idea in the four, five days I spent there. And yet, if I could, I'd head straight back there, even now.'

Husseini looked at him with a mixture of admiration and pity. 'You didn't get enough, did you? Listen to me. You'd better forget all about it because next time you won't get a second chance. It's just too dangerous: fences, thieves, drug barons, people who don't forgive and forget. You wouldn't come out alive.'

'Not that the idea frightens me much any more.'

'You'll change your mind. Mark my words, one day you'll wake up and you'll want to start all over again . . .'

Blake shook his head. 'Start what?'

'Anything. As long as we're alive, we're alive. What about the papyrus?'

'Haven't heard anything more about it. When I got back here I was overwhelmed by the consequences. The loss of my job, my wife . . .'

'What are you going to do now?'

'Now as in "right now"?'

'Exactly.'

'I'll find my way back to the car and go home. I've got a little place not too far from here. By the ballpark. I'm not going to kill myself, if that's what you're worried about.'

'I don't know . . .' said Husseini. 'I don't think there's much I can do for you. I'm just an assistant professor and I don't have tenure but, if you like, you can tell Olsen when he comes back that I'm willing to give you a hand if I can.'

'Thank you, Husseini. You've already helped me. And we've never even been . . . friendly.'

'That's normal. You can't have relationships with all of your colleagues.'

'Well, it's late. Time for me to go.'

'Listen, it's no problem for me. If you like you can sleep here on the couch. It's pretty comfortable.'

'No, thanks. I really appreciate you taking me in like this but . . . I should be going now. Thanks again. You know, if you'd like to come out to my place, it's not as nice as here but there's always something to drink and . . . Well, I'll give you the address. It's in Bridgeport . . . If you feel like it, you know.'

'Count on it,' said Husseini.

Blake went to a table to write out the address and noticed a photograph of a little boy of maybe five, and a phrase in Arabic that said: *In memory of Said. Dad.* He would have liked to ask about the little boy, but instead he just scribbled down his address, put on his coat and went to the door. It was still snowing.

'Listen, can I ask you one last question?' asked Husseini.

'Sure.'

'Where does the name William Blake come from? It's like being called Harun al Rashid or Dante Alighieri or Thomas Jefferson.'

'Just chance. I've never liked being called Bill, because Bill Blake is awful.'

'I see. Well, goodbye, then. I'll come and visit, and you can come here whenever you like, if you feel like talking.'

Blake waved briefly and trudged off through the deep snow. Husseini watched him as he passed from one ring of light to the next under the street lights, until he disappeared in the dark.

He closed the door and returned to the living room. He lit another cigarette and sat in the dim light, thinking about William Blake and the papyrus of the Exodus.

At eleven he switched on CNN. The crisis in the Middle East was old news, but he liked seeing the places anyway: the horrible roads of Gaza, the ruined buildings, the piles of filth. It reminded him of his childhood: the friends he'd played with in the streets, the scents of tea and saffron in the bazaar, the taste of unripe figs, the smell of dust and youth. But at the same time he found unutterable pleasure in living in this comfortable American apartment with a salary in dollars and a girlfriend, warm and uninhibited, a secretary at the university who came by two or three times a week and never set any limits in bed.

The telephone rang as he was getting ready to go to sleep.

He thought that William Blake must have changed his mind and decided to spend the night in his apartment instead of facing the long trip through snow and icy wind.

He picked up the receiver and was about to say, 'Hi, Blake, changed your mind?' but the voice on the other side froze his blood.

'*Salaam alekum*, Abu Ghaj. It's been a long time . . .'

Husseini recognized the voice. There was only one person in the world who would call him by that name. For a moment he was speechless, but then he forced himself to react and said, 'I thought that phase of my life was over a long time ago. I've got my life here, my work—'

'There are promises that we must remain faithful to our whole lives, Abu Ghaj, and there's a past from which no one can escape. Aren't you aware of what is happening in our country?'

'Of course I am,' said Husseini. 'But I've already paid all I can. I've played my part.'

The voice on the other end fell silent and Husseini could hear a train passing in the background. Maybe he was calling from a phone booth near the El or was in the lobby of the station.

'I have to meet you as soon as possible. Now, actually.'

'Now . . . I can't. There's someone here with me,' improvised Husseini.

'The secretary, huh? Send her home.'

He even knew that, then. Husseini stammered, 'No, really, I can't. I—'

'Then you come here. In half an hour, at the Shedd Aquarium parking lot. I have a grey Buick La Sabre with Wisconsin plates. I'd advise you to be there.' He hung up.

Husseini felt his world cave in on him. How was this possible? He'd left the organization after years of fierce battles and furious gunfights. He thought he'd paid his debt to the cause in full. Why this call? He would have given anything not to go. On the other hand he knew very well, from personal experience, that they were not people who fooled around. Least of all Abu Ahmid, the man whose voice he had heard and whom he knew only by his *nom-de-guerre*.

He sighed, turned off the TV and put on a fur-lined parka and gloves. He switched off the lights and closed the door behind him. His car was parked down the block. He scraped the ice and snow off the windscreen and left for his appointment.

The snow was falling hard and fine, blown by an icy wind from the east. He left the neo-Gothic buildings of the university campus on his left and drove up 57th Street to Lake Shore Drive, which was nearly deserted at that hour.

The spectacular scenery of the city centre loomed up before him: the serried ranks of the glass and steel giants, lights sparkling against the grey sky. The top of the Sears Tower was lost in low cloud and the beacon at its tip throbbed inside the foggy mass like lightning in a storm. The John Hancock stretched its colossal antennae into the clouds like the arms of a Titan condemned to hold up the sky for all eternity. The other towers, some encrusted with gilded ornaments on ribs of black stone, others bright with anodized metal and fluorescent plastic, fanned open at the sides of the street like enormous stage settings in the magic atmosphere of falling snow.

He passed slowly alongside the Field Museum, its Doric columns bathed in a green light that made them look like bronze. On his right was the long peninsula, with the Shedd Aquarium at one end and the stone drum of the planetarium at the other. He drove with care, leaving deep grooves in the white blanket, following tracks already covered by the snow that continued to fall incessantly in the glow of his headlights, in the continuous alternating rhythm of the windscreen wipers.

There was a car pulled over with its side lights on. He stopped, got out and walked towards it through ankle-deep snow. It was him. Husseini opened the passenger door and sat down.

'Good evening, Abu Ghaj. *Salaam alekum.*'

'*Alekum salaam*, Abu Ahmid.'

'I'm sorry to have interrupted your evening.'

'You did not interrupt my evening, Abu Ahmid. You interrupted my life,' said Husseini, his head low.

'You should have expected it. We always find deserters sooner or later, wherever they are.'

'I'm not a deserter. When I joined the organization, I said that I would leave as soon as I couldn't take it any more. And you accepted this condition. Don't you remember?'

'I remember very well, Abu Ghaj. Otherwise you would not be here now, alive and well and talking with me. The fact remains that you left without a word.'

'There was nothing to say. It was as we'd agreed.'

'That's your story!' exclaimed Abu Ahmid sharply. 'I'm the one who decides. And I could have condemned you to death then.'

'Why didn't you?'

'I never act on impulse. I wrote your name in my book. On the you-owe-me side.'

Husseini lowered his head. 'So now you want me to settle up, is that it?'

Abu Ahmid did not answer, but his silence made Husseini realize that his life alone would not be sufficient to settle his debt.

'Is that it?' he repeated.

Abu Ahmid began to speak, as if he had been asked to express his opinion on a philosophical matter. 'Circumstances are so dramatic and so pressing that all of us are called upon to make our contribution. Our private lives have no significance in such a moment.'

'Mine does. Leave me out of it. I don't have that kind of energy any more, or the motivation behind it. I can contribute some money, if you want, but please leave me out of it. I can't be of any use to you.'

Abu Ahmid turned towards him suddenly. 'Your attitude could be taken as a full confession to the charge that has been hanging over your head for years: desertion! I have the power to pass judgement on you and to execute the sentence, right now, this very instant.'

Husseini felt like saying, 'Do it, then, you bastard, and go to hell,' but as he watched the snow dancing down in the glow of the street lamps and the myriad lights of the city glimmering in the dark mirror of the lake, what he actually said was, 'What do you want me to do?'

Abu Ahmid began to speak in a low voice with his hand on his chest. 'When I have told you what is about to happen, you will thank me for having sought you out, for having given you the chance to participate in such a historic moment for us and for our nation. The Zionists will finally be wiped forever from the face of this earth and the city of Jerusalem will be restored to the true believers.'

Husseini shook his head. 'I can't believe that you're planning yet another bloodbath. More slaughter? More massacres? Hasn't all the blood that's been spilled, futilely, all these years been enough for you?'

'This time it's different. This time our victory is certain.'

'My God . . . that's exactly what you've said each time, and each time the defeat has been more humiliating. Look around you, Abu Ahmid. See these colossal towers? Each one of them contains more people than the inhabitants of many of our villages. Each one of them represents an economic power that is stronger and richer than a single one of our states. They are the symbol of an imperial power that has no comparison – and no competitors – anywhere in the world, equipped with weapons and instruments so sophisticated that they could listen in on our every word and hear our every breath right now, from miles and miles away. And this power does not want any changes in the current political order in our region. They don't care about any trouble this may cause or any violations of so-called agreements.'

Abu Ahmid turned and stared at him with a strange smile. 'It almost seems . . . as if you've become one of them.'

43

'I have, Abu Ahmid. I've been an American citizen for years.'

'Citizenship is just a piece of paper. The roots of your soul are another thing . . . something which can never be cancelled. Never. But you're wrong in what you say. This time the battle will be on equal terms. They won't even have the chance to deploy their potential for destruction. This time the Islamic armies will take Jerusalem by force, like in the times of Salah ad Din. We will fight hand to hand, and the men who live on the top of these towers won't be allowed to change the outcome of the battle. This time we will win, Abu Ghaj.'

Husseini fell silent and his breath condensed into little clouds of steam as the winter air invaded the parked car. He wondered just what those words could mean: was he bluffing or did Abu Ahmid really have a trump card that he could play at the table of history? He still couldn't believe what was happening.

He pressed on with his weak protests. 'Do you really want to start a war? Unleash destruction on thousands or millions of human beings? I want you to know that, for me, there is no cause worth all of this. I believe that history has something to teach humanity, and that the most important lesson is that war is too high a price to pay, under any circumstances.'

'Moving words, Abu Ghaj. That's not the way you talked when you lived in the refugee camp, when you saw poverty and death up close every day, disease and hunger, when you saw your family annihilated by an enemy mortar . . .'

Husseini felt a hard knot in this throat.

'Then you thought fighting back was the only way out. Think back. Think back and you'll find that your wise, conciliatory words are just coming out of the tranquil existence you lead now. They are nothing more than an expression of your egotism. But I won't insist. This is not the moment to debate such complicated, difficult problems. I just want to know whose side you're on.'

'Do I have a choice?'

44

'Certainly. But your choice, whatever it is, will involve consequences.'

'I see.' Husseini nodded, thinking. 'If I give you the wrong answer tomorrow morning they'll find my body lying stiff right out here in the bloody snow.'

'Listen,' said Abu Ahmid, 'we need you. I can guarantee that you will not be involved in operations which result in the spilling of blood. We need someone beyond suspicion. I'm the only person who knows your true identity. You'll just be the point of reference here, inside the system, for the cells that are about to enter this country.'

'Isn't that the same thing?'

'We don't want to spill blood in vain. We only want to fight our enemy on equal terms. That means we have to immobilize America until the duel is over. Whether we are victorious or have been annihilated, it doesn't matter. But this will be the last battle.'

'What is it that I have to do?'

'Three groups made up of our best men, completely trustworthy, will be operating within the United States for as long as necessary. They do not know each other, they've never seen each other, but they will have to move in unison, in perfect coordination, timed to a fraction of a second. They will act as a deadly weapon pointed at the head of a giant and you will be the man holding your finger on the trigger.'

'Me? Why me?' asked Hussein, incredulous. 'Why don't you do it, Abu Ahmid?'

'Because my presence is required elsewhere. And because here no one knows who you are, Abu Ghaj.'

Omar al Husseini realized that everything had been provided for and decided upon and that there was no way out. All Abu Ahmid had to do was provide the American authorities with proof that Professor Husseini was in reality Abu Ghaj, the terrorist hunted by all the police of the Western world for years.

The man who had mysteriously vanished into thin air. Husseini would end up in the electric chair.

'When is the operation scheduled to begin?'

'In six weeks, on 3 February.'

Husseini lowered his head in surrender.

Abu Ahmid gave him a gadget that looked like a small black box. 'All the instructions will be sent in code to your computer, which will transmit them in turn to the destinations indicated. This is the reserve unit. You must never lose it. You must carry it with you at all times. The password for access is the name of the operation itself: Nebuchadnezzar.'

Omar al Husseini put the box into his jacket pocket, then walked back to his car, started it up and disappeared into the swirling snow.

3

William Blake parked his car in front of the house at one in the morning and walked towards the entrance of his small rented apartment. It would be the worst Christmas of his life, and yet those few hours spent with Husseini had warmed his heart, as well as his numbed limbs, and if it hadn't been for a residue of self-pride, he would have accepted the invitation to sleep on Husseini's couch. At least he'd have had someone to talk to tomorrow morning over a cup of coffee.

He heard a sharp click as he turned the key in the lock, but it wasn't the door he was opening. It was a car door snapping shut behind him. He tried to slip in quickly; the neighbourhood wasn't the best and, at that late hour, he had reason to worry. But an arm stretched out in front of him, preventing him from entering.

He wheeled around to try to get back to the car but bumped into another person who was standing directly behind him.

'Don't be alarmed, Professor Blake,' said the man who had stopped him from entering. 'And do excuse the antisocial hour, but we've been waiting for you because we need to speak to you urgently.'

'I don't know you,' said Blake in an unsteady voice. 'If you just want to talk, come back in a couple of days. People usually spend Christmas with their families, you know.'

The man who had spoken to him was about forty. He was wearing a Gore-Tex jacket and a fake-fur hat. The other was about fifty and was wearing a tailored coat and a fine felt hat.

'I'm Ray Sullivan,' the older man said, extending his hand. 'I work for the Warren Mining Corporation, and this is Mr Walter Gordon. We have to talk to you now.'

Blake rapidly reflected that if they were criminals there was no way they would be interested in someone like him in a place like this, and this convinced him to grant their request. He wasn't busy, after all, and had no pressing plans.

'Please allow us just a few minutes,' said the man with the coat. 'You'll realize that we had no choice.'

'OK,' said Blake, nodding, 'you can come in, but the place is small and I'm afraid it's a bit of a mess.'

'We'd just like to have a few words, Professor Blake,' said the man with the jacket.

Blake turned on the light, let them in and closed the door.

'Please, sit down,' he said, reassured by the respectable appearance of the pair and their politeness.

'Please excuse our intrusion, Professor. We thought you'd be back for dinner. We certainly didn't plan on such an unsettling encounter, at this time of night.'

'It doesn't matter,' said Blake. 'But please fill me in on the reason for this little visit, because I'm very tired and would like to go to bed.'

The two men exchanged a perplexed glance, then the one who had been introduced as Walter Gordon began to speak.

'As my friend Ray Sullivan was saying, we work for the Warren Mining Corporation and we're doing some exploratory drilling in the Middle East. We're looking for cadmium.'

Blake shook his head. 'My God, you've made a huge mistake: I'm an archaeologist, not a geologist.'

Gordon continued, unperturbed. 'We know very well who you are, Professor Blake. As I was saying, we'd been doing this exploratory drilling, and three days ago a team led by Mr Sullivan was coring when suddenly the ground started to cave in, as if sucked into a chasm.'

48

'I went over to the opening we had just drilled,' interrupted Sullivan, 'to see what could have happened. I thought at first that it was a natural sink hole: the area we're working in is full of them due to the calcium carbonate deposits that are found there. But all I needed was one glance to realize that this was totally different.'

Blake's eyes, bleary with fatigue, suddenly snapped to attention. 'Go on,' he said. 'I'm listening.'

'The drill had penetrated the ceiling of an underground room and the sun filtering through shone against something metallic in the darkness. I immediately interrupted the operation, moved out the team and referred everything to Mr Gordon, my direct superior, back at the camp. When everyone was sleeping that night, we went back.

'It was a clear night and the chalky colour of the sand reflected the moonlight, so we could see almost as well as by day. As soon as we got there, we leaned down into the hole and lit up the inside with torches. What we saw left us, literally, breathless. We were so amazed we didn't know what to say. Although our angle of view was limited, we could see objects made of bronze, copper, gold and ivory down there. What we could see clearly looked like an unspoiled tomb.'

'I don't know how you feel when you find yourself in front of a great discovery,' Gordon took over, 'but I swear that for a few minutes I just couldn't believe what I was seeing. I was shaking. I could barely control my excitement . . . We calculated that the tomb below us had to be pretty vast. The chamber measured about four metres by five. It was a couple of metres high, and we supposed there could be side chambers as well.

'It looked like a natural cavity which had been adapted to contain those incredible treasures. The shape of the sarcophagus, which we could partially see, the statues of the divinities and the style of the decorations left us in no doubt. We had found the tomb of some very high-ranking Egyptian dignitary. We're no specialists, but as far as we could guess, it looked like the tomb of a Pharaoh!'

'A Pharaoh? My God, it would be the first inviolate royal tomb since Carnarvon and Carter opened the tomb of Tutankhamun.'

'That's just what we thought. But then—'

'Although it could be a Hellenistic age tomb. The Ptolemies had begun to imitate the Pharaonic order completely. But without examining the finds directly, there's no way to tell. You didn't actually drop down into the room, then?'

'No, the opening wasn't big enough. And that's the reason we're here,' said Sullivan. 'We'd like you to take charge of the discovery. Up until now we've kept it a complete secret. The site is under the surveillance of armed guards with orders to shoot on sight.'

Blake ran his fingers through his hair and sighed. He was exhausted and this interminable day, instead of allowing him to rest, kept dragging on in a sequence of increasingly emotional experiences. 'I'd like to thank you for thinking of me,' he said. 'It's the last thing I could have expected on a day like today. But I'm afraid I can't accept. Two reasons. First of all, you have to notify the authorities. They will then nominate an inspector who will direct the preliminary inspection and catalogue the materials. Second, due to a series of misfortunes which I have no intention of boring you with, I'm *persona non grata* in Egypt. And I honestly don't understand the reason for all this urgency at one o'clock in the morning.'

'In reply to your first objection, Professor Blake,' said Gordon, 'our activity is being carried out in territory which is absolutely off-limits. The military have ruled out informing the Minister of Antiquities. Too many people would come into the area and the stir caused by the discovery would attract too much attention. For this reason, in mutual agreement with our hosts, we've decided, for the moment, to rely on the collaboration of a trustworthy specialist whose absolute discretion we can count on. As far as your second objection is concerned, we're well aware of your misfortunes. The fact that you're not allowed to enter Egyptian territory has no bearing on the matter.

'You'll have to leave with us, now. That's why we were waiting for you to come home.'

Blake turned to them with a strange expression, having suddenly understood what they wanted from him. 'Now?' he asked.

Gordon nodded. 'The company's private plane will be taking off from Meigs Field in less than an hour. If you need to get some things together, we can give you about fifteen minutes.'

Blake fell silent.

'It's understood,' said Sullivan, 'that you will be paid for your work. And given the circumstances and the inconvenience that we've caused you, your remuneration will be quite generous.'

Blake didn't answer. He wasn't interested in the money at that point. He would have worked for free, given the chance.

He thought of Judy, whom he probably would never see again, and was a little shocked to realize that losing her probably wouldn't drive him to desperation, and he thought of Husseini, the servant of Allah who had offered him hospitality on Christmas Eve. It all seemed incredibly distant, as though it had happened a long time ago.

'All right,' he said. 'Just let me get my toothbrush and throw some things in a suitcase.'

The two men exchanged a satisfied look.

'You've made the best decision, Professor Blake,' said Gordon. 'I can assure you that what you'll find waiting for you is beyond your wildest expectations.'

'There's just one thing I want to make clear. I'm not in this for the money. I see that you're well informed about my status in Egypt and you may know I've had problems in my personal life, but that doesn't mean anything. I'm not on sale for any price. The only thing I'm interested in is publishing the find.'

'Your views are certainly understandable,' said Sullivan. 'But that's something you'll have to take up with our superiors. We're sure that you'll be able to come to a satisfactory agreement with Warren Mining.'

Blake knew all too well that he was getting himself into a potentially difficult situation, but his only alternative was looking for work in some remote city college or private high school.

'Alea jacta est,' he said as he got up and walked into the bedroom to pack a suitcase. The embarrassed smiles of his guests revealed their ignorance of Latin, even the most common of quotes.

He put his working clothes into the suitcase, along with his trowel and scalpel for the dig, Gardiner's *Egyptian Grammar*, the disk with his hieroglyphic translation program, his underwear, shaving kit, suncream, a bottle of aspirin and one of antacids. He picked up the Prozac, but then threw it in the rubbish bin, knowing that he wouldn't need it any more now that he would soon be treading the sands of the desert. He found his camera bag and, in less than five minutes, rejoined his travelling companions.

'Let me lock up and I'll be right out,' he said. 'Go ahead and start the car.'

The black Mercury drove through the deserted metropolis and Blake, sitting on the back seat, seemed hypnotized by the yellow flashing light on the snowplough which preceded them, raising a white cloud which fell in soft waves on the right-hand side of the street. The long day was nearly behind him and he thought with amusement that Gordon was like a benevolent Santa Claus who had brought him his Christmas present nice and early in the morning: an entire unspoiled Egyptian tomb and Lord knew what else.

He was excited by the idea that he would soon be flying over the Nile and plunging into the dry, clear atmosphere of the desert, his natural element. He would soon be breathing in the dust of the millennia and nudging an important someone out of thirty centuries of slumber.

At Meigs Field, Sullivan showed some credentials to a security guard, who let them pass. They drove out on a service runway to the ramp where a Falcon 900EX was waiting with its engines running. When they got out of the car, they were hit by a blast of snow and Gordon held his hat down until they'd got into the plane. Before entering, Blake turned around for a last glance at the snow-covered city, glittering with coloured lights. He remembered how, when he was a kid, he would anxiously scan the sky on Christmas Eve, hoping to see Santa with his sleigh and reindeer flying over the skyscrapers in a cloud of silver dust like in the cartoons, and he wondered whether he would ever set foot in the city again.

Sullivan got in behind him and they settled into the comfortable seats. The Falcon accelerated down the runway and took off into the grey night sky like a dart. It was soon soaring towards the cold northern constellations.

THE OLD MERCEDES advanced in a cloud of dust that the moonlight bleached white against the black rocks and steppe-like plain, towards the colossal ruins of Baalbek. When it reached the entrance to the Valley of the Temples it stopped and switched off its headlights. The six columns of the Great Temple rose towards the starry sky, like the pillars of infinity, and the man in the back seat marvelled at the spectacle in silence, listening to the voice of his soul. He thought of all those he had seen die in the countless clashes that had punctuated his life: dying in bombings or in battle, mowed down by machine guns, ripped apart by mines and grenades. He thought of those he had seen die of starvation and desperation, of disease and injuries, and he thought of all their restless souls wandering through the desert night.

53

Despite everything, this was one of the rare moments when he could rest his body and his mind, this moment of waiting. He rolled down the window and lit up the last of the three cigarettes a day his doctor allowed him and looked up at the starry black sky. It was times like this that reminded him of his childhood and his youth, the parents he had known for such a short time, the women he hadn't been able to love, the studies he hadn't been able to finish, the friends he hadn't been able to see. Because there had never been time enough.

He thought of the people he had had dealings with: petroleum princes and emirs, tyrants out only for power and money, religious leaders who were sometimes cynical and sometimes visionary, young men devoured by hate and fanaticism, consumed by their frustration at not being able to possess the fetishes of Western wealth, secret service agents playing on both sides, bankers who'd got rich on the poor through the most filthy speculation.

He had used them all, as much as he had despised them, and not a single one of them had learned his real identity. He was waiting for the day of reckoning, when the most ambitious plan ever conceived by an Arab since the time of the Battle of Tours would give him victory over his enemies, the leadership of a nation extending from the Himalayas to the Atlantic Ocean. And the control of a third of the energy resources of the entire planet.

He started when a man dressed in black emerged from the darkness and began to walk towards the car, drawing closer and nodding at him. He nodded in response, got out of the car and followed to a low mud-plastered house. The man let him in.

He was an old man with curved shoulders and eyes dimmed by cataracts. 'Welcome, effendi,' he greeted him.

'What news do you have?'

'Good news. I was told to tell you: "Three donkeys have been bought at the market of Samarkand as you ordered, paying a proper price. Now the donkey keeper is bringing each one to its stable, as you ordered." '

The guest nodded his approval. 'Praise Allah,' he said. 'Everything is proceeding for the best. Now, my good friend, you will tell the young men who are coming on the pilgrimage with me that I need to see them. Three of them will meet me in Bethlehem, three in Nablus and three in Gaza.'

'Shall I arrange lodging for you at Mecca, effendi?'

'No, my friend. This is a pilgrimage that we'll be doing the old way, on camelback. You needn't do anything else.'

They embraced and the guest walked back to his car, which was waiting at the foot of the columns of Baalbek. The old man watched him go, disappearing like a shadow from his uncertain sight, then he turned to the Temple. The columns seemed like giants on sentry duty in the middle of the night, ensuring that no curious eyes would see the small man hurrying off.

The old man had never seen him before, and would not have been able to describe him later, except for his black-and-white-checked keffiyeh and his grey jacket worn over a white jellaba. But he knew that he had spoken with the man most wanted on the face of this earth, he who above all others his enemies dreamed of having within their grasp.

Abu Ahmid.

THE AIR OF Bethlehem was still fragrant with incense and the city still bustled with activity so soon after Christmas. Thousands of pilgrims swarmed through the city streets and past the shops and stands at the bazaar.

It was a crowd that spoke many languages. An Orthodox priest dressed in black with a long-veiled *polos* on his head and silver icons around his neck, a humble Franciscan friar with his dusty sandals and a rope belt, a mullah with his head swathed in a white turban: the crowds milling around saw them all; they were living proof of how many different ways there were to reach a single God.

No one noticed the man with a black-and-white-checked keffiyeh, wearing a grey jacket over a white jellaba and carrying a woollen shoulder bag, as he entered the city and went to a little two-storey crumbling plaster house at the crossroads of Suk el Berk and Ain Aziza.

An elderly widow was waiting for him in the deserted house and she led him from the entrance to the main room: a modest place, the floor covered with old kilim carpets and a few cushions. The woman lifted one of the kilims, uncovering a wooden trapdoor that led into a cellar illuminated by a dim electric bulb. The man went down a ladder as she closed the trapdoor behind him and put the kilim back in place.

The man walked along a narrow passageway and entered another room about two metres by three, with a mat on the floor and a single light bulb hanging from the low ceiling. Three men were waiting for him, sitting on their heels, their faces completely covered by their keffiyehs.

The man's face was concealed as well and his voice sounded dull through the strip of cloth covering his mouth. 'Brothers,' he said, 'your mission is about to begin and it is of such importance that the success of Operation Nebuchadnezzar and the victory of our cause depend on it. We have spent years pondering the reasons for our past defeats, and these errors will not be repeated. This time we won't move until we've received the signal that the packages have been delivered. As you know, these packages are quite large and would attract attention, and so they have been divided into three parts, one for each of you.'

He reached into the bag and extracted three envelopes, handing them out. 'Here you'll find cash, International City Bank credit cards and the instructions for collecting and delivering your package. You will learn them by heart now, here in front of me, and then I will destroy them. The instructions will also tell you how to contact the coordinator of the operation on American soil. His code name is Nebuzaradan. You will communicate with him only in code. Unless it is an absolute emergency or I instruct you to do so, you will not meet with him in person.

'If you are discovered, set off the charge you will have on you and try to take as many victims with you as you can. Have no pity on the elderly, or on women and children, as our enemies have shown no pity for our fathers, our sons, our wives. Once you have terminated the mission, you will return to base, because we need brave, well-trained combatants like you to fight in the final battle.' He articulated his last words as if pronouncing a sacred formula: 'The siege and the conquest of Jerusalem.'

The three men opened the envelopes, removed the money and credit cards, and read the instructions carefully. One after another, ending with the one who seemed youngest, they handed back the sheets, which were immediately burned in a copper plate placed on the mat.

'*Allah Akbar!*' said the man.

'*Allah Akbar!*' responded the other three.

Shortly after, the man was walking through the sun on a lovely winter's day in the crowded bazaar. He passed under a banner that said, in three languages: *Peace on earth to men of goodwill.*

The three combatants of Allah left the house one at a time, at intervals of about an hour. They departed, each towards his own destination, like the horsemen of the Apocalypse. The first had instructions to reach Beirut and from there go by plane to Limassol, from where he would leave on a Cypriot cargo boat bound for New York. The second was to drive to Alexandria, where he would board an oil tanker heading towards New Haven, Connecticut. The third would travel by ship from Jaffa to Barcelona, where he would take an Iberia flight for San José in Costa Rica, and from there board a United Fruits banana boat from Puerto Limon going to Miami, Florida.

Two days later Abu Ahmid contacted three more young men

in Nablus, in a mosque in the old city, and then, two days after, three others in Gaza, in a hovel in the refugee camp. All six, like the three in Bethlehem, were suicidal combatants sworn to death and trained to face any kind of situation. They also received instructions and itineraries.

They were, and always had been, pawns on Abu Ahmid's chessboard, replaceable as necessary. Each group, having completed its mission, could detach a member to remedy any losses in the other groups, until all three of their objectives were attained.

All nine of them spoke English without the hint of an accent and were experts in the use of firearms and knives of any sort; they were proficient in the martial arts, could pilot an aeroplane or helicopter, parachute from any height, climb a rock or concrete wall and swim underwater with an aqualung.

They had no names, but were known by their numbers. They had no mothers or fathers, sisters or brothers, and the documents they carried were false but perfectly forged. They did not prize their lives because they had been taught for years to be ready to sacrifice life at any moment for their cause, upon a signal from their leader. They could survive for days on a hard biscuit and a few sips of water. Inured to hunger and thirst, heat and cold, they could endure any suffering and withstand any torture.

Each of the three groups had a leader who had absolute power over his companions, and could decide whether they lived or died. The whole of Operation Nebuchadnezzar, from start to finish, would depend on their abilities and their endurance.

When they had all reached their destinations with their packages, they would contact 'Nebuzaradan', who would in turn advise him, Abu Ahmid. That moment would mark the beginning of phase two of the operation, the military attack they had been planning day and night for two years in minute detail.

Now all he had to do was find a good vantage point from which to wait and review the operation from beginning to end.

He reached Damascus and went from there to his tent in the desert not far from Deir ez Zor.

It was there that he'd been born about sixty years before, and his small Bedouin tribe was still faithful to the memory of his father and to him, whom they knew as Zahed al Walid. He would awake every day at the break of dawn to contemplate the waters of the Euphrates enflamed by the splendour of the rising sun and to watch the herds as they set out for pasture behind their shepherds, while the women washed their clothes in the river and lit fires in the mud ovens to bake the bread that they served him hot and fragrant, smelling of fire and ash. The sun glittered on the coins that they wore on their foreheads and made them seem ancient queens of burnished beauty: Sheba who had seduced Solomon, or Zenobia who had so fascinated Aurelian.

He would take long rides through the desert, towards Qam-ishli, and would ride so far out that he could see nothing around him, in any direction. Feeling alone between earth and sky on his horse's back gave him an intense and terrible sensation of power. Then he would dismount and walk barefoot on the desert which once had nourished the lush soil of the Garden of Eden. Or sit on his heels and meditate in silence for hours, his eyes closed, attaining nearly absolute concentration, touching a transcendental dimension, as if in his bent knees were distilled the forces of the sky and of the earth.

He would usually return at dusk and have dinner in his tent with the tribal chiefs, eating bread and salt and roasted lamb, and sit there until late, drinking ayran and talking about completely futile and irrelevant things like pregnant camels and the price of wool at the Deir ez Zor market. This was how he would fortify his spirit and sharpen his mind in preparation for the biggest game that had ever been played on earth, since the day on which Esau had lost his birthright over a bowl of lentils.

He did not want to admit it, but he knew very well, in his heart, that on the other side of the chessboard there was a player just as cunning and as dangerous as himself. A man whose appearance was humble and unassuming like his own, capable of keeping a thousand different situations under control at the same time, wary and tireless, probably lacking any human sentiment save an arrogant pride in himself and his capabilities: the head of Mossad, Gad Avner. In the end, it would be the two of them playing the game to its finish and the stakes would be the City of God: Jerusalem.

The world would not be any better, or any worse, than it already was, whoever the winner turned out to be, but you play to win, you fight to prevail; offences must be avenged and wrongs must be righted.

After many millennia, Ishmael had returned from the desert to which he had been banished, to lay claim to his role as Abraham's firstborn son.

ABU AHMID remained in his tent in the desert for ten days and then returned, first to Damascus and then to Amman, to resume contact with the men who would fight his battle on the field: the bishops, the rooks and the knights of his gigantic chessboard.

He waited a few days in a hotel in the centre of town until he received the message he had been waiting for: the date and time of an appointment in the middle of the desert, thirty miles north-east of the F7 oil pipeline pumping station.

Towards evening he hired a taxi and travelled on the road to Baghdad until he'd crossed the border, then he left the taxi at a service station and joined a small caravan of Bedouins headed south-east, towards the pipeline.

They left him at the agreed spot and he waited, alone, until the roar of a helicopter engine could be heard coming from the east, a large Mi–24 Russian-made combat helicopter armed with missiles, cannons and rocket launchers.

It was flying just a few metres from the ground, raising a dense cloud of dust as it passed. It flew over the oil pipeline, came to a standstill in the air and then landed about 100 metres away from where he was standing. The rotor blades continued to spin for a few minutes, then slowed down and came to a complete stop. The door opened and an officer wearing a tanker's beret and a leather pilot's jacket came towards him on foot. The helicopter turned off the lights on board, plunging the area into darkness and silence.

The two men were now standing opposite each other.

'*Salaam alekum*, General Taksoun,' said Abu Ahmid.

'*Alekum salaam*,' replied the officer with a slight nod of his head.

'I'm glad that you agreed to meet me.'

A cold wind was blowing and the sky threatened rain. The general was a thick-set man of about fifty. He had the dark complexion and large hands of the peasants from the south, but an uncommon pride in his bearing and gaze.

'This meeting is very dangerous, Abu Ahmid,' he said, 'and it will have to be as quick as possible.'

'I agree, General. I asked for this face-to-face encounter because what I have to tell you is so important that no message from any intermediary could communicate its full impact. Furthermore, the response can pass through no middleman; I must hear it directly from your lips. I will lay out my plan and my proposal. You have to abandon your . . . collaboration with the Americans and come over to our side.'

The man started. 'I will not remain here one more minute if you attempt to insinuate—'

'Don't bother protesting, General. We have indisputable evidence of what I've just said, and we are ready to hand it over to your chief if you don't calm down and listen very attentively.'

Taksoun looked at him in astonishment, without attempting a reply. He could see only the man's eyes, because the rest of his face was covered, and it was difficult to catch the expression in them, the fleeting light of an unstable, restless spirit.

'You need not modify a single detail of your agreement with

them. You can even count on our collaboration. We are much more reliable than those friends of yours, who know nothing about the men or the territory.

'Trust me,' he said, seeing the other's bewildered expression, 'no one, besides myself and another person whom I can trust completely, is aware of this situation, so you have nothing to fear. You are actually quite highly considered in this part of the world. The Iranians, in particular, are pleased to have a Shiite like yourself on their side. As am I. To demonstrate my own esteem I have brought you a little gift.' He took a photograph out of his pocket and handed it to the general.

'What is this?' he asked.

'A jihad combatant sworn to suicide, a soldier in the President's guard. He will be the one to blow up your Reis the day of the parade, much more reliably than the commando unit you have chosen for the same task. It's quite likely that you would be exposed before you managed to succeed in your goal, which would mean your immediate execution. So allow us, if you don't mind, to take care of this one.

'After the explosion, you will preside over the solemn funeral rites for any bits and pieces of al Bashar they may find scattered over the parade ground, and then you will take supreme command of the armed forces and have yourself named temporary head of state that very day, pending elections to be held at a future date.

'Your first step will be to confirm official diplomatic relations with the Americans. Then you will immediately establish, secretly of course, a plan for a close alliance with the new Syrian president, who supports our project. You will contact the Iranians as well, who are already behind us, and several fundamentalist groups in Egypt and Jordan, according to our instructions.

'I will take care of arranging the appointments and meetings, in absolute secrecy.'

General Taksoun raised his eyes to the clouds gathering in

the sky and tried to make out Ahmid's expression in the darkness beneath the keffiyeh that hid most of his face.

Abu Ahmid nodded, looking up as well at the thickening black clouds driven by the khamsin. 'A storm is coming up,' he said, and seemed to be listening to the sound of the wind growing stronger, 'a storm the likes of which the world hasn't seen since the last world war. And this will be Armageddon.'

Taksoun shook his head. 'You think you can set off another war, Abu Ahmid? It won't work. There's only one superpower left in this world and their military supremacy is overwhelming. Alliances or no alliances, the times of Salah ad Din and Harun al Rashid will never come back. My choice was not a betrayal of the Arab cause; rather, it is the only way out, the only way to set this country free from poverty and from civil and political degradation.'

'I believe you, General. But listen carefully. This time there won't be any superpowers in the arena. The battle will be between the powers in play in our little corner of the world. I can't tell you yet how this will happen. When the first part of my plan attains its goal, you'll understand. What I can absolutely guarantee is that the United States will be in chains on the other side of the ocean, without being able to move a single ship, plane or man. America will have a gun pointed at its head and I, in person, will have my finger on the trigger.'

Taksoun looked hard for a hint of what might be going through the man's mind, and listened closely as he continued.

'At that point, our forces will move, lightning swift, in two directions.' He used the tip of a stick to sketch out his plans in the sandy soil. 'One part will go south, with the backing of the Iranians, advancing day and night until they reach the Kuwaiti and Saudi oil wells, which they will proceed to mine. Ensuring one third of the planet's energy resources in our hands. The bulk of our forces will move west, where they will join with the other Arab nations at the walls of Jerusalem.

'You will lead the largest part of this army and I can guarantee that you will be the supreme commander.'

The first drops of rain fell on the sand with small dull thuds, releasing the pleasant odour of doused dust.

'What is your answer, General?'

Taksoun nervously bit his lower lip. 'Afterwards . . . what will happen then? A threat like the one you've devised can't be kept up indefinitely. If you keep a pistol pointed at someone's head for too long without pulling the trigger, sooner or later he'll manage to surprise you and disarm you.'

'This has been foreseen as well,' replied Abu Ahmid. 'It should suffice for you to know that when we're ready to negotiate, our position will put us at an absolute advantage. Well, General, what is your answer?'

'You seem very sure of yourself, Abu Ahmid,' said the officer. 'But if I were to . . .'

Abu Ahmid watched calmly as the general's hand settled on the butt of his gun.

'You forget that there's another person, besides myself, who knows everything about you. If you were to take such a risk, you would never make it back to headquarters, my friend. Isn't your pilot, by chance, a young lieutenant from Zahko who served up to two weeks ago at the Erbil base and who has the habit of wearing his gun on his right side?'

Taksoun took a startled look at the helicopter, then seemed to think for a minute. 'All right.' He nodded. 'Yes, you can count on me.'

'And you on me,' said Abu Ahmid. 'At any time of day or night and in any weather.'

The wind blew harder and a flash of lightning lit the swollen clouds waiting on the horizon.

'But how will I—'

'You will never be able to contact me, for the simple reason that you will not know who I might be or where I can be found. I will come looking for you. And find you.'

'Farewell, then, Abu Ahmid.'

'Goodbye, General Taksoun. The day of the military parade is not far off. *Allah Akbar.*'

'*Allah Akbar,*' answered the general.

He nodded and turned towards the helicopter. The pilot started up the engine and the blades began to rotate faster and faster until the craft lifted into the air. Beneath them, the man wrapped in his keffiyeh became very small, until he disappeared behind a veil of rain. The general looked away and sat thinking as the helicopter flew over the deserted banks of the Euphrates.

He suddenly turned towards the pilot. 'Where are you from, lieutenant?' he asked.

'Town called Zahko, sir,' the young officer answered.

THE SAME DAY, but much later that night, Gad Avner left the National Security Council meeting in a very bad temper. The politicians, as usual, had spent the whole time tearing each other to pieces without reaching any decision regarding his request for a special allocation to reinforce the intelligence services.

They had asked him for proof, solid evidence that would justify such a large financial commitment, but all he had to offer was an old bloodhound's sixth sense of danger in the offing. Yes, but something solid, they demanded. Unusual activity in certain circles, edginess in several banking institutes, suspicious transfers of massive sums of capital, disturbing euphoria among political prisoners. And two words: Operation Nebuchadnezzar.

'And you're asking us to allocate five hundred million shekels on the basis of two words?' asked the leader of the opposition. 'What kind of an idiot are you?'

'Do you know who Nebuchadnezzar was?' replied Avner. 'The King of Babylon who took Jerusalem in 586 BC, destroyed the Temple and deported the remaining population to Mesopotamia,' he said, leaving the room and slamming the door after him.

Now he was a few steps away from the Wailing Wall,

alongside the courtyard where he had parked his car. The neighbourhood was very quiet and almost no one was out on the streets.

He started up the car and drove past the square that was guarded by soldiers in combat fatigues, towards the King David Hotel, where one of his men was waiting for him with urgent news.

He was a recent acquisition but a good one: a young secret service agent, a second lieutenant of Italian origin, the son of a Venetian rabbi. Fabrizio Ferrario was working for him under-cover as a social worker in an international charity organization with headquarters at the Jerusalem Plaza. Good-looking, he dressed with effortless but unmistakable elegance, nothing but perfect Armani shirts, whether under a blazer or a bush jacket.

They met at the bar in the lobby. Avner lit up a cigarette and ordered an ice-cold Maccabi.

'What was so important that it couldn't wait until the end of the meeting?' he asked.

'Two things,' said the young man. 'The first is that Operation Nebuchadnezzar does exist and is, in all probability, ready to go.'

'And the second?' asked Avner without looking up from his drink.

'We have to take a walk. You have to see this for yourself, and right away.'

'A walk? Where to?'

'Follow me, as soon as you've finished your beer. It isn't far.'

'What else have you found out about Operation Nebuchad-nezzar?'

'Not much. What I have learned is from some wire-tapping we've done, mainly in the prisons. There are transfers in progress from several of the Middle Eastern banks, like the Banque du Liban and the Saudi Arabian, and we're talking about considerable sums.'

'Payments? In which direction?'

'Swiss accounts. Nassau. We're investigating likely recipients, especially in the Sicilian and Russian mafias. It shouldn't take us long.'

Avner had finished his beer and followed his companion out as the bartender turned to a couple of American tourists who weren't ready to call it a day. Tourists in Jerusalem had become a rare commodity lately.

They walked down the deserted street to the great Antonian Fortress archway.

'What do you think they're buying with that money?'

'Arms, electronic surveillance devices, missile systems, bacteriological and chemical weapons . . . who knows?'

'No, I don't think so,' said Avner. 'Those kinds of goods are bought and sold by state ministers in this part of the world. The Palestinian Authority doesn't have a cent and Hamas is already being financed by the Iranians and Libyans. They're giving away plastic explosives on practically every street corner. Have I left something out?'

'The ex-Soviet arsenal. You can get anything from them, at a good deal.'

'Yeah,' said Avner, pulling his coat collar up around his neck.

They had reached the centre of a large underpass and could see a weak halo of light filtering through a section of the wall between two soldiers armed with Uzi machine guns.

'We're almost there,' said the lieutenant. 'It's this way.'

Avner followed him into a sort of tunnel dug into the wall of the fortress, cut through the solid rock. They could hear voices coming from inside and the passage was lit by a couple of neon lights hanging on the walls.

'What is this?' asked Avner.

They'd already reached the end of the open part of the passage, where a group of people with miner's hats and digging tools were at work. Avner recognized the archaeologist Ygael Allon among them; he had been a cabinet member during the Shimon Peres government.

Lieutenant Ferrario introduced Avner as 'Engineer Nathaniel Cohen of the civil engineers'.

'Pleased to meet you,' said Avner, grasping the archaeologist's dust-covered hand. Then he turned towards the tunnel which appeared to be partially caved in. 'But what is this?' he repeated.

Allon showed him a few ceramic fragments and shone a torch on a short inscription in the wall. 'It's a tunnel from the age of the kings of Judah. And it seems to lead to the Temple.'

4

WILLIAM BLAKE had dozed off for a couple of hours, trying to get a little sleep before they landed. He was woken by a voice over the intercom that wished them all a merry Christmas and asked them to fasten their seat belts. When he opened his eyes he saw that the plane's window shades had been lowered. Gordon was nowhere to be seen; he must have gone into the cockpit.

'Where are we?' he asked Sullivan.

'Nearly at our destination, Professor Blake,' was the reply.

Not much of an answer. But Blake thought they must be somewhere west of Luxor if the descriptions of the terrain that his companions had provided him with at the beginning of the flight were accurate.

Sullivan and Gordon had shown him a few snapshots that they had taken inside the tomb, but it was still rather difficult to get an overall idea, because of the constricted angles of the shots. What was clear was that the tomb was definitely untouched. It was in the same condition, at the time of its discovery, as when the person lying inside had been buried.

A few more minutes went by until the wheels touched down and the engines were reversed. When the plane had nearly come to a complete stop, the pilot opened the side hatch to allow the passengers to exit. Blake stepped into the doorway and inhaled the dry, scented air of the desert. Then he looked around to try to get a bearing on where he was.

The aeroplane had come down on a dirt runway that was smooth and even enough to permit landing without any problems.

It was situated at the centre of a valley which stretched between two mountain ridges. The hillsides were furrowed by a series of gullies joining in the bed of a wadi which meandered across the valley, more or less parallel to the runway. The river bed was completely dry but flanked and shaded here and there by low thorny vegetation, broom and tamarisk bushes.

A station wagon pulled up alongside the plane and loaded on the passengers and their luggage. They set off as the Falcon rolled down the runway towards the hill where a hangar hatch was opening.

They travelled up the river bed for about half an hour, until they reached a group of trailers: the camp of the Warren Mining Corporation. Off to one side was a power generator run by a petrol engine and to the other a large black Bedouin-style tent, probably used for meals and meetings.

Behind the site, on the hillside, was a wheeled cistern connected to pipelines which distributed the water to a number of trailers. One of them was much larger than the others, and Blake imagined it was the residence of the site manager or mining foreman.

All the company vehicles were lined up in a rectangular area marked off by a row of stones: a tracked drill, a dump truck, three Jeeps, a truck and two three-wheeled ATVs.

About 200 metres away from the camp was a cabin with a sack outside full of white powder, also sprinkled liberally all around the structure. Obviously the latrine, with its supply of quicklime to dump into the pit, replacing the toilet flush. He decided immediately that he would never use it; the desert was a big place, and there was nothing worse than the shared latrine in a camp.

On the right, looming over the main valley, the mountain took on the shape of a crouching lion or sphinx. The hammada terrain was typical, a geological formation common to the entire Middle East and most of North Africa: compact soil and sand covered by flint and limestone pebbles. But the setting sun helped to soften the eroded landscape, cloaking it in a rosy glow and making the dried satinpod fruit sparkle like so many silver coins.

The sky had already turned cobalt blue. A full white moon was rising at that moment opposite the setting sun, hovering over the deserted, silent mountain crest. It looked like it was rolling forward over the rugged peaks.

The car stopped in front of the main trailer and a well-dressed man in a khaki-coloured bush jacket came forward to welcome them.

'My name is Alan Maddox,' he said. 'Welcome to Ras Udash, Professor Blake. I hope you had a good trip.'

'Pleased to meet you, Mr Maddox,' replied Blake. 'The trip was fine and I'm feeling much better than I had expected.'

Maddox was a hefty man of about sixty, with wide black eyebrows, a grey moustache and beard. He wore an Australian ranger's hat, grey cotton trousers and a pair of military boots.

'This is your lodging,' he said, pointing to a grey trailer off to the left. 'I'm sure you'd like a shower. The water is always nice and hot here. Dinner will be ready in half an hour, here in my accommodation. I hope we'll have the honour of your company.'

'You can count on it, Mr Maddox. I never manage to eat on planes, not even luxury planes like your Falcon. I'll see you in half an hour.'

Gordon and Sullivan also went to their living quarters, located to the right of the main unit.

Blake entered his trailer, which smelled dusty. Someone had hastily wiped down the floor and the bathroom, smearing the mirror above the sink. The place was sparsely furnished, but he was relieved to see that there was a computer on the desk with what looked like a modem connection and a small portable television.

He got into the shower and let the water run hot. He couldn't help but remember the last shower he'd taken, curled up on the floor like a dog, his stomach gripped by cramps.

He rubbed himself dry with a towel, combed his hair carefully and arranged his toiletries, while the TV blared with news of rioting and skirmishes at the outskirts of Jerusalem and in Hebron. Fifteen Israeli schoolchildren killed before the gunman took his own life. Blake couldn't shake a feeling of dismay; he couldn't remember when the situation had ever been quite so bad in the Middle East.

Would a fifth war break out between the Israelis and the Arabs? And what would the consequences be? He turned off the television, threw a jacket over his shoulders and went outside.

The camp was deserted but he could see lights on in the other trailers and hear the distant rumbling of the generator. For a moment, he thought he saw men moving about on the mountain crest in front of him; it looked as if they were carrying guns.

Suddenly, two trails of flames streaked across the sky as the silence was torn by a thunderous roar. Two jets were chasing each other at low altitude, as if simulating an aerial duel. One of them launched a couple of decoys and managed to get his pursuer off his tail. The decoys fell into the desert, scoring the darkness with two cascades of silvery sparks.

'Never touch anything around here that isn't wood or stone,' said a voice behind him.

'Gordon, it's you! Where did you come from?'

'From my lodgings – that yellow trailer down there on the left. Just enough time for a shower. Maddox is a stickler for punctuality. He's from an old Virginian family and he's used to crystal and silver at dinner. What did you think of him?'

'He seems . . . polite, pleasant.'

'Yeah, but don't let yourself be fooled. He's a tough one. He's old fashioned, very righteous. There's only one thing he cares about: the best interests of the company, and getting the work done.'

'He knows all about the tomb, right?'

Gordon nodded. 'Right.'

'Has he seen it?'

'Yes, he has. We took him over one evening before we left

for Chicago. He was very impressed. Anyway, you'll soon be hearing about it all from him. Come on. He's waiting for us.'

They walked towards the trailer which was being used as the camp headquarters.

Blake stopped suddenly. 'Did you see those two fighter planes, Gordon?'

'Sure, I saw them, why?'

'They were Jaguars, if I'm not mistaken. French-made stuff. What were they doing here? What I mean is, those had to be Israeli fighters, right?'

Gordon was uncertain how to answer. 'I'm not sure,' he said. 'I don't know much about weapons. Anyway, the situation is incredibly tense in the whole Middle East. Nothing would surprise me. But don't worry, the area we're working in is far off the beaten track. No one will bother you.'

They had reached Maddox's trailer. Gordon knocked and their host answered the door personally. His hair was still wet from the shower and he had changed: a Panama suit, blue shirt and cotton neckerchief.

'Merry Christmas to you all!' he greeted them. 'Gordon, Professor Blake, please, come in. I was just getting myself a drink. What do you say to a martini?'

'A martini would be wonderful,' said Blake.

'Fine for me too,' said Gordon.

Sullivan was sitting in a corner of the room and was already sipping his cocktail. He greeted them with a nod.

The table was set with real porcelain, crystal and silver, a carafe of water and one of white wine, and a basket on the white tablecloth held freshly baked Bedouin bread. A synthetic Christmas tree sat on a table in the corner, decorated with dried desert fruits that had been decorated by hand and some coloured lights that blinked on and off.

Maddox had them sit down, with Blake to his right. 'I'm pleased that you accepted my invitation, Professor Blake,' he said. 'Mr Sullivan will already have explained everything, I assume.'

'Yes, he has indeed.'

'What do you think?'

Blake tasted his martini. Exactly the way he liked it: the glass had been just rinsed with vermouth, then filled with straight gin and ice.

'It's hard to say without having seen anything, but from what Gordon tells me it would seem to be a very important discovery. Too important to be investigated like this.'

Maddox looked him straight in the eye. 'You are quite . . . forthright, Professor. That's fine with me. I don't like beating around the bush myself. Do you mean that you don't feel up to the task, or you don't approve of our methods?'

An Arab waiter came and began to serve them. 'I hope you like couscous. It's all we have.'

'Couscous is fine. I love it. Mr Maddox, if I've understood the situation, what I feel doesn't make much of a difference, and I hardly think it would cause you to change your mind. On the other hand, I'm virtually washed up in my field and quite frankly I'm grateful for this opportunity. In other words, I'm in no condition to make demands. I would only like it to be clear that I've accepted this job purely in the interest of science, and in the hopes of publishing the results of my preliminary exploration and the studies that will follow.'

Maddox poured him a glass of wine. 'I'm not sure that you will have the possibility of conducting any further studies, other than viewing the tomb and the objects it contains.'

'I have to, Mr Maddox. You can't be saying that you expect me to understand everything at first glance. Let me tell you, I don't think anyone could.'

Maddox listened quietly and Sullivan looked at him from the corner of his eye.

'I could provide with you access to the Internet on the company computer, under our surveillance, naturally. Would that be sufficient?'

'It would help,' answered Blake. 'I could consult the library at the Oriental Institute and other research institutions. I would say that might be sufficient.'

'As far as publication goes,' continued Maddox, 'it's a problem that can't be dealt with now. I'll have to think about it and consider all the repercussions. Please, let's face one problem at a time, shall we?'

The Arab waiter passed with some beans and poured wine into their glasses.

'It's a Californian Chablis,' said Maddox. 'Not bad, is it? As I was saying, one problem at a time. We would like you to examine the tomb and to determine, if you can, when it was built, and to describe and appraise the objects it contains. I can assure you that we have no intention of doing anything illegal. The fact is that this discovery came as a complete surprise and has considerably interfered with our schedule. We will continue to work as you occupy yourself with the excavation. You'll be able to count on the collaboration of our staff, who have already cleared away the entrance, and use all the technical means at our disposal. Your fees will be paid in cash, when the work is completed, or into an account of your preference, in the United States or elsewhere.'

'One question,' said Blake.

'Yes?'

'Where am I?'

'At the Warren Mining Corporation site at Ras Udash.'

'What I mean is, in what region?'

'I'm afraid I can't tell you that.'

'Then I must warn you that my inability to locate the tomb topographically may very well interfere with its identification.'

Maddox stared at him without blinking an eye. 'That's a risk we'll have to take, Professor.'

The waiter began to clear away the plates and Maddox got up. 'I would suggest that we have our coffee outside, in the Bedouin tent. It's much cooler and you can smoke if you like.'

His guests followed him into the tent and settled on wicker

chairs arranged around a little cast-iron table. The generator was to the leeward and the noise it made was carried off by the evening breeze.

Maddox passed around a box of cigars. 'Always so difficult to find in the States,' he said. 'If only they'd lift that damned Cuban embargo. Here it's not a problem. In the Fertile Crescent, all the heads of states, ministers and members of parliament smoke them.'

'That's not all they smoke,' snickered Gordon.

Blake drank his coffee and lit a cigar. 'When do you want me to start?' he asked.

'Tomorrow's fine,' said Maddox. 'If jet lag isn't a problem. The sooner you begin the better.'

As they were still talking, Blake noticed a light approaching in the midst of a cloud of dust on the track that led to the camp, and the two-stroke engine of an ATV could soon be heard over the noise of the generator. The ATV stopped in the vehicle parking area and a person wearing a dark work suit and a helmet got out. When the helmet was removed a wave of blonde hair settled onto the shoulders of a young woman of about thirty who approached the tent with a quick, light step.

Maddox got up and walked towards her. 'Sarah, come on over. Have you eaten? Sit down and I'll have something brought out for you.'

The girl stepped out of her overalls and hung them on a pole, remaining in jeans and a T-shirt. Blake watched her admiringly as a light wind lifted her hair around her face.

'Let me introduce our guest, Professor William Blake.'

'The Egyptologist,' said the girl, extending her hand. 'I'm Sarah Forrestall. Welcome to Ras Udash. I hope you'll like it here in this inferno. Thirty degrees by day and two or three below zero at night, but it could be worse. This is the best time of day: not too hot and not too cold.'

'I'm used to it,' Blake said.

'Sarah is our topographer. She may be useful for your work,' said Maddox.

'Right,' said Blake. 'A topographer would be just the thing, if you'd let me know where we are, that is.'

Maddox didn't seem to notice, and not even Sarah picked up on his comment as she sat down to eat a cold chicken sandwich that the Arab waiter had brought, together with a bottle of mineral water.

'Professor Blake will be starting tomorrow. Can you give him a ride out and help him if he needs it?' asked Maddox.

'With pleasure,' said the girl. 'I'll meet you at the parking area at seven, if that's all right with you. What do you need?'

'Not much. A ladder to begin with. A rope ladder would be fine. A harness, a torch, a ball of string and a pad of graph paper. I'll take care of the rest. Tomorrow I'll just be doing a general survey and setting up a work schedule. I still don't have a precise idea of what I'll find and what problems may come up. Later you can help me to map out the elevations and position the objects inside the tomb.'

The girl seemed disappointed. 'I had imagined that you'd be bringing in a load of sophisticated instruments, but all you seem to need is a rope ladder and a torch.'

'I'm old-fashioned,' said Blake. 'When the time comes I'll show you some advanced methods of research, but for now that's all I'll be needing. I want to figure out who the person buried in that tomb is. All the way out here, so far away from everything and everyone.'

Gordon got up, said goodnight to them all, and walked off to his trailer, soon imitated by Sullivan.

Maddox looked at his watch. 'We turn in early here,' he said. 'And I've got a long day tomorrow. Goodnight, Professor Blake.'

'Goodnight, Mr Maddox.'

Sarah got up and walked towards a camp stove. 'I'm going to make some coffee,' she said. 'Would you like some?'

'Love it,' said Blake.

'It'll keep you awake. Aren't you tired?'

'Dead tired, but I'm not sleepy. It'll come, sooner or later. A cup of coffee more or less won't make much difference.'

'Well, we don't have any more than ten, fifteen minutes before they turn off the generator. Maddox can't sleep with the noise of the engine.'

'I see.'

'And it will get freezing cold out here before you know it. The temperature drops from one minute to the next.' She poured him some boiling coffee in a plastic cup. 'How do you feel?'

'Eager as all hell to get started. I'm afraid I won't close an eye tonight. I still can't believe all this actually.' He took a sip of coffee and glanced over at the girl sitting in the circle of light cast by a single bulb with a jacket thrown carelessly over her shoulders. She was very pretty and she knew it.

'What's a girl like you doing in a place like this?' he teased.

'They're paying me well,' she said. 'What about you?'

'What do you say to a fire?' he asked in reply.

'You mean a camp fire?'

'Well, there's plenty of dry wood around here and it's starting to get cold.'

The generator suddenly went off and the camp was lit only by the light of the moon.

'If you like.'

Blake went towards the dry river bed, uprooted an old tree trunk and dragged it to the tent, then gathered some brushwood, dry tamarisk and broom branches, and used his lighter to set fire to the pile he'd arranged. The flames rose crackling and enveloped the trunk in a ball of lively orange light.

'Beautiful, isn't it?' He took a chair and went to sit next to the bonfire, lighting up a cigarette.

'Well, what about you? What are you doing in a place like this?' the girl asked again.

Blake turned towards her and noticed her slim figure caressed by the light of the flames.

'I was an Egyptologist at the Oriental Institute in Chicago, and not one of the worst. I got burned doing something stupid and my superiors and colleagues couldn't believe their luck. I accepted this job because I had no future.'

'Are you married?'

'Divorced. For . . . two days now.'

'Fresh wound, huh?' She studied him with an odd expression that to Blake looked like condescension.

'When it rains, it pours, I guess,' he said. 'Things happen. You survive. A change of air and starting to work again will do me good.'

Sarah met his glance for a moment through the flickering light and read emotion much deeper than the perfunctory words he'd pronounced. She felt a wave of desire for him, but pulled back instinctively.

'You can count on my technical assistance,' she said. 'Anything else you can forget about.'

Blake didn't respond. Instead, he poked at the ashes under the fire to stoke up the flame, then stood up. 'Thanks for the company,' he said, and walked away.

In his trailer, he felt a wave of claustrophobia mixed with anger at Sarah's needlessly scornful words, and he realized that he wouldn't be able to bear staying inside.

He took a sleeping bag and went out of the back door, walking off along the edge of the hills that bordered the camp to the east.

He was soon under the shadow of the sphinx-shaped mountain and he continued to walk along a dry river bed that descended towards the valley. In a corner he found a strip of fine, clean sand and stretched out, taking in the incredibly bright, clear constellations.

He thought angrily of Sarah's blonde hair and her body

sculpted by the light of the fire, seething at the thought of what she must think of him, until the silence of the desert, the cosmic silence of complete solitude, entered into his spirit and calmed him. All of the ghosts crowding his mind began to fade away, and he gradually became aware of the creatures of the night, heard the trotting pace of the jackal and the timid, watchful gait of the gazelle.

He realized that he couldn't be west of Luxor. Perhaps he was about to fall asleep in some hidden corner of the desert of Wadi Hammamat, where the fabled gold mines of the Pharaohs were said to lie.

He stared languidly at the celestial image of Ra, its belt of shining stars, until his eyes closed.

SARAH FORRESTALL had gone to Blake's trailer right after he'd walked off and knocked on the door. 'Blake, I'm sorry. I didn't mean to offend you. Blake?' She got no answer and so returned to the campfire he had lit for her to enjoy the last warmth of the flames. Professor Blake was totally different from what she'd expected. A very special breed of loser, the kind who waits patiently at the river's edge until the corpse of his enemy floats by. His kind always come back, sooner or later, and when they do, they leave no survivors.

BLAKE REACHED the parking lot slightly before seven and saw that Sarah Forrestall was already there, warming up the Jeep's engine.

'You could have opened the door last night,' she said. 'You could have let me explain—'

'You explained yourself very well. Anyway, I wasn't in. I slept in the river bed.'

'In the wadi? You're crazy! Snakes and scorpions are attracted by body heat. You might have been bitten.'

'I'm OK.'

'Have you had breakfast at least?'

'A glass of water. It helps me get over the jet lag.'

Sarah started up the Jeep and they drove south along a barely visible track that sometimes disappeared completely into the river bed.

'You really should eat something. Look in my bag. There's plenty there: sandwiches, fruit. I've taken them for lunch but there's more than enough.'

'Thanks,' said Blake, but he did not move. He gut was filled with anger and anxiety. There was no room for anything else.

'Hold on,' said Sarah, 'this is where we leave the wadi.' She downshifted and accelerated. The Jeep climbed up the steep wadi wall, hurling a hail of pebbles backwards from under its wheels until it finally settled into a horizontal position.

They faced a vast, flat black expanse scorched by the sun.

'Is it that way?' asked Blake.

'Yeah, about an hour's drive from here. Apart from the heat, the worst is over.'

Blake had pulled out the graph paper and a compass and continuously checked the mileage counter, sketching out a rough itinerary and adding natural elements as they came.

'You don't give up, do you?' asked Sarah.

'No. And I don't understand why no one will tell me where we are. I'm sure you know, right?'

'No. They brought me here more or less like they did you and I'm keeping my nose out of things. Maddox doesn't kid around and I have to watch my own butt.'

'I'll figure it out anyway,' said Blake. 'I know this country like the back of my hand. Give me three, four days at most and I'll surprise you.' But inside he wasn't so sure. He'd left in such a damned hurry. If only he'd thought to bring the LORAN. In two seconds the satellite navigator would have given him their exact topographical position.

The track had taken them close to the mountain ridge that bordered the plain on the east and Blake suddenly noticed something on the rocks. 'Could you stop, please?'

'Sure, no problem,' Sarah replied, braking. 'What is it that you see?'

'Rock carvings. Look! Over there on that wall.'

'Oh, there are tons of them around here. I've even sketched some of them. I have a whole album full back at the camp, if you're interested.'

'I'd like to see them,' said Blake. 'But just let me take a look at these,' he said, moving towards the rock.

'I don't get it,' said the girl. 'There's an entire Egyptian tomb waiting for you and you stop to look at these scribbles on the rocks?'

'These scribbles were put here to leave a message for whoever passed this way and I'd like to understand it. Any evidence on the territory is precious.'

The terrain near the rock wall was surrounded by boulders, some of which were ringed by smaller stones, as if someone had wanted to attract attention to them.

Blake walked to the wall and examined the incisions. They had been formed using a sharp stone as a percussion tool and represented a scene of ibex hunting. The hunters wielded bows and arrows and were circling the animal, which was drawn with its long horns curved backwards. He took a few photographs and marked the position on his map. Then they got back into the Jeep.

'Have you ever gone up the wadi towards the mountain?' Blake asked.

'A few times.'

'And you didn't notice anything strange?'

'I wouldn't say so. Stones, snakes, scorpions.'

'The rocks show signs of high-temperature fires.'

'What does that mean?'

'I don't know, but I noticed that the sand was vitrified in a couple of spots.'

'You know, it could have been a phosphorous bomb. There have been a lot of wars out this way.'

'No, I don't think it was a bomb. The vitrified sand was on the bottom of a couple of pits dug artificially in the rock and there were carvings of the type we just saw on the inside of the wells.'

'Which means?'

'That someone was capable of lighting high-temperature fires more than three thousand years ago in the midst of all this desolation.'

'Interesting. What for?'

'I don't know. But I'd like to find out.'

The landscape had become even more barren and the warming air created the illusion of water in the distance.

'This place must be a furnace in the summer,' said Blake.

'It is,' said Sarah. 'But in this season the weather can change quite suddenly. You'll see a cloud passing and then boom! There's an abrupt drop in temperature and a very violent storm breaks. The wadis fill up completely, because the soil can't absorb all the rainfall, and that can lead to disastrous flooding. Nature here is decidedly . . . hostile.'

Back on the road Blake watched as the landscape changed again and the Jeep jolted at every crag in the hard, white calcareous crust. Sarah slowed down and downshifted and then turned towards the hills on their left.

Blake motioned for her to slow down again.

'What is it now?' complained Sarah, stepping on the brake.

'Another rock carving. Look! Over there on the mountainside, on that slab of flint.'

Blake got out of the Jeep and walked over to the carving. It represented a curved shepherd's crook and a serpent.

'Extraordinary!' he exclaimed. 'This reminds me of something . . . Let me get a photograph, please.'

'We're very close to the tomb now, you know. See that caved-in part of the rock?' She pointed at a barren area a couple of hundred metres in front of them. 'That's where it is. We're here.'

Blake took a deep breath as he got back into the vehicle. He braced himself to feel the strongest emotion of his whole life.

As soon as the Jeep stopped, he got out and examined the surrounding terrain. He noticed a small depression at the centre of a calcareous slab where pebbles and sand had been mounded. 'It's there, isn't it?'

Sarah nodded.

Blake shook his head. 'I don't get it. All this secrecy and the site is left completely unguarded. I'd have been told otherwise.'

'It may look that way,' said Sarah, 'but no one can get near this place unless Maddox wants them to.' She looked him straight in the eyes. 'And most of all, no one can get away. To reach the nearest settlement you have to cross a hundred miles of this desert, without a blade of grass or a drop of water.'

Blake didn't reply. He took off his jacket, got the shovel out of the Jeep and approached the small depression, removing the pebbles and sand. He soon hit an iron plate that must have been placed there to cover the opening.

'Why did you choose this precise spot to drill?' he asked.

'Pure chance,' answered Sarah. 'We do sample boring and analyse the cores on the basis of either previous geological surveys or statistics. I can guarantee that this was nothing more than extraordinary luck.'

The heavy iron plate had a ring at its centre. Blake hooked up the Jeep cable and signalled to Sarah to drag it off. A cylindrical aperture which had perforated the calcareous layer was uncovered. He could see the signs left by the drill on the sides of the hole, but the bottom was completely dark.

'Have you gone down yet?'

'Not yet,' Sarah replied, getting the rope ladder and torch from the Jeep. The sun had risen high on the horizon, but it wasn't unbearably hot because the air was so dry. Blake took a couple of long drinks from his canteen, then put on the harness. He took the ball of string, tied one end to his belt and left the ball sitting next to the driver's seat in the Jeep.

He hung the torch from one of the clips on his belt and then instructed Sarah: 'Get into the Jeep and start it up. I'll hook the winch cable onto my harness and you'll lower me very slowly into the underground room. You hold this end of the string and stop the winch when you feel me pulling on it. When I yank it again, lower me some more. OK?'

'Yes, I've got it. But why don't you use the rope ladder?' she asked.

'Because by unrolling it in the dark I could bump into or break something that's fragile or off balance. I have to see what's down there first.'

He hooked the end of the winch cable to the harness, and began his descent.

He dropped down a couple of metres, and realized that he was suspended in the middle of the tomb. He tugged on the string. Sarah stopped the winch and he switched on the torch.

A world which had lain sleeping for thirty centuries leapt to life before his eyes and in the intense silence of the tomb the beating of his heart seemed enormously amplified. Odours imprisoned for thousands of years filled his nostrils with strange, unknown scents. Violent, contrasting sensations crowded all together inside of him, arousing awe, anxiety, fear.

The sun's rays, filtered through the fine dust that had been stirred by opening the hatch and descending into the tomb, struck a panoply, with a copper and enamel helmet and bronze breastplate in the shape of unfurled falcon's wings, set with precious stones, amber, quartz and lapis lazuli. A golden belt with a lapis lazuli buckle shaped like a scarab held a sword with an ebony hilt ornamented with silver studs. There were two lances and two bronze-tipped javelins and there was a huge bow, its quiver still full of arrows.

Sarah pulled the handbrake and shouted down, 'Blake! Blake! Everything all right?'

All she heard in response was a muted voice murmuring, 'Oh, my God . . .'

Blake shone the torch over the rest of the tomb. At the northern end of the funeral chamber was a dismantled war chariot. The two four-spoked wheels rested on top of each other in a corner, while the cart was leaning against the wall, with its shaft nearly touching the ceiling. The remains of the reins hung from the shaft, while two bronze horse's bits had fallen onto the ground on either side of the chariot.

On the northern wall there were other extravagant objects: a bronze candelabrum, a painted wooden throne, a headrest, a four-branched candlestick, a chest which had probably held precious fabrics. He turned the torch towards the southern wall and a wave of disappointment hit him. The sarcophagus was nearly completely buried under a mass of rubble and stones, some of them quite large.

He was so dazed and astonished that he had forgotten to have himself lowered to the floor. He gave a tug on the string and called to Sarah, 'You can drop me to the bottom, Miss Forrestall. There's nothing below me. You can come down too, if you like. Fasten the rope ladder on that end and send it down. I'll catch it.'

Sarah started up the winch and Blake soon hit the ground, softly, nearly at the centre of the tomb, on the heap of detritus which had fallen during the drilling. The girl soon lowered the ladder and descended into the tomb with Blake.

'This is incredible,' she said, looking around.

Blake pointed the torch at the southern wall. 'Look. Unfortunately, a cave-in has almost completely buried the sarcophagus. Must have been an earthquake. It'll take days of work to get it free. Removing all that debris won't be easy. What's more, we'll have to pile it up outside. The colour is so different from the surrounding soil that it will certainly attract attention, even from quite a distance.'

They approached the walls and examined them carefully. They had been chiselled in a limestone which was not very hard and rather crumbly, but there were no traces of decoration, besides the beginnings of a hieroglyphic inscription on the left-hand side of the sarcophagus.

Blake's gaze shifted to the floor in front of the sarcophagus. 'That's strange,' he said. 'There are no canopic jars. Very, very strange. I've never seen that before.'

'What are they?' asked Sarah.

'They were jars used to hold the internal organs of the dead person, after the embalmers had extracted them from the chest cavity. It's as if the body of this person did not undergo the traditional embalming rites. And that's very strange in itself, seeing as he's obviously very high-ranking. Unless the jars are inside the sarcophagus.'

They walked over to the front of the landslide and examined it carefully. That was strange, too. If an earthquake had caused the pile-up, why were all the other objects in perfect order? Why hadn't the chariot wheels leaning up against the wall fallen over and why was the armour still perfectly arranged?

He noticed a number of other anomalies: a haphazard air in the assortment of objects, which seemed to be from different time periods, a hurried look to the burial chamber, as if the walls had been adapted from a pre-existing natural cavity. The sarcophagus itself seemed to be carved into the rock. The stone-dressers had cut and removed the rock all around it until they had excavated a rectangular shape that was then hollowed out. But it was too early to say; all the debris would have to be removed before he could confirm his impressions.

He tried to climb up the pile of rubble but it slid forward, filling the room with a dense cloud of dust.

'Damn!' he cursed.

Sarah held out her hand to help him up. 'Are you OK?'

'Yes, of course,' he replied. 'It's nothing.'

He waited until the dust had settled a little and approached the landslide again. The further sliding of the rocks had uncovered a dark corner on the right wall above the sarcophagus that hinted at a bigger opening. Beyond he thought he could perhaps make out the start of a corridor. He tried to climb up again, much more cautiously this time, and nearly made it to the opening.

He couldn't see anything, because the corridor curved almost immediately, but when he turned and used the torch to light up the rest of the wall, he noticed something at the foot of the heap, sticking out from the rest.

'What is it?' asked Sarah.

'Could you shine the light on it, please?' he asked her, and took the trowel from his pocket, scraping and cleaning all around the protruding mass. He uncovered a femur and then a skull, and in a few minutes' time a tangled jumble of skeletons.

'Who could they be?' wondered Sarah.

'I have no idea,' replied Blake. 'The bodies were burned and then covered with a few shovels full of earth.'

He was baffled and upset. This admittedly superficial inspection had raised enormous problems of interpretation. Would he ever be able to crack the mystery of who this person, buried like a Pharaoh in the middle of nowhere, was?

He took out his camera and photographed every visible detail of the tomb, then began to measure and sketch each piece, while Sarah did the surveying work and recorded the position of each object on the graph paper.

He didn't stop working until heat and fatigue overwhelmed him. Nearly three hours had passed without his noticing. He suddenly felt very weak and deadly tired; looking at Sarah, he realized that she must be exhausted as well.

'Let's go,' he said. 'We've done enough for today.'

They climbed up the rope ladder and when they got to the surface Blake felt so light-headed he had to lean against the Jeep to keep from falling.

Sarah reached out a hand. 'Blake, you are so stubborn. You've been down in that hole for hours without anything in your stomach and a ten-hour flight behind you, not to mention all the rest. Divorces are tiring, from what I hear.'

'You're right,' said Blake. He went to sit in the shade of the

Jeep and had something to eat. There was a slight, cooling breeze.

'Well, what do you think?'

Blake drank a half-bottle of water before answering because he felt so dehydrated, then began, 'Miss Forrestall—'

'Listen, Blake, it seems pretty silly to continue with all these formalities, seeing as we're going to be working side by side for quite a while. If you're not still angry with me for that stupid thing I said last night, I'd like you to call me Sarah.'

'OK, Sarah, fine with me. But don't treat me that way again. You're a beautiful girl and you seem to be very intelligent as well, but I'd like you to know that I can do fine without a woman for a couple of weeks, without having to beg anyone for anything.'

Sarah seemed to hesitate, but Blake smiled as if to play down what had happened and returned to the topic at hand. 'I'd say the complex is extraordinarily interesting, much more so than I expected, but it's going to be difficult to unravel all this evidence. There are enormous problems.'

'There are?'

'First of all, the fact that I don't know where I am is creating practically insurmountable problems of interpretation.'

'OK, besides that?'

'The funeral objects are from different ages, the tomb is very different from any I've ever seen, and the burial seems to have been very hurried. People were killed inside before the tomb was sealed, and what's more, the landslide that we saw was not caused by an earthquake, otherwise the armour would have fallen to the ground, along with the chariot wheels, which are just propped up against the wall.'

'What time period do you think it's from?'

Blake took an apple from the bag and bit into it.

'It's difficult to say with any precision, but what I've seen would lead me to place it in the New Kingdom, in the age of Ramses II or Merenptah, but I could be wrong. I noticed, for example, a plaque from Amenemhat IV on the headrest which is much, much older. It's a real puzzle.'

'No idea of who could be buried inside?'

'Not yet. But I have to decipher the texts and get that landslide out of the way so I can open the sarcophagus. The characteristics of the mummy and the objects inside should give me the key for ascertaining his identity. I can only say that he seems to be a very high-ranking person, perhaps even a Pharaoh. Tell me where we are, Sarah, and it will be so much easier for me ... We're at Wadi Hammamat, right?'

Sarah shook her head. 'William, I'm sorry, I can't help you. Don't ask me any more, please.'

'Fine,' said Blake, tossing aside the apple core. He lit up a cigarette and quietly watched the sun as it began to descend over the boundless desert plain. There was not a stone, not a single feature of the terrain that recalled anything familiar. It was all so strange and different; even the sun looked different in this setting, as absurd as it seemed.

He buried the cigarette butt in the sand and said, 'Let's get back to camp now. I'm really tired.'

It was nearly dusk when they arrived and Blake went to make a report to Maddox after a quick shower in his trailer. He explained his point of view and the doubts that had arisen during his exploration of the tomb.

Maddox seemed very interested and attentively followed every word of his report. When Blake had finished, Maddox accompanied him to the door.

'Relax a little, Blake,' he said. 'You must be dead tired. Dinner is at six thirty in the Bedouin tent, if you'd like to join us. Last night we ate later because we were expecting you, but usually we eat early, American style.'

'I'll be there,' said Blake, and then, before leaving, 'I have to develop and print some photos.'

'We have all the necessary equipment,' replied Maddox, 'because we often take aerial photos from the balloon and develop the film in our own darkroom. Sarah Forrestall will show you where it is.'

Blake thanked him and walked south towards the wadi to while away the time until dinner. He was too tired to work.

The air was a little cooler. The tamarisks and broom cast long shadows over the clean gravel on the bottom of the river bed. Blake watched the lizards scatter at his arrival and for a moment saw an ibex, standing with its great curved horns against the disc of the sun descending behind the hills. The animal seemed to consider him for an instant and then turned with a quick sidestep and vanished, as if into thin air.

He hiked for nearly an hour before turning back and that long walk calmed and relaxed him, dissolving the tension that always gripped the nape of his neck when he was absorbed in his research. The sun had nearly disappeared behind the line of hills, but its rays skimmed the peaks that rose up from the plain, sculpting and cloaking them in a clear, tawny light.

Just then, as he returned towards the camp, his gaze was attracted by a rise to his left which was about half a mile away. Its peak was lit up by the rays of the setting sun.

It looked exactly like a pyramid. The horizontal layers of its stratification accentuated the impression, creating a perfect illusion of a man-made structure. He thought of the other mountain dominating the camp; it looked like a crouching lion or a sphinx. What place was this, where nature and chance had combined to recreate the most emblematic and suggestive landscapes of ancient Egypt? He turned it over and over in his mind as the valley of Ras Udash sank slowly into the shadows of the night.

5

It took Blake a few days to photograph, describe and survey all the objects in the tomb, with Sarah's help. He decided to leave each item in its original position and built a partition with wooden boards and plastic sheeting to isolate the sarcophagus and most of the rubble around it from the rest.

Ray Sullivan helped him to build a kind of vacuum cleaner to remove the dust, which would be especially useful when he began to remove the debris and to transfer it all up to the surface. To make the job easier, he built a framework over the opening and equipped it with a pulley so he could let down the Jeep's winch cable with a big hanging bucket-like container that he'd had made at the camp to hold the rubble. When he was ready to start clearing it away, he went, as usual, to Maddox's trailer shortly before dinner.

'How are things going, Professor Blake?'

'They're going well, Mr Maddox. But there's a problem I have to talk to you about.'

'What's the matter?'

'Well, I've finished all the surveying work, but now I have to free the sarcophagus from the landslide that's covering it. I'm calculating that it'll be about twenty cubic metres of material – dust, pebbles and sand, mostly – and the only way to get it out is by hand. Now, I'm wondering how many people are aware of what we're doing. You, Sullivan, Gordon, Miss Forrestall and me make five. We'll need workers if we want to get it done in a reasonable amount of time, but that means other people will have to be involved in the find. I'd say that it's up to you to decide.'

'How many men do you need?'

'Two for removing the rubble. No more, because there's not enough room. One working the vacuum cleaner and another at the winch.'

'I'll give you three workers. Sullivan can take care of the winch.'

'How many other people, at the camp, know about the tomb?'

'No one, besides those you've just mentioned. I don't think we have a choice as far as the three workers are concerned.'

'I'd say not.'

'How long will it take to remove this slide?'

'If they work hard, we can get up to two or three cubic metres out a day, which means that in a little over a week we'd be ready to open the sarcophagus.'

'Fine. We'll start on this tomorrow. I'll choose the workers personally. At seven tomorrow morning they'll be waiting for you at the parking lot. Will you still need Miss Forrestall's help?'

Blake hesitated for a minute, then said, 'Yes. She's been a great help.'

The only people present at dinner, perhaps not by chance, were those who knew about the tomb, and so they continued talking about it until they went to have their coffee in the Bedouin tent. Listening and watching them attentively, Blake realized that Sullivan, besides being an excellent technician, was Maddox's right-hand man, maybe even his bodyguard. Gordon seemed to be the middleman between Maddox and the company administration, and Maddox himself seemed to think very highly of him, if not to fear him. There was no doubt that Sarah Forrestall was the most independent of the bunch, and that wasn't easy to explain.

After Gordon and Sullivan had turned in, Maddox asked him,

'Professor Blake, in your opinion, just what are those things down in the tomb worth?'

It was a question that Blake had been expecting for some time. 'In theory, they're priceless. Certainly in the field of tens of millions of dollars.' And he tried to look for a reaction to his words in the eyes of both Maddox and Sarah.

'In theory?' asked Maddox.

'Yes, that's right. Getting the material out of here would be almost impossible. You'd have to corrupt half the public officials of the Arab Republic of Egypt and even if you did, that wouldn't be enough. In theory, you could use your Falcon, but you'd have to practically rebuild it inside to make it suitable to transport such goods, and out here that wouldn't be simple. Without considering that you'd have to build a protective framework around each piece, increasing their bulk tremendously. Some of the pieces wouldn't even fit through the door.

'And even if you did manage to move a certain number of objects, the smaller ones, say, you wouldn't be able to exhibit them or allow potential buyers to make them public in any way. The sudden appearance of all this material from such a rich archaeological find, completely undocumented, would lead immediately to an investigation and Egypt would demand the return of the goods. It would be a very big mess to talk your way out of.

'My opinion, once again, is that the discovery should be announced officially and the findings published, Mr Maddox.'

Maddox didn't answer and Sarah Forrestall continued to sip her coffee, as though it were none of her business.

'It doesn't depend on me, Professor Blake,' said Maddox finally. 'In any case, we need a detailed estimate of the value of the tomb contents, as accurate as possible.'

'I'll do that,' said Blake, 'but only when I've finished with the excavation. It wouldn't make sense now. We don't even know what's in the sarcophagus.'

'As you wish, Blake, but keep in mind that we won't be here for long. Goodnight, Professor.'

'Goodnight, Mr Maddox,' replied Blake. Then, as soon as Maddox had left, he turned to Sarah. 'What is this story about the estimate?'

'Shall we take a walk?' asked Sarah.

Blake followed her and they crossed the camp, passing in front of the tents of the workers, who were sitting around playing cards and drinking beer. It was almost time for the generator to go off.

'It's logical, isn't it?' observed Sarah. 'There are tens of millions of dollars down there in assorted antiquities and it's more than understandable that Warren Mining is eager to do business.'

'I thought that cadmium exploration and processing were Warren Mining's core business.'

'They are, but the company's in financial trouble.'

'How do you know?'

'Rumours.'

'Just rumours?'

'No, not only. I accessed a restricted file in the host computer. These guys owe me a lot of money. I had the right to find out more about the company's financial situation.'

'But this is crazy! You really think they want to solve their financial problems with archaeological finds?'

'Why not? All they are to them are goods with an extremely high market value that could save them from bankruptcy. You tell me why else they would have organized this whole thing, and why they picked someone like you.'

'You mean, why did they pick a failure?'

'I mean a man who's an outsider, isolated, out of a job.'

Blake didn't answer. The generator abruptly went off and the camp was plunged into darkness, leaving the mountain peaks to hold up the miracle of the night sky. Blake's gaze wandered through the infinity of stars teeming across the diaphanous veil of the galaxy. 'Maybe you're right,' he said. 'But it's not important compared to the enigma that's hidden in that tomb. You have to help me save the evidence that destiny has protected over thousands of years.'

'How? Maybe you don't realize how tightly controlled we are. We are always being watched, every time we leave the camp, and I can guarantee that every time we drive back in, someone checks the mileage on the Jeep. Are you thinking you could just load it all up and carry it off with you across the desert? With what?'

'Damn,' burst out Blake, realizing how totally powerless he was. 'Damn!'

'Come on,' said Sarah. 'Let's go back. We've got a tough day ahead of us tomorrow.'

They walked in silence to Sarah's trailer and, as she inserted the key into the lock, Blake put a hand on her arm. 'Sarah.'

The girl turned towards him, trying to make out his expression in the dark. 'What is it?'

'You have got to have a topographical map of this area.'

Sarah seemed disappointed by his question. 'Yes, of course, but it won't help you. All the coordinates have been taken out. All the place names are in Arabic. You know that this place where we are is called Ras Udash, but that hasn't answered any of your questions, has it?'

'Sarah, I want to see that map. Please.'

'This isn't an excuse to get into my room, is it, Professor Blake?'

'That's a possibility. So, can I come in?'

Sarah opened the door. 'Let me light the gas lantern,' she said, feeling her way in the dark to find some matches. She placed the lantern on a drawing table with the map tacked onto it. 'Here it is. See, just like I told you. No references. Just about ten named places in all, including Ras Udash.'

Blake put on his glasses and examined the map carefully. 'It's like I thought. This map is a computer printout. That's how they deleted all the references. There's got to be a master copy somewhere that contains all the coordinates.'

'Very probably.'

'Do you have a mobile hard disk?'

'Sure.'

'What capacity?'

'Two gigabytes.'

'Great, that's more than enough.'

'I get it,' said Sarah. 'You think you can find the master, copy it onto a disk, transfer it onto your computer and print it. Right?'

'That's the idea.'

'Fine, but I have no idea where to look for the master, if it exists. And how could I manage to fool around with Maddox's computer without anyone noticing or getting suspicious?'

'You told me that you'd accessed a restricted file on the main computer. If you wanted to help me, you could do it again.'

'It's not the same thing. What you're asking me to do would take too long. The guy in charge of the computer is one of Maddox's must trusted men, a technician named Pollock. He sits there the whole time the generator is on.'

'Well, how did you do it the first time?'

'Pollock has his habits. Every morning at ten he goes to the latrine and spends ten minutes there, if not more. It depends on whether he takes a magazine to read or not. But for your problem, Blake, ten minutes or even fifteen would not be enough. A topographical map takes up a lot of memory. Finding it will take time and copying it even longer.'

'I realize that,' said Blake. 'But I absolutely have to know where I am. It's the only way I'll be able to figure out who is in that tomb and why it's located in such an out-of-the-way place. If what you've said is true, as soon as I've finished excavating they'll send me packing, leaving them free to ransack the chamber and take away all their goodies. Sarah, I didn't come here to help a bunch of tomb raiders. This is an extraordinary scientific discovery and a unique opportunity for me. Help me, for God's sake.'

'Tomorrow I'll give it a go. I have an idea I could try.'

'I really appreciate it,' said Blake. 'If we succeed it will really give me a fighting chance.' He turned towards the door. 'Goodnight, Sarah. And thanks.'

'Goodnight, Will. No problem.'

'Know something?'

She looked at him with curiosity. 'What?'

'This thing about turning off the generator at this hour seems totally idiotic.'

'It's Maddox,' said Sarah. 'He can't sleep with the noise the generator makes. Or maybe he can't fall asleep if he knows someone is doing something he doesn't know about. It does give us some interesting opportunities, though. Like they say, every cloud has a silver lining, right?'

Blake looked at her as if seeing her for the first time and lowered his gaze, confused. 'Sarah, don't play games with me. I'm not the type of man who could have an affair with a woman like you and come out smiling the day it was over. Just a week ago, you invited me to stay out of your life and that's no problem for me. My balance is still a little . . . off.'

He caressed her hand lightly, then nodded goodbye and walked towards his own lodgings. In the distance he could hear the insistent noise of helicopter blades, and lights were flashing in the same direction, behind the hills. He could hear Jeeps rumbling over the mountainside and noticed the wake left by a couple of tracer shells. It was certainly the strangest mining camp he'd ever heard of.

He lit his gas lantern as soon as he got in and began to study the photographs he had taken of the inscriptions from *The Book of the Dead* on the walls of the tomb. There was something strange, something peculiar, in those hieroglyphics that he couldn't quite get a handle on. Something familiar nagging at the back of his memory. Was it the type of expression? Or the style of the writing, the ideograms?

He boiled water for tea and lit a cigarette, walking back and forth in the little room, trying to focus on what was disturbing him.

He poured the dark, clear tea into a glass, Oriental-style, dropped in a couple of sugar cubes and drank, enjoying the strong, sweet beverage. He inhaled a puff of smoke from his cigarette and for a moment felt that he was back in Omar al Husseini's apartment in Chicago, on that freezing, desolate evening. His heart skipped a beat: the Breasted papyrus!

That's what the writing on the tomb wall reminded him of! The use of certain ideograms with given meanings, the way the scribe had drawn the signs for 'water' and 'sand'. Could it possibly be the same person? Maybe it was just a casual coincidence, Breasted's handwriting that for some weird reason looked like that of a scribe who had decorated the walls of a tomb in the desert.

He sat down at his desk, took paper and pen, and wrote out a letter that he would email the next day. His hands trembled with excitement.

Dear Husseini

I'm studying a series of wall hieroglyphics, mostly taken from The Book of the Dead. *What is extraordinary is that they seem drawn by the same hand as the Breasted papyrus. Maybe it's just an impression, or a strange coincidence, but I absolutely must know whether I'm on to something. Could you please:*

a) email me an exact reproduction of the first three lines of the Breasted papyrus, as soon as possible,
b) check if the Breasted transcription is considered a reliable reproduction or just a rough copy of the original.

I really appreciate your help and hope to hear from you as soon as

*possible on this. Thanks again for having taken me in on
Christmas Eve. Maybe you saved my life. Or maybe you ruined it,
who can say, but the Good Samaritan was certainly no better
than you.*

Blake

THE NEXT MORNING, as soon as he woke up, Blake went to
knock on Sarah's door. She answered in pyjamas and he handed
her a disk.

'Sarah, there's a file that has to be emailed on this. You could
take it with you into Maddox's office and if Pollock comes back
while you're still there you can say that you just came to send an
email. What do you think?'

'Good idea, even though this whole thing is nuts.'

'Thanks, Sarah. You won't be coming to the dig, then,
today.'

'No, seeing as I'll be busy here at the camp.'

'I'll miss you,' said Blake.

'Me, too,' said Sarah. And she seemed sincere.

Blake reached the Bedouin tent, where the other members of
his expedition were already having breakfast. He had a cup
of milky coffee with cereal and some dates. Then he packed
something for lunch and headed for the parking lot, followed by
Ray Sullivan.

'Miss Forrestall won't be coming out to the site, today, Mr
Sullivan,' he said, before getting into the Jeep. 'She has important
business here at the camp. We'll have to make do.'

'Fine, Professor Blake,' replied Sullivan, starting up his vehicle
and accommodating the three new workers.

The sky was partially overcast, with a front of clouds coming
up from the north-east. A gentle wind blew over the expanse of
desert. Half an hour after they'd set off, Blake turned back
towards the camp and could distinctly see the pyramid-shaped
mountain and, in the distance, the other mountain that looked

like a sphinx. If Sarah managed to get him a topographical map with coordinates, he'd surely be able to interpret those bizarre natural phenomena.

When they got to the site it was nearly nine o'clock, and the sun was already quite high. Blake descended into the tomb with the three men who would be digging and using the vacuum cleaner, and he couldn't help but notice their astonishment as they took a first look around. He realized that the discovery really had been kept a secret that only a very restricted group of people were privy to.

He left Sullivan outside to operate the winch and empty the buckets as they sent them up. At each shovel stroke, the pile of debris slipped further forward, until slowly the side of the sarcophagus was uncovered. Blake was becoming increasingly excited; each time he stole a glance at the massive stone tomb, he felt as if he could perceive the awakening of a voice that had remained silent for millennia. As if a cry were about to explode out of that block of stone.

The two men working with the shovels kept up a steady rate and filled a bucket every three or four minutes.

Blake suddenly noticed something dark on the tomb floor and stopped the diggers. He knelt down, took his trowel out of his jacket pocket and started to clear away the rubble and clean the area with a brush. The object was a piece of wood, darkened by time and oxidation: a board of some sort.

He took a sample of it, then ordered the workers to continue to clear away the slide, being very careful not to damage the wooden board that lay there for no apparent reason. When it was nearly lunch time, one of the workers called him: they had found something else in the middle of the debris.

'Let's see,' said Blake, coming nearer.

About halfway down the slide, as the material on top had slid forward, an indefinable object that seemed to be made of leather had come to light. Blake extracted it with wooden pincers and looked at it closely: it was what remained of a sandal! He wrapped it carefully in aluminium foil and placed it alongside the sample of the wooden board.

SARAH FORRESTALL remained in her trailer and kept an eye on Maddox's movements. He finally drove off towards the north in his Jeep with Gordon, as they did nearly every day, usually not returning until shortly before dusk. The camp was practically deserted if you didn't consider the guards posted on the surrounding hills, a couple of hundred metres away.

At about ten o'clock, Pollock walked out of the office with a copy of *Playboy*, a roll of toilet paper and a plastic bottle full of water in his hand, and headed towards the latrine.

Sarah quickly slipped out of the back door and walked along the row of trailers towards Maddox's lodgings, hoping that Pollock hadn't thought to lock the door. She pushed; it was open. She figured that she had between ten and fifteen minutes and took a quick look at the digital clock hanging on the wall. The computer was on and the screen displayed diagrams reporting the mineralogical analysis of the soil in the various zones of Ras Udash.

Sarah sat down and started to go through the files on the hard disk. She had taken a pair of binoculars with her and in the distance – through the window on the wall opposite the desk – she could see the latrine, and Pollock's feet with his trousers covering his shoes. An excellent observation point.

There was a series of protected directories that obviously contained confidential documents. Sarah reached into her shirt pocket for a disk which she had previously taken from Maddox's office and used it to launch a program to decipher the passwords. The directories began to open up, one after another, and Sarah copied them onto the mobile hard disk that she had with her, without any idea of whether one of them might contain the master of the topographical map. It was starting to get hot and the overheated trailer was giving off waves of heat.

She checked the latrine with her binoculars and saw that

Pollock was pulling up his trousers. She had no more than three minutes before he walked through the door.

She restored the original display while Pollock closed the latrine door behind him and started to fiddle with the bag of quicklime. She slipped out to wait until he had returned to the office and then knocked on the door.

'Come in,' said Pollock.

Sarah couldn't help but wrinkle her nose; he'd brought the stench of the latrine back in with him.

'I see you've decided to stay at the camp today, Miss Forrestall.'

'That's right. I have office work to do.' She took a disk from her pocket and handed it to him. 'Professor Blake gave me this. Would you email it as soon as you can; he's written the file name and the email address on the label. As soon as you get an answer, be sure to inform Blake. I think it's very important.'

'You know, Miss Forrestall, that all outgoing and incoming mail has to go through Mr Maddox. As soon as he comes back, I'll show him the message and get his authorization.'

Sarah returned to her trailer, connected the hard disk to her computer and began going through the files one by one.

BLAKE GOT BACK to camp just after dusk and went straight to Sarah's trailer without even stopping to clean up. 'Any news?' he asked as soon as she let him in.

Sarah shook her head. 'No, I'm afraid not. Take a look for yourself. Here's the master of the map I showed you, but there are no references. I guess they didn't want to run any risks.'

Blake dropped onto a chair, discouraged.

'What about the dig? Anything new?'

Blake took a little packet out of his pocket. 'I found a wooden board,' he said, 'on the floor, under the rubble. Very strange. And something else, a piece of leather sandal. We'll have to do a radiocarbon analysis right away to date the finds.'

'Radiocarbon? How can we do that? I don't think anyone at

the camp will know where to find a laboratory doing that kind of work.'

'I'd know just where to find one, if only I had some idea where in the hell we were.'

Sarah lowered her head. 'I did everything I could to try to help. It wasn't easy concentrating on all those computer operations with so little time and worrying that Pollock might come in from one moment to the next and start asking embarrassing questions.'

Blake stood up. 'I'm not angry with you, Sarah,' he said. 'It's just that everything is crazy out here. I don't even know what I'm doing any more. It's like I was digging on another planet. No references, nothing to check my results against. Thanks, anyway, I really appreciate what you did. See you in a little while, at dinner.'

He opened the door and walked out. Sarah waited for a moment, as if certain that he would turn back, but Blake walked straight to his trailer and went in, slamming the door behind him.

The evening was so mild, with a hint of spring in the air, that dinner was served in the Bedouin tent. Blake sat down next to Sarah, waiting for Maddox's usual query about how the dig had gone so that he could request a radiocarbon analysis of the material that he had taken from the tomb.

Maddox seemed embarrassed. 'You must realize that we don't have that kind of equipment here,' he said. 'But if you can tell me which laboratories do this type of work here in the Middle East, I'll see to it as soon as possible.'

'There's a centre at the Egyptian Museum in Cairo,' he said. 'And another very well-equipped lab at the Hebrew University of Jerusalem at the Institute of Archaeology, another at the University of Tel Aviv—'

'Leave the finds with Mr Pollock, please, and I'll have him make arrangements.'

Pollock approached their table and handed an envelope containing a disk to Blake, taking the little aluminium foil packets with the wood and leather samples from him. 'This is the answer to the message that Miss Forrestall asked me to send for you this morning,' he said. 'I had to wait for Mr Maddox to return and OK it. The reply just came in.'

Blake put it into the pocket of the jacket he had left hanging on the back of the chair and began to talk with Sarah. He seemed to be in a good mood again.

When the coffee was served, Pollock left for a few minutes. He returned almost immediately and whispered something to Maddox, who finished his coffee quickly and got up, excusing himself to his table companions. 'There's a call from Houston, I hope you don't mind my leaving. Miss Forrestall, would you please come to my office as soon as it's convenient for you?'

Sarah got up to comply and quickly glanced over at Blake, looking perplexed: could Pollock have discovered her raid on his office?

He noticed Sarah's jacket hanging on the back of her vacant chair. He slipped his hand into the right pocket, felt for her keys and got a sudden idea.

'Please excuse me,' he said to Sullivan and Gordon. 'I left my cigarettes in the trailer and I need a smoke after the coffee. I'll be back in a minute or two.'

Gordon gave Blake a condescending little smile, as if he'd just admitted to needing his daily dose of heroin. 'Go right ahead, Professor, go right ahead. We're not going anywhere.'

Blake walked quickly towards the trailers. When he got to Sarah's, he turned around to make sure no one was watching, then opened the door, switched on her computer and began looking through the desk drawers to find the mobile hard disk. Nothing. He looked out of the door again to make sure that nobody was coming, then returned to the desk. He saw that one of the drawers was locked, checked her keys and found one that opened it. There were papers, notes, photographs. And the hard disk. He took it out, loaded it into the drive and scanned the list of files.

Blake felt his heart beating wildly. What could he say to Sarah if she walked in? Maybe it had all been a trick to trap him? Suddenly one of the file names leapt out at him: TPC-H-5A. Tactical Pilotage Chart H-5A. A topographical map put out by the Department of Defense! It had to be what he was looking for.

He copied it onto another disk, turned off the computer, closed the drawer and left, checking his watch: six minutes had gone by.

Sarah and Pollock were still in Maddox's office. He walked back towards the Bedouin tent after checking that he had a packet of cigarettes in his pocket.

He took his seat as the waiter was pouring another cup of coffee and slipped the keys back into Sarah's jacket pocket. He lit a cigarette and took a couple of long drags.

'I've never even been tempted,' said Gordon. 'Every time I see a smoker going through his pockets hysterically I realize how lucky I am.'

'You have a point there, Mr Gordon. On the other hand, consider that it is vice, and not virtue, that separates us from brute beasts. Have you ever seen a horse smoke?'

Gordon cracked a sour smile and changed the subject. 'Ray told me about that wooden board you found on the tomb floor under that heap of debris around the sarcophagus. Funny, no? Finding an object like that in the middle of all the rubble. What do you think it could be?'

'I've been thinking about it all day, but I still don't have an explanation. However, I can easily narrow down the possibilities. Originally, that board had to be in either a horizontal or a vertical position. If it were horizontal it might have covered some sort of a hole dug in the tomb floor. But that hypothesis doesn't work because the weight of the landslide would have caused the board to collapse into the hole it was covering sooner or later over all these years, no matter how sturdy it was. So the board had to have been upright.'

'So?' Sarah had just arrived and sat down next to him.

'Well, the way I figure it, it could mean only one thing.'

'What?'

'That the landslide was provoked intentionally to cut off access to the tomb.'

Sarah considered this quietly. The daylight had nearly completely disappeared and the wind brought with it distant noises, echoes of mysterious activity somewhere beyond those chalky hills that bordered the plain to the north-east.

'That seems strange to me,' she said after a while. 'All the Egyptian tombs were inaccessible. And we still don't know where the entrance was, originally, or what direction it led in from.'

'You're right. And yet that landslide seems artificial to me. The board was vertical because it was holding back a mass of rubble. Then someone, for some reason, deliberately tipped it forwards, and the material it was holding back spilled into the tomb and covered the sarcophagus. The person who set off this landslide probably thought it would destroy everything inside, but that's not what happened. It didn't work out as planned.'

'That is a daring hypothesis,' said Sarah.

'Not as daring as you think. Most probably, the mass of rubble had been there for such a long time that it had begun to conglomerate, which stopped the whole mass from sliding forward into the tomb. But if that were true, as I think it is, it means that someone visited that tomb long after it was closed up.'

'But why?'

'Don't have the slightest idea. But I'll figure it out, sooner or later.'

'So now what are you going to do? Free the sarcophagus or pursue this problem of the board?'

'If it were up to me, I'd concentrate on the board. That's where the key to the secret lies. But I doubt that Maddox would approve. And he's the boss here, right?'

'Yeah,' said Sarah.

Silence fell over the table as everyone was absorbed in their

107

own thoughts. Maddox came out but didn't sit down. He walked towards the parking lot and they could hear him starting up his Jeep.

Sarah glanced towards the lot and looked nervous.

Blake stood up. 'Well, I'd better get to work,' he said. 'I have to read my colleague's answer to my email. I may very well stay up all night working.'

'I'm going to sleep,' said Sarah. 'It's been an intense day.' She shot Blake a significant look.

Blake accompanied her to the door of her trailer. 'Where do you think Maddox is off to, alone at this hour?'

'I don't know,' answered Sarah. 'And I'm not all that interested. I've learned to mind my own business since I've been here, and you should do the same, as far as you can. Goodnight, Will.'

She gave him a light kiss on the lips and went inside, closing the door after her.

Blake felt a wave of heat rise to his face, as though he were a kid falling in love for the first time. Thank God it was dark enough for her not to have noticed. He walked to his own trailer and noticed that there was no longer anyone in the Bedouin tent.

He powered up his computer and immediately inserted the disk with the file he'd copied from Sarah's hard disk. The map appeared, with the coordinates at its sides. Sarah had lied to him!

At the same time he heard a very slight noise, like the creaking of a door. He looked out of the window, just in time to see Sarah leaving her trailer and disappearing around the corner.

He left as well and went towards the parking lot, keeping out of sight behind the trailers. When he got there, Sarah was gone and an ATV was missing. After several minutes, he heard the distant rumble of the vehicle being started up. Sullivan, Gordon and the others were housed close to the generator and wouldn't have heard a thing.

The noise faded completely, carried away on the northerly wind. For a few seconds, Blake thought he saw headlights reflected on the top of a ridge. Sarah was probably following

Maddox towards an unknown destination, alone, in the middle of the desert.

Even though she had tricked him he still felt worried for her, thinking of the danger she might be headed for. But there was nothing he could do.

He went back to his trailer and sat in front of the computer. He transcribed the coordinates and printed them, but could not manage to localize them precisely, since he didn't have a general map of the Middle East. He'd have to get someone outside to look them up for him. Husseini, maybe. But how could he get around Pollock?

He couldn't ask Sarah to repeat her performance while Pollock was in the can, nor could he attempt a break-in himself, being off at the dig all day.

An idea: he'd use hieroglyphics!

There was probably no one in the camp who could read hieroglyphics, and a text in ancient Egyptian wouldn't arouse Pollock's suspicions, given the circumstances. He could send an uncensored message without being found out.

He remembered Husseini's answer to his message and pulled the disk that Pollock had given him out of his pocket.

Hi Blake

Your news is extraordinary, and I'd give anything to be there with you to work on the text.

The answers to your questions:

a) Following is a reproduction of the three lines of the Breasted papyrus in our possession.

A text in hieroglyphics followed.

b) The text is almost certainly a faithful transcription of the original, with all of its palaeographic characteristics. Breasted was famous for being scrupulous to the point of being a stickler.

109

A transcription of his can practically be considered a photocopy of the original, if you'll permit the anachronism.

Let me know how the situation develops. I'm anxious to hear more.

Husseini

Blake uploaded his hieroglyphic translation program and with the help of the grammar he'd brought, tried to work out a message for Husseini which would ask him to identify the place and region that the coordinates referred to. It wasn't easy to find the terms in ancient Egyptian to express modern geographical concepts, and when he reread the message he wasn't at all sure that Husseini would understand what he needed, but he had no choice. He intended the message to say:

The place in which I read the words is the place where a great man of the Land of Egypt is buried. I entered and saw that the place is intact. I don't know where I am, but the numbers of this place are: thirty-eight and eighteen and fifty towards the night; thirty-four and forty-three towards the rising sun.

Hoping that Husseini would understand: northern latitude 38°18'50", eastern longitude 34°43'.

When he finished he called Pollock on the phone. 'Sorry to disturb you, Pollock. It's Blake and I have to send an email.'

'Can you be more specific, Professor Blake?'

'It's a text in hieroglyphics that I have to consult a colleague about, the same person I sent the last message to.'

'I'm sorry, Professor, but seeing that Mr Maddox is not here, I can't accept your request.'

Blake reacted aggressively. 'Listen, Pollock, this colleague is the only person I can trust on this, and he just happens to be leaving town tomorrow. He'll be gone for a couple of weeks. That means that I won't be able to fully decipher the texts that I've transcribed, and that information is absolutely essential for my work. If you want to take the responsibility for hindering my work, go right ahead, but I don't think Mr Maddox will be happy about it.'

Pollock didn't answer immediately. Blake could hear his breathing on the other end of the phone, and the noise of the generator in the background, much louder than it was outside.

'All right,' said Pollock, 'if you guarantee that's all there is in the message.'

'That's it, Mr Pollock,' insisted Blake. 'If your computer is on, I'll send you the text directly by modem so you can email it right away. I might even get an answer back quickly, if you could leave the generator on for a little while longer.'

'Well,' replied Pollock, 'I did plan to take advantage of Mr Maddox's absence to take care of a few things and to let the refrigerators run a little longer. Send me through the message.'

Blake hung up and breathed a sigh of relief. He immediately transmitted the text he'd prepared to Pollock's computer, hoping that Husseini was still in the house. He figured that in Chicago it would be between twelve and one in the afternoon.

After he'd sent the message he pulled up Husseini's response again and printed the three lines of the Breasted papyrus, comparing every line and every palaeographic detail with the figures from the tomb he was excavating. They matched incredibly. It really looked as if the same scribe had written the two texts. But how could that be?

He suddenly realized that he'd been working on his analysis for nearly two hours and the generator was still on. It was a quarter to ten. Evidently Maddox hadn't returned yet, and probably neither had Sarah.

He opened the door and walked outside. The air was cold and crisp and the waning moon wandered between a thin layer of clouds and the wavy profile of the mountains.

He thought of Sarah out all alone in the desert. Sarah who had lied to him and used her beauty to manipulate him. No one in that camp was who they seemed to be and he realized that he couldn't allow himself to feel any emotion other than diffidence. His only remaining contact was Husseini, the colleague who had taken him in off the street that lonely Christmas Eve. And even that contact felt very precarious; he could be cut off at any time.

He lit up a cigarette and tried to relax, but with each passing moment the situation seemed even more difficult and dangerous. And he realized that he had absolutely no influence on the outcome. Those people roaming around at night through the desert, those distant noises, those strange flashes of light on the horizon: what did any of this have to do with their presumed mining activity?

He imagined that they might even be planning to take him out, once they'd got what they'd wanted from him. Or blackmail him, forcing him to keep his mouth shut about everything.

The ringing telephone interrupted his thoughts and he jumped to his feet. He went back in and picked up the receiver.

'Hello.'

'It's Pollock. There's an answer to your email. If your computer's on, I'll send it through.'

'Thanks, Mr Pollock. I'm ready on this end.'

Husseini answered him in the same way, in hieroglyphics. He seemed to have understood perfectly what Blake needed to know. He had to make a rough interpretation of the answer; some parts of it weren't entirely clear. But there was one phrase that left no doubt: *Your place is in the desert called Negev, near the low land called Mitzpe Ramon, in the land of Israel.*

He added: *How could that possibly be?*

GAD AVNER left archaeologist Ygael Allon's company at one in the morning. 'A thrilling tour, Professor,' he said, as soon as they'd come up from the tunnel under the Antonian Fortress archway. 'How long do you think it will take to reach the end of the tunnel?'

Allon shrugged. 'Hard to say. It's not a construction like a house or a sanctuary or a thermal bath where we know the approximate dimensions. A tunnel can be ten metres long or even three kilometres. The extraordinary thing is that it seems to lead to the Temple.'

'I can see why you had me called,' said Avner. 'I'll give immediate orders to have the area with access to the dig cordoned off, and I'll ensure that you have everything you need to finish your investigation as soon as possible. Because of where we are, I'm sure you'll agree with me that this whole operation must remain completely secret. Tension is so high that news like this could have unforeseen consequences.'

'Yes,' admitted Allon. 'I think you're right. Goodnight, Mr Cohen.'

'Goodnight, Professor.'

He walked off, followed by his companion. 'Ferrario,' he said as soon as they'd taken a few steps, 'give immediate instructions to have the area blocked off and infiltrate a couple of our agents among the excavation crew. I want to be continually informed of what's going on down there.'

'But sir,' protested the officer, 'blocking off the area will draw attention to it and—'

'I know, but I'd say we have no choice in the matter. Do you have a better idea?'

Ferrario shook his head.

'See? Do as I ask. I'll see you tomorrow afternoon in the King David lobby at five, for a cup of coffee.'

'I'll be there,' answered Ferrario. He turned and disappeared into the shadows of the Antonian Fortress.

Avner reached his private residence in the Old City and took the elevator up to the eighth floor. He never had a bodyguard with him at home, having given his agents firm orders that no one should cross into his private territory. He had always calculated the risks and he preferred it this way. He turned the key in the lock and went in.

He walked through the apartment without even switching on the light and walked onto the terrace to look down at the city, as he did every night before going to sleep. He let his gaze roam over the domes and towers, over the city walls, over the Mosque of Omar rising on the mount that was once the site of the Sanctuary of Yahweh. He needed to know that he had the situation under control before calling it a night.

He lit a cigarette and let the stiff, cold wind from the snowy peaks of Mount Carmel numb his face and forehead.

This was the time when he thought of his dead. Of his son Aser, killed at twenty in an ambush in the south of Lebanon, and his wife, Ruth, who had died shortly after, incapable of surviving without him. He thought of his own solitude at the top of that apartment building, at the top of his organization and at the turning point of his existence.

He scanned the eastern horizon in the direction of the desert of Judah and the high Moab plain and he felt his enemy moving like a ghost somewhere beyond those barren hills, through that sterile land.

The elusive Abu Ahmid.

The man who had been directly responsible for the death of his son and the massacre of the boy's comrades. Avner had sworn that day to hunt him down relentlessly. But since then he'd only managed to catch a glimpse of him once and only after the bastard had already slipped out of his hands, during a parachute raid on a refugee camp in southern Lebanon. But he was sure he would recognize him if he ever saw him again.

The cigarette burned quickly, helped by the wind. Gad Avner walked back into the house and switched on his table lamp: the light on his private telephone line was flashing in the dark.

'Hello,' he said.

'It's the night porter,' replied a voice on the other end.

'I'm listening.'

'I'm working, but it's not easy in these surroundings. There have been unforeseen newcomers . . . intruders, you could say.'

Avner fell silent, as if taken by surprise. 'The risks of the profession. Who are they?'

'Americans. A commando unit. And there's talk of an operation in progress.'

'Can't you find out anything else?'

'A date: 13 January. And the situation seems to be moving along quickly.'

'Anything else going on at the front?'

'Lots. But I have to cut off, sir. There's someone coming.'

'Be careful. If something happens to you there's no one who can replace you. Thank you, night porter.'

The little green light went out and Gad Avner turned on the computer. He connected to the databank at headquarters to access a schedule of events for the entire Middle East: local functions and festivities, religious celebrations, political and diplomatic meetings.

One in particular attracted his attention: a military parade commemorating Gulf War casualties. The parade was scheduled to take place in front of the newly restored Palace of Nebuchadnezzar in Babylon. At 5.30 p.m. on 13 January, in the presence of President al Bashar.

He turned off the computer, switched off the lights and went into his bedroom. The alarm clock by his bedside told him it was 2 a.m., on 4 January. Nine days, fifteen hours and thirty minutes to go.

6

Two days later, Gad Avner got home about midnight and turned on the TV as he often did to wind down a little before going to bed. As he was switching channels, he paused at the CNN news, and realized just how nervous the media was getting about the turn that events had been taking in Israel and the Middle East.

Vague hopes were expressed for a political solution, not forthcoming, to what had become an irremediable situation. But he, in the meantime, he, Gad Avner, commander of Mossad, had to take action. No matter what the politicians were up to. Time was running out and he still didn't know what was behind Operation Nebuchadnezzar.

He turned to look out of the rain-streaked window and noticed that the little green light on his private line was flashing. He switched off the TV and picked up the receiver.

'Avner.'

'It's the night porter, sir.'

'Hello, night porter. Any news?'

'Quite a bit, actually. I've discovered who the Americans are. A commando unit sent as support for an assassination. At Babylon. President al Bashar, during a military parade.'

'Who will kill him?'

'A group of Republican Guards, led by a certain Abdel Bechir. They say that his real name is Casey. His father was American, his mother Arab, and he's totally bilingual. Something like the assassination of President Sadat in Cairo. But the powers behind the plan are different this time.'

'Who are they?'

'I don't know. But it seems that General Taksoun will be succeeding him.'

'Too predictable to be true,' commented Gad Avner, perplexed. 'Taksoun most probably won't make it to 13 January alive. If I were al Bashar, I'd already have had him shot. Too capable, too popular, too open to new ideas, too well connected in diplomatic circles all over the Middle East. Here too. If al Bashar ever survived an assassination attempt, Taksoun would immediately be accused and executed, whether or not he was involved. Al Bashar is just waiting for an excuse. What else?'

'The American SOF unit belongs to the Delta Force and is under cover at Mitzpe Ramon. They're preparing for an air raid. In support of Taksoun, if it becomes necessary.'

Avner was struck dumb. It seemed impossible that the Israeli air force could have handed a training base over to an American commando unit at the Mitzpe range without him knowing about it. What seemed even more impossible was that the Americans were keeping him out of something so big. There'd be hell to pay for this.

He said, 'Anything else?'

'Yes . . . sir,' replied the other with some hesitation. 'I haven't mentioned it because it's still completely unclear to me – inexplicable, actually, although at first I thought that it could be directly related to my primary mission. But I really don't know what to think.'

'What is it?'

'A dig, sir. An archaeological dig near an area called . . . Ras Udash.'

THE CAR STOPPED in front of the American consulate general and the guard peered inside.

'Excuse me, sir,' he said. 'The consulate is closed. You'll have to come back tomorrow morning.'

'I won't hear of it,' replied the man sitting on the back seat. 'Announce me to the ambassador.'

'Sir, you must be joking. It's two o'clock in the morning.'

'No, I'm perfectly serious,' answered the man. 'Tell him that Gad Avner wants to see him, immediately. He'll receive me.'

The guard shook his head. 'Wait here a minute.' He dialled a number at the front switchboard and exchanged a few words with the person on the other end. He returned to the car with an astonished look on his face: 'The ambassador will see you now, Mr Avner.'

The guard accompanied him to the building and led him into a little sitting room. The ambassador arrived, and it was clear that the unexpected visit had disturbed his slumber. He was wearing a robe over his pyjamas.

'What's happened, Mr Avner?' he asked with an alarmed expression.

'Mr Holloway,' began Avner without any small talk, 'President al Bashar will be assassinated at 5.30 p.m. on 13 January. Probably with your support if not on your direct orders. You've installed a Delta Force unit under cover at Mitzpe Ramon without asking for my consent or my opinion. This is completely unjustifiable and extremely dangerous in the light of the situation in which we find ourselves. I demand an immediate explanation.'

Ambassador Holloway acknowledged his accusations without protesting. 'I'm sorry, Mr Avner, but the instructions I've received will not allow me to give you an answer. I can say that we are in no way directly responsible for any assassination plot, but that we are in favour of General Mohammed Taksoun taking over the reins in Baghdad.'

'Fine, Mr Holloway. The damage is done, but I want you to realize that nothing can happen in this country – understand, absolutely nothing – without me finding out about it. Refer that to your president and to the CIA and tell them that no decision at any level can pass without considering the opinion of Gad Avner.'

Holloway lowered his head and did not dare to object when his guest nervously lit up a cigarette, despite the notice on the wall which clearly said: THANK YOU FOR NOT SMOKING

'What else is there, Mr Avner?' he said, trying to mask his irritation at Avner's blatant violation of the rules.

'One question, Mr Holloway. Do you know what Operation Nebuchadnezzar is?'

Holloway seemed genuinely surprised. 'I have no idea, Mr Avner. Not the slightest idea.'

Avner leaned close, enveloping him in a cloud of blue smoke, and stared straight into his eyes. 'Mr Holloway,' he said, 'I want you to know that if you are lying to me I will do everything in my power to make your life here in Jerusalem very, very uncomfortable. You know that I will not hesitate to do so.'

'I've told you the truth, Mr Avner. I give you my word.'

'I believe you. Now, tell your superiors in Washington that I want to be consulted before any decisions are made about moving that commando unit you've got in the Mitzpe Ramon crater. And that they should start considering the possibility of pulling them out in very short order.'

'I will do so, Mr Avner,' said the ambassador.

Avner looked around for an ashtray and, not finding one, put out his cigarette butt on a Sèvres plate resting on a console, further scandalizing the American ambassador.

Just then they heard a soft knock on the sitting-room door. The two men exchanged surprised looks: who could it be at that hour?

'Come in,' said the ambassador.

A consulate official came in, nodded to both of them, and turned towards his superior. 'A report has just come in for you, sir. Could you come with me a moment?'

Holloway excused himself and walked out behind the official. Although Avner had been about to leave, he took his seat again. The ambassador returned almost immediately, visibly shaken.

'Mr Avner,' he said, 'we've been informed that General Taksoun has just arrested Abdel Bechir and had him shot, along with five Republican Guards, accusing them of conspiracy and high treason. The execution took place just after midnight at a barracks in Baghdad.'

'That was to be expected. Taksoun knew that if the assassination attempt failed, there would be no way out for him. He has decided not to take risks and to put all his cards on the table. You have placed your trust in the wrong person, Mr Holloway, and now you have a number of dead people on your conscience and a traitor in your midst. Excellent results, no doubt about it. Goodnight, Mr Ambassador.'

Avner left and had a taxi driver take him to the Old City, where he got out and continued on foot. He passed alongside the Wailing Wall and stopped to look at the base of the Antonian Fortress. The cordons were still up and two soldiers in fatigues were guarding the entrance. So Ygael Allon was still digging through the bowels of Mount Moriah. Avner had been told that they would reach the Temple within a couple of days. He had instructed them to let him know when the time came: he wanted to be with them in that tunnel under the Mount which had borne the Throne of God and the Ark of the Covenant for centuries. He wondered, if this was somehow a sign, what would happen if the Diaspora were once again forced upon Israel. He crossed the threshold and disappeared down the dark hallway.

THE LAST COUPLE of days had been so quiet that Omar al Husseini began to tell himself that perhaps the whole thing had just blown over.

He'd got back to his apartment at five and had sat down to take care of a few letters and prepare his lesson for the next day. The prints made of the microfilms that reproduced the first three lines of the Breasted papyrus were still on his desk. What could Blake have meant with that strange message? Husseini had asked to meet that evening with Blake's assistant, the one who had gone with him to El Qurna in Egypt to search for the Breasted original. He was a young man from Luxor who had got his degree in Cairo and then won a scholarship to the Oriental Institute. His name was Selim, and he came from a very poor family of peasants who farmed the land along the Nile.

He arrived right on time, at six thirty, and greeted Husseini respectfully. Husseini made him a cup of coffee, then got around to the business at hand.

'Selim, what do you know about the Breasted papyrus at El Qurna? Is there any chance it was authentic, or was it a set up to get money from Blake? It's just you and me here, and nothing you say will go any further. There's no need for you to lie—'

'I have no intention of lying, Professor Husseini.'

'Selim, Professor Blake has made an extraordinary discovery: an Egyptian tomb of an important figure from the New Kingdom, intact. But somehow this tomb has something to do with the Breasted papyrus. I'm not sure just how it may be connected, but the discovery seems very important. As you know, Selim, he's always been fair and honest with you, and he still would be, if he were here. He lost his job, he was abandoned by his wife – a terrible thing for an American – and now this is his one chance to show the world that he is a great scholar. To show his colleagues that that they were wrong to kick him out. To show his wife that he isn't a loser. Personally, I didn't know him well at all, until I met him sitting outside on a street bench on Christmas Eve, half frozen. He was very grateful for the meagre hospitality I offered him, and I could tell he was a man of feeling, rare among these people who only think of their careers and of business.

'Selim, listen to me well. Professor Blake seems to have found himself in very exciting, but very complicated, circumstances. I'm not sure I understand what has happened, but it seems that the discovery he has made is so important, and the mystery it involves so difficult to solve, that those who engaged him for this work are holding him prisoner. We are the only chance he has. Now, you have to tell me if you are willing to help him even though there's nothing he can do for you. Not only can't he further your career, but being associated with him might hinder it.'

'You can count on me, Professor Husseini. What is it that you want to know?'

'Absolutely everything you know about the Breasted papyrus. And whether it can still be found.'

Selim took a deep breath, then said, 'I'll tell you everything I know. It was about five months ago, around mid-September. Professor Blake had got a sizeable grant from the Oriental Institute for his research in Egypt and he had asked me to assist him in this investigation. I was born near El Qurna and I know everyone down there. You could say that the inhabitants of that village have been in the antiquities trade for generations and generations. Any scholar or researcher who has come through the area has had to come to terms with the El Qurna tomb raiders.

'I have a dear childhood friend who lives there, a boy named Ali Mahmudi. We used to swim in the Nile and snatch fruit from the market stands together. Both of us were already interested in Egyptian antiquities before we'd even lost our milk teeth. One of his ancestors had accompanied Belzoni to Abu Simbel, his grandfather had dug the tomb of Tutankhamun with Carnarvon and Carter, and his father was at Saqqara with Leclant and Donadoni.

'Our paths separated when my father managed to sell a set of ushtabi figures and some bracelets from a tomb of the Twelfth Dynasty and got enough money to send me to study at the University of Cairo. There I was awarded the scholarship that brought me here to the Institute, where I met and learned to esteem Professor Blake. Ali, my friend, continued to pillage tombs, but that hadn't changed anything between us.

'As soon as we got to Egypt he invited us to dinner. He didn't say anything that was particularly interesting then, we just talked about old times and the adventures of his ancestors in the Valley of the Kings. After we had gone, he came knocking on the door to my room and asked me why I had come back and what I was looking for.

'It was so hot that I certainly wouldn't have been able to sleep in that stuffy room. So we went up to the rooftop and I told him all about my work and about what we were looking for: a papyrus that an American had seen in a house in El Qurna about eighty years ago. We knew the name and the first few lines of the papyrus. Nothing else.'

' "Why do you want that papyrus?" he asked me. "There are more interesting things on the market."

' "Because my professor is interested in it," I told him, "and if I help him he will help me. He will extend my scholarship and perhaps find me a position at the university."

'Ali didn't answer. We watched the waters of the Nile sparkling under the rays of the moon. It was as if we were boys again, dreaming about what we'd do when we grew up, planning to buy a boat and sail to the delta of the Nile and continue our voyage over all the seas of the world. Suddenly he asked me, "Do you want to become an American?"

'I answered, "No, I don't want to become an American. I want to finish my studies in a good American university and then come back to Cairo and become the general director of antiquities one day. Like Mariette, like Brugsch and Maspero . . ."

' "Wouldn't that be the life?" said Ali. "Then we could really do business." '

Husseini wished he would get to the point, but realized that it was important for Selim to give him all this background information. It was his way of confiding in Husseini and making his story credible.

'Go on,' he said.

Selim continued, 'Ali got up to go and I walked down the

stairs with him to the gate outside. He turned to me and said, "You're looking for the Breasted papyrus." And then he left.'

'And what did you do?' asked Husseini.

'I know Ali very well. I knew what that way of talking without saying meant. I didn't do anything. I waited for him to come back. A few days later, he was waiting at the door when I got home shortly before midnight. I had become worried, because Professor Blake was beginning to think that we'd never find anything and he knew that in Chicago there were people ready to write him off.

'Ali had a sheet of paper in his hands with several lines of hieroglyphics: the beginning of the Breasted papyrus. I nearly dropped dead, Professor—'

'Go on,' urged Husseini, looking him straight in the eye.

'I told him that I had the same lines and then he pulled out a Polaroid. I'm sure it was what we were looking for, Professor Husseini. The Breasted papyrus!'

'What made you so sure?'

'The snapshot showed a papyrus along with several other objects from a tomb. Theoretically, it could have been just about anything, but then he showed me another old, yellowed picture with the same papyrus and the same objects on the table in the house of a fellah.

'Now, Professor Husseini, even though James Henry Breasted himself wasn't in the picture, I think it was legitimate to assume it was his papyrus. First of all, it looked absolutely identical: the top right-hand corner was ripped in just the same way and there was a missing piece on the left edge about three-quarters of the way down. I could have sworn that the objects in that old, yellowed photograph were the same ones in the Polaroid taken eighty years later.'

'What did you do then?'

'You can't even imagine how excited I was. The most logical thing was to ask him if I could see the papyrus immediately, in the name of our old friendship. I couldn't wait to tell Professor Blake. I could already see his face when I told him the news!'

'Well?'

'Well, what I asked him was how come this stuff had suddenly reappeared after almost ninety years.'

'Yes. That is an interesting question.'

'Well, the story was just incredible. I hope you have the patience to listen to it, Professor Husseini.'

Husseini nodded for him to continue and poured out some more coffee.

Selim went on, 'Ali's grandfather had participated in the exploration of the cave at Deir el Bahri as the foreman of Emil Brugsch, who was then director of the Antiquities Service. Brugsch had always been suspicious of him, because he was a friend of the two fellahin of El Qurna who had found the cave of the royal mummies. Remember, they managed to sell a quantity of precious objects before they were found out and forced to reveal the source of their trafficking.

'Brugsch had reason for suspicion, as it turned out. His foreman, that is, Ali's grandfather, was a handsome, vigorous young man, but poor as a dog and madly in love with a girl from Luxor, a waitress at the Hôtel du Nil. He needed to find enough money to make a suitable gift to the family of the girl, whom he wanted to marry. So what did he do? He tried to sell a few of the things he'd taken from the cave of the royal mummies.

'If he had been in his right mind, he would have waited months or even years before putting those things on the market, but love is love. He was so eager to ask for permission to marry this girl that he threw caution to the wind and, against his friends' advice, he let certain guests of the Winter Palace Hotel know that he had several extremely old and valuable pieces to sell.

'James Henry Breasted was among these guests, and when he heard that there was also a papyrus among the objects for sale, he asked to see it immediately. They made an appointment, but in the meantime the affair had reached the ears of Emil Brugsch, his boss. He was the director of the Antiquities Service, you see, and he had always had his informers in the hotels in Luxor and especially at the Winter Palace. There had always been bad blood between him and Breasted, because Brugsch had begun to suspect that many of the important objects that formed the collection of the Oriental Institute in Chicago hadn't exactly been acquired legally.

'Towards the end of that spring, Breasted met with the grandfather of my friend Ali somewhere along the Nile and he was brought on horseback to the house where the objects were being kept. Breasted was mostly interested in the papyrus, but the foreman wanted to sell everything at once. He knew that the fewer buyers and transactions there were, the greater his chances of getting away with it.

'Breasted tried to insist, but the seller wanted nearly as much for the papyrus alone as for the whole lot together. Breasted realized that the funds he had available to him in Cairo would not suffice for the deal. He wanted the papyrus so badly that he had no choice but to telegram Chicago with a request for more funds. He asked Ali's grandfather if he could photograph the finds. He refused, but allowed Breasted to copy the papyrus. Breasted had just begun when a breathless fellah arrived to tell them that Brugsch's men were on their trail.

'Breasted certainly couldn't allow himself to be found in such a compromising situation. He left all the money he had with him as a kind of down payment and quickly slipped away. Ali's grandfather hid everything and took a photograph of the objects together with the papyrus, but later realized how closely he was being watched by the Antiquities Service. He never succeeded in meeting with Breasted again.

'The poor devil had to forget about his dream marriage with the waitress from the Hôtel du Nil. A couple of years later he married a girl from El Qurna whose family was so poor that the father accepted a few sacks of millet and a bushel of rice in exchange for his daughter's hand.

'Just a few months after their marriage, while Ali's grandfather was working on a ridge near Deir al Bahri, he slipped and fell. He was dying when they brought him home, but he managed with his last breath to tell his wife, who was already expecting their child, where he had hidden those objects.

'And the secret was handed down from generation to generation—'

Husseini interrupted him. 'It seems very strange that a such a treasure would stay hidden for generations. I imagine that Ali's father wasn't swimming in gold either.'

'You're right, Professor Husseini. They would have sold it off instantly had they been able to. The fact is that they could not. Breasted was not the only one to be cheated out of his prize. You see, shortly after the poor man's death, the Director of Antiquities had a guard house built for the surveillance of that vast area which had become of such great archaeological and historical interest.'

'I get it,' said Husseini. 'This shack was built right where Ali's grandfather had buried his treasure.'

'Exactly. But that's not all. What was a shack at first was transformed over the years into a little brick barracks – in other words, a permanent structure. However, it was just recently demolished to allow for the passage of a new road. And so one night, when there was a full moon, my friend Ali followed his father's instructions and dug up the small treasure of Deir el Bahri.'

'But you . . . why did you think of asking this friend Ali in the first place?'

'Well, because there's always been talk at El Qurna of a hidden treasure and an incredibly valuable papyrus that both Breasted and Emil Brugsch had tried to find. I had told Professor Blake about it when I saw that he was interested in those three lines of the Breasted papyrus and that's why he decided to transfer his research to El Qurna, in Egypt.'

'No doubt about it,' admitted Husseini. 'You were on the right track from the start. What happened then?'

'Well, more or less what you've already heard, Professor Husseini. I started to negotiate for the purchase of the finds, because Ali, like his grandfather, wanted to sell everything at once, but the sum he wanted was very high.'

'How high?' asked Husseini.

'Half a million dollars, paid to a Swiss bank account.'

Husseini let out a long whistle.

'I was able to talk him down to 300,000 dollars, but it was still an enormous amount of money. Blake had to lay his reputation on the line to get 100,000 dollars immediately, in cash, as a down payment.

'As soon as the money came through, they set up a meeting, but right after Professor Blake got there, the Egyptian police raided the place. They managed to sneak up on us totally by surprise, as though they'd been expecting us.'

'And the papyrus?'

'To tell you the truth, I don't know what happened to it. Ali managed to slip off and he probably had it on him. Or maybe he had never brought it: he's very suspicious, very careful. He had some of the other things: two bracelets, a pendant . . . beautiful, real masterpieces. They were on the table when the police burst in.'

'There's something you haven't told me,' said Husseini.

Selim raised his eyes and seemed upset, as though he felt guilty or had behaved badly.

'Professor Blake told me that there was one thing above all that convinced him that the papyrus was authentic: the fact that other unknown and powerful buyers were after it. Do you know anything about them?'

'No, sir. Nothing . . .'

Husseini went to the window. It was snowing outside and the

white flakes wafted in the air like confetti during a parade, but the street was deserted. In the distance, a low call like that of a hunting horn could be heard. Maybe some boat trying to find its way through the mist on the lake to an invisible port.

'What did you do afterwards?' asked Husseini.

'I wasn't there when the police burst in, because I was waiting outside in the car. I got out of there as soon as I saw them driving off with him with their sirens wailing. Poor Professor Blake.'

'Where do you think the papyrus is now?'

'I don't know. Maybe Ali has it, or those other . . . buyers, if what you said is true.'

'Or the Egyptian government, or the American government, or even Blake.'

'Blake, sir?'

'You never know. In reality, we know nothing about what happened that day at Khan el Khalili. Ali got away. You weren't there. The only one who was there . . . was Professor Blake.'

'That's true. And you may not be the only one who suspects him.'

'What do you mean?'

'The other day I was working late in my office at the Institute and I saw Professor Olsen going into what used to be Professor Blake's office with a key.'

'Do you know what he was looking for?'

'No, I don't. But I started keeping an eye on him and I found out something else. Professor Olsen is having an affair with Professor Blake's ex-wife. And has been for some time. I think that must mean something.'

'I'm sure you're right about that, Selim. But now we have to figure a way out of this and decide what to do. Let me think about it. I'll get back to you very soon.'

'I'll be going, then, Professor Husseini. Thank you for the coffee.'

'It was a pleasure, Selim. Continue to keep me informed about what's going on with Olsen.'

Husseini saw him to the door and waited until Selim's car disappeared down the street before going back in. He sat in his silent apartment and felt oppressed by his solitude. There was nothing in his life that could arouse any feeling or emotion. He didn't even care about his academic career any more. There was just one thing that held any interest for him: the possibility of reading the complete Breasted papyrus.

His mobile phone rang. Husseini looked at the clock and did not move. The phone continued to ring and ring, filling him with a sense of dread. Finally he picked it up with a mechanical gesture.

'Hello,' he said.

'Good evening, Professor Husseini,' said a voice. 'Please consult your email. There's a message for you.'

Husseini hung up without responding and sat there unmoving. When he finally went to the computer, he realized that nearly an hour had passed.

He connected to the Internet and opened his email messages. There it was: $3 \times 3 = 9$

He switched off the computer and sat on the floor, lighting up a cigarette. All three of the commando units had arrived. They were on American soil and ready to proceed.

The phone rang again at midnight as he was getting ready for bed.

'Husseini,' he answered.

'Professor Husseini,' said a metallic voice on the other end, 'Los Angeles and New York are the most beautiful cities in America, but you're better off staying in Chicago to meet your friends. You know the addresses.' The voice was perfect, without any hint of an accent, sterile.

So these were their final objectives: the choices had been made. And now they wanted Abu Ghaj to enter the field. But Abu Ghaj was dead. And had been, for a long time.

And if he wasn't dead, maybe it was better to kill him. Abu Ghaj couldn't rise from the past to determine the life or death of millions of people who had never done anything wrong, just because he had received an order.

He turned off all the lights and lay awake thinking. He hadn't expected everything to move with such stop-watch precision. He hadn't imagined that Abu Ahmid's plan would grind forward like a perfect war machine. But he knew Abu Ahmid well and an atrocious suspicion struck him. When he was sure that the weapons were in place and ready to go, would he stop at merely using them as a threat? After Jerusalem was in his hands, would he not be tempted to deal the final blow to his hated enemy?

Husseini thought of how he could kill himself. He could see the suicide scene perfectly in the darkness: the police would come in tomorrow, take measurements, check for prints. He saw himself lying in a pool of blood (a gunshot?) or dangling from the ceiling by his trouser belt.

He pictured William Blake searching through a Pharaoh's tomb absurdly dug into the rock in Israel, of all places. Blake had no one there to help him. He was being held captive by strangers and prevented from acting on his own. Husseini realized that even if he did kill himself, the machine might slow down but would not stop, and that William Blake would remain alone in that tomb.

He thought of the cruelty that Abu Ahmid was capable of and a shudder of terror ran down his spine. Scenes from the past that he thought he had long buried came back to him vividly: the traitors who fallen into his hands, tortured slowly for days to squeeze the very last drop of pain from their tormented bodies. He knew that if he betrayed the cause or refused to carry out his orders, Abu Ahmid would devise an even more atrocious punishment for him. He would find a way to keep him alive for weeks, for months, maybe for years. Dragging out an endless hell devised especially for him.

Who could disobey such a man?

He decided that he would play his part but that he would also prepare an escape route for himself: suicide. He looked up a phone number in his book and, seeing that it wasn't too late, called his doctor and made an appointment for six the next evening. That was done, at least.

He sat down at the computer and sent his response by email. It said: *DR115.S14.1.23*. In the code that had been devised for the commando units, the message meant that he would meet one of them at the south 115th exit of the Dan Ryan Expressway on 14 January at 11 p.m. or 2300 hours. So, the next day he would find himself face to face with one of the horsemen of the apocalypse.

He felt deadly tired but he knew that if he lay down again he wouldn't be able to sleep. There was no longer the smallest space in his brain that was free from nightmares.

He turned on the TV and the breaking-news logo filled the screen. The speaker's voice announced that Iraqi president, al Bashar, had been the victim of an assassination attempt at 5.10 p.m., 13 January, as he had been watching a military parade in front of the walls of Babylon.

The CNN coverage showed scenes of total confusion: thousands rushing to escape from the stands which had been set up on either side of the route; the soldiers who had been parading shooting wildly as if under attack from an invisible enemy; enormous Soviet-built tanks that clattered horribly as they reversed, turning their turrets as if aiming at an aggressor who would not enter into their sights.

There were flashing lights everywhere, ambulances and police cars. And at the centre of the platform, under a canopy bright with national slogans and symbols, a pool of blood. The footage included shots of a stretcher being transported towards a helicopter which dropped down in the centre of the street and immediately took off again. The lens on another camera followed the flight of the helicopter over the gilded domes and minarets of the mosques of Baghdad.

The speaker reported that, according to a national press release, President al Bahsar had been admitted to hospital in a critical condition but surgeons were hopeful that his life could be saved. Doubts were immediately expressed regarding the credibility of this report. Eyewitnesses had seen the flash of the bomb very close to the President and had watched as medical personnel gathered pieces of his body, which had been blown to bits by the explosion. The most probable hypothesis was a suicide bomber from the opposition, who had adopted the techniques of Hamas commandos. It was impossible that a bomb had been planted on the platform beforehand, since it had been thoroughly checked by security forces minutes before the ceremony.

Husseini lowered his head as an ad came on and he wondered just who could be behind the assassination of such a key figure at such a critical moment for the Middle East.

When the news started again, the cameras were framing a high-ranking officer wearing a tanker's cap, encircled by his guards. His left shoulder was bandaged and bloodstained, and he was barking out orders. General Taksoun, already filling the power void left by al Bashar. A man who could count on the esteem and loyalty of the army's elite troops and who had a certain reputation abroad as well.

Husseini considered the hard, decisive expression of the general, his sharp, rehearsed gestures. It looked as though he had been preparing for this moment for a long time. Perhaps American intelligence was behind the bombing. The Americans saw General Taksoun as someone who could be negotiated with.

The telephone rang and Husseini picked up the receiver.

'It was us, Professor Husseini,' said a metallic voice.

7

SARAH FORRESTALL took the ATV to the top of a hill overlooking the camp, turned off the engine and coasted in neutral almost all the way to the parking lot. She got out and pushed it to its spot next to the other vehicles; catching her breath, she surveyed the area. Everything was quiet and peaceful and the trailers could be made out in the dark, thanks to the crescent moon that illuminated the chalky dust of the parking lot. Suddenly she saw a light flashing on one of the hills that framed the camp to the west and ducked behind a truck. She could now hear the sound of the Jeep that Maddox had used to leave the camp.

The vehicle came to a stop near her hiding place. Maddox got out and exchanged a few words with the men who were with him. They were wearing fatigues and carrying automatic weapons.

She strained to hear as they continued to talk in low voices. She then saw the soldiers get back into the Jeep and drive south, while Maddox headed for his lodging. She waited a little longer until he was inside and then slipped towards her own trailer. She slid the key into the lock and opened the door, but just as she was about to step in an arm blocked her way.

'William,' she gasped, startled. 'You scared me.'

'And you had me scared.' Blake retorted. 'What were you trying to do out there in the desert in the middle of the night? Is this any time to be getting back?'

'First, let's go inside,' the girl replied. 'I don't think it's a good idea for us to be standing around out here, making small talk at two in the morning.'

'Whatever you say,' said Blake, as they went in.

The girl lit the gas lantern, set it to low and pulled down the window blinds.

'But I do think you owe me an explanation,' Blake went on.

'Why?' Sarah asked.

'Because I've fallen in love with you and you know it. You led me to believe that you felt something for me as well, but then you run off and leave me here like an idiot. You refuse to help me in any way, although you know how desperate I am. I think you know what I'm driving at.'

Sarah turned towards him and Blake could tell that his words had had an effect. 'Yeah, I think I do know what you're driving at, but you're wrong. I risked my neck to get the information you wanted. It's not my fault that it wasn't there.'

'Not your fault?' asked Blake. 'I copied your master and examined it on my computer. The coordinates are all there and they refer to a place in the Negev desert in Israel. We are roughly forty miles south of Mitzpe Ramon, about fifteen miles west of the Egyptian border. And you knew it. Plus, I'd really like to know what you were up to, driving around in the ATV at this hour. I assume you were following Maddox and his men, but why and for whom?'

Sarah leaned back into a chair, letting out a long sigh. 'Then you really do love me,' she said, looking into his eyes. 'Why didn't you tell me before?'

'Well, for starters, I don't know who the hell you are, what the hell you're up to in this place or even who you're in cahoots with.'

'What's that to you anyway?' the girl asked. She got up and moved towards him, allowing him just enough time to sense the heady mix of her perfume and her perspiration before she kissed him boldly, pressing her body against his.

Blake felt a burst of heat rising from his chest, fogging his brain. He had forgotten how violent desire could be, how overwhelming the fragrance rising from a beautiful woman's breasts.

He tried to keep his head. 'Sarah, why did you lie to me?' he asked, pulling away slightly from her embrace but continuing to look her in the eye.

The atmosphere in the trailer was sticky: the room around them seemed to be shrinking, as if the walls were closing in on them, forcing them into an increasingly cramped space that was saturated with their feelings and desire.

Right there in front of him Sarah pulled off her shirt and dusty jeans, announcing, 'I'm going to take a shower. Please don't go anywhere.'

Blake waited alone in the middle of the small space crammed with papers, books and clothes hanging in plastic bags. He just stood there, listening to the splatter of the water in the foggy shower cubical and the increasingly powerful beating of his heart. He felt himself trembling inside, thinking about when the rush of water would suddenly come to a halt. It had been six months since he had made love with Judy. A lifetime. And Judy was still a part of him: the colour of her eyes, the perfume of her hair and her graceful way of moving.

He tried to turn his thoughts to the tomb in the heart of the desert on the other side of the sphinx-like mountain and the pyramid mountain, to the mystery of the Pharaoh buried so incredibly far from the Valley of the Kings. The place where nature and destiny had conspired to create the most majestic architecture of the Nile Valley. And yet, at the same time, the savage beating of his heart obliterated all thought; the voice of that man buried by the millennia and oblivion in a godforsaken spot in the most arid of deserts could not compete with the compelling power of the force calling to him from the other side of the steamy curtain.

And suddenly, there she was, standing naked before him; only then did he realize that the thundering of the water had ceased.

Water dripping from her hands, she slowly took his clothes off, caressing his body and face as if finally taking possession of a long-desired territory.

Blake carried her to the bed and took her into his arms in a fever of desire, caressing her with incredulous passion. His kisses grew increasingly ardent, liberating his soul of its painful memories, as she enveloped him with intense, all-encompassing, hungry sensuality. As he raised his glance from her body to look into her eyes, he found her transfigured by pleasure, becoming more beautiful than ever, radiant with a mysterious splendour, a soft, faint light.

He continued contemplating her after she had surrendered herself to exhaustion, her entire body limp in the lassitude that precedes sleep. He suddenly shook off his languor, as if returning from a dream.

'Will you answer me now?' he said. 'Please.'

Sarah looked into his eyes as she sat up in front of him, taking his hand. 'Not yet, Will,' she said, 'and not here.'

PROFESSOR HUSSEINI switched off all the lights in the house, turned on his answering machine and slipped a little black box into the inside breast pocket of his jacket. He left the house and began walking down the pavement to where his car was parked. He ran into a colleague, Dr Sheridan, a professor of Accadian studies, who was out walking his dog, greeting him with a slight nod of the head. Husseini was convinced that the man would be wondering where he was going at that hour in such cold weather and would no doubt have come up with a salacious but presumably innocent explanation.

He started the engine and drove off, passing the spires of the university buildings capped with snow and, further in the distance, the chapel tower. The view was both enchanting and spectral at the same time and he had never lost his wonder at it, remembering the first time he set foot in the chapel and how it was barren of any sign or token that might have revealed a particular religious faith. It could have even been a mosque. 'This is America,' he had thought. 'They couldn't decide on a single faith, so they chose no faith at all.'

Before long he was pulling onto the wide boulevard that flanked the little lake on the old World's Fair grounds, shimmering under the street lights that cast a greenish halo across the ice. A few minutes later he was getting on the almost deserted Dan Ryan, taking the overpass that headed south.

He passed a police car lazily patrolling the expressway and could make out the corpulent body of the black officer behind the wheel. He followed an oil tanker gleaming with chrome and brightly coloured lights as far as the 111th exit, where he got into the right-hand lane. A little further on, he noticed an old Pontiac station wagon with Indiana plates proceeding at a steady speed of forty miles per hour. He thought it might be his contact.

He saw him turn off at 115th street at five to eleven and pull into the parking lot of a liquor store; now he was sure.

He took a deep breath and pulled over, leaving his parking lights on. A man got out of his car and just stood immobile for several seconds in the middle of the deserted parking lot. He was wearing jeans, running shoes and a jacket with the collar turned up. He had a Chicago Bulls cap on. It seemed to him that the youth was looking his way, as if he wanted to make sure he had sized things up correctly. Next he saw him lower something over his face, a ski mask. He approached Hussein's car with quick, light steps, opened the door and got in.

'*Salaam Alekum*, Abu Ghaj,' he said, as he sat down. 'I'm the number one man of group two and I bring you greetings from Abu Ahmid. Please excuse me covering my face, but it's a safety measure that we all have to comply with. Only Abu Ahmid has ever seen our faces and is capable of identifying us.'

This was the metallic voice he had heard over the telephone. Husseini looked at him: he had the demeanour, the voice and the posture of a young man, perhaps between twenty-five and thirty years old, a sturdy build and long, powerful hands. Husseini had observed his movements as he was approaching the car and opening the door: loose, almost fluid, confident yet careful, and those eyes, gleaming from the depths of the ski mask, seemed indifferent, but were actually very intent upon checking out the surrounding area. This man was obviously an extremely efficient precision fighting machine.

'It's an honour,' he said, 'to work under the direction of the great Abu Ghaj. Your actions are still a source of inspiration throughout the Islamic world. You're a genuine role model for anyone fighting in the jihad.'

Husseini didn't answer, waiting for the man to continue.

'Our operation is about to be completed. The three donkeys bought at the market in Samarkand are about to reach their destination. One of the three was on the truck ahead of you on the expressway, remember it?'

'I do,' Husseini confirmed.

'Listen now, Abu Ghaj,' said the man. 'Group one will reach its destination in two days, group three the day after that, and group two . . . is already in position. The three donkeys can be saddled at any time.'

Husseini realized that his fears were falling into place. 'Saddling the donkeys' was evidently a coded expression for assembling the bombs. Presumably such language was thought necessary even in private conversation in case a bug had been planted in his car. Or was it just another florid expression of the rich Arabic language?

'Abu Ahmid says you are to forward the message as soon as the final donkey is put into its stall.'

'Three days in all,' Husseini thought. The situation was coming to a head with unstoppable momentum. The megalomania of Abu Ahmid was about to reach unprecedented new heights. And yet Husseini still couldn't understand why Abu Ahmid had chosen him and, more significantly, how he could be so certain that Husseini would carry out everything he was asked to do. He lowered the window and turned towards the young man seated next to him. 'Do you mind if I smoke?' he asked him, reaching for a packet of cigarettes.

'No,' the young man answered, 'but not only is it bad for your health, it is harmful for the people around you.'

Husseini shook his head. 'Incredible,' he exclaimed. 'You think like an American.'

'I have to,' the other man answered, without batting an eye.

Husseini leaned back in his seat, taking a deep drag of his cigarette and blowing the smoke out of the window along with a cloud of steamy breath.

'What else did Abu Ahmid say to you?'

Oddly, the young man didn't even glance at him; he simply reached into his jacket and pulled out an envelope.

'He told me to give you this and ask you if you know him.'

Husseini roused himself from the strange torpor he had slipped into and reached out to take the envelope, something he had not anticipated at all.

He opened it and saw that it contained three photographs of the same person, as a child, an adolescent and a young man.

The young man continued to stare straight ahead into the void of the black night. Once more, he mechanically repeated, 'Abu Ahmid wants to know if you know him.'

Husseini continued to look at the photographs in silence, at first without grasping their meaning and then, as if struck by lightning, with an agonized expression, his eyes glistening. 'It could be . . . but it's not possible . . . Could it be . . . my son? Is that who it is? Is it my son?'

'That's who it is, Abu Ghaj. Abu Ahmid says it's your son.'

'Where is he?' he asked with his head bowed, as tears began streaming down his cheeks.

'I don't know.'

Husseini tenderly fondled the pictures of the boy he had for so long believed dead. Many years ago, Abu Ahmid had sent him a little coffin with the unrecognizable remains of a child who had been mutilated by a mortar during the bombing of a refugee camp. He was the little boy in the first photo. It was thus that Husseini had always thought of him, wondering what he would have been like as an adolescent, as a young man, if only he hadn't been cruelly denied his future. But in reality Abu Ahmid had kept the boy hidden away secretly for years, just waiting for the day when he could be used as a hostage . . . And now the day had arrived to force him, Omar al Husseini, to obey without question. That's why Abu Ahmid was so confident that his orders would be carried out . . .

Now, with his son in the hands of the most cynical, ruthless man he had ever known, Husseini could not even consider suicide as a viable way out . . . He was trapped.

'Abu Ahmid says that the boy is fine and not to worry.'

A tomb-like silence descended in the cold car.

It was the young man who again picked up the conversation. 'Is something wrong, Abu Ghaj?' His mechanical words rang with a tone of derision.

Husseini dried his tears on his sleeve and gave back the photographs.

'Abu Ahmid says you can keep them,' the young man explained.

'I don't need them,' answered Husseini. 'His face has always been etched on my soul.'

The young man took the envelope and finally turned to face him. Husseini was able to meet his eyes for an instant, but all he really encountered was an immobile, glacial glare.

'Your soul is distressed but, believe me, what you feel is infinitely better than nothing, than complete emptiness. I'm about to die, perhaps, but I have never had a father or a mother, nor do I have any brothers or sisters. I don't even have any friends . . . No one will mourn me. It will be as if I'd never existed. Goodbye, Abu Ghaj.'

He walked back to his car. After he had driven away, Husseini kept staring for a long time at the tracks his Reeboks had left in the snow, as if deposited by some uncanny dream creature. Finally, he started the engine and drove off.

WILLIAM BLAKE descended slowly into the underground tomb, waited until Sarah had lowered herself down and then turned on the light. He started moving towards the place where he had been removing the debris and discovered the wooden board.

'The secret of this tomb lies right here,' he said, facing Sarah, 'but before we go on, I want you to answer my questions. No one can hear us down here; Sullivan's ears are full of the sound of the generator and the winch.'

Sarah leaned up against the wall and said nothing.

'You knew we were in Israel and didn't say anything to me. You are also aware that Maddox is involved in more than mineral prospecting. There were two armed men in battle gear with him last night when you got back and you were on his heels, shadowing him with the ATV right up to that point.'

'Whatever I hid from you up until now has been for your own good. Knowing where we are would only have stirred up your curiosity, and that meant putting you in danger, given the circumstances.'

'You could have helped me avoid a wild-goose chase. I thought I was in Egypt.'

'Egypt's only a few miles to the east . . .'

'The Egypt I'm talking about is on the Nile.'

'And knowing what Maddox is up to would only have made things more dangerous for you.'

'I don't give a damn. I want to know everything, and that means about you too. We've made love. Don't you think it's about time we levelled with each other?'

'No, I don't. And I still think you shouldn't get involved in this business. You already have a mystery to solve. One should be enough for you.'

Blake glared at her. The situation was getting a bit tense and the air started to feel close. 'If you don't answer my questions, I'll tell Maddox that you followed him last night and that you sneaked into his office the other day to copy some files from his computer.'

'You wouldn't dare!'

'Oh, yes, I would. Plus I can prove it, because I've got a copy of the master you reproduced. Believe me, it's not worth the risk. I'm not bluffing, Sarah.'

'You son of a bitch!'

'This is nothing. I'm capable of much more.'

Sarah moved closer to him. 'Do you seriously think you can influence me with your threats? Just keep this in mind, honey. You can't count on anybody in this camp except me. If your presence happened to get a little inconvenient for any reason, no one would think twice about killing you and getting rid of your body under a couple of hasty shovelfuls of sand and gravel. Maddox wouldn't bat an eye, and Pollock would gladly give him a hand.'

'You're not telling me anything I don't know. But I didn't have a choice about coming here.'

'Sure you did. You could have stayed in Chicago, found a new life for yourself . . . but there's no use talking now. Things are looking pretty bad around here. I'll tell you what I can. Our government was planning a secret operation and had decided to use one of the Warren Mining Corporation camps as their base. One reason for this choice was the fact that Alan Maddox had worked for the government before becoming the manager of Warren Mining. The operation has failed, so to speak, although, as fate would have it, the actual goal was nevertheless achieved. Unfortunately, the entire matter has caused a great deal of resentment in the Israeli intelligence force – who happen to be indispensable to the American government in this country – because they were kept completely in the dark about the whole matter. At this point, no one trusts anyone any more and, besides, Maddox's idea of having you work on this excavation has turned into a headache all round.'

'Why did Maddox send for me anyway? Is it true that they really have financial problems or did you just make the whole thing up?'

'It seems to have been simply one of Maddox's brainstorms. He's absolutely infatuated with Egyptology. I have my own theory: our government obviously guaranteed Maddox healthy remuneration for his efforts, but this money was supposed to be put into the company to save it from bankruptcy. When he discovered this damn tomb, he figured he could kill two birds with one stone, personally pocketing the proceeds from the treasures, apart from a more or less equal share going to Sullivan and Gordon. I bet they even tried to make some sort of deal with you.'

'That's right. But I didn't go for it.'

'The problem is that the whole situation in this part of the world is degenerating fast and we are in for some major trouble. There's no more time for all your painstaking archaeological work. If you want my opinion, clear away the rubble from that damn landslide by getting the men to work day and night; catalogue your findings and get the hell out of here – if you can. When this whole thing's over, I'll look you up and we can enjoy some more peaceful time together and maybe even get to know each other a little better. Who knows? I'm still game . . .'

Blake remained silent, gazing into her eyes, trying to control his feelings, the fear and all the uncertainty her words had stirred up. Lowering his head, all he could muster was, 'Thanks.'

He went back as far as the entrance and signalled Sullivan to send in the workmen and lower the winch.

Once again, he set about removing the rubble, but not without some major professional qualms. Each time he saw a piece of wood from the mysterious board hauled out on a work-man's shovel and tossed into the big dump bucket attached to the winch he got a sinking feeling in the pit of his stomach, but he had no choice. If he had opted to work instead with a brush and trowel it would have taken weeks and he realized that his time was drastically limited. He only interrupted the job for a half-hour lunch break, climbing up into the fresh air and sitting down with Sarah in the shade of the tent to eat a chicken sandwich and drink a beer. As he was about to go back down into the tomb, he noticed a cloud of dust approaching from the direction of the camp. Gradually he was able to make out what it was: one of the mining company vehicles. It pulled up at the entrance to the little work site, the door flew open and out hopped Alan Maddox.

'Surprise, surprise,' said Blake. 'To what could I possibly owe the honour of this visit to my dig site?'

'Hi there, Sarah,' proffered Maddox, seeing the girl still seated not far away. Turning to Blake, he added, 'Got some news. The results of the radiocarbon tests on the samples we sent in for analysis have come back. It cost a fortune, but they did it in record time. I just thought you would want to have the results as soon as possible.'

'Thanks a lot,' said Blake, without any attempt at hiding his excitement. 'Can I see them?'

'That's what I came for,' said Maddox, handing him a still-sealed envelope.

Blake opened it and hurriedly pulled out the sheet of paper with the test results. He read them aloud:

'Wood sample: mid XIII cent. BC, +/ − 50 years
Leather sample: early VI cent. BC, +/ − 30 years'

Maddox watched him nervously, waiting for his reaction. 'Well? What kind of news is it, anyway?'

Blake shook his head. 'It's a very precise finding, but I just can't figure it out—'

'Why? What does it mean?'

'All the factors that I have thus far taken into consideration lead me to date this tomb some time between the twelfth and thirteenth centuries BC, and the radiocarbon dating of the wood from the panel confirms my theory. But the results for the leather date the sample at the beginning of the sixth century BC and that just doesn't make sense.'

'Someone broke into the tomb six centuries before Christ to rob it. What's so strange about that?'

'Just that. It wasn't robbed. What, then, brought our mysterious visitor into the tomb?'

Maddox stood in silence for a few moments, as if pondering this strange set of circumstances.

'Thirsty?' Blake asked him. 'There's some water and the orange juice should still be cold.'

'No, thanks, I've already had something to drink. By the way, Blake, how much time do you think you'll need to clear away the rubble from the landslide?'

'Not much,' said Blake. 'Maybe by tomorrow evening . . .'

'And then what will you do, open the sarcophagus?'

Blake nodded yes.

'I definitely want to be present when you do it. Send for me, Blake. I want to be down there with you when you open that damned lid.'

'All right, Mr Maddox. Thanks for coming by. If that's all, I'd like to get back to work.'

Maddox had a brief discussion with Sullivan, said goodbye to Sarah, hopped back into his Jeep and left. Blake had himself lowered into the tomb so he could continue.

Sarah joined him shortly. 'Do you really intend to open the sarcophagus tomorrow evening?'

'Quite possibly.'

'How do you plan on doing it?'

'The top slab sticks out about ten centimetres all the way around. All we need are four blocks of wood and four hydraulic jacks. We will use two more blocks to slide the lid down onto the ground. Do you think we can find what we need around the camp?'

'I'll take care of it this evening. If we have to, we can always use the jacks from the Jeeps. They should do the job.'

By this point the workmen had already uncovered most of the board and gradually, as more debris was removed, on the eastern side of the tomb a kind of door frame appeared, through which rubble and debris kept falling.

Blake drew nearer and pointed his torch at the frame.

'What's this?' Sarah asked.

Scrutinizing first the frame and then the board, which had been almost completely cleared of debris, Blake was suddenly overcome by a strange excitement. 'Maybe I've got it,' he said. 'Hand me the tape measure.'

Sarah took a tape measure out of the tool kit and handed it to him. Blake climbed up the heap of debris, slipping back down several times before managing to reach the frame structure and measure it. Next, he came back down and measured the width of the board.

'I knew it,' he said. 'It's exactly as I thought. This board was originally positioned vertically in such a way as to close that opening . . .'

'So then, at some later time, someone made it fall to permanently seal off the entrance to the tomb,' Sarah broke in.

'Right. And I bet, when we've removed the board, we'll also find the latches that held it in place. Tell the workmen to be careful and damage the board as little as possible when they remove the debris.'

He picked up a shovel and began digging at the side of the sarcophagus, while the men continued to work on the side where the board was. He was starting to hit lighter material now, sand mostly, mixed with pebbles as big as grains of corn, and the removal operation began proceeding at a quicker pace than he had anticipated.

Sarah also was possessed by a mounting excitement that wouldn't allow her to simply stand idly by and observe. She began filling buckets and emptying them into the dump container, revealing amazing reserves of physical energy. She was sweating so hard that her light cotton shirt began sticking to her body, revealing even more of her physical attributes, causing her supple tan skin to glow in the shadows of the burial site, like the patina of an ancient statue. Both of them had tied handkerchiefs over their mouths to keep out the thick dust that the work of the four people was raising from the heap of rubble; too much for the vacuum to adequately draw outside.

Blake suddenly stopped and took a little whisk broom and a brush from the tool kit, then began removing the dust that had coated the surface of the sarcophagus.

'What do you see?' asked Sarah.

'The stone of the sarcophagus is inscribed. All the way down to the base, it looks like.'

Sarah left the workmen to their task and joined Blake, kneeling down beside him.

'Light the lantern and give me some bright light,' he said as he continued to clean the calcareous surface, first with the little whisk broom and then with the fine paintbrush. Sarah did as she was told and stood observing her companion as he delicately fingered the fine grooves cut into the stone. The bright light revealed a line of hieroglyphs that still displayed traces of the original colours wielded by the ancient scribes: ochre, indigo, black and yellow.

'What does it mean?' Sarah asked.

'Nothing,' answered Blake. 'It doesn't make sense.'

'What do you mean?' the girl enquired.

'This isn't a horizontal sequence of signs; each one is rather the top of a buried vertical line. I won't be able to make any sense out of it until we reach the floor. Let's get to work.'

Blake picked up his shovel again and managed to dig out a space between the heap of debris and the side of the sarcophagus

148

that was big enough for him to manoeuvre into. He began cleaning the surface to see what the inscriptions said.

When he had finished the cleaning operation, he realized that the scribe must have been the same one who had made the other inscriptions found in the tomb, the same one who had written the Breasted papyrus.

He began reading and Sarah observed his reaction as his eyes coursed along the lines written from top to bottom. When he stopped, she approached him. He had a puzzled expression on his face, almost distressed, as if the text had thrown his mind into great confusion. Sarah placed her right hand on his shoulder and looked him straight in the eye.

'What does it say, William? What does the inscription mean?'

Blake shook his head. 'I can't say for sure . . . If what I'm thinking were true, it would be so outrageous that—'

'Why? Will, come on, tell me what it says!'

The workmen noticed the agitated tone of the girl's voice and turned towards her, letting their shovels hang limply at their sides. Blake made a gesture intended to halt her insistence. But all he said was, 'Take a couple of pictures while I copy out the text. I have to be sure . . . have to be sure . . . And it's not easy. A person can always make a mistake . . . We'll talk about it later. Help me, now.'

Sarah didn't persist. Instead she got the camera and took several photos of the inscription, as Blake began carefully to copy the hieroglyphic symbols into a sketch pad.

In the meantime, the workmen had almost completely freed the board of all debris and had cleared the structure on the eastern wall of the tomb: a lintel and two jambs which framed an opening that was just slightly smaller than the board itself.

'Clean the board completely and clear away the rest of the debris from the sarcophagus,' said Blake. 'There are still a couple of hours and we can do it. If you finish by evening, I guarantee you that Mr Maddox will give you a nice bonus.'

The two workmen nodded in assent and Blake began to dig

at the spot where, several days before, they had found the remains of some skeletons. There were just the bare bones of four adults, most probably male. Around them were traces of sulphur and bitumen, the substances used to burn the bodies. He gathered the bones into a little box and set it in a corner of the tomb. When he had finished, he signalled for Sarah to follow him out into the open. They were hoisted to the surface by the winch.

'How are things progressing?' asked Sullivan.

'Fine,' answered Blake. 'If everything proceeds as it should, we'll have all the debris removed by evening. I'll see you later, Sullivan. You carry on while we take a little stroll.'

'That's fine with me,' said Sullivan, riding the bucket back down into the tomb. 'But don't go wandering off too far and be careful of snakes and scorpions.'

'Don't worry, Sullivan,' said Sarah. 'I'll take care of him.'

Blake drank a little cold water from the thermos as they set off in the direction of a hill that rose to the east, not far from the excavation site. The sun was very low in the sky, casting unnaturally long shadows towards the base of the hill. He walked quickly, as if he were in a hurry to get to a certain predetermined destination.

'Why are we going so fast?' asked Sarah.

'Because I want to get up there before the sun sinks behind the horizon and by now it's just a question of minutes.'

'I don't get it,' said Sarah, trying to keep up with him. 'What are we going to look for up there? And what did you read that was so extraordinary in that inscription?'

'I told you,' Blake replied. 'I'm not sure. The hieroglyphs could be interpreted in different ways. I have to find confirmation, some other evidence, before I want to commit myself. And, above all, I have to open that sarcophagus.'

By now he was walking uphill, panting. The light was growing dimmer with every step and the sky above him began darkening to a deeper and deeper blue. He finally got to the top of the hill and turned round to look over the plain, where Sullivan's Jeep and their equipment stood out against the total emptiness.

'What are you looking for?' Sarah asked again.

'Don't you see anything?' asked Blake, observing the surrounding territory.

'No,' replied Sarah, 'nothing other than Sullivan's Jeep, our Jeep and the equipment around the dig.'

'Look more carefully,' said Blake with an enigmatic expression. 'You really don't see anything?'

Sarah just shook her head, her eyes scanning the deserted plain below. 'Nothing other than rocks, that is.'

'That's right,' said Blake, 'rocks. But if you look closely you'll make out patterns that delineate a kind of perimeter. And the tomb is more or less in the middle.'

Sarah observed more closely as the sun sank completely behind the horizon and now she could make out the four corners of an enormous rectangle and other stone arrangements inside it that almost seemed to trace further divisions of the space.

Just then a solitary night hawk took wing, leaving its nest perched on a distant peak of the Mitzpe crater, flying towards the centre of the sky to take possession of the night.

'How did you know about these patterns on the landscape?' asked Sarah.

'This place is full of patterns, drawings and signs – on the ground, on the rock walls. I was struck by them from the very first time we came out here. There are rock carvings, alignments of the stones, a language that has remained mute up until this moment. I have studied and sketched out a great number of patterns whenever I've had free time away from the dig . . . And now the time has come to let them speak . . . Sarah, do you have a Bible in your quarters?'

'A Bible?'

'That's right.'

'I'm not very religious, William. I'm afraid I don't have a Bible . . . But maybe Pollock might have one. He's an old lech, but he's also a bit of a fanatic, as far as I can tell.'

'Ask him for it. I need it. I'll explain later. Let's get going now. I'm curious to see how the work is proceeding.'

They walked past Sullivan, who was dumping the bucket. 'I think they're about to finish,' he said. 'The bucket is coming up half empty.'

'I'll go down,' said Blake.

Blake lowered himself with the winch and saw that the rubble had been almost completely removed. The two workmen were cleaning the board with brooms. Their beards and hair were white from the fine powder that was floating around in the motionless air.

'When you have finished,' he said, 'close the opening but don't remove the plastic sheeting, because there's still too much dust in the air.'

He had himself hoisted to the surface and got into the Jeep with Sarah, while Sullivan put away the tools and hooked the bucket to the slab used for sealing the opening, so he could set it over the entrance to the tomb.

Sarah drove the Jeep along the road that was still illuminated by the last rays of light from the sunset, as Blake scrutinized the sheets of paper on which he had copied the inscription from the sarcophagus.

'So you're not going to tell me what's written on that stone?' the girl asked suddenly.

'Sarah, this isn't a matter of telling or not telling. You see, hieroglyphics is a system of writing in which the majority of signs have a variety of meanings, depending on their position in the phrase or in the overall context . . .'

'Nonsense. I saw how upset you looked . . . You can't hide it. I could tell there was something . . . special about those symbols. Wasn't there?'

'Yes,' Blake admitted, 'but that's not enough to make me

want to go out on a limb with my opinion. Just give me tonight and tomorrow. I promise, you'll be the first one to know.'

The Jeep proceeded along the southern rim of the Mitzpe Ramon crater and began to descend into the rugged basin of the wadi. The lights of the camp glimmered in the distance. It was almost time for dinner.

As soon as they got to the parking lot, Blake got out of the Jeep.

'Are you going out traipsing around tonight?' he asked Sarah.

'No, I don't think so. Tonight I'll be here if you should happen to need me.'

'For any reason at all?'

'For whatever reason.'

'And find me that Bible, please.'

'I'll do everything within my power, and more, if necessary.'

Smiling at him, she tossed her backpack over her shoulder and headed towards her quarters. Blake sat down on a boulder and lit a cigarette. How much time had passed since that freezing night in Chicago? It seemed like an eternity to him and yet it had been little more than two weeks. He wondered what Judy must have thought when he disappeared without even a phone call . . . He liked the idea of suddenly vanishing like that from her life. She, no doubt, had expected him to call, to somehow get a message to her, to try to invent some excuse for seeing her again. And what about Sarah? He thought he could bet on her disappearing once her mission had been accomplished. What then? He would have to start all over again, dealing with the miserable life he was left with, unless they decided to get rid of him first . . . So what if they did? At least he had experienced the most intense moment of his life and that was probably much more than any number of men who move about over the face of the earth as if they had never really existed. By the evening of the next day, he would have faced the greatest mystery in the history of mankind, of this he was sure, and he would have looked the Pharaoh of the desert in the face for the first time.

After lingering a little while longer to enjoy the warmth of the day that still radiated from the rocks, he finally rose and went back to his trailer.

As soon as he had closed the door, he switched on the radio he kept by his bedside, turned up the volume and got into the shower. It was news time and the station he was listening to was from Cyprus and in English. The announcer was very excited, as if there were some sort of emergency: he was speaking of a concentration of Iranian troops at the southern Iraqi border, just a little north of Kuwait and the islands of the Shatt el Arab. The speaker added that General Taksoun had asked the United Nations and the American government for permission to mobilize at least part of the army in order to defend the threatened border and that the American government had given him the go-ahead. It was a well-known fact that Taksoun was held in high regard in certain State Department circles.

In Israel there had been another suicide-bombing incident, this time inside a synagogue on Saturday, the Sabbath, resulting in a real bloodbath. The police figured that the explosives had been brought into the place of worship the day before. That's the only way the commandos could have got around all the strict security checks. Prime Minister Benjamin Schochot had just narrowly escaped an attempt on his life and the Minister of the Interior had issued orders to beef up security measures, closing all checkpoints leading in and out of the Palestinian territories.

Blake turned off the shower and moved closer to the radio, drying his hair briskly.

Just then Sarah walked in and, pointing at the radio, asked him whether he had heard the news.

'Yes,' answered Blake, 'and I don't like the sound of it at all. Evidently the situation in this region is completely out of control. No wonder Maddox wants to hightail it as fast as he can.'

Sarah was holding a book. 'I found it for you,' she announced. 'Pollock loaned it to me. You should have seen the strange look that came over his face when I asked for it. He must have thought I was in the throes of some sort of mystical rapture.'

Blake got dressed as Sarah thumbed absent-mindedly through the thick volume.

'What do you hope to find in it?' she asked, raising her face towards him.

'Confirmation of a hunch,' answered Blake.

Sarah closed the book and went towards the door. Taking hold of the doorknob she reminded her companion: 'Dinner's served in five minutes.'

And out she went.

8

GAD AVNER went into Prime Minister Schochot's office, where he was faced by a very stern chief executive.

Avner greeted him with a nod. 'Mr Prime Minister . . .'

'Have a seat, Mr Avner,' the Prime Minister said. 'Can I offer you something? Some whisky, a cigar?'

Avner knew very well what these pleasantries were leading up to and was aware that this calm would be followed by a storm. He shook his head politely, declining these tokens of hospitality. 'No, thank you, sir, I don't want anything.'

'Mr Avner,' Schochot began, 'I don't want to speak about the attempt on my life just yet . . .' He put a certain emphasis on the 'just yet'. 'Instead, I want you to explain to me how a bomb could have gone off in a synagogue in the middle of the day on the Sabbath. Nothing like this has ever happened before. If our security forces can't keep terrorists from profaning our nation's places of worship we are really in bad shape. This has been a severe blow to public morale. The polls say that increasing numbers of our people are considering emigrating to America, France or Italy. Some are even considering Russia! Does this mean we have to stand by helplessly in the face of a new Diaspora? Mr Avner, you know as well as I that if the people of Israel leave their homeland, it will be forever. There will be no coming back.'

He spoke with personal conviction and trepidation, and Avner got a glimpse of the man behind the politician.

'Mr Prime Minister, the bomb was carried into the synagogue

from below. Under the flooring we found a fifty-metre tunnel that was connected to the municipal sewage system, a system that your government had built to service the new settlements . . .'

The Prime Minister appeared momentarily disarmed, but he immediately returned to the attack. 'Don't they run a security check in synagogues before beginning services? I mean, we're talking about a whole kilogram of Semtex. That's a hefty little bundle, hardly the sort of thing that goes unnoticed.'

'Sir, this is how we have reconstructed the incident: a commando unit of terrorists dug the tunnel right through to the floor without actually breaking through, completing their task Friday evening or early Saturday morning. The last security check found nothing unusual and allowed the worshippers to come in. Once the synagogue was full, probably upon a signal from outside, the terrorist burst through the floor of the passageway by means of a small explosion and then leapt up into the synagogue, detonating the explosive material attached to his body. Caught completely off guard, the people inside the temple had no chance to defend themselves.

'Now, Mr Prime Minister, you will rightly insist that it is our job to prevent this sort of thing, rather than just clean up the mess afterwards, but you know as well as I that there's a limit to what any organization can do. The availability of men and equipment is always limited. It is physically impossible to patrol the whole country both above and below ground. Nevertheless, my technical squad is installing sensing devices in all synagogues and other public places. This equipment can pick up suspicious underground noise and vibrations. It's a complex and costly operation and this too, of course, is part of our enemy's plan. By maintaining relentless pressure on us, they force us to keep investing more and more in terms of money, effort and precious human resources . . . We cannot hold out if this pressure doesn't let up. I'm not referring to myself, and if you have any doubts about me, don't hesitate to act; I'm ready to step aside. I have no ambitions, sir, other than to protect you and our citizens . . . But if you know of a man better suited than me and more qualified, you should call him in and give him my job right now. I'm at your complete disposal . . .'

He got up to go, but the Prime Minister stopped him. 'Sit down, Avner, please.'

Gad Avner sat down and the two men looked at one other in silence for several seconds. The noise of the traffic below had almost ceased; most of the population had already closed themselves up at home, because of the descending night.

Schochot got up and went over to the window. 'Take a look, Avner. There's nobody on the street. Everyone's terrified.'

Avner got up and walked over to the window of the big office, which looked out over the Old City and the gilded Dome of the Rock, just like the view from the window of his terrace.

'Our soldiers are out there,' he said. 'See them? And so are my men, but I can't point them out to you.'

The Prime Minister sighed. 'What do you plan on doing?'

Avner lit a cigarette, took a deep drag and then coughed hard.

'You smoke too much, Avner,' the Prime Minister told him, almost solicitously. 'You know it can be bad for you, don't you?'

'I won't die from smoking, sir. I don't have that much time, I'm afraid. So why worry about it? Listen to me, now, because I have to give you some bad news.'

'What could be worse than what we already know?'

'Do you remember how a couple of weeks ago I spoke in a cabinet meeting about a certain "Operation Nebuchadnezzar", requesting more funding for something I considered a grave and imminent threat?'

Schochot frowned. 'Are you saying that these attacks are the beginning of the operation?'

'I'm not sure, of course, but it would certainly appear so . . . The thing I'm really concerned about is that we will have to fight on two fronts: internal terrorism and a frontal attack from outside.'

'That's not possible. We have always won by fighting in the open. And so far, we have always maintained a devastating technical advantage. They wouldn't dare.'

'I'm afraid they would.'

'Do you have any evidence, any proof?'

'No . . . just a hunch.'

Schochot looked at him in disbelief. 'A hunch?'

'It's difficult to explain . . . A detective just smells these things in the air. I don't need proof. It has to be that bastard who's behind all of this. He's the one who arranged the murder of al Bashar . . . and Taksoun's coming to power, catching the Americans totally off guard.'

'What bastard?'

'Abu Ahmid, who else?'

'But Taksoun has the respect, if not the friendship, of the Americans.'

'But they weren't the ones who murdered al Bashar. Although they had deployed a squad of commandos at Mitzpe Ramon for the operation. Didn't you know about it, sir?'

Schochot remained dumbfounded for a moment as Avner insisted with a tone of ill-concealed reprimand, 'Of course you knew, didn't you?'

'I did know about it, Avner.'

'And why didn't you inform me, then?'

'Because I thought you'd be against the operation and that . . .'

'Go ahead, you can speak freely.'

'That you would create problems for me at a time when I couldn't afford to make a fool of myself in front of the Americans.'

'I would have deferred to you without publicly opposing your initiative. I would have only tried my hardest to make you change your mind in private.'

'But why? The Americans trust Taksoun and even you would agree that he's much better for us than al Bashar.'

'I don't trust anyone, least of all Taksoun. If he's a friend of the Americans, he's a traitor and a mercenary. But if he's not, as I believe, then someone bailed him out of a really ticklish situation for a completely different reason than our friends in Washington could ever imagine.'

'Does this also have something to do with the mysterious "Operation Nebuchadnezzar"?'

Avner lit another cigarette and Schochot noticed that they were Syrian 'Orients'. One man's vice . . .

Avner coughed drily, peevishly, then said, 'I don't understand this story about the Iranian troops on the border of the Shatt el Arab. It doesn't make sense. And the mobilization requested by Taksoun makes even less sense. It all sounds like a bad film to me . . . I don't like it, not one bit. Plus, I know that Taksoun's men are talking to the Syrians and Libyans. I would have expected him to contact the Jordanians and the Saudi Arabians. Wouldn't that make more sense under the circumstances?'

'Are you sure of all this?'

'Yes.'

'And why didn't you report it sooner?'

'I'm telling you now, Mr Prime Minister, and I have also informed the chief of staff of the armed forces.'

Schochot shook his head. 'No, I can't believe what you're saying. The Americans would mobilize another army, like during the Gulf War. It's absolutely impossible, believe me.'

Avner extinguished his cigarette in the ashtray on the Prime Minister's desk and got up. Schochot got up too and walked him to the door.

'Mr Avner,' he said, 'you worked for the last government and with the previous coalition, but I have the utmost confidence in you. I want you to stay on at your job and continue your work. In the future, I shall avoid making decisions without consulting you.'

Avner stopped with his hand on the handle of the door. 'Mr Prime Minister, have you ever read Polybius?'

Schochot looked at him in bewilderment. 'The Greek historian? Yes, a bit in high school.'

'According to Polybius, history isn't entirely in the hands of the men making it. There exists something imponderable that he calls "thyche", or fate. I believe that this time our enemies have prepared everything very carefully. Only fate can help us now, or the hand of God, if you prefer. Goodnight, Mr Prime Minister.'

HE HAD HIS driver take him home and, as usual, went up to the top floor. On the kitchen table he found some cold chicken and slices of bread in the toaster. A bottle of mineral water and the pot of coffee ready on the stove completed his evening repast.

He opened the terrace door and breathed in the air that came in off the Judaean desert, carrying a sweet hint of early spring. Considering all the cigarettes he smoked, it sometimes amazed him just how sensitive his sense of smell still was.

He sat down to eat something while thumbing through the newspapers and the file with his agenda for the next morning. When he had finished he went to the bathroom to get ready for bed and as he was coming out, he heard his private line ringing.

He picked up the receiver and heard a familiar voice greet him in the usual way.

'This is the night porter, sir.'

'I'm listening, night porter.'

'The Mitzpe commando unit is demobilizing, but there's something that escapes me. I'm trying to find out who the mission leader is really reporting to.'

'What do you mean?'

'I have the feeling that this person is playing two games at once, but I still can't work out who the second contact is.'

'Last time you spoke to me about an archaeological dig. How's it coming along?'

'By the end of tomorrow the sarcophagus should be opened and the mummy could be identified. If this operation is concluded there might not be any reason to stay, unless something unforeseen happens. The situation as it stands is very complex. If I'm not mistaken, I think some deals are being made, but I can't tell yet who's on the other side of the table. The tomb's treasure, which is certainly of inestimable value, may be involved in these negotiations, but I'm not sure. I'm starting to get suspicious, though. That treasure could come in handy for someone right here in Israel . . .'

Avner remained silent upon hearing these words, wondering who they could be referring to. He too was beginning to have some suspicions of his own, but said only, 'Be careful, and call me if you can as soon as there are any new developments. Goodnight.'

'Goodnight, sir.'

After hanging up, Gad Avner lay down exhausted on his bed. He felt besieged by an omnipresent enemy, but didn't know where to strike first to defend himself.

MADDOX SIGNALLED for the camp cook to serve coffee and pass around the box of Cuban cigars. There were just six of them at the table: Pollock, Sullivan, Gordon, Sarah, Blake and himself. Maddox, therefore, felt free to talk about the dig.

'Tomorrow Professor Blake is going to open the sarcophagus and examine the mummy, exposing it to the light of day for the first time in three thousand years. I have asked to be present for the operation. It's something I don't want to miss. I imagine you will all want to be present as well. Do have any objections, Professor Blake?'

'No, Mr Maddox, that's fine with me. All I want to know is what you have decided to do with the artefacts found in the tomb.'

'This is something that will be decided at the last moment. Right now, though, I would like you to explain what your excavation efforts in the tomb have accomplished so far. Clearing away the debris inside was certainly necessary in order to lift the lid of the sarcophagus, but I gather this also enabled you to more clearly evaluate exactly how the slide may have occurred. Isn't that so?'

'As you all know,' Blake began, 'the burial site was partially blocked by a slide of debris, sand and rocks that had to be cleared away to expose the two sides of the sarcophagus which were completely enclosed by it. I had hoped that by removing the rubble, I would be able to understand the circumstances under which this slide occurred. At first I thought it must have been an earthquake, but I was forced to change my mind when I saw that all the objects accompanying the mummy were still intact and in their original positions. If there had been an earthquake strong enough to cause a slide of this proportion, all sorts of objects would have fallen over and many of the ones made from glass and ceramic materials would have broken. So the cause was not an earthquake, but rather a slide that was set off on purpose. It was just a question of discovering when and why.

'I began to remove the rubble by loading it into a dump-bucket hooked up to the winch on Mr Sullivan's Jeep and disposing of it on the surface. I soon discovered that under the slide there was a wooden board or panel resting on the floor of the tomb, something I couldn't figure out at first.

'A little later we found what appeared to be the remains of a leather sandal, not far from this board. I had some radiocarbon tests done on samples of both these finds. The results that came back yesterday are very surprising. The board is made from very tough acacia wood and dates back to the middle of the thirteenth century BC. The sandal, however, only dates back to the sixth century BC. A very peculiar situation.

'When I had finished clearing away the slide, it became clear that the board was almost certainly part of the ancient tomb's security system. If robbers had attempted to break in, they would have caused the board to fall to the ground, unleashing a slide of sand and rock that would have blocked the entrance and probably buried the intruders. A similar device was discovered in the great mound tomb of the Kings of Phrygia in Asia Minor.

'The presence of the sandal, carbon-dated to the beginning of the sixth century BC, leads me to believe that the slide occurred then. This particular scenario, however, gave rise to a number of unanswered questions. Who was the owner of the sandal? A grave robber? If so, why wasn't he buried under the slide? The fact that he lost only one sandal suggests to me that he knew exactly what he was doing. My theory is that it was a priest who for some reason knew about the location of this tomb and, having got wind that it might be profaned or robbed, purposely triggered the slide mechanism, sealing off the entrance forever.'

'And this series of events,' interrupted Maddox, 'supposedly took place five centuries after the actual mummy had been placed in the tomb.'

'That's how I see it,' confirmed Blake.

'Over those five centuries, the board could have collapsed on its own; the slide could have been spontaneous.'

'It could have been,' Blake allowed, 'but it wasn't, for two simple reasons. First of all, the board was reinforced with two bronze bars and the wood itself is naturally very hard and strong, and was well preserved by the dry climate. Secondly, the sandal indicates that someone was present when the slide occurred, someone who was not caught unawares by the event, but rather set it off. Otherwise, I would have found his remains under the rubble along with his sandal.'

Blake paused for a moment in his presentation, and everyone sat in complete silence, waiting for him to continue his account. Seeing that there were no questions, he proceeded. 'The presence of the security device and the fact that a priest knew how to trigger it after five centuries means that knowledge of this tomb's location was handed down from generation to generation for an as yet unknown reason.'

'Do you hope to discover it tomorrow when you open the sarcophagus?' asked Maddox.

'That's what I'm hoping,' answered Blake.

'Now, however, it's best that we all get a good night's sleep.

Tomorrow's going to be a very strenuous and exciting day. Goodnight to everyone.'

They all got up and headed back to their quarters. After just enough time to brush their teeth and slip into their pyjamas, the generator turned off, plunging the camp into darkness and silence.

Blake got back to his quarters, lit the gas lantern and sat down to read the Bible, taking notes in a little notebook. The silence was broken every now and then by the shrill howl of fighter jets as they flew over the camp at low altitude. He remained immersed in his reading until he suddenly heard what sounded like the whirr of helicopter blades in the distance. He checked his watch: it was one in the morning.

He got up and walked to the back window to look out over the desert in the direction from which the noise was coming. He saw Sarah lowering herself out of the back window of her trailer and sneaking off into the dark. He caught a glimpse of her one last time from behind a bush before she disappeared for good. He was just starting to get back to work when he was interrupted by the distant sound of a car engine. Looking up, against the background of the dunes he was able to discern the silhouette of a Jeep driving with its headlights off, moving towards a point on the horizon where he could just make out a faint glow.

Letting out a quiet sigh, he went out of the back door to have a cigarette on the step. It was completely dark and the sky was overcast. He picked up a stick from the ground, split it with his pocket knife and stuck it into the soft ground. He placed his cigarette in the groove and proceeded to slip around to the back of the trailer, continuing on to the parking lot. Maddox's Jeep was gone.

He went back to his trailer and picked up the still-lit cigarette to finish it. The air was chilly and scented with the distant odour of damp dust. It was raining somewhere over this parched and sterile land.

He felt like an inexperienced soldier on the eve of his first battle. What was in store for him the next day? What would become of the tomb's treasure and what would he do if the crazy theory he was nursing in the back of his mind turned out to be right?

He returned to his papers and put his head between his hands, trying to see if he could think of a way to save the tomb in the desert. The Falcon alone surely couldn't carry away all the objects, but they could use the Jeeps or have trucks sent across the desert. All they would have to do then is set up a meeting at some secluded spot in the desert, transfer the stuff and then load it all onto a ship anchored off some deserted stretch of the Mediterranean coast.

IT WAS THREE in the morning and William Blake got up from his desk to wash his face and make some coffee. As he was lighting the stove, he made out the barely perceptible sound of footsteps on the path behind the trailer. He peeked out of the window and saw Sarah slip into her trailer. He waited a short while and then went outside barefoot, in order to make as little noise as possible. He went over to her trailer and leaned his ear up against the metal wall. He heard her voice talking quietly to someone, probably on a mobile phone or short-wave radio. Then the conversation suddenly ended, followed by various sounds: the running of water, steps and then silence. He went back and returned to his work, but before long he heard the sound of an engine coming from the parking lot. Maddox must be returning from his nocturnal expedition.

Blake drank his coffee, an Italian blend he had found at the little camp shop and with which he was able to prepare something vaguely similar to an espresso. Lighting a cigarette, he went over to the map he had laid out on the only available table. All of a sudden, things began to come together: apparently absurd theories assumed credible new substance and forgotten itineraries suddenly disentangled themselves right before his eyes. From a drawer he took out the pictures of the rock carvings he had taken here and there along the road in the desert that led to the tomb and they too began to form a succession of signs and new meanings. He thought of the two mountains shaped like a sphinx and a pyramid, as the face of the Pharaoh of the desert slowly started to emerge from the mysterious depths, like the great solar disc rising out of the morning mist.

IT WAS FIVE in the morning when Blake left his trailer to go and knock on Alan Maddox's door.

'Excuse me, Mr Maddox,' he said when he saw him appear with sleepy eyes, wearing his dressing gown. 'I need your help.'

'Don't you feel well?' asked Maddox, looking at him in alarm. In the tentative dawn light Blake's complexion was ashen and his eyes, reddened by his long vigil, had a half-crazed, disturbing, glazed look.

'No, I'm fine, Mr Maddox. I just have to send an email before going off to work. It's urgent.'

Maddox gave him a rather perplexed look. 'Really, you know the rules we have in the camp. Restricted contact with the outside world until the operation has concluded. I made an exception for you once but you must understand—'

'Mr Maddox, I've already communicated with the so-called outside world when you weren't here and, as you see, nothing has happened.'

'Well, how—'

'Let me in, please, and I'll explain everything.'

Maddox stepped aside, grumbling, 'Pollock will pay for this.'

'As I say, nothing has happened. I'm a man of my word and I made a deal with you that I intend to keep. It was just about a hieroglyphic text that I needed some help interpreting. I received the help shortly afterwards, once again by email, and it enabled me to continue my investigations. Listen, Mr Maddox, just think if I were able to identify the actual person buried in the tomb at Ras Udash. The value of those artefacts would triple, just like that. Doesn't that interest you?'

'Come on in,' said Maddox, 'but I'm going to stay here while you send the email. I'm sorry, but I have no choice.'

'That's fine. Pollock did the same thing: he checked the attachment to make sure that the text was really a hieroglyphic inscription. I have a special program. Watch.'

He sat down at the computer, turned it on, loaded the writing program with a couple of diskettes and then started to compose a text of hieroglyphic characters.

'Extraordinary,' muttered Maddox, watching from over the shoulder of his unexpected early-morning guest as the ancient language of the Nile began its dignified procession across the screen of this new-fangled electronic contraption.

OMAR AL HUSSEINI went into the apartment, poured himself a coffee and sat down at his desk to try to correct the first-term exams of the few students he had, but he couldn't concentrate and he couldn't help but look at the picture of the little boy on his desk. The picture of his son. His name was Said and his mother had been a girl from the village of Suray. He had met her on the day of their wedding, after his family had successfully concluded lengthy negotiations with her family to establish an adequate dowry. He had never really loved her, which was only normal, since he hadn't chosen her and didn't find her all that attractive, but he was fond of her because she was a good, devout woman and because she had given him a son.

He had mourned the death of both of them when the house they were living in was hit by a mortar. He buried them in the shade of the village cemetery, surrounded by a few carob trees, on the top of a rocky hill parched by the sun.

His wife had been hit by a piece of shrapnel and bled to death, but the boy, they said, had been hit directly and was unrecognizable, so he wasn't even allowed to see him one last time before putting him in the ground.

That very same evening, while he was still weeping for his loss in front of the ruins of his house, a man came up to him and offered him a chance to get even. He was around fifty, with a full grey moustache, and told Omar he wanted to make him into a great warrior for Islam. He wanted to offer him a new life, a new reason for living and new companions with whom he could share the dangers and ideals of this glorious new life.

He accepted and swore to serve the cause to the death. They took him to a training camp near Baalbek in the Bekaa Valley. There they trained him how to use a knife, a machine gun, grenades and missile launchers. They rekindled the hatred he already harboured for the enemies who had destroyed his family and then they deployed him in a series of increasingly daring and destructive missions, until he had become a ruthless, unassailable fighter, the legendary Abu Ghaj. Then the day came when he was deemed worthy to meet, face to face, Islam's greatest fighter, the arch enemy of the Zionists and their supporters: Abu Ahmid.

They had been years of hard combat and impassioned dedication, during which he felt like a true hero, seeing and actually meeting very highly placed people, sleeping in expensive hotels, wearing fancy clothes, eating in the best restaurants and enjoying the company of the most glamorous and obliging women. Abu Ahmid knew how to treat his boldest, most intrepid fighters very well.

Then suddenly, one day, all the bloodshed and the constant danger started to get to him and he just couldn't take it any more. He had made a pact with Abu Ahmid: that he would continue fighting only as long as his strength and courage lasted. So one night he boarded a plane and, equipped with false documents, went first to Paris, where he completed his studies in Coptic, and then to the United States. Sixteen years had passed since then and during that whole time he had heard nothing from Abu Ahmid. He had disappeared completely from his life.

Omar himself had managed to forget about everything, cancelling his entire previous existence as though it had never taken place. He no longer kept up with the politics and actions of his former movement, nor did he even take much interest in what was going on in his native country. He blended into his new surroundings, immersing himself in his academic responsibilities and the quiet, peaceful lifestyle of a respectable upper middle-class American. He had a girlfriend, cultivated various hobbies, played golf and took a lively interest in following basketball and American football.

The only memory that had remained alive all this time was that of Said, the son he had so tragically lost. His portrait had always been there on his desk and every day he imagined him growing, sprouting his first manly hair and taking on the deeper voice of an adult. At the same time, he continued to consider himself the father of the little boy in the photograph who had never grown up, and this somehow kept him feeling young. That was why he had never wanted to remarry or have any more children. Then, one day, all the skeletons in his closet came tumbling out with that photograph of the young man he immediately recognized as his son. He still couldn't quite believe it.

As he was on the way to the medicine cabinet to get a tranquillizer, his mobile phone rang. He went to answer it.

'*Salaam alekum*, Abu Ghaj.' It was that same metallic voice, slightly distorted by the poor reception. His caller was also using a mobile phone. 'All the donkeys have been saddled. We are ready to go to market.'

'Yes, I understand,' answered Husseini. 'I'll transmit the message.'

He waited a few more minutes, thinking about how he could get out of this situation, wipe away all of it, past and present, and return to his peaceful existence in America as a professor. No matter how hard he tried, though, he just couldn't think of any way out. Not even death was an option now. Would he ever see the columns of Apamea, pale in the dawn light and red at sunset, like flaming torches? The sky outside was grey; the street was grey and so were the houses, just like his future.

And then the doorbell rang, startling him. Who could it be at this hour? He was a nervous wreck and could hardly keep a handle on his emotions; and to think that once, for a long time, he had been known as Abu Ghaj, a killing machine, a ruthless robot.

He went to the door and asked, 'Who is it?'

'It's Sally,' an almost childish voice answered timidly. 'I was just going home and noticed your lights were on. Can I come in?'

Husseini let out a sigh of relief and let her in. She was his girlfriend and he hadn't seen her in several days.

'Sit down,' he told her, ill at ease.

Sally slipped past him, then turned around. She was blonde and buxom with two big, rather perplexed, blue eyes: 'I haven't heard from you for quite a while,' she said. 'Did I do something wrong?'

'No, Sally. You haven't done anything wrong. It's my fault. I'm going through a really rough time.'

'Don't you feel well? Can I help you?'

Husseini was very nervous. He knew he should have made the call immediately and without meaning to he looked at his watch. The girl felt humiliated and tears started welling up in her eyes.

'It's not like you think, Sally. I have to take medicine at regular intervals and that's why I was checking my watch . . . Really, I'm not well.'

'What's the matter? Can I do something for you?'

'No,' he said. 'You can't do anything. No one can do anything, Sally. It's something I have to resolve by myself.'

She drew close to him, stroking his cheek tenderly. 'Omar . . .' But Husseini stiffened.

'Really, I'm sorry, but I just don't feel . . .'

She lowered her head to hide the tears.

'I won't be calling you for a while, Sally, but don't blame yourself . . . I'll get in touch as soon as I'm better.'

'But I could—'

'No, it's best this way, believe me. I have to find some way out of this mess by myself . . . Why don't you go on home now? It's getting late.'

The girl dried her eyes and left. Husseini stood in the doorway watching her as she walked to her car, then closed the door, picked up his mobile phone and rang. An answering machine responded and so he left a message: 'All the donkeys are saddled. The drivers are ready to go to market.'

He kept looking at the boy's face in the photograph and at that moment it felt like the mortar that had destroyed his house all those years ago was exploding again in his heart, tearing it to pieces. He no longer knew who he was or what he was doing. All he knew was that he had to keep moving forward, no matter what. Sooner or later the real man would re-emerge and he would be ready to fight again. On one side or the other.

His glance fell on the computer and he thought of William Blake. He turned it on and hooked up to the Internet so he could check his emails. He found a couple of messages from colleagues and then, the last one, was a message from Blake.

In hieroglyphics.

The most accurate translation would probably have been:

The Pharaoh of the sands will show me his face before this day's sun sets.
And before sunset perhaps I shall know his name.
You'll have his name within twelve hours. In the meantime, look for the lost papyrus.

It was a precise appointment and Husseini checked his watch. The message had been sent at 6 a.m. Israeli time, so the next message would arrive the next day before noon, local time in Chicago. He should be ready and waiting at the computer on line in case Blake needed an immediate response. In the meantime he composed a message confirming receipt, hoping that Blake would be able to interpret it as: *I'll be here in twelve hours. Am looking for the lost papyrus.*

He sent the message, turned off the computer and tried to get back to his work, but he couldn't manage to concentrate. When he finished he realized that it had taken him twice as long as usual to correct half a dozen papers. It was nearly eleven and he still hadn't eaten. He took two antacid tablets instead of dinner and swallowed a tranquillizer, hoping he'd be able to fall asleep.

He slipped into a troubled sleep as soon as the medicine began to take effect and remained in that sluggish state for almost five hours. Then he went into a sort of half-slumber, tossing and turning, trying to find a comfortable position. But every time he seemed to be about to settle a message from the dream world thwarted him: someone seemed to be ringing the doorbell. He couldn't tell if the sound was really part of a dream, as he hoped, or real.

It finally stopped and he imagined that Sally was on the other side of the door, waiting for him to let her in. He thought it would be nice if she crawled into bed with him. It had been a long time since they had made love. But it wasn't the doorbell, the doorbell didn't have that off-and-on regular sort of pattern. It was something else . . .

He sat bolt upright, squeezing his temples between the palms of his hands. It was his mobile phone. He answered it.

At the other end he could hear the usual metallic voice: 'Orders have arrived. The attack begins in thirty-four hours, by night. An unusually violent sandstorm is expected in the area . . . Look in your mailbox. You'll find a package with a video cassette that contains the message. Deliver it in exactly nine hours. Have a nice day, Abu Ghaj.'

He got up, threw his dressing gown over his shoulders and went out to the mailbox, trudging through the snow. He found the package and went back into the house to fix himself some coffee.

He sipped on the boiling brew, lighting himself a cigarette, all the while eyeing the package wrapped in plain brown paper that was sitting on the kitchen table. He wanted to open it and see what was inside, but he realized that if he did so his anxiety would soar, and he had a class to teach at nine. He had to force himself to appear absolutely normal.

He left home at seven thirty and by eight was walking into the Oriental Institute. He picked up his mail and university bulletins from his pigeonhole and read them, killing time until he had to start teaching. There was a knock on the door.

'Come in.'

It was Selim, Blake's assistant.

'I have to speak with you, Professor Husseini,' he said.

'Come in and sit down. What do you have to tell me?'

'My friend Ali from El Qurna has contacted me.'

'The one with the papyrus?' asked Husseini.

'That's him.'

'What's the news?'

'He says that he still has the papyrus.'

'Great. But can he be trusted?'

'I think so.'

'What do you suggest we do?'

'If we want to get it back, we need some money. Ali won't wait forever. He's still got Blake's down payment and is willing to keep his word.'

'Only the Institute can write a cheque for 200,000 dollars, but they'll never do it. They were burned too badly by the story with Blake.'

Selim shrugged his shoulders. 'Then I don't think there's any hope. Ali has had another offer. It's very generous but he won't tell me who made it.'

'I see,' answered Husseini.

'Well, then?'

Husseini drummed nervously with his fingers on his desk, chewing his lower lip. An idea was beginning to suggest itself to him.

'Go back to your office, Selim. I'll join you after my class and I'll come up with 200,000 dollars. Can you get a message to Ali?'

'Sure.'

'Then do it immediately. Tell him you're coming with the money.'

Selim went out and Husseini remained for a few moments to ponder the situation, still drumming his fingers against the top of the desk. Finally he got out his mobile phone and made a call. At the sound of the signal, he said, 'Emergency. What sort of availability is there on the funds deposited at the International City Bank. I need some cover money.'

He terminated the connection and sat waiting, still drumming with increasing obsessiveness on the desk top. His class was scheduled to begin in five minutes.

At last, his mobile phone rang and a synthesized voice said, 'Availability confirmed up to 500,000 dollars. Withdrawal code: Jerash.*200\x. Repeat Jerash.*200\x.'

Husseini jotted down the information and put away the phone. It was time for class. He took out the file containing his notes, texts and slides and headed towards the classroom, where his students were waiting.

The seats were almost all taken and so he began.

'Today, we're going to talk about the Great Library of Alexandria, which is commonly held to have been destroyed by the Arabs. I shall demonstrate the falsity of this position, using two fundamental facts: first, the library had been gone for centuries by the time the Arabs conquered Egypt; secondly, the Arabs were always champions of culture and never its enemies . . .'

WILLIAM BLAKE watched the sequence of characters that appeared on his screen and interpreted them as:

When the day has reached the border of night I shall be present.
I am looking for the papyrus.

He imagined this meant that in about eleven hours Husseini would be in front of his computer hooked up to the Internet.

'Thank you, Mr Maddox,' he said. 'Now we can go.'

They left as the horizon was just starting to brighten up in the east. Blake let Maddox go ahead, then stopped in front of Sarah's door and knocked.

'I'm coming,' she answered, appearing shortly in the doorway. She was wearing a pair of khaki shorts, desert boots and a military-style shirt. She had pulled her hair up, exposing her neck, and looked absolutely beautiful.

'You look really beat,' she said when she saw Blake. 'What have you been up to?'

'I worked all night.'

'Me too,' said Sarah. 'Well, not quite all night.'

'Wait for me at the parking lot. Just give me enough time to take a shower and make myself some toast and I'll join you. In the meantime, you can get the equipment ready. Maddox is coming too. You knew that, right?'

The girl nodded in assent. She closed the door behind her and started walking towards the parking lot.

Maddox went up to her. 'Well, this is the big day. Has Blake mentioned anything to you about what he's got in mind?'

'No. But I don't think even he's sure what we're in for. He'll tell us what he thinks once the sarcophagus has been opened.'

'I don't know why, but I have the impression that he's hiding something. Keep an eye on him. I want to know everything that's going on in his mind. You won't regret it. In the end there'll be enough for everyone.'

'What about him?'

'For him too,' said Maddox.

Sullivan and Gordon showed up and then Blake joined them, a bundle of papers under his arm, saying, 'Well, shall we be off?'

9

WILLIAM BLAKE GOT INTO the Jeep with Sarah and they headed towards the Ras Udash camp. Behind them Sullivan was driving Maddox's Jeep.

'You really look awful,' said Sarah, eyeing her companion furtively.

'I've never been much to look at, but not shutting my eyes all night certainly doesn't help.'

'Were you able to translate the inscription?'

'Yes.'

'Anything interesting?'

'Something that can derail the destiny of the world, traumatize two-thirds of humanity and leave anyone else capable of understanding totally stunned,' Blake said in a monotone, as if he had recited a telephone number

Sarah turned to him. 'Are you kidding?'

'It's the honest truth.'

'And are you sure of your interpretation?'

'Ninety per cent.'

'What's missing?'

'I have to open that coffin and look him in the face.'

'The Pharaoh, you mean?'

'Whoever's buried inside.'

'Why?'

'The tomb could be empty. It wouldn't be the first time. I'd have to reconsider my thinking completely. Or else the person buried there could be someone other than who I think it is.'

'And who do you think it is?'

'I can't tell you, not yet.'

'Will you tell me later?'

Blake was silent.

'You don't trust me, do you?'

Blake said nothing.

'And yet I'm the only person in this camp who can save your life. And you've even been to bed with me.'

'That's right. And I'd like to again.'

'Don't change the subject.'

'Revealing the identity would have a devastating impact.'

'And that's why you don't trust me, isn't it? Not even if I told you what Maddox is up to and what they're going to do with your tomb?'

Blake turned to her sharply.

'You're interested, then,' said Sarah.

'I'll tell you. When I've opened that lid.'

'Thanks.'

'I burned the toast. Got anything in your bag?'

'There're some cookies and coffee in the thermos. Help yourself.'

Blake waited until they were on more level ground, then with some difficulty poured himself coffee from the thermos. He took a handful of cookies from the bag and started to eat them distractedly.

'Well,' Sarah resumed, 'last night I followed Maddox and saw whom he was meeting.'

'Did you manage to hear what they were saying?' asked Blake between mouthfuls.

'I took a very useful little toy with me: a high-fidelity directional microphone.'

'You're well equipped.'

'That's my job.'

'Well, then?'

'Maddox met with Jonathan Friedkin. Do you know who he is?'

'No.'

'He's the head of the Orthodox Israeli extremists. A group of extremely dangerous fanatics.'

'Fanaticism is always dangerous, no matter where it comes from.'

'They have dreams of overthrowing the government of the republic and setting up a monarchy inspired by the Bible.'

'I've heard about this—'

'But there's more. Their plan is to destroy the Al Aqsa Mosque on Mount Moriah and build a fourth temple in its place.'

'An interesting plan, certainly. And how do they think they're going to do that?'

'I don't know. But the current situation is so dramatic in the Middle East that it can only fuel the extremist positions on both sides.'

'Yeah ... they're dreaming, all right ... But the power of dreams is greater than any other. Their power is overwhelming. Do you want to know something? If I were Jewish, I would dream of rebuilding the temple, too.'

He lit a cigarette and slowly exhaled the smoke into the desert air.

'And would you be willing to slaughter people for the cause?'

'No, not me.'

'Will, Maddox is in with these guys. They're going to sell the objects in the Ras Udash tomb and split up the money. It's a colossal amount. They showed buyers the photos and sheets of your documentation. There's a total offer of 100 million dollars, twenty of which will go to Maddox. More than enough to solve his problems. The rest will be used to finance Friedkin's group.'

'Bastards. And when do they plan on doing all this?'

'Tomorrow night.'

'You're joking? That's not possible.'

'They're going to do it. Two trucks from Mitzpe are going to come to load everything up, then they'll head towards the coast, where a boat will be ready to take the things on board. The payment will be made when the cargo gets picked up. I see camel, I pay for camel, as they say around here, you know?'

'Yeah.'

'Won't you tell me what you've read in the inscription?'

'I'll tell you. After I've opened the sarcophagus.'

'Thanks.'

'Sarah?'

'Yes.'

'I love you.'

'Me too.'

They passed in front of the area with the boulders and then the inscribed rocks. They had almost reached the stretch of hammada that covered the tomb of Ras Udash.

'How are you feeling?' asked Sarah.

'Sometimes I feel like I can't breathe, other times I feel like I have a hole in my stomach. Shitty.'

'You've got to be strong. It's a crucial day and you worked all night.'

'What do you think they're going to do to me?'

'I don't think they have any reason to hurt you. Maddox originally offered you money. I think you should accept it. They'll put you on the Falcon and drop you off in Chicago. They'll wire a nice sum of money to a Swiss bank and that's that. I wouldn't worry if I were you.'

'I'll try. But I keep on thinking about how difficult this whole situation has become.'

They stopped at the site and got out, waiting for the other two vehicles to arrive: the first with Maddox and Sullivan, the second with the workers and Walter Gordon.

Whey they arrived, Sullivan locked the wheels of the Jeep, then slipped out the winch cable, inserted it into the pulley and attached it to the plate covering the tomb. He lifted it and moved it to the side.

'If you want to go down, I'm ready,' he said.

'OK,' said Blake, 'drop the ladder down and then the tools. When you've lowered everything, come down yourself, because we'll need your help.'

As soon as the ladder rested on the bottom of the tomb, he went down, followed by Sarah. The workers were next and Maddox and Sullivan last.

'If Mr Gordon wants to see, he'd better wait until we open the sarcophagus. There are already too many of us in here. We might break something.'

The stagnant air of the tomb was immediately filled with the odour of sweat and the atmosphere soon became oppressive.

Blake arranged four wooden blocks as shims at the corners of the sarcophagus and then placed a truck jack on top of each one. He lay wooden boards on the jacks, two parallel to the long sides of the sarcophagus and two along the short sides.

Using a spirit level, he adjusted the shims under the jacks until the four boards were completely horizontal. On the north side of the sarcophagus he positioned a piece of tubular scaffolding to act as a ramp, setting a wooden plank coated with grease on it for the purpose of sliding the lid of the sarcophagus to the ground when the time came to remove it entirely.

When the support mechanism was finished, squared and levelled, Blake put two workers at the southern corners of the sarcophagus. Sullivan and Sarah stood ready at the northern corners.

'Now, be very careful,' Blake said. 'This is not the right equipment for the job, but we don't have anything else, so we'll have to make do. We need to try to push the four jacks upwards slowly and steadily, otherwise we might break the slab. The wood underneath and on top will cushion any uneven pushing, so we shouldn't have too much trouble.

'I'll be guiding you step by step, but you'll all have to keep an eye on the person facing you and the one beside you, and apply an even, constant pressure on the lever of the jack. Look to me for any signal. Every push should stop at the end of its stroke and start again upon my order.

'Be careful. The first push is crucial, because it's the one that will detach the lid from its support. If necessary, the two jacks on the north side can be pushed upwards later to create a slanted surface so that the slab can slide towards the ramp to the ground. But this is something we'll consider when I've seen the inside of the sarcophagus. Any questions?'

No one spoke. Blake drew a deep breath. 'Ready?'

The workers too could feel the tension pervading the cramped space of the tomb. Maddox, who was already dripping under his arms and at the nape of his neck, nervously wiped a handkerchief across his brow and under his chin.

Blake looked at the sarcophagus and the support system he'd built, then fixed his eyes on Sarah, who was exactly in front of him. There was violent emotion in them, and yet he seemed possessed by total calm. He had the look of someone who was playing the biggest game of his life, but was doing so in the cold-blooded fashion that circumstances required.

'Now!' he said.

And he started to lower his hands, moving slowly and steadily. Sarah, Sullivan and the two workers pushed the lever downwards, following the movement of his hands. The shims groaned and the limestone lid creaked as it was coaxed away from its resting place after three thousand years of immobility. The four arms continued to descend, while Blake moved his own hands to coordinate their movement, like an orchestra conductor keeping time for his musicians.

The levers were at the end of their stroke and Blake examined the lid that had been lifted a few centimetres. The slab had not been recessed into the sarcophagus, it had simply been set on the edges. For an instant he could detect a vague smell of resinous substances, then just the odour of dust thousands of years old. His brow was sweating profusely and his shirt was soaking. The two workers looked like ancient statues, only a few beads of sweat glistening on foreheads framed by keffiyehs. They were accustomed to the extremes of the desert.

'Now the second push,' he said. 'Raise the lever to the end and pay attention to the movement of my arm when I give the signal to go down. Are you all right, Sarah? Do you want Mr Gordon to take your place?' he asked, noting a flash of uncertainty in her eyes.

'Everything's OK, Blake. I'm ready.'

'Good. Then, careful . . . go!' He started to lower his left arm slowly to guide the movement of the four arms that were pushing the levers. The wood creaked again and the slab was raised another three centimetres. Sarah drew a nearly inaudible sigh of relief.

Blake observed the columns of the jacks: they were extended to about half of their stroke. He took the blocks of wood and placed them between the lid and the sarcophagus in order to unload the jacks and increase the shims under the bases.

'Ingenious,' said Maddox. 'You are very clever, Blake.'

'I'm used to handling emergencies, that's all. I don't trust these jacks and I don't want to draw the pistons out of the cylinders too much further. I prefer raising the bases. With any luck, in a little while we will have completed the first stage without any difficulties.'

He had Gordon lower the bucket with more wooden planks and laid them at the bases of the jacks until they were lifted seven or eight centimetres. Then he returned the boards to their positions and readjusted the squares and the levels. When everything was ready, he signalled to the others to get back into position and to place their hands on the levers of the jacks.

Maddox moved towards Sarah's end. 'Let me do it,' he said. 'You're tired.'

Sarah offered no resistance and went to lean against the wall.

Her shirt was drenched and sticking to her body, as if she'd been immersed in water.

Blake signalled with his hand again and the four levers were slowly lowered at the same time, then stopped at the end of their stroke. Blake could now see the inside wall of the sarcophagus thanks to the ambient light that reached down about thirty centimetres.

He repeated the movement a fourth time and raised the shims underneath the lid. The moment had come to look inside.

'Would you like to be the first, Mr Maddox?' he asked.

Maddox shook his head. 'No. You've led this whole operation brilliantly, Professor Blake. It's only right that you be the first.'

Blake nodded, took a torch and got on a stool to illuminate the inside of the sarcophagus. He searched an instant for Sarah's eyes before peering into the open tomb of the Pharaoh of the sands.

There was the body of a man inside, completely wrapped in bandages, but there was no trace of the canopic jars that should have contained the viscera. Perhaps embalming had been carried out hastily.

The face bore a typical Egyptian mask with a bronze-and-enamel Nemes headdress, but it did not portray a conventional or mannered image. The face was incredibly realistic, as if the artist had been working from a live model rather than respecting the dictates of some remote Amarnian style.

A sharp, wilful nose, strong jawbone and two thick eyebrows under a slightly wrinkled forehead gave those solemn features an aura of uncompromising yet troubled might.

Crossed over the chest, his arms gripped two extremely unusual objects: a curved acacia-wood staff and a bronze serpent with slightly gilded scales.

From his right elbow hung a solid gold ankh and on his heart was a tourmaline scarab.

Blake realized immediately that this object was within his reach and, after some hesitation, stretched his arm inside. The space was not big enough to get his head between the lid and the sarcophagus, and so he had to make several attempts, lowering his hand a few millimetres each time so as not to cause any damage.

He suddenly felt the smooth curved surface of the scarab, clasped it between his fingers and withdrew it from the tomb.

He turned it slowly in his hand to expose the bottom part to the light. It bore an inscription in hieroglyphics:

This he interpreted without any doubt as the word: MOSES.

He felt faint and started to sway.

Sarah ran to help him. 'Are you all right, Blake?'

'He's under too much stress,' said Maddox. 'Give him a glass of water.'

Blake shook his head. 'It's nothing,' he said, 'just nerves. You take a look too. It . . . it's extraordinary.' Then, leaning his back against the sarcophagus, he slowly lowered himself to the ground.

Maddox got on the stool, turned on the torch and looked inside.

'Oh, my God.'

SELIM KADDOUMI stopped the car in the Water Tower Place parking lot, took his brown leather briefcase, pulled up the collar of his coat and proceeded along the street. Turning down Michigan Avenue, he felt the icy blast of wind in his face and thought of the warm nights along the banks of the Nile so far away. He wondered what would await him over the next twenty-four hours.

He hurried towards the entrance and was greeted by the artificial atmosphere of the mall, the monotone music of the waterfalls that fell into each other amid the lavishness of green plastic plants. He took the escalator to the second floor. Those falls fascinated him and he enjoyed observing the shimmering coins on the bottom of each of the marble pools.

Someone had told him that it was a custom of tourists to throw a coin into one of the great fountains of Rome so that they would be sure to return to the eternal city. But what sense did it make to throw coins into those fountains? People came back every day to shop anyway. There were some aspects of Western society that still escaped him.

He took the elevator to the third floor and walked into the Italian bookstore there. He began looking along the shelves until he came across the art books. He set the case down on the floor and started leafing through a splendid volume in a black and gold cover on the baptistery in Florence. The title on the spine read *Mirabilia Italiae*, Marvels of Italy.

Soon another man appeared, set down an identical case and started examining a book of Piranesi prints. Selim placed back his book and took the other case, leaving his own behind before wandering to another shelf. He chose a guide to Italy entitled *Off the Beaten Track*, paid for it and left without looking back.

He returned to the elevator, went down to the second floor and descended the escalator to the atrium, where the falls poured into each other down to the ground floor. When he got out onto the street, the air was even icier and he felt a sharp, almost painful spasm in his lungs. Coughing, he hurried to his car in the parking lot and got in. He set the case down on the passenger seat and opened it. There was an envelope with ten stacks, each with twenty one-thousand dollar bills, and a ticket for Cairo on British Airways.

Soon he was on the expressway headed towards O'Hare. It was drizzling but the rain soon turned to sleet, and small pearls of ice silently bounced off the windscreen.

OMAR AL HUSSEINI left the lobby of Water Tower Place with the brown leather case and headed towards a telephone booth. He put a quarter in the slot and dialled a number.

'*Chicago Tribune,*' answered a female voice.

'Give me the news department, please.'

'Excuse me, could I have your name, please?'

'Just do it, damn it. This is an emergency.'

The operator was silent for a moment. 'All right. One moment, please.'

A jingle played over the phone while he waited, then a man's voice answered. 'News.'

'Listen. In five minutes FedEx will be delivering a dark grey package addressed to your editorial department. There's a video cassette inside. Look at it immediately. It's a matter of life and death for thousands of people. I repeat: this is a matter of life and death for many thousands of people. It's no joke.'

'What—'

Husseini hung up and went to the parking lot. He started up his car and drove towards the Gothic-styled *Chicago Tribune* building. After a quarter of a mile he stopped, faking a breakdown because there was nowhere to park in that area.

Armed with a jack and the spare tyre, he saw a FedEx van stop in front of the *Tribune* building and a man get out with a grey package. He took a powerful pair of binoculars from his pocket and framed the entrance. A man with white hair quickly made his way towards the delivery man, signed the receipt, tore open the package and took out the video cassette it contained.

Husseini put back the jack and the spare tyre just as a police car pulled up beside him.

'Need some help?' said the policeman, sticking his head out of the window.

'No, thanks, Officer, just a flat tyre. All taken care of. Thank you.'

He got back in his car and returned home as fast as he could to wait for the evening news.

Night was descending upon the streets of the city like a harbinger of death.

ALAN MADDOX emerged from the tomb and approached Gordon who was sitting under a length of canvas that Sullivan had stretched between the ground and the roof of the Jeep.

'Go down there, Gordon. Go down and look. It's incredible. In my entire life, I've never known such a feeling. There's ... there's a man in there who's been sleeping for three thousand years. And yet his mask emanates an overwhelming vitality, a real ... presence. I stared at his chest all wrapped in bandages and for a moment I thought I saw him breathing.'

Gordon eyed him in bewilderment. Maddox was almost unrecognizable. His face was smeared with dust and sweat, his shirt was soaking and his eyes looked as if he had undergone enormous strain. Gordon said nothing, but cautiously climbed down the rungs of the ladder.

Soon Blake came out into the open, followed by Sarah. For a moment he looked at the sun, which was starting to set, then turned to Maddox.

'We've finished.'

Maddox looked at his watch. 'The time flew. We were down there for hours and it seemed like just a few minutes.'

'Yeah.'

Gordon came out.

'Well?' asked Maddox.

'Astonishing. Absolutely astonishing.'

'What are you going to do now?' asked Maddox.

'Nothing else today,' answered Blake. 'If you want, you can go back to the camp. I'll stay here for a little while to make sure that the workers seal the sarcophagus well. Exposure to air might damage the mummy. I'll meet up with you for dinner.'

'OK,' said Maddox. 'I sure need a shower.'

Blake descended back into the tomb. The lid was resting on the wedges and was raised on the edge of the sarcophagus by almost thirty centimetres. He waited for the workers to cover it with a sheet of plastic and remained after they had gone back up. He climbed onto the scaffolding and pointed the torch inside the sarcophagus. The face carved into the wood assumed an even more disturbing appearance behind the confused transparency of the plastic, as if it were immersed in a milky liquid.

Blake stared at it intensely for a long time, as if hypnotized by the magnetic expression. He jumped when Sarah's voice called to him, 'Is everything all right down there?'

'Yes,' he said. 'Everything's fine.'

He climbed down the scaffolding and approached the ladder, but before going up he turned his glance to the sarcophagus, murmuring, 'You deceived everyone . . . But why? . . . Why?'

Sullivan waited for him to come out and then closed the hole back up with the iron plate and covered it with sand. Then he started up his Jeep and drove off with the workers.

It was starting to get dark.

'Should we be on our way too?' Sarah asked.

'Let me have a smoke,' answered Blake. 'I need to relax.'

Sarah sat on a rock and Blake lit a cigarette as he leaned back against the side of the Jeep.

'Did what you see confirm what you were thinking?' she asked after several seconds of silence.

'Totally.'

'Do you want to talk about it?'

'I had promised you.' Blake turned towards her. His eyes were shining, as if he were about to cry.

'What's wrong?'

'I know who the man buried in that tomb is.'

'I realized that when I saw you read the hieroglyphics carved into the scarab. You seemed struck by lightning. Is it that distressing?'

'More than distressing. It's beyond belief. Sarah, what's down there is the mummy of Moses.'

Sarah shook her head incredulously. 'That's not possible.'

'I had my first hunch when I first saw those rock carvings: a staff and a serpent . . . a man with his arms raised in front of a fire . . .'

'The burning bush?'

'Maybe . . . and then traces of the high-temperature fires on the mountain. Don't you remember the Book of Exodus? Smoke and flashes of flames covered the sacred mountain while God dictated his law to Moses amid the crash of thunder and the blaring of trumpets. Sarah, do you realize what this means? The Warren Mining Corporation camp lies at the foot of Mount Sinai!

'I became even more suspicious when I found out that we're in Israel, not Egypt. No Egyptian dignitary would ever have had himself buried so far from the Nile.'

'And the inscription? What did that say?'

'Let's get into the Jeep,' said Blake. 'I don't want to raise suspicions.'

Sarah started up the Jeep and put it in gear. Blake took a crumpled piece of paper out of his pocket and started to read aloud:

> 'The son of the sacred Nile
> and of the royal princess Bastet Nefrere,
> – Prince of Egypt, favourite of Horus –
> crossed the threshold of immortality
> far from the black soil
> of his beloved lands
> along the banks of the Nile,
> while leading the people of the Habiru
> to settle at the borders of Amurru
> so that even in these arid and distant places
> a nation could be founded obedient to the Pharaoh,
> Lord of Upper and Lower Egypt.
> Here may he receive the breath of life
> and from here cross the threshold of the celestial world
> to reach the fields of Yaru and the home of the Setting Sun.'

'Is that all?' asked Sarah.

'More or less. It finishes off with the ritual formulas from *The Book of the Dead*.'

'His name isn't in the inscription. Is that why you were waiting to open the sarcophagus for the final confirmation?'

'Yes. But I was just being extra cautious. I already had an incredible amount of evidence. The inscription speaks of a prince who is son of the Nile and an Egyptian princess. That fits perfectly with Moses. According to the tale, he was saved from the waters of the Nile and adopted by a royal princess. What's more, this man dies far away from Egypt in an arid, desolate place while leading a group of Habiru, or Jews, to settle at the border of Amurru, that is Palestine. This could easily be referring to the story of the Exodus. There is no other way we can account for an Egyptian prince being buried outside Egypt.

'I have pored over the pages of the Bible. The death of Moses is wrapped in mystery. It is said that he climbed up Mount Nebo on the eastern banks of the Jordan with some of the elders and died there. In fact, no one has ever known where his tomb was. How is it possible for an entire people to forget the burial place of its father and founder?'

'Well, how do you explain it, then?'

'Sarah, before going down into that tomb I was firmly convinced that Moses had never existed, that he was a legendary founder like Romulus or Aeneas.'

'And now?'

'Now everything's different. The truth is not only was Moses a real person, but he remained an Egyptian to his very core, no matter what his people thought. He may have been attracted to the monotheistic cult of Amenhotep IV, the "heretic" Pharaoh, who instituted worship of just one God, Aten. But Moses himself actually remained true to his Egyptian upbringing to the very end, demanding an Egyptian burial with Egyptian rituals.'

'Wait a minute, Will. That just doesn't make sense. How could he have prepared a tomb like this for himself? Who decorated it? Who carved the sarcophagus and devised the protection mechanisms without his people ever finding out?'

'The tent sanctuary. That explains it. Remember? No one had

access to that sanctuary except him and his closest assistants and friends, Aaron and Joshua. Officially, because God manifested himself in that tent. But in reality because it served to cover up the preparations for his Egyptian immortality, his eternal resting place.'

'Do you mean that the sanctuary covered the access to the tomb?'

'I'm practically certain. Don't you remember the stones we saw from the hill overlooking the site? The stones that formed a perimeter around the tomb opening? I made measurements. They match the measurements given in the Book of Exodus perfectly.'

Sarah shook her head, as if she couldn't or didn't want to believe her ears.

'But there's more. The Bible says that one day a group of Israelites led by a man named Korah quarrelled with Moses over his right to lead the people and impose his rules. Obviously these men represented the leadership of the opposition movement.

'Moses challenged them to appear before the Lord – that is, to enter with him in the tent sanctuary. There a vortex opened beneath them and they were swallowed into the earth. So here's what I think: a kind of trap made them fall inside the tomb which had already been dug to a large extent. There, their bodies were burned and hastily buried. Confirmed by those skeletons we found at the back of the eastern wall.

'From a distance the people must have seen ominous flashes of light, smelled sulphur and burning flesh, heard desperate cries coming from the tent. In their obedient terror, they stayed in their own tents trembling with fright in the dark of night.'

'Will . . . I really don't know if you can take this so far. Your hypothesis is actually outrageous.'

'It's frightfully logical . . .'

'But it depends on the Book of Exodus being read literally as a faithful transcription of events that actually occurred.'

'You're wrong. It's just the opposite. What we have here is solid testimony that confirms the claims of the Book of Exodus. I found traces of sulphur and bitumen inside the tomb too, and you yourself saw those bones piled up in a corner and covered with a few handfuls of dust. Isn't that enough?'

'The remains of Korah and his reckless followers who dared to challenge Moses?'

'Why not? And if I could chemically analyse the traces of fire I found in the tomb and compare them with what I found on the mountain, I'm sure that they would reveal the presence of the same substances. Probably the substances that caused the pillar of fire that led the people by night and the smoke that led them by day. The same that caused the flames and thunder on the sacred mountain while he was receiving the two tablets of the law.'

'Enough!' cried Sarah. 'I don't want to hear any more!'

But Blake continued to speak more urgently. 'It's this place! Think of what a place he chose. We are near a pyramid and a sphinx, two natural formations that uncannily recall the most famous sacred landscape of Egypt. That's not a random circumstance for an Egyptian prince who is forced to build his eternal resting place outside his country.'

But Sarah continued to shake her head. She was obviously upset.

'That's not all,' resumed Blake, 'Moses personally gave orders to exterminate the Midianites, a tribe he had blood ties with, given that his wife, Zipporah, was a Midianite. The only plausible explanation is that he, or others for him, wanted to create a vacuum around the location of the tomb to preserve the secret.'

'My God,' murmured Sarah.

'I . . . I didn't think that you were such a believer,' said Blake.

'It's not that,' she replied. 'I'm not, not at all. It's the idea that two-thirds of humanity – that is, all three of the great monotheistic religions – would be threatened with destruction by your theory.'

'It's not a theory, unfortunately. I am giving you proof.'

'But do you realize what you're saying? That the father of universal monotheism was simply an impostor.'

'Sarah, that mummy down there was wearing a scarab on his heart with the inscription "Moses".'

'How can you be so sure?'

Blake took the pen and drew the sequence of ideograms he had seen inscribed on the scarab on his notepad. 'See?' he said. 'The first two marks mean M and S. If the inscription stopped there, the word would be open to question. The Egyptians never transcribed vowels, you see, so the two consonants could have also had other meanings. But the other three ideograms that follow specify "Leader of the Asians", who were the Jews. No, Sarah, I have no doubts.

'What's more, the cadaver wasn't embalmed using traditional methods. Why? Because it was impossible to use the embalmers of the House of the Dead from Thebes. Everything matches up. The inscription carved on the sarcophagus clearly refers to the story of Moses being saved from the waters of the Nile and to his journey in the desert of Sinai, just as it was described in the Book of Exodus. I can only acknowledge what I have seen, read and discovered.'

'But why? There has to be a reason why. If there's no reason behind it, all the evidence in the world isn't enough to make it plausible.'

'I thought it over all night, trying to find an explanation.'

'And?'

'I don't know ... It's very hard to find an answer. We are talking about a man who lived over three thousand years ago. The basic problem is that we don't know if the words of the Bible should be taken literally or if they should be interpreted. And in what way. Maybe he was driven by ambition: the ambition of becoming the father of a nation, like the Pharaoh in Egypt. An ambition he could never have achieved, since he was, in reality, the son of unknown parents. And in the end, at the supreme moment of his death, he was not able to resolve the conflict that had torn him his whole life: blood and body of a Jew, education and mentality of an Egyptian.'

'And the landslide in the tomb? The wooden panel? The sandal? What do they have to do with your theories? Maybe if you consider these elements, you could find a different, more plausible answer.'

'I have already found an answer. The man who lost his sandal knew where the tomb was and went off searching for it. I imagine that, in some way, a closed circle of people handed down information about the location from generation to generation, but probably no one had ever gone in there. And so it had to be a Jew, maybe a priest, maybe a Levite, maybe a prophet. I don't know what he came looking for in this place twenty-six centuries ago. But what he saw must have had such a tremendous impact on him that he tripped the mechanism to seal off the tomb forever. If he had had explosives available he would have blown it up, I'm certain.'

The light of the sunset dimmed over the sands of the Paran desert. The peaks of the barren mountains and the gentle ripples of the earth were covered by a sheen of bronze. The ghostly outline of the moon came forward against a pale blue sky that darkened at the centre of the vault.

Sarah said no more. She kept her hands tight on the steering wheel and only let go to downshift when she had to negotiate a difficult stretch.

Blake was silent too. Before his eyes he saw the countenance of the Pharaoh of the sands, the unreal fixedness of his stare, the proud austerity and harsh purity of his features.

Suddenly, when the lights of the camp came into view, Sarah turned to him again.

'There's something I still don't understand. You spoke of traces of high-temperature fires on the mountain.'

'Yes.'

'And you connected them to the God of Israel manifesting himself to Moses.'

'That's what I think.'

'And this would imply that the mountain lying above our

camp is Mount Sinai, where Moses received the tablets of the Ten Commandments.'

'With all probability.'

'But I always thought that Mount Sinai was at the southern-most part of the peninsula, and we're in the north, in the Negev.'

'True. But this is the territory of the Midianites and a little further north is the territory of the Amalekites, the people of the desert who attacked the children of Israel. It makes perfect sense that Sinai is in this area. What you're referring to – the thesis claiming that Mount Sinai is in the far south of the peninsula – is Byzantine and perhaps dates back to the pilgrimages to the Holy Land by Helen, the mother of Constantine. But that has never had any real basis in fact. No one has ever found the slightest physical trace of the biblical Exodus there. All the relics to be found there are fakes that take advantage of the beliefs of the gullible.'

'I don't know,' said Sarah. 'It all sounds so absurd. For centuries and centuries hundreds of millions of people, including scientists, philosophers and theologians, have accepted the epic of the Exodus as a relatively coherent account. How could they all have allowed themselves to be so deceived?'

'And now you, William Blake from Chicago, say that the faith of two and a half billion people actually hinges on the acts of an impostor. I understand your arguments, but nevertheless I just can't accept them completely. Are you sure of your theory? Isn't there anything that casts some doubt on it?'

Blake turned to her slowly.

'Possibly,' he said.

'What, then?'

'The look in his eyes.'

OMAR AL HUSSEINI reached home in the early afternoon and turned on the television immediately, switching from one channel to another to catch the news, but there were no revelations about the cassette that had been delivered to the *Chicago Tribune*.

He went into his study and switched on the computer, seating himself at the console to get onto the Internet quickly. He checked the mailbox and saw the name 'Blake'. He opened the file and found himself looking at the five ideograms in hieroglyphics:

and then the signature: William Blake.

He sank back, as if struck by lightning, barely managing the murmur, 'O, Allah, clement and merciful.'

10

'IT'S A SHORT ONE this time,' said Pollock with a half-witted smile, observing that Blake had sent his colleague only five ideograms transcribed from a sheet.

'That's right,' Blake said tersely.

'Is that it?'

'That's it. We can go to dinner. Mr Maddox and the others should be waiting for us.'

While Pollock turned off the computer, Blake joined his other dinner companions in the Bedouin tent, acknowledging them with a nod as he sat down.

There was an almost palpable tension around the table and the unease on Maddox's face was plain, as if his schemes for the next twenty-four hours were written on his forehead. When Blake arrived, however, he said, 'I should like to compliment our Professor Blake for the brilliant job he has done, and I hope that very soon he will let us in on the contents of the inscription he has transcribed from the sarcophagus and his interpretation regarding the landslide found inside the tomb.' He was speaking as if he himself were an eminent archaeologist. Yet another of his affectations.

Blake thanked him and said that several more hours would be needed to draw up a full report, but that he was close to concluding his research. The conversation became stilted and intermittent, as if there was little to talk about after what they had seen and experienced that day.

It was obvious, instead, that everyone was lost in their own thoughts and plans, or maybe a strange electrical charge hung in the air, affecting their mood and behaviour.

This held especially true for Maddox and Blake, who seemed to have little to say to each other, despite the fact that they had worked side by side all day. Maddox could only express himself in general terms, announcing, 'It was the most exciting experience of my whole life, and that's saying a lot, with everything I've seen over the years, in every country in the world.'

Sarah cut in, no less predictable: 'If anyone had told me what I was getting into when I accepted this job, I would have thought they were crazy, but it's true, it's been an absolutely fantastic experience, especially since I was involved personally day by day.'

Sullivan hung his head over his plate the entire evening without uttering a word. At a certain juncture, Gordon started talking about the weather, falling back on his British-Bostonian upbringing, but his choice of topic shocked everyone into the realization that any plans they had for the next twenty-four hours might very well fail due to something so simple as a sudden change in meteorological conditions.

'I heard the weather forecast on the satellite,' he said while coffee was being served. 'There's going to be a huge sandstorm, starting some time within the next twenty-four hours and lasting for at least a full day or so. It will affect a good part of the Near East, and it could easily hit our camp. They're predicting disturbances in communication, interruption in flights and poor visibility for thousands of square miles.'

'We're well equipped to face such an event,' replied Maddox. 'We have plenty of food and water and our trailers have air filters that can be powered by the auxiliary generator. Pollock, make sure that everything is in perfect order and ready to deal with this situation.'

Pollock got up and went to the trailer housing the auxiliary generator, while Maddox bid them goodnight and left.

'What are you going to do?' Sarah asked Blake when they were alone.

'I'm staying. I have to talk to Maddox.'

'Do you want some advice? Don't.'

'I have no alternative.'

'I imagined so . . . but listen to me anyway.'

'What is it?'

'Don't give Maddox the slightest idea that you know about the operation scheduled for tomorrow night or you're dead, and I'll be up to my neck in trouble too. He'll have no problem figuring out the source of your information. Another thing, Will, I'm serious about this: if he offers you money, take it. If you refuse, he'll be convinced that he can't trust you and he'll eliminate you. Trust me on this one, Will. Maddox won't even think twice. It's very easy to dig a hole in the sand. No one knows that you're here, nobody is going to come looking for you. It'll be like you just disappeared into thin air, got it?'

'There are my emails.'

Sarah shrugged her shoulders. 'In hieroglyphics? Sure.'

'You aren't worried? You were with me.'

'No, with me he'd be biting off more than he can chew.'

'Is that so?'

'Please, do as I say. If he offers you money, accept it. I think he likes you. If he doesn't think it's absolutely essential to kill you, he'll have no problem sparing you. But if you refuse any money he's offering you, I think you're signing your death sentence. Especially with that Friedkin character involved and the turn things have taken. It feels like everything's going to explode any minute.

'Will, I'll be waiting for you. Don't be stupid. I'd still like to pick up where we left off the other night.'

'Me too,' said Blake, almost to himself. Then, as Sarah started to leave, he held her back. 'Sarah, there's something I haven't told you.'

'What's that?'

'It's about the inscription.'

'The one on the sarcophagus?'

Blake nodded.

Sarah smiled. 'I'm not an Egyptologist but I could tell that you were keeping something from me. You looked like a cat with a mouse in his mouth . . . So?'

'It's not true that the text I read you ended up with *The Book of the Dead*. What followed was a curse.'

'That makes sense. I would have been surprised if it were otherwise. But don't tell me that a scientist believes in such nonsense. Curses have never managed to keep thieves away – in any century.'

'Of course not. But there's something particular about this one. Wait up for me if you're not too tired.'

'I will,' said Sarah, and she went off across the moonlit camp.

For an instant Blake yearned to be with her, anywhere but here. He stubbed the cigarette out with his heel and caught up with Maddox, who had nearly reached his quarters.

'Mr Maddox,' he said, making a move to enter, 'could I have a word?'

'Of course,' said Maddox. 'Come in.' But he had the look of someone who was being disturbed by an unwanted guest. He turned on the light and opened the liquor cabinet. 'Scotch?'

'Scotch is fine, thank you.'

'What do you think about this sandstorm, Blake? Sounds like it's going to be a bad one.'

'It will be a nuisance, at any rate, and could even cause serious damage. But that isn't what I came to talk to you about.'

'I know,' said Maddox pouring him a glass of Macallan from his personal stock. 'You want to talk to me about the Ras Udash tomb, but I—'

Blake raised a finger, looked Maddox straight in the eye and spoke all at once. 'Mr Maddox, I have to ask you if you intend to plunder the Ras Udash tomb and scatter its treasures to the four winds.'

'Blake, what the devil—'

'No, listen to me, Maddox, or I won't have the courage to go on. You have to stop, immediately. Nobody has the right to do such a thing.'

'That's what you think, Blake. I'm in command here and if you get in my way I won't hesitate to—'

'Maddox, before you say another word, just listen to me. You can't touch that tomb, because the extraordinary collection of things it contains is hiding a mystery that my preliminary research has only touched the surface of. If you disperse those objects, we will have lost a heritage that remained intact for over thirty centuries until we came upon it. We'll never be able to recover the information that will be lost, and that information could be vital for the whole human race.'

Maddox shook his head, as though he were listening to the ravings of a madman. 'You told me that you were about to discover the identity of the person buried in the tomb and that knowing that would enormously increase its value. I also gave you permission, more than once, to send – at my own risk – emails to your colleagues for consultation. Isn't that so?'

'That's right,' said Blake, lowering his head.

'Well, then?'

'That is exactly the point. The odds are that we are dealing with a high-ranking person, maybe even a great historical figure. Imagine . . .' Blake took a deep breath. 'Imagine that the mummy of a great Pharaoh was threatened by desecration during a period of anarchy. In that case, it's reasonable to believe that the priests would have transported him to somewhere that was absolutely inaccessible. Or let's say that a great leader, involved in a military campaign, died far from the capital because of his wounds or an illness, and that it was impossible, for reasons we don't know, to transport the corpse to the Valley of the Kings for embalming. Mr Maddox, you must believe me. I have done everything possible to squeeze information out of that tomb, but there are still too many questions. I suspect that the side opening, where the debris poured out of, may stretch back further into some sort of tunnel, but I have no idea how far that might go. And I still don't know exactly what purpose it served.'

'Unfortunately, we're out of time.'

'What's more, you've never wanted to tell me where we are.'

'I've had no choice.'

'Please, don't do it, Maddox. Don't sell off the pieces to the highest buyer.'

'Sorry, Blake. Our agreement was clear. You were asked to perform a certain job and you did so, very quickly and very well. The rest is my business, isn't it?'

Blake looked away.

'I'm sorry that you weren't able to do more or understand more. I am perfectly aware of your curiosity as a scientist, which in this particular moment is extremely frustrated, but you also have to take into account that you have been given a unique opportunity, a true privilege.

'If you're smart, you'll be satisfied with that. You'll receive a sum of money that should allow you to live comfortably for the rest of your life, or even to start a whole new life if you wish. Alan Maddox is no ingrate. You'll have the money within forty-eight hours maximum. I can give you an amount in cash or, even better, wire it to a Swiss bank account and have the statement forwarded to you. This means that you renounce any right to publish these finds. Should you breach this agreement, I am sorry to tell you that you will do so at serious risk to yourself.'

His words were very clear and Blake nodded.

'Very good,' said Maddox, interpreting his gesture as a sign of acceptance. 'You have reservations for a direct flight on El Al at 9.30 p.m. on Friday from Tel Aviv to Chicago.'

'From Tel Aviv? Why not Cairo?'

'Because we have an arrangement with El Al.'

'Isn't there anything I can do to dissuade you?'

Maddox shook his head.

'At least let me supervise the packing and loading. You risk doing enormous damage.'

'All right,' said Maddox. 'Obviously, I didn't feel I could ask you.'

'One last thing. Do you intend to touch the mummy?'

Blake's eyes held an uncanny uneasy expression, like a warning of deadly danger. Maddox hesitated, at a loss to know how to respond.

'Why do you ask?' he said after a while.

'Because I need to know. Maddox, I would not touch that mummy if I were you. Under any circumstances.'

'If you think you can scare me, you're wrong. You don't expect me to believe in the curses of the Pharaohs and all that other rubbish.'

'Well, no. Or yes, rather. I want you to know that the inscription on the sarcophagus contains one of the most atrocious and frightening curses that I've read in my twenty-five years of research. And it's not just a curse. It's a prophecy that specifies with considerable precision what will happen to the plunderers.'

'That includes you, then,' said Maddox with an ironic smile.

'It's possible.'

'And what makes you think that this curse is so much more powerful than all the others, which were never enough to protect even one of the tombs on which they were carved?'

'The beginning. It says, "Whoever shall open the door to his eternal resting place will see the bloodied image of Isis."'

'Oh, well, then,' said Maddox, adding even more irony to his tone. 'So?'

'There's going to be a total eclipse of the moon tomorrow night. The moon is going to turn red: the bloodied image of Isis. If that's a coincidence, it's quite something.'

'In fact, Blake, that's just what it is. A coincidence.'

'But then it says that the next day the breath of Set will darken a large part of the earth, from east to west, for a night, a day and another night. If Mr Gordon was right about the weather forecast, it seems to me that we can expect a sandstorm over a good part of the Near East, starting, incidentally, tomorrow night, including bad visibility and communication cut-offs in some areas for over twenty-four hours. You must admit that that's some coincidence, seeing that the "breath of Set" is universally known as the desert wind.'

'Close the sarcophagus back up, Blake,' said Maddox without concealing a streak of nervousness, 'and spare me this nonsense. The contents of the tomb are already worth a fortune. I don't need those few objects inside the sarcophagus. Anyway, to get out just the funeral mask of the mummy, which is the only piece of any real value, we would have to lift the lid another twenty centimetres, which would mean extra hours of work. Time we don't have. Anyway, it has very little importance for me.'

'Just as well. Goodnight, Mr Maddox.'

GAD AVNER walked behind Ygael Allon, who held a neon lamp in his right hand to light the tunnel. They had been walking for almost a quarter of an hour.

'After clearing blockage from collapses that date to the late empire and medieval periods, the tunnel has proved to be largely accessible. Look here,' he said, holding the lamp to the left wall, 'these are graffiti from the early sixth century. They may even go back to the siege of Nebuchadnezzar.'

That name gave Avner a slight start. He passed a handkerchief across his forehead to wipe the sweat and observed the graffiti.

'What does it mean?'

'We haven't quite figured that out yet, but it looks like a topographical sign, perhaps indicating that the tunnel went off in another direction. The letters carved under the drawing say "water" or "stream on bottom".'

'A well?'

'It's possible. During a siege people would often dig tunnels like this one to ensure a water supply. But that inscription could also mean something else.'

'And what's that?'

'Come,' he said, and resumed walking along the tunnel, which bent left in a narrow curve at a certain point and then straightened out into the distance. On the left there were traces of drilling on the wall; on the right was a wooden plank secured to the wall with a lock.

'Here we are,' said Allon. 'Over our heads are thirty metres of compact rock and then the platform of the Temple. Look at this,' he said, kneeling on the ground and raising the lamp again.

'There are steps,' noted Avner.

'Yes. Which disappear into the side of the mountain. I think that it's a stairway that came from the Temple. Maybe even from the Sanctuary. We drilled at that point, see, and found incongruous materials, ash, fragments of plaster, lime mortar. It may be material from the destruction of the Temple in 586 BC that fell from the upper levels into the staircase, partly filling the room.'

'You mean that following those steps might lead us to the level of the Temple of Solomon or to its underground compartments?'

'It's very likely.'

'Extraordinary. Listen, Allon, who other than you knows about this?'

'My two assistants.'

'And the workers?'

'They're recent arrivals from the Ukraine and Lithuania and don't understand a word of Hebrew. Especially the technical Hebrew that we're speaking.'

'Are you sure?'

'As sure as I am of being here with you.'

Allon took a key out of his pocket and opened the lock. 'And here we made the most startling discovery. The find is still *in situ*. Come.'

A new tunnel opened before them. It presumably headed southward. 'Maybe towards the pool of Siloah and the Kidron Valley,' said Allon. 'This may be what the graffiti is referring to.

At this very moment we are following the directions we found carved into the wall of the main tunnel and are going through a passage that must have been the continuation of both the main tunnel and the steps that came down from the Temple. The point where we first stopped must have been the intersection of the two.

'We had to remove part of the rubble that was nearly blocking the passage at this point. And underneath we found this.'

Allon stopped and cast light on a lump of clay that had a gleaming object set into it.

'Oh, Lord,' said Avner, kneeling down into the wet mud. 'I have never seen anything like this in my entire life.'

'Me neither, to tell the truth,' said Allon, crouching down on his heels. He brought the lamp nearer and swung it to bring out the flashes from the sapphire, carnelian, amber and coral on the tawny gold shining through the mud.

'What is it?'

'A thurible. And the mark you see here on this side means that it belonged to the Temple. My friend, this object burned incense to the God of our Fathers in the Sanctuary built by Solomon.'

His voice trembled as he uttered the words and, in the reflection of the lamp, Avner saw that his eyes were glistening.

'Can I . . . touch it?' he asked.

'Go ahead,' replied Allon.

Avner stretched out his hand. This was a cup of extraordinary perfection, whose base was embellished with gems mounted to form a sequence of winged griffins, stylized to the point they seemed just an elegant succession of geometric patterns. Around the rim was a circle of palmettes that continued onto the lacy cover. They were surrounded by damascened silver that had been burnished through time. The knob on the cover was a small golden pomegranate filled with minuscule coral balls.

'Why should such a precious object be here?' asked Avner.

'I have only one answer to that. Someone tried to save the

sacred vessels to protect them from desecration by the Babylonian invaders. It's also clear that this thurible must have been made and donated to the Temple shortly before that time. It looks like the product of a Canaanite workshop in Tyre or Byblos, or may be the work of an artisan from the city of Canaan who transferred his workshop here to Jerusalem to work on an order for the Sanctuary. These ornamental motifs that you see are characteristic of a style we archaeologists call "orientalizing". It dates back to some time between the end of the seventh and the first quarter of the sixth century BC.'

'The time of Nebuchadnezzar's siege.'

'Exactly. Now, it is very likely that the people who tried to save the sacred vessels did so at the last minute, when it was certain that the Babylonians would be storming in at any minute. It might have been when King Zedekiah fled through a breach in the wall near the pool of Siloah ... to meet his excruciating destiny.

'In the rush the objects couldn't be arranged and packed carefully enough, so the thurible fell to the ground and remained where it was until last night, when we found it. We can also imagine that whoever was carrying it was walking so fast that he wouldn't have even noticed if something, though hardly insignificant, fell out of his bundle.'

'You mean that at the end of this tunnel we might find the treasure of the Temple?'

Allon hesitated. 'That could be. We certainly can't exclude the possibility that this tunnel led to some secret room, but that's not necessarily so. Tomorrow we'll resume work. I'm about to take this thurible outside now. There's an escort of military police who are waiting to take me to the National Bank, where it can be locked up in the vault.

'This object is the most precious relic that has ever been found in the land of Israel since the time of our return to Palestine.'

Allon took the thurible very gently and placed it in a box lined with cotton wadding which he strapped over his shoulder.

They turned back towards the entrance of the tunnel under the arch of the Antonian Fortress. Just as they emerged, Avner's eye was caught by the red flashing light on his mobile phone, signalling an emergency.

He shook the archaeologist's hand warmly.

'Thank you, Professor Allon. This has been a great privilege. Please let me know of any new developments in your investigation, no matter how small. I must go now. There's an urgent call I have to attend to.'

'Goodbye, Mr Cohen,' said Allon, who then went with the policeman to an armoured car parked a little way off.

AVNER LISTENED to the message. 'Urgent call from the Ministry of Defence.' The voice sounded like Nathaniel Ashod, the Prime Minister's cabinet secretary.

He looked at his watch: it was eleven o'clock. He thought it best to have someone from the office pick him up and started dialling the number, but in that instant a dark Rover pulled up alongside and Fabrizio Ferrario got out.

'Mr Avner, we have been looking for you in every corner of the city. Have you checked if your telephone is working? We couldn't get through.'

'Because I was underneath thirty metres of rock.'

The young man opened the door for Avner and slid into the back seat beside him. 'Go ahead,' he said to the driver, then turned to Avner. 'Excuse me, sir?'

'You heard right, Ferrario. I was in the tunnel with Professor Allon of the Hebrew University. And now what in God's name is happening?'

'I'm afraid we've got serious trouble, sir,' said the officer. 'The minister will explain everything.'

They entered the ministry from a service door and Ferrario

led Avner down stairs, along corridors and up in elevators until they reached a small lounge, sparsely furnished with just a table and six chairs.

Around the table sat Prime Minister Schochot, Minister of Defence Aser Hetzel, Chief of the General Staff Aaron Yehudai, Minister of Foreign Affairs Ezra Shiran and the American ambassador, Robert Holloway. In the middle of the table there were two bottles of mineral water and each man had a plastic cup in front him.

When Avner entered, they turned towards him, most with distressed, almost shell-shocked expressions. Only Yehudai maintained his usual soldier's demeanour.

Fabrizio Ferrario went out, closing the door behind him.

'Have a seat, Avner,' said the Prime Minister. 'There's some bad news.'

Avner sat down, certain they were about to announce that Operation Nebuchadnezzar had been launched. He was primed to be furiously angry, telling them that for at least two months he'd been warning of serious danger and that no one had ever deigned to listen to him.

The American ambassador started to speak. 'Gentlemen, several hours ago someone phoned the news bureau of the *Chicago Tribune* announcing the imminent delivery of a video cassette and asking that it be watched immediately because the lives of many thousands of people were at stake. The package arrived shortly after, delivered by a FedEx van.

'The managing editor of the *Tribune* watched the video along with the editor-in-chief, then proceeded to call the FBI. A few minutes later the video was transmitted to the Oval Office in Washington. The video shows three different groups of terrorists assembling three nuclear devices in three different locations in the United States.'

'How can you be so certain that they are really in the United States?'

'They offered proof, adding insult to injury. In another

anonymous call, they gave clues to the places where they assembled the bombs, which proved to be identical to the video. With the only difference that the bombs were missing, but all the packing was there.'

'They could have been computer-generated images.'

'We're ruling that out,' said Holloway. 'Our experts say that the video's an original that shows no traces of having been tampered with. In any case, a copy is on its way here for our examination.'

'Might the bombs not be perfect mock-ups, like the ones you see in the movies but full of sawdust?'

'Unlikely. The video shows close-ups with a detail of a Geiger counter working.'

'What do they want?'

'Nothing. There's a statement that says that other messages are to follow. The FBI, CIA and every special police unit in every state have orders to sift through the country from top to bottom and find those bastards, but this is most dramatic situation that has hit the United States since Pearl Harbor.'

'No clues?'

'Not for the time being. The President and his staff think that it's a commando squad of Islamic fundamentalists. But the men in the video have their faces hooded and aren't identifiable.

'Pentagon experts are trying to identify the bombs, but the shots are only partial and never give a full view. The hypothesis is that they are the famous "portable" bombs that have been so widely talked about, jewels of ex-Soviet technology, mechanisms that can fit in a suitcase and be transported easily.'

'How powerful?'

'According to some, they are tactical bombs of five hundred kilotons, easy to assemble, transport and conceal. But if they were to explode in a densely populated urban area, it would cause a massacre. We could estimate between five hundred and seven hundred dead on impact, half a million wounded and another three hundred thousand people exposed to possibly fatal doses of radiation who might die within three or four years of the explosion. Enough to bring a country to its knees. And it appears that these bombs can be triggered directly by the same person who's carrying them, without requiring that famous black briefcase always accompanying the presidents of Russia and the United States.'

Avner looked Yehudai in the face. 'General, this is the beginning of Operation Nebuchadnezzar. They'll attack tomorrow when the storm is at its worst. They'll use land vehicles, while we won't be able to use our air supremacy to advantage. No one will come to our rescue. The United States has its own death threat to worry about. They won't move and they'll compel their European allies to stay put as well.'

'My God,' said the Prime Minister.

'I should have expected as much,' grumbled Avner. 'Here I was, watching the mountains over the Judaean desert . . . I never thought the attack would be launched from the other side of the Atlantic . . . God damn him, that fucking bastard.'

Yehudai stood. 'Gentlemen, if this is the status of things, I ask permission to launch a preventive attack using our air force and missile systems to destroy the Arab air forces on the ground, as far as possible. I will meet immediately with my general staff, launch the red alert and organize the defence plan for our territory. We can have all the reserves operative within six hours and the combat units on duty in one hour.'

'I think General Yehudai's proposal is the only viable one, gentlemen,' said the Prime Minister. 'Given the current state of affairs, there's not a minute to lose.'

'One moment, Mr Prime Minister,' said Ambassador Holloway, 'I don't think it's wise to make such a decision. We've had no declaration of war from any Arab country, none of our satellites have detected massive troop movements, and we've received no demands from the terrorist commandos who have allegedly assembled nuclear bombs on our national soil.

'To all intents and purposes, your attack would be an act of war and would destroy – once and for all – any chance of achieving peace in this area. Something very important to my government.'

They all stared at each other without uttering a word. Avner was the first to speak.

'Mr Prime Minister, I am absolutely positive that the two events are related. The terrorists brought those bombs onto American territory to immobilize the US while the decisive attack was being launched here. The man behind this is Abu Ahmid, and the assassination of al Bashar was part of his strategy.

'I don't trust your friend, Taksoun,' he said, turning to Holloway. 'I'm sure that at this very moment he is preparing his battle plan in some accursed bunker in al Bashar's palace. I'm for attacking even without the endorsement of the Americans. It's our skin,' he said, and lit a cigarette, ignoring the no-smoking signs threatening severe penalties hanging everywhere.

Holloway became livid.

'Mr Avner, your conduct is unacceptable.'

'Because of the cigarette? Come on, Holloway, millions of people are risking their lives and you're worrying that your fucking lungs are going to get a little ration of tar. My father and mother ended up in smoke in an oven in Auschwitz. Damn you, go to hell!'

'Gentlemen,' intervened the Prime Minister, 'gentlemen, we must arrive at the best decision together. This is certainly no time to argue. You, Avner, do me the favour of putting out that cigarette and, when everything's over, I promise I'll send you a whole case of the best Havana cigars money can buy. And at the expense of the taxpayers. Now, Mr Holloway '

'I'm sorry, Mr Prime Minister, I have precise instructions from my government. No rash acts until we've found out what they want.'

'And if we ignored your advice?'

'You would be left on your own. Not a dollar, not a spare part, no information. This time my government is seriously determined not to get involved in another war. The public just wouldn't stand for it.'

'Nevertheless, the decision is ours,' said Prime Minister Schochot, turning to Yehudai. 'General, take all measures for a state of readiness, but do not launch any attack until you receive my order.'

Yehudai got up, put on his beret and left the room, crossing a soldier who was delivering a parcel to the guard at the door. The guard took it, then knocked.

'Come in,' said the Prime Minister.

The guard entered and handed him the package. 'Just arrived, Mr Prime Minister.'

Schochot opened it. It contained a video cassette. 'Do you want to see it?' he asked Holloway.

The ambassador nodded.

'I already know everything there is to know,' said Avner with a shrug. 'Goodnight, gentlemen. God willing it won't be our last.'

He nodded goodnight to everyone and left.

Fabrizio Ferrario was waiting for him in the car. As soon as he saw the expression on his face, he offered Avner a cigarette and lit it for him. 'It's as bad as it looks?' he asked.

'Worse. Take me home. I'm afraid I'll be doing without sleep tonight.'

Ferrario asked no questions, started up the car and headed towards the old part of the city, to his boss's residence. Avner was silent the whole time, brooding on his thoughts. When the car stopped in front of his house, he got out and then turned back to the agent. 'Ferrario, anything could happen in the next twenty-four hours, even another Holocaust. You're pretty new here, after all. If you want to go back to Italy, I won't blame you.'

Ferrario didn't acknowledge his words. 'Do you have any orders for me tonight, sir?'

'Yes. Stay in the neighbourhood, because I might need you.

And if you feel like taking a walk, go by the Antonian Fortress, to Allon's tunnel. You know where it is?'

'Of course I know where it is. It's where you were today.'

'Exactly. Keep an eye on the situation. Make sure that the soldiers maintain strict surveillance. If even the slightest thing seems suspicious, call me.'

Ferrario left and Avner took the elevator to the eighth floor. He opened the door of the terrace and stood in silence as the night slowly enveloped the mountains of the Judaean desert.

'That's where you'll have to come from to kill me, you son of a bitch,' he mumbled between his teeth. 'And I'll be here waiting for you.'

He closed the window and went back into the living room. He sat in front of the computer to access the copy of the *Tribune* video that Mossad had already forwarded to him. He ran through all the information in the database of every known, or presumed, nuclear device to see if he could identify a precise object based on the details in the video.

Suddenly out of a corner of his eye he saw the flashing signal on his private line. The clock read a few minutes after midnight.

'It's the night porter, sir,' said the voice.

'What's new, night porter?'

'The sarcophagus was opened and the mummy has been identified.'

'Is it certain?'

'Yes. The man buried under the sands of Ras Udash is the Moses who led Israel out of Egypt.'

A stony silence from Avner.

Then he spoke. 'Impossible. Absolutely impossible.'

'There is incontestable proof. The inscription found on the sarcophagus identified him, without the shadow of a doubt.'

'What you are telling me is very serious, night porter. You are telling me that the leader of Israel was, in reality, a pagan who wished to die among gods with the head of a jackal or a bird. You are telling me that our faith has no foundation and that God's covenant with Abraham was not kept.'

'I am telling you that the man inside that tomb is Moses, sir.'

'And there is no chance of a mistake?'

'Minimal, I believe. On the chest of the mummy there was a scarab inscribed with his name.'

'Oh,' said Avner, completely dumbfounded. Since the day they had brought him the news of the death of his son in combat he hadn't thought that anything could shake him.

'There is more, sir.'

'What more could there possibly be, night porter?'

'Tomorrow at sunset, the entire contents of the tomb will be removed and sold to a group of Orthodox extremists. Jonathan Friedkin's people. There may be items that have not been examined yet, evidence that may provide further proof of the identification. And Friedkin is completely untrustworthy. He may even have instructed his men to attack rather than pay.'

'Do you know where the pick-up site is?'

'Not exactly. But I assume that they'll come in on the road from Mitzpe. They'll need trucks and that is the only viable route. But they might also come from Shakarhut. There are some small settlements there.'

'I understand.'

'Is there anything more you want to know?'

Avner thought for a few moments, then said, 'Yes. As far as you know, is the Delta Force command still in the vicinity of Ras Udash?'

'No more than half a dozen men are left, I think, but I assume they'll be leaving soon.'

'Very good. That is all. Goodnight.'

'Goodnight, sir.'

Avner hung up, then took another phone and dialled a number.

'Yehudai,' answered a hoarse voice on the other end.

'It's Avner, Commander. Where are you?'

'At IDF general headquarters.'

'Listen, I have some very serious news. A group of Hamas fundamentalists has caused a stir in the Warren Mining camp near Mitzpe Ramon. They are using the camp as a base to launch a series of terrorist attacks in the southern part of the country. And Beersheba is out that way. Do you realize what this means?'

'I do. They could try to disarm our nuclear retaliation system.'

'Destroy them, Commander. This very night. We can't risk a threat coming from that area with everything else that is going on. Do not spare a single one of them. Do you understand? Not one.'

'Understood, Avner,' replied General Yehudai. 'Not one. You have my word.'

Avner hung up and went to the terrace window to ponder the full moon rising over the Judaean mountains. Out of a corner of his eye he saw the private telephone line on his desk, mute.

'Goodbye, night porter,' he murmured. '*Shalom.*'

11

WILLIAM BLAKE went back to his trailer and sat on the front doorstep to smoke a cigarette and think about what he was going to do during the next twenty-four hours. He knew he had been right not to tell Maddox the identity of the person buried in the tomb of Ras Udash, because he couldn't have predicted the effect the news might have had on him and what the consequences might have been.

The more he dwelled on the plunder and scattering of the objects in the tomb, the more his heart ached with the realization of what an irremediable loss that would be. He had to prevent it from happening, whatever the cost. His mind had, almost automatically, started to turn over a rescue plan, one which, at this point, seemed to be the only possible course of action. Now he was annoyed at how unassertive he had been in his talk with Maddox. He knew that he was going to have to take care of things himself, as quickly as possible. But he wouldn't be able to do it alone.

He went and knocked on Sarah's door.

'How did it go?' she asked as she let him in. Her hair was wet from the shower and she was wearing only a T-shirt, as if she had been going to bed.

'I tried everything to persuade him, but it was no use.'

'I'm not surprised. There's no way you could have! All that intellectual posturing of his is just a front. The only thing he's interested in is money. Speaking of which, did he offer you a reward?'

'Yes. A fat little sum in a Swiss account.'

'And you accepted, I hope?'

Blake said nothing, embarrassed.

'You haven't done anything stupid?' Sarah went on, alarmed.

'No, no. I accepted . . . or at least I led him to believe that I was ready to accept.'

'Well, the main thing is that he believed you. Otherwise you're a dead man.' She pulled his head towards her and gave him a kiss. 'I've got used to you being around. It would be a real pain to have to think of you as being extinct.'

'Me too, believe me.'

'So let's not do anything stupid. Tomorrow evening, Maddox will hand over everything to those fanatics. We'll take our money, get out of this hole and it'll be as though we were never here. I've done my part. So have you. If we could have done it better, we would have. But right now it's time to split, take my word for it. You have no idea what kind of hell could break loose here at any moment. Instead, the day after tomorrow, we're going to be on a flight for the good old United States and that'll be that. Just as soon as I finish off a little bit of business I have to see to, we'll go away together for a weekend on the lake. We can rent a cottage and stay for a few days. You know, I can even cook—'

'Sarah, I'm thinking of going back to Ras Udash.'

Sarah was speechless.

'And I want you to help me.'

'You're out of your mind. What's there to do at Ras Udash?'

Blake took a notebook out of his pocket and made a fast sketch.

'Listen, when we cleared the debris away from the opening above the sarcophagus, I didn't remove it all. The top part of the heap was fairly compact. I smoothed it out with my trowel so that the opening would look like a niche, but with just a little work with a pick we could open a way into what I am sure is a tunnel to the side of the tomb. I want to see where it goes. It may lead outside some way or perhaps to another chamber.'

'And if it does?'

'This is my idea. If we can find a way out, I want to try to save as much as I can, and then close the sarcophagus back up and block the entrances.'

'Will, you have no idea of—'

'No, Sarah. I've thought of everything. In the tomb, there are five biggish pieces. Three are wooden and two are painted plaster. The plaster ones probably weigh fifty kilos or so, but between us we can easily move them. The wooden statues are light. The other pieces, thirty-four in all – perfume burners, headrests, candelabra, vases, cups, weapons and jewels are all small. It won't take more than an hour and a half. And another hour to close the sarcophagus. We can do it bit by bit, using thinner and thinner wedges. We'll need another half-hour to place the charges and then we'll bury the whole complex under a few thousand tons of sand. There's that rise just to the west of the opening Maddox made. If we set off a charge halfway up the slope, it'll be enough to create a landslide that'll close up the entrance.'

'I see,' said Sarah. 'You don't give a damn about me or about anything else. The only thing you care about is your goddamn academic glory. You'll go to the States, present a paper and then rush back here to "bring it all out" again. The most fantastic archaeological discovery of all time, apologies and applause for the great William Blake and, guess what, the director's chair at the Oriental Institute.'

'You've got it all wrong. I—'

'Haven't you thought of the consequences? Your discovery will dash to smithereens the hope of an afterlife for two-thirds of the people living on this earth. It will undermine Judaism, Islam and Christianity.'

'Ra, Amon, Baal and Tanit, Zeus and Poseidon are all dead. Even Yahweh, the Lord of Israel, can fade away without God ceasing to exist.'

'Look, I'll help you place a charge inside the tomb. It's the best thing, believe me.'

'No, Sarah. If that tomb has come down to us still intact after more than three thousand years, we don't have the right to destroy it.'

'But your plan is impossible. We can't leave the camp without anyone realizing—'

'You've done so at will.'

'We don't have any explosives.'

'They won't be hard to get from the storehouse. The workmen have the keys. Find some excuse.'

'But we don't know what the hell is beyond the landslide opening. We could cause another cave-in. We could be trapped and suffocate to death.'

'If you don't help me I'll do it by myself.'

Sarah lowered her head.

'Well?'

'I'll help you. Otherwise you'll just get yourself killed. But there'll be some talking to do when all this is over.'

'That's OK by me.'

'You do realize that we won't be able to come back here. Have you thought of what we'll do afterwards?'

'There's always water and gasoline in the ATV. We'll take a couple of packs of survival rations and leave. I'd avoid the trail to Mitzpe Ramon. Better to head south down the Arava Valley to Yotvata and Eilat. There we'll have to decide what to do. If that's all fine with you, I'm going to the warehouse.'

'You'd better not. You'll only arouse suspicion. Let me do it. You get your things together. Fill up the water bottles and meet me at the parking lot in fifteen minutes. Don't forget the suncream: we don't want to end up getting burned.'

Blake went into his trailer and began to pack his things. A feeling of excitement was sneaking over him; this place had become an unbearable prison and the thought of getting out of these people's clutches seemed like a dream. He kept checking his watch, counting the minutes as he nervously smoked a last cigarette before going out.

VALERIO MASSIMO MANFREDI

The moon hadn't emerged from behind the hills yet but a
pale light was spreading to the east, announcing its imminent
appearance over the Paran desert. With just a few minutes to go,
Blake stubbed out his cigarette. He went into the bathroom and
jumped out of the back window after tossing his rucksack onto
the ground.

He stopped for a moment to look towards the camp and saw
a dark shadow slowly approaching the parking lot: Sarah.

He crept in the same direction until he was quite close to her.

'I'm here,' he whispered.

'So am I,' said Sarah. 'Come on. We'll be out of here in a
minute.'

She approached the vehicle and was leaning forward with her
rucksack when they heard the generator start up and suddenly
the whole area was lit up like day.

'Freeze where you are,' a voice said.

'Maddox! Damn!' swore Sarah. 'Move it! Let's go!'

'Stop them!' cried Maddox to a group of men running in their
direction.

Blake jumped into the open back of the vehicle as Sarah fired
the engine and set off at high speed.

Maddox's men had reached the parking lot and were shooting
and shouting at them to stop.

'What are they doing?' yelled Sarah, without taking her eyes
off the track.

Blake looked back and what he saw made his blood freeze in
his veins.

'Oh, God,' he said, grabbing Sarah by the arm. 'Look. Look
down there!'

Sarah turned for a second and saw searchlights criss-crossing
the dark sky. Then she heard a steady beating of rotors and the
screeching of engines pushed to their limits.

'Assault helicopters!' she yelled. 'We're getting out!'

She rammed the accelerator down as hard as she could, while

Maddox's men jumped into Jeeps to spin them around and out of the parking lot.

They didn't get the chance. The darkness behind them was suddenly shattered by a series of blinding flashes and the deafening explosions of heavy guns hitting the trailers, machines and depots with murderous accuracy. The hammering of the guns was punctuated by the sharp chatter of automatic weapons spraying bullets. In the cone of light projected from the front of the choppers, the bullets raised spouts of sand along the ground and loosed off hundreds of glowing chips of stone that shot like meteorites up across the dark backdrop of the night.

The Jeeps jumped around like toys, then a boom shook the mountain and a gigantic globe of fire lit up the area for miles around when the explosives depot was hit.

'What's happening? What the hell's happening?' shouted Sarah, who couldn't take her eyes off the track.

'The helicopters have attacked the camp and they're flattening it,' yelled Blake. 'It's like an inferno. They're firing for all they're worth at everything they can see.'

Sarah had turned off the headlights and was using the side lights so they wouldn't be seen.

'They're landing now!' shouted Blake, who was looking backwards. 'The camp is hidden behind the hills, but I can see the helicopters circling as they're going down.'

The choppers had disappeared behind the outline of the hills, but the light coming from them and the tracers lit up the sky like the glow of a surreal dawn.

For a while, only the beating of the rotor blades could be heard, then the crack of the automatic weapons started again.

'They've landed. They must be combing the terrain inch by inch. Step on it! We've got to get away as fast as we can.'

'We've done almost three miles,' said Sarah. 'We should be pretty safe by now.'

Meanwhile, the moon had begun to rise in the sky, spreading

a wide expanse of light over the pale desert, and Sarah was able to keep up a steady speed that she increased when they hit the flat plain of the hammada.

The ATV streaked along like a shooting star, leaving a milky-white cloud of moonbeam-crossed dust in its trail.

When they approached Ras Udash, Sarah switched the engine off, slid out of the seat and fell to the ground, completely exhausted.

Blake went to her. 'I've never driven a contraption like that, but I would have taken over from you if you had told me how.'

'Forget it,' said Sarah. 'We got out by the skin of our teeth. One more minute and—'

'But who were they?'

'I don't know. I couldn't see anything because I had to look where we were going. Did you see any markings on the sides of the helicopters?'

'All hell had broken loose. What with the explosions, tracer bullets and flashes, I couldn't make out anything. You were driving so fast . . .'

'Maddox must have stamped pretty hard on someone's toes and they were out to get him,' said Sarah. 'God, we only just escaped in time.'

'You can still see the light of the fires towards Mitzpe. Look.'

Sarah stood up and narrowed her eyes looking north to the horizon, where a confusion of lights flickered behind the low line of the hills.

'Yes,' she said. 'And now what are you going to do? It looks like your plan doesn't make much sense any more.'

'True,' replied Blake. 'But I still want to go down into the tomb to check out that side opening and close the sarcophagus. And after that, I'll set the charges.'

He took the shovel from the ATV and cleaned off the iron plate. Then he took the winch cable and hooked it to the lifting ring.

'Listen,' said Sarah, 'let's get out of here now. Someone might have noticed we've got away. We may not be safe even here.'

'Help me, quick,' said Blake as if she hadn't spoken. 'Start up the engine and drag off the cover plate. I just need to open it enough to get in. We'll go down on a rope.'

Sarah obeyed. She put the ATV into reverse and accelerated. It sank several times into the hammada and swung left and right until it got a grip and started to pull. The plate slid back slowly, uncovering part of the opening.

Blake tied a rope round his waist, secured the other end to the lifting ring on the iron plate and slipped down inside.

He lit a neon torch and looked around. Everything was in order and the sarcophagus lid was still resting on the crude raising mechanism he had used. He removed the plastic sheet that was wrapped round the sarcophagus and got up onto the stool from where he looked motionlessly at the mask which covered the face of the mummy.

The startling realism of the likeness was austere yet majestic, highlighting the powerful, severe expression of a man whose mere look had held multitudes in sway.

He came to suddenly, as if from a daze, when he felt Sarah's hand touch his arm.

Silently, he got down and connected the levers on each of the pairs of jacks with a rod so they could be operated simultaneously by a single person. With Sarah's help, he raised them until the weight of the lid was off the blocks. Gradually, by placing smaller and smaller blocks, he lowered the jacks, two centimetres at a time, until the lid was completely closed.

'It's taken us sixty-five minutes,' he said, wiping his brow as he looked at his watch. 'Longer than I expected.'

'Things always take longer than planned,' said Sarah. 'Now, please, Will, let's get away while it's still dark.'

Blake turned towards the side opening, where he had cleared away the debris.

'I want to see what's in there,' he said, grabbing a small pick.

'Come on. Let's get out of here,' Sarah insisted. 'I don't like this place. And you never finished telling me that story about the curse.'

'There wasn't enough time for explanations.'

'I know. But anyway, it's time to get away. Let's close up this hole on top, set off the charges and head out for Yotvata. If that hunk of tin out there stays in one piece, we can probably expect to reach Eilat before the weather changes. The ATV's top speed is seventy, which means an average of forty or fifty. Have you thought about that? Christ, you can always come back here when all this has blown over and dig down right to the centre of the earth if you want. But for now let's go.'

'Just half an hour,' said Blake. 'Just give me one half-hour and then we'll go. I don't know if I'll ever be able to come back here. I want to see what's behind there. Shine the light here, please.'

Sarah pointed the neon light towards the opening and Blake started to work at the compacted mound as if he were demolishing a wall. After a while, the pick broke through.

'I knew it!' he said, his excitement rising. 'There's a cavity on the other side.'

He widened the opening and had Sarah pass the neon through to light up the space beyond the mound of debris.

'What's there?' asked Sarah.

'The rest of the slide, which is partly blocking a tunnel that goes up like a ramp.'

'You only have a quarter of an hour,' said Sarah. 'You promised.'

Blake continued digging with the pick, throwing the rubble behind him until he had finally opened up a gap big enough for a person to get through.

'Come on,' he said, and started to go through to the other side.

Sarah followed him uncertainly, lighting the way with the

neon. They had gone about twenty metres along the narrow passage when she stopped suddenly to listen.

'What is it?' asked Blake.

'The helicopters . . . damn! They waited until it was light enough, then they followed the tracks of the ATV.'

'Sarah, you can't be sure of that. We've seen helicopters passing this way at other times.'

But the noise was getting louder and nearer. And soon they could hear the crackle of machine guns.

Sarah yelled, 'Let's get out of here, quick!' She started to run back, but, at that very moment, an explosion shook the earth under their feet. A flash filled the tomb and the corridor with light, and immediately afterwards there was a dull crash as they were plunged into darkness.

'They've hit the ATV and the explosives. We're buried in here!'

'Not yet,' said Blake. 'Quick! This way. Shine the light!'

They heard another explosion.

'The gasoline tanks,' said Sarah, crawling up the ramp. At that moment, they heard a sinister noise behind them, a sort of crunching and then sliding rocks.

'Oh, God! The vibrations are making the tunnel cave in!' shouted Sarah. 'Hurry! Run! Run!'

The tunnel had got narrower and began to slope upwards slightly. Sarah and Blake scrambled up desperately, pouring with sweat, their hearts beating wildly as a growing sense of oppressive claustrophobia assailed them.

In the midst of their dash, clambering over the fall of rocks and sand and through a suffocating dust that the light barely penetrated, all of a sudden Blake came to a dead halt. He stared as if made of stone towards the left of the tunnel, where a kind of niche had unexpectedly appeared.

'Come away!' shouted Sarah. 'What are you waiting for? Come on!'

But Blake seemed to be paralysed by what he was seeing, or what he thought he was seeing. Within the cloud of white dust, there was a dazzling confusion of golden wings under a stone vault and a veiled shimmering of treasure.

'Oh, my . . . God!'

Sarah grabbed him by the arm and pulled him away just a second before the whole vault collapsed onto where his head had been and she kept pulling him until she thought her heart would burst.

They sank onto the floor of the gallery, exhausted.

Not a sound could be heard now, except for the occasional pebble that continued to fall from the walls. Bit by bit, the dust settled and they could see that a gentle draught was coaxing it upwards. 'There's an opening there,' said Sarah. 'We might be able to get out.'

Blake pulled himself to his feet first. His forehead was bleeding where the stones falling from the vault had grazed him. His hands were skinned and his face was grubby with a mixture of sweat and white dust. He was still brandishing the pick and seemed to be out of his mind.

'I have to go back,' he said, turning round. 'You don't know what I saw there.'

Sarah grabbed him by both arms and pushed him against the wall.

'For the love of God, Will. We have to save ourselves. If we don't get out of here, we'll die. For the love of God, let's get out of here. We have to go!'

Blake seemed to come out of his dazed state and started walking upwards. He continued his backward glances until, finally, they both saw a stream of light. It was a thin sun ray filtering through a crack at what seemed to be the end of the tunnel.

Blake approached it and lifted the pick to widen the crack, but, at that very moment, he saw some dust fall and heard the muffled sound of voices. He signalled to Sarah not to move or make any sound and put his ear up to the crack. Now he could hear the noise of steps moving away and, further still, there was the beating of a helicopter's rotor blades turning slowly.

'They've landed,' he whispered. 'They're patrolling the area, probably looking for us.'

'Can you hear what language they're speaking?' asked Sarah.

'No. They're too far away and I can't hear them because of the helicopter. We could try to get out so we can see.'

He opened the crack with the pick just enough to get his head and shoulders out and found himself in a small cave which was rank with the smell of urine. On the ground were fresh prints of military boots.

When Blake had got out he helped Sarah do the same.

'Jeez!' said the girl. 'What the hell is this stench?'

'It's only ibex urine. They use caves like these for shelter at night and the sand on the floor is completely impregnated with their excrement. I've seen tons of these places in the Middle East. Let's go and see what's happening.'

But even as he spoke, he heard the helicopter engine speed up and heard the whir of the blades as they spun through the air. They slipped across the cave floor to the entrance and found themselves on the side of the hill at Ras Udash, above the site where they had worked for so many days and from which a dense column of black smoke was now rising. The helicopter was already far away.

'What a disaster,' said Blake, his eyes filling up.

The ATV had suffered a direct hit and bits of it were lying all over the place. The explosion had blasted a crater and the fallout had formed an enormous heap where the entrance to the tomb had been.

'Two explosive charges and four tanks of gasoline. Quite a bang,' said Sarah. Her eyes followed the helicopter, which was, by now, barely a speck in the grey sky. 'Did you see any markings?' she asked.

Blake shook his head. 'I didn't see anything. Have you seen the boot tracks?'

Sarah glanced at the footprints that had been left all around the entrance of the cave.

'NATO combat boots. They're the most common type of all and loads of armies use them. As far as I can tell, they could have been Egyptians, Americans, Saudis, Israelis . . . But the helicopter was Western-made. Not that that tells us very much.'

She opened her rucksack.

'We've only got the stuff we were carrying with us. What've you got?'

Blake opened up his pack.

'A water bottle, a few cereal bars, a couple of cans of meat, some crackers, a box of dates and one of dried figs.'

'Anything else?'

'Matches, string, needle and thread, Swiss Army knife, soap, suntan cream. The usual junk . . . and a topographical map and compass.'

He started down towards the deserted plain. The sky was beginning to lighten and a cold wind had sprung up from the north. It forced the column of smoke down to the ground, where it meandered at length between the rocks and stones of the hammada.

At a certain point, Sarah saw Blake turn towards something on his left and bend down to pick it up. She went over to him.

'What is it?'

Blake turned round. In his hands he was holding a Bible whose pages had been charred by the explosion.

'There's nothing else left,' he said, 'nothing at all . . .'

'If they'd been Christians, they would have picked it up, don't you think? Maybe they were Arabs . . . Oh, it's no use racking our brains. I'm afraid we aren't going to find out anything anyway.'

They sat on the ground and drank sparingly from their water bottles.

Blake took a packet of cigarettes out of his pocket and lit one while he continued to stare at the cloud of smoke that snaked across the expanse of desert. He seemed to be miles away.

'The road to Yotvata seems to be the best to take,' said Sarah. 'If we ration the water and the food, we can do it. It's about eighty miles.'

'Yes,' said Blake. 'If we aren't surprised by the storm tonight.'

'There's no saying it will hit this area.'

'No, I guess not. But it might.'

'Will?'

'Yes?'

'Why did you stop in the tunnel? You could have died.'

'I saw—'

'What?'

'Angels' wings . . . of gold.'

Sarah shook her head. 'You're exhausted. You were seeing things.'

'Maybe I just wanted to believe I was seeing them.'

'Seeing what, for Christ's sake?'

'Golden angels, kneeling . . . on the Ark. And there were other things too, vessels, incense burners.'

Taken aback, Sarah looked into his eyes. 'My God, William Blake, are you sure you're all right?'

'Yes,' said Blake. 'It all makes perfect sense now. I know why that sandal was in the tomb and perhaps whom it belonged to as well.'

He leafed through the charred Bible. 'See? It's here in a passage from the Book of the Maccabees.'

Sarah stared at him in amazement and she pulled her cotton jacket more tightly around her. It wasn't equal to the biting wind that was blowing even more strongly from the north.

'That sandal goes back more or less to the time when the Babylonians, under King Nebuchadnezzar, laid siege to Jerusalem. Somebody there must have realized that the pagans were about to break into the city, desecrate the Temple, steal the treasure and carry away the Ark of the Covenant. That person would have tried to take the treasure to safety, using a secret passage that only he knew about. His destination was a place in the Paran desert, where his people's first sanctuary had been raised in a tent at the foot of Mount Sinai. His intention was to hide the Ark there, where it had come from originally. Perhaps he found that little cave by chance and thought that it would be a good hiding place. Or perhaps he knew there was a cave nearby where the ancient sanctuary had been and went there on purpose. He began to make his way through the tunnel and put his treasure in a niche in one of the walls—'

'And then?' asked Sarah, her head spinning with the enchantment of such a faraway past.

Blake was trying to light another cigarette, shielding the lighter from the insistent wind. When he finally succeeded, he blew out a great mouthful of bluish smoke and continued.

'The man had carried out his duty and he was about to retrace his steps, but the tunnel that went down into the bowels of the earth seemed to have been waiting for his visit for many years and beckoned to him irresistibly. Instead of going up again, he started to descend.

'He must have had some sort of light so he could see where he was going and, when he got to the tomb entrance, without realizing it, he unknowingly triggered the protection device and an enormous pile of rubble slid down into the tomb. That was when he lost his sandal. It was dragged down into the tomb by the unexpected rock slide and was the only object in that funerary world that came from another period.

'He probably got dragged down as well, but the slide stopped because an infiltration of water had solidified some of the plaster. The entrance wasn't completely blocked, and he could probably see the inside of the tomb and read the first part of the inscription. It's likely that he knew Egyptian hieroglyphics.

'If he guessed the truth, he must have had the shock of his life. He turned and fled without leaving a trace behind him.'

'Who was the man?' asked Sarah. 'You said you knew who the sandal belonged to.'

Blake turned the last pages of the large, half-burnt book.

'This volume has a very special appendix: the Apocrypha of the Old Testament. I've read it many times in the course of my research but, when I was reading one particular passage the other night, the penny dropped.'

'Which passage?' Sarah asked. She still couldn't really fathom how he could be gathering clues from thirty centuries ago, like a detective does at the scene of a crime just a few hours after it has been committed.

'It's a passage by Baruch. He says that during the siege of Jerusalem, his master disappeared from the city and was absent for two weeks. His master was the same man the Book of the Maccabees talks about: that is, the Prophet Jeremiah! And two weeks is exactly how long it takes to get here and back from Jerusalem on a mule. Surely the man with the sandal was Jeremiah, the prophet who wept for the desolation of Jerusalem, abandoned by its people and by its kings, who had been dragged off into slavery.'

Sarah said nothing and just stared at him as he smoked his cigarette and looked off into the void, the wind blowing through his dusty hair and his empty soul.

'Come on, Blake,' she said suddenly. 'We have to get a move on. It's a long way and it won't be easy. If we get caught by the sandstorm on the way, we'll get completely lost.'

'Just a minute,' said Blake. 'I've told you everything about me, but I still don't know who *you* are.'

'I really am a topographical engineer, you've seen that for yourself. And I did the work I had to do for Warren Mining. But I was put there by a private organization that does jobs on commission for certain government agencies.'

'Like the CIA?'

'I couldn't say. But I can't exclude the possibility. In any case, I have the impression that the powers-that-be don't trust Maddox completely and are keeping an eye on him.'

'I'd be surprised if they weren't. There's nothing that's not suspicious about this set-up. The only thing that works is the season. It's the only time of year you can do any sort of mining out here in the desert.'

'Well, that's all I know. But I don't simply take orders sitting down. I have my own points of view and my own way of doing things. And when I'm involved in something, I move the way I think is best.'

'I've noticed.'

'All right. At the start I didn't trust even you, because in my line of work I know I can't afford to trust anybody. Then I tried to keep you out of it as much as possible because, one way or another, I figured you would find some means of getting yourself killed. And now, please, let's get moving.'

They made their way over an empty wasteland – a bleak, flat expanse, scattered here and there with thorn bushes parched by the lack of water. Meanwhile, the sun had risen above the horizon and was beginning to warm the air. The boundless plain glittered with countless fragments of black flint that covered it for as far as the eye could see.

When the sun was high in the sky, they stopped to eat some food, but there was nowhere to take refuge from the burning rays of the sun.

Blake tried to find their position on the map while Sarah nibbled at a cereal bar. 'I figure we must have covered about ten miles,' he said. 'If we keep this pace up, by evening, we should be crossing the trail of Beer Menuha, which is approximately here,' he said, putting his finger on the map.

He looked over to the east, where the sky was veiled in milky mist.

'You haven't told me yet what the rest of the inscription was about,' said Sarah.

'True,' replied Blake, folding the map, putting away the compass and walking into the blinding sun.

SELIM KADDOUMI landed on the evening of 5 February at Luxor airport. From there he took a taxi to the outskirts of the city, paid the fare and continued on foot. It took him twenty minutes to reach the old house where his mother now lived alone. At first, she didn't want to open the door, not believing that it was indeed him, showing up at such a late hour without letting her know beforehand.

'Mother,' he said, 'I'll explain everything later. Right now I've got a very important matter to attend to.'

He wasted no time in removing his Western clothes and putting on a jellaba before hurrying out of the back door. He walked for nearly half an hour until he found himself in a solitary spot at the edge of the desert. There was a grove of palm trees not far away from a well. Shortly afterwards, a boy arrived, carrying under his arm a pitcher which he started to draw water with.

He went up to the boy and said, 'Salaam alekum. Isn't it a little late to be drawing water out of the well? You could risk falling in when it's dark like this.'

'Alekum salaam, el sidi,' answered the boy without hesitation. 'One draws water when one is thirsty.'

Selim uncovered his head and came nearer.

'I am Kaddoumi,' he said. 'Where's Ali?'

'Let's get away from here,' the boy said. 'Follow me.'

They followed a path which the full moon had lit almost as brightly as day and came to the top of a small hill. At the bottom, they could see the village of El Qurna in the middle of the valley. They continued until they reached a little house halfway down the slope. The boy pushed the door open and let his companion in.

'I can't see anyone,' said Selim.

'Ali must have told you he is being watched. The same people as before are around, understand? We have to be very careful. Have you got the money with you?'

Selim nodded.

'Then wait here. He'll come during the night. If you haven't seen him by sunrise, come back here tomorrow night, without being seen, and wait until, *inshallah*, he comes.'

'*Inshallah*,' said Selim.

The boy closed the door and the sound of his steps faded away along the path down to El Qurna.

Selim blew out the light and waited in the darkness and silence, smoking a cigarette. When his eyes had got used to the gloom, the bare mud-plastered room seemed almost light in the bluish rays of the moon. He was tired after his long journey and very sleepy at this late hour. He smoked cigarette after cigarette and forced himself to get up and pace back and forth in the tiny space. Every now and then, he would glance out of the cracks in the blinds to see if someone was coming up from the valley.

At a certain moment, he was overcome by fatigue. His head flopped against the back of the chair and he fell asleep. He slept for as long as his exhaustion was stronger than the sense of discomfort caused by the hard chair. When he opened his eyes and looked around, the shadows seemed strange and the room was immersed in a soft red light. He went over to the window to look outside and saw the disc of the moon suspended over the houses of El Qurna. It was obscured by a red shadow that covered it almost completely.

An eclipse. He had never seen such a thing before in his whole life. The shadow did not hide the moon's shape, but rather veiled it with a blood-red mist, and the dusky face of the night star had caused a deep silence to fall over the valley, as if the night creatures themselves had been struck dumb by the disquieting metamorphosis.

He felt dead tired and thought about leaving, but as he was

picking up his bag, he saw the door open and a dark shape nearly filled the room. He stumbled to his feet.

'Is that you, Ali?' he asked.

The figure seemed to sway for a moment, then fell forwards. Selim caught him before he collapsed on the floor and tried to make him comfortable by putting his jacket under his head.

'Ali . . . is it you?' He flicked on his lighter and recognized the face of his friend. It was deathly pale and, when he withdrew his hand, he saw that it was bathed in blood.

'O merciful Allah, my friend, my friend . . . What have they done to you?'

'Selim,' gasped the youth. 'Selim, the papyrus . . .' His forehead was beaded with drops of cold sweat.

'Where is it? Where is it?'

'Winter Palace . . . The bald man with a red moustache . . . has a bag with silver . . . buckles.'

He turned his terror-stricken eyes to the red moon and, with a long sigh, passed away.

Selim looked around, feeling lost and bewildered, and then pricked up his ears at a distant sound: sirens. In just a few minutes he would find himself in the same situation as Professor Blake, but one that was far more dangerous. He had to get away immediately. He closed his friend's eyes and set off into the night, running as fast as he could towards the foot of a wadi that cut the valley in two on his right, about half a mile away.

He threw himself down behind a boulder seconds before he saw two police vehicles roar up the hill and come to a stop in front of the little house where his friend lay dead. If he had waited just a few moments longer, he would have been caught with blood on his hands, standing beside a corpse.

He waited until they had left and, making sure that there was no one around, he walked slowly back the way he had come. In the courtyard of his home, he drew a bucket of water from the well and put his hands into it. The water turned red.

12

FABRIZIO FERRARIO entered Avner's office carrying a stiff-sided black suitcase, which he put down on the floor in front of his chief's desk.

'This is how they move during sandstorms,' he said, unzipping it.

Avner stood up and walked around his desk.

'What is it?' he said, looking at the contraption sitting inside the case.

'A beacon transmitter. They've placed them all the way along the lines of invasion. They can move through the densest fog guided by the signals sent out by this gadget.'

'And here we are down to only 20 per cent of our potential helicopter and aviation strength. The weather conditions to the east of Jordan are impossible. How did you get your hands on this thing?'

'They've installed them in the Bedouin tents, pretty well all over the place. Someone tipped me off about where I could find this one. What's the weather forecast?'

'Bad. It's going to get worse over the next twenty-four hours. When it clears, we'll probably find them at our front door.'

Ferrario zipped up the case.

'I have to go to a meeting with the general staff and experts who've been sent by the Americans. You'll come with me. Unfortunately, I already know we're going to get bad news, but at least we'll find out how we're going to die. Bring the case with you.'

Ferrario grasped the handle on the large case and pulled it over to the elevator. He waited for Avner to get in, then he pressed the down button. The staff car was waiting for them in the street and the two men took the rear seats.

'It seems that the people who sent the video have shown signs of life. That's why the Americans will be at today's meeting as well. I should kick their arses. They prevented us from acting early and now they'll say they can't make a move,' said Avner. 'You can bet on it.'

'If they've got three atomic bombs in their own backyard, they can't be blamed,' commented Ferrario.

The car drew to a halt at 4 Ashdod Street and Ferrario entrusted the guards with the task of carrying the cumbersome case he had brought with him up to the fourth floor, where the meeting was being held.

The men who had been at the first meeting were there. Avner came in at the same time as General Yehudai, who was both the chief of the general staff and commander of the ground forces.

Sitting on the other side of the table were three men in civilian clothes who had just arrived from the American consulate. Avner signalled to Ferrario to wait outside with the case and walked in, greeting all those present. From their faces, it was easy to see that they weren't expecting good news.

One of the three Americans, General Hooker from the Pentagon, started speaking in an embarrassed tone.

'We regret to admit that we were mistaken,' he said. 'General Yehudai was right. The presence of the nuclear arms on our territory, as seen in the video sent to the *Tribune*, is directly connected to what's happening in this part of the world. Our State Department has received this recorded message.'

He pressed the start button on a cassette recorder. A metallic voice, without a trace of an accent, spoke:

As you listen to this message, an attack by Islamic forces is taking place against the Zionists. It will sweep them away once and for all from the lands that they usurped with the help of the imperialist

Americans and Europeans. This is a fair battle because, this time, there cannot be any outside intervention. If the American government or the governments of any of its allies should act, the nuclear devices which you have seen, and which are now in place on American territory, will be activated.

There was a buzzing sound and then silence.

Each one of the men looked around at the others. Avner said nothing, aware that everybody already knew what he had to say, but his expression was more eloquent than a thousand words.

'Unfortunately, the threat has to be taken seriously. Our experts have ascertained that the video is genuine and original and, as you already know, the terrorists have become so cocky that they have even shown us where the bombs were assembled. The evidence they left behind is such that there can be no doubt about the authenticity of their threat.'

'Am I right in thinking that the news has been kept secret so far?' said the Minister of the Interior.

'Certainly,' said General Hooker. 'But if we can find out where the bombs are currently located, then we'll be able to neutralize them and evacuate the population at the same time. Already aircraft equipped with highly sophisticated radiation-detection equipment are flying back and forth over the United States. I'm sorry to say, however, that the results of this operation haven't been very encouraging.

'The enemy has probably hidden the devices carefully so as to prevent detection. Our attempts to intercept their communications have so far met with failure. Unfortunately, the whole country is being held hostage by these criminals and, right now, we're not in a position to help anyone because we are helpless ourselves.

'From now on, we can't even risk holding consultations like this one, which could be considered a sort of assistance and could result in reprisals.'

He lowered his head and was silent.

'Thank you, General Hooker,' Prime Minister Schochot said. 'We understand your situation and we are sensitive to the terrible danger you are facing because of the friendship you have always shown us.'

He turned to his chief of staff. 'General Yehudai, can you tell us what is happening now?'

'Three army corps, two of them Iraqi and one Syrian, are advancing through the storm, apparently without suffering any negative effects from the terrible weather. Mr Avner will explain later how they are doing it.

'A fourth corps, which is Iranian, is crossing Kuwait, headed towards the Saudi Arabian oil fields. It seems obvious that they intend to take control of them.

'Our informers think that a coup d'état by fundamentalists with Libyan and Sudanese support is imminent in Egypt, so we are keeping a close eye on that area. The danger is that, if such a coup were successful, the Egyptian government would cancel its peace treaty with us and go to war alongside the other countries.

'There are already ultra-nationalist demonstrations and activities taking place. There could also be an attack at any time on the Sinai front. Our air forces have informed me that our fighters are having great difficulty taking off because of the terrible weather conditions, but at least the enemy is in the same situation.

'The problem will come when we have to face the massed air forces of our enemies. In addition, the Iranians have returned the Iraqi planes taken during the Gulf War to their old enemy. Now Mr Avner will show you how the armoured divisions are managing to advance towards our border in spite of the sandstorm.'

Avner went to the door and let Ferrario in. The youth opened the case and showed the gathered group what was inside it.

'Beacons,' he said. 'Run on batteries or recharged wherever they can find electricity. They emit a steady signal that guides armoured cars along set routes.'

'Has there been a declaration of war?' asked General Hooker.

'No, obviously not,' replied the Prime Minister. 'Taksoun has let it be known that there are joint exercises with Syria. That shows you just how brazen he has become. He obviously knows he has nothing to fear.'

There was a knock at the door and Ferrario went to see who it was. Shortly afterwards he returned, pale and tense.

'Gentlemen,' he said, 'we have just been told that swarms of Hezbollah have moved into Galilee with rockets and, even worse, three bombs went off in Tel Aviv, Haifa and West Jerusalem ten minutes ago. Over seventy people are dead and hundreds are wounded, many of them seriously.

'It is feared that there will be more Hamas suicide commando units acting in the next few hours.'

'What are you going to do?' asked Hooker.

'Fight. What else? We have defeated the united Arab forces before,' said Yehudai. 'I'll drop my parachutists all over south Lebanon to fight Hezbollah. We'll send up all the bombers that can fly and we'll drop all the bombs we have on them. The armoured forces and the artillery are ready to engage on the Jordanian front. It's very likely that Jordan will join the others or be dragged into the conflict, and then Egypt won't have much choice but to go along too. Even if we can't stop them, we still have one card to play. We won't be pushed into the sea. We will not go back to being a landless people!'

General Hooker got to his feet and looked him in the eye. 'General Yehudai,' he said, 'are you saying that you're considering the use of nuclear arms?'

'Without the slightest hesitation,' replied Yehudai after exchanging glances with his Prime Minister. 'If that becomes necessary.'

'You do realize that our enemies may well have been able to get atomic weapons from the Islamic former Soviet republics? That's certainly where the bombs they've positioned on our territory come from. A nuclear response would bring about a similar reprisal. Their missiles have limited range, but it would be enough.'

Yehudai looked at the Prime Minister again and then at the

American general. 'Armageddon,' he said. 'If that's what they want, so be it. And now, if you will excuse me, General Hooker, I must join my men on the front line.'

He bowed his head, took his leave of the Prime Minister and Avner, and then walked away, his combat boots echoing ominously in the silence-filled room.

THE THREE Americans prepared to go as well, standing up and moving towards the door. As Ferrario was opening the door to let them pass, Avner nodded to him and the Italian turned to General Hooker, the last one to leave.

'General,' he said, 'Mr Avner would like a word in private. He will be waiting for you in an hour's time at the King David Hotel. May I tell him that you'll be there?'

Hooker hesitated for a moment and then replied, 'I'll be there.'

The American arrived at around four o'clock and was shown to a private room.

'This place is quieter than the chief of staff's headquarters and I think it's more private too. Do you mind if I smoke?' Avner asked, lighting a cigarette.

'Go ahead,' said Hooker. 'You may as well. Things are shot to hell anyway.'

'General, I need your help.'

'I'm sorry, Avner, I can't do anything. What I just said at the meeting still stands.'

'I know. It's not about that. It's another problem.'

'Another problem? You mean there's another problem besides the one we already have?'

'Yes, not as important, I hope ... You are aware of the Warren Mining operation at Mitzpe Ramon, aren't you?'

'Yes, I am. But that's all over now, I think. Our forces have almost completely withdrawn.'

'I'm not talking about that, General. Unfortunately, there have been some complications. Last night, the Warren Mining camp suffered a massive attack. It may have been a preparatory incursion by enemy forces, clearing the way in a highly strategic area, or it may have been a reprisal. There are still many officers in the Iraqi high command who are faithful to the dead president. They may have learned about the force you had there to kill al Bashar.'

'But we didn't do it.'

'If I know them, it won't make any difference. In any case, we did a bit of reconnaissance down there and we didn't find any survivors. Those bastards hit with surgical precision. However, my informants tell me that someone may have escaped the massacre, someone who would be a valuable witness to that attack in which so many of your compatriots were killed. I tend to think that if someone got out, it was because he was allowed to do so. I don't know if I am making myself clear.'

'Loud and clear,' said Hooker. 'Whoever escaped was the one who talked in the first place.'

'There's no other explanation that makes sense to me. The camp was completely surrounded, every square foot sprayed with machine-gun fire and torn apart by huge explosions. But an ATV left the scene just minutes before all hell broke loose. A bit odd, wouldn't you say? It was found abandoned near the Egyptian border at a place called Ras Udash. So, it's plain that if whoever was in it came from the Warren Mining camp, they were headed for Egypt, where someone was waiting for them.

'We were also able to intercept radio messages from the Warren Mining camp and we know that someone there was in contact with a group of Islamic fundamentalists. We don't know why.

'We found profiles of the camp staff on the company's remote computer system. Two of them concerned people whose bodies we haven't been able to find. They could be the people we are looking for. What I'm asking you is to let us know if you should find out where they are or if they should come directly to you, even if they are American citizens.'

'I'll do what I can, Mr Avner. If we locate anyone, you'll be the first to know.'

'Thank you. I knew you would help us.'

Hooker left and Avner sat and finished his cigarette, while he thought about the secret that was once again buried in the middle of the Paran desert, a secret that, should it ever get out, would destroy the soul of his nation, but would also put an end to wars like the one that was about to break out once and for all.

He thought for a long time, watching the embers slowly die and turn to ashes. Deep inside, he knew all too well that the one thing he could never let happen was the destruction of the people of Israel, the destruction of their history and their soul. No price was too high for him to pay to prevent that from happening.

A step behind him brought him out of his reverie.

'Ferrario! Any news?'

'Yehudai has sent out the air force and the army helicopters despite the storm, but they're meeting stiff resistance from the enemy forces. There have already been losses and it looks like it's going to get worse in the next few hours. The United Nations have given the Iranians a final ultimatum to withdraw immediately from Saudi territory but it might as well have been the Pope for all the good it'll do.'

'The Saudi troops are retreating anyway. Without American help they can't even blow their noses.'

'And the northern front?'

'Incursions by the Syrian air force. Rockets on Galilee. On the Golan, Hezbollah are attacking like mad all the way along the front line. We're dropping paras behind them to take the pressure off, but it's heavy going. The government is evacuating all civilians in a ten-mile range.'

'Egypt?' said Avner. 'I don't want anything to move down there without my knowing about it.'

'Yes. Our network is working at full capacity, so nothing should get past us.'

Avner looked at him. 'Don't say stupid things, Ferrario.

Nobody on God's earth can expect to know everything there is to know. It's the unexpected that has always changed the course of history over the millennia. Always the unexpected. Remember that.'

'Shall I take you back to headquarters, Mr Avner?'

'No, Ferrario, I'll get there on my own . . . In the meantime, I want you to do a little job for me.'

'Yes?'

He held out a folder. 'Someone should tell the Egyptians about the people in this file. At least two of them may already be on their territory. They represent a mortal danger for us, but we can't move about in Egypt freely enough to take care of the matter ourselves. We have to get the Egyptians to eliminate them. Have I made myself clear?'

'Very clear, sir,' said Ferrario, leafing through the files in the folder. 'I'll see to it immediately.'

'Oh, and by the way, I want to know what's happening in the Allon tunnel. Keep me informed.'

'Certainly, sir.'

Out on the street, Avner stopped to look up at the sky, which was still clear over Jerusalem, while the wail of sirens from ambulances carrying bomb-blast victims reached his ears from every direction. Then he set off along a path he hadn't followed for many years.

He walked alone with his hands pushed deep into his pockets and his scarf pulled up for almost half an hour, until he came to the Damascus Gate. He followed El Walid Street, crossed over Hashalshelet and found himself in the open space by the Western Wall of the Temple.

Soldiers in combat fatigues were guarding all the entrances to the square and checked everyone coming in or out, fingers ready on the triggers of their Uzis. Avner crossed the square, swept by a cold wind, and approached the Western Wall. A few orthodox faithful with their hair shaved at the top and with long black locks falling from their temples rocked rhythmically as they chanted their centuries-old lament for the lost sanctuary.

Avner stared at the great blocks of stone smoothed by the piety of millions of sons of Israel, forced into exile by the Diaspora. Exiles in their own countries. For the first time since the death of his son, he felt like praying and, by a strange twist of fate, was unable to do so because his mind was filled with a secret that left no room for anything else.

His anger and disappointment turned to profound grief and Gad Avner, who had buried his son without shedding a tear, now felt his eyes fill. He touched his tears with his fingertips and wet the stone of the Temple, adding his tears to those of all the Jews who, for centuries before him, had done the same.

There was nothing left for him to do, so he turned to go. But when he had reached the other side of the square, he saw an old man sitting on the pavement, begging. Avner looked at him and saw a strange light in his eyes, almost like divine inspiration.

'Give me some money so I can eat,' said the beggar. 'And I'll give you something in return.'

Taken aback by the unexpected words, Avner took out a five-shekel note and handed it to the old man, then said, 'What can you give me in exchange?'

The old man put the money into his satchel, raised his eyes to Avner's face and said, 'Perhaps . . . hope.'

Avner shivered suddenly, as if the wind blowing down from Mount Carmel had got under his clothes.

'Why do you say that?' he asked.

But the old man did not reply and his empty eyes stared into space, as if just for an instant he had been the unwitting messenger for a mysterious force which had now disappeared.

Avner looked at him for a while without saying anything, then continued on his way, absorbed in his thoughts.

THE LAST GLOW of the sunset faded from the immense desert and the first stars began to shine in the darkening sky. Blake continued onward, even though his feet were bleeding inside his boots. Sarah was wearing running shoes and moved more easily with lighter steps, but both of them were at the limits of their endurance.

Suddenly the wind knifed across the enormous empty space and the two looked at each other anxiously, reading in the expression of the other the knowledge of what was about to happen.

'It's coming,' said Blake. 'We have to prepare ourselves.'

'But where do you think we are?'

'By now, we should be almost at the Beer Menuha road. We should be able to see it when we've gone over that little hill up ahead. But that doesn't mean much. Just that on the road we may find someone who'll pick us up.'

'What'll we do if we get caught by the storm?'

'What I've already told you. If we find some shelter, we'll use it. Otherwise we'll lie on the ground and try to protect each other by covering our heads, our mouths and noses. And then we'll wait until it passes.'

'But it could last for days.'

'Yes, but there's nothing else we can do. The alternative is to die of suffocation. The dust is as fine as talc and it stops you breathing in minutes. Come on now. We'll make it.'

Blake turned to the east and saw that the line of the horizon was disappearing in a white mist. He hurried as fast as he could to the little hill, which was now only a short distance away. When he got to the top, the Beer Menuha road was visible, deserted for as far as the eye could see. However, at the foot of the hill there was a boulder as tall as a man, a large outcrop of flint surrounded by smaller stones that had broken off it over the years because of the drastic swings in temperature.

Blake turned to call Sarah and heard her saying, 'Oh, God, the moon! It's red . . .'

Blake looked up at the surreal sight. The disc of the rising moon was veiled by a bloody shadow which expanded and reflected over the endless plain.

'The eclipse,' said Blake. 'The bloodied face of Isis . . . Hurry now, before the storm catches us. It's getting near. I can feel it.'

Sarah joined him and saw that he had put down his pack and was frantically piling stones on the north-west side of the big boulder to form a windbreak. She set to, helping him as the wind gathered strength and the air grew thicker and denser with every minute that passed.

'We should try to eat and drink something,' said Blake. 'Who knows when we'll get another chance?'

Sarah dug into her pack and passed him a packet of biscuits and a few dried figs and dates. Blake took his water bottle out of his own pack and handed it to her. After she had finished, he drank a few long draughts himself.

He was beginning to taste the dust in his mouth. He glanced towards the moon, which was gradually being covered by that bloody veil, and then said, 'We have to find some way of protecting ourselves, otherwise we'll die. It's nearly here.'

He looked around desperately and then again at the horizon.

'What are you looking at?' asked Sarah before she tied a handkerchief over her mouth.

'This shelter isn't going to be enough and neither will that handkerchief . . . Oh, God . . . there's no time left, no time . . .'

Suddenly his eyes fixed on Sarah's pack.

'What are these things made of?' he asked.

'Gore-Tex, I think,' answered the girl.

'Then maybe there's some hope for us. If I remember rightly, the pores in Gore-Tex only release water vapour, so they should keep the dust out and let us breathe at the same time.'

Sarah shook her head. 'You aren't thinking of—'

'That's exactly what I'm thinking,' said Blake, and emptied the contents of the packs into a plastic bag that he jammed between some rocks. He held out the upside-down pack towards Sarah. 'Put this over your head,' he said, looking her in the eyes. 'We don't have any choice.'

The girl obeyed and Blake pulled the cord, tightening it

around her neck. Then he wrapped her scarf several times round her neck and the pack opening. 'How's that?' he asked.

A muffled reply that could have meant anything was the answer, but Blake took it to mean that everything was all right. He squeezed her hand hard, then carried out the same operation on himself and closed the opening of his pack as best he could with two handkerchiefs knotted together.

When he had finished, he felt for Sarah's hand and pulled her down. They curled up on the ground with their heads against the wall, held each other tight and awaited the arrival of the storm.

Barely a few minutes had passed before it broke in all its fury. The surface of the desert was stripped bare by the violence of the wind and the cloud of dust enveloped everything, eliminating the sky and the earth, the stones and the hills. Alone, the moon managed to keep a vague, orange glow alive in the western half of the sky, but there was no one in the wide, deserted expanse to see it.

Every now and then, Blake held Sarah tighter to him, as if to transfer the will to resist and survive this challenge, or perhaps to take courage from her instead.

He could hear a sound like hail battering the big rock because the wind was so strong it was raising thousands of tiny pieces of stone and dashing them against it. The words of Elijah came to him: 'And there came to pass a wind so powerful as to shake the mountains and to split the stones . . .' This was the hell of the Paran desert, a place where only prophets guided by the hand of God dared to venture.

The shrill whistling went on and on. The incessant rattling of stones against the boulder and the complete darkness that surrounded them made them lose all sense of time. He tried to concentrate on Sarah's body, on the beating of her heart; tried to overcome the terrible mental strain and the increasing sense of being suffocated. Now the dust was everywhere, covering every millimetre of their skin, passing through their clothes as if it were water, but their nostrils and lungs were safe for now and they knew that although breathing was difficult it wasn't impossible.

The only question he asked himself was how long they would be able to hold on in these dreadful conditions. He was fully aware that, in any case, it would only be a simple question of time. Sooner or later, the humidity from their breathing would form a paste with the tiny particles of dust coating the Gore-Tex. And at that point, they would have to choose between suffocating because of lack of oxygen or because of the dust. How long would it be until nature, in all her awful might, dealt the final blow to crush them like insects in the dust?

The grip of tension and fatigue began to loosen as they drifted into a semi-conscious state. Blake realized that he had let go of Sarah's body, but something was telling him that the force of the storm had let up slightly. Even the wind needed time to gather its forces again.

He stood up and untied the handkerchiefs round his neck, pulling his head free of the sack. A ghostly apparition met his eyes: a dark mass, enormous and luminescent, casting forth two pale milky lights. In the background, a continuous rhythmic sound like slow wheezing.

He took a better look and managed to focus on the shape behind the haloes of light penetrating the powdery thickness of the night's atmosphere. It looked almost like a submarine sitting on the bottom of the ocean but was, in fact, a desert bus, one of those strange vehicles that managed to carry as many as fifty passengers from Damascus to Jeddah, from Oman to Baghdad along the most frightful tracks. Vehicles that were sealed like spacecraft with powerful filters and air conditioning.

He shook his companion, who seemed to be almost unconscious, and freed her head.

'Sarah! Sarah, get up for Christ's sake! We're saved! Look! Look in front of you!'

Sarah sat up and sheltered her face with her hand, while Blake started walking towards the headlights.

'Hey! Hey!' he shouted. 'Help! We got lost in the sandstorm. Help us!'

At that moment men bearing arms got out of the vehicle and one of them turned Blake's way, pointing his gun towards the noise he thought he had heard. Blake was so overwhelmed by the thought of being saved that he didn't realize what peril they were in. As he started shouting, though, he was thrown to the ground.

'Shut up!' a voice hissed into his ear. 'Look! They're armed!'

The man pointing his gun came towards them a bit, waving his torch back and forth through the thick dust. But Blake and Sarah, flattened as they were on the ground and covered with dust from head to foot, were totally camouflaged. The man kept peering into the gloom for a long while, listening hard. Then, reassured, he went back to the bus.

Three or four men wearing keffiyehs wound tightly round their heads and carrying machine guns came out of the rear door of the bus and took up positions at the four corners of the vehicle. Two more seemed to be checking the wheels.

'But they might be—' protested Blake.

'We can't risk it. They certainly aren't Israelis. Let's go back to our shelter. What time is it?'

Blake cleaned the face of his watch. 'It's just past midnight. Six more hours before the sun comes up.'

As they made their way back to the stone, they felt the wind start to rise again, but it seemed to have already spent the worst of its strength.

Then new shapes, seemingly coming from nowhere, were caught in the beams of the headlights.

'Camels,' said Sarah. 'How the heck did they get here in this storm?'

'The Bedouins,' muttered Blake. 'They can move through the desert like fish in water. Can you see anything?'

'Yes, I can. Well, well. What do you know. Here come some

more, and they're all armed to the teeth. It looks like some kind of arranged meeting. Amazing.'

'They could have got here with their eyes closed,' said Blake. 'After spending thousands of years in the desert, they've developed an incredible sense of direction. In weather like this, they can move about like ghosts, almost invisible.'

One of the men opened the rear door of the bus and let the newcomers in. They were all carrying machine guns. When the last one had entered, the bus started off again and disappeared shortly afterwards, going north, into the clouds of dust.

Blake and Sarah crouched down again behind the pile of stones, once more covered their heads with their packs and remained motionless beneath the fury of the storm. The lack of oxygen, their fatigue and their disappointment following the brief thrill of thinking they were about to be saved combined to take them into a sort of stupor in which they were neither sleeping nor waking. The only thing they felt was the keen cold that cut through to their bones and the fine dust that was starting to get inside the packs, forming a paste round their mouths and up their noses.

Suddenly Blake lifted his head to the west.

'What is it?' Sarah managed to mumble when she felt his movement.

'Cordite,' said Blake. 'Smell that stuff in the air? That's the smell of war.'

Blake loosened the pack on his head for a moment and listened, and for a few moments it seemed that the wind carried the roll of distant thunder.

Dawn arrived. They took their packs off their heads and pulled themselves into a sitting position, leaning against the pile of stones. The wind continued to blow strongly, but the worst was over. The air was still thick, as if there was a dense mist over the desert, but towards the east they could just make out a watery lightness in the distance.

'Ready to get going again?' asked Blake.

Sarah nodded. 'We haven't got much choice, have we? If we stay here, we'll die. We have to get to the track going south. Sooner or later, we'll find something. If our strength doesn't fail us.'

They collected their things, put them in their packs and started off again. They dragged on wearily for hours until they were about to drop from exhaustion, when Blake saw a low concrete block to his left. The roof was made of corrugated iron and the doors and windows were half wrecked.

He entered and looked around. There was dust everywhere but there was a small room where the wind hadn't done quite so much damage. Here they sat on the floor to drink what water they had left and to eat two cereal bars, their last. The packets of dried figs and dates had been open and the fruit was completely coated with dust.

They rested for half an hour and then continued on the long way to Beer Menuha. Hour after hour they walked, buffeted by the wind, protecting themselves as best they could and resting when they felt their energy flagging. They reached the Beer Menuha fork in the late afternoon and took the road to Yotvata.

Before very long, a van carrying goats stopped and gave them a ride to Yotvata. It was dark and they managed to find a room without any trouble. The owner, a man in his sixties, regarded them with suspicion. They looked liked ghosts with white dust all over their bodies, on their clothes, in their hair, their eyelashes and eyebrows. And their faces were scratched and bleeding.

'We're tourists,' explained Blake. 'We had no idea there would be a storm and our car broke down around Beer Menuha. We've been walking for hours and hours through the sandstorm.'

'I see,' said the man. 'You must be nearly dead.'

'And we are hungry,' said Blake. 'Is there anything we can have sent to our room now?'

'Not very much, I'm afraid. The government has requisitioned everything for the troops at the front and there's not much left.

But I think we can manage some hummus and tuna sandwiches and a couple of cool beers.'

'The front?' asked Blake. 'We've been in the desert for so long ... we hadn't heard ...'

'There's a war going on,' said the innkeeper, 'and, as usual, we are on our own, nobody bothers to help us ... If you could just give me your passports.'

'We lost everything in the storm,' said Blake. 'If you like, we can write our names and details and so on, so you won't have a problem if anyone checks.'

The man looked worried for a moment, then he nodded. Sarah watched as Blake wrote out a false name and particulars so she could do the same.

They went up to their room as Mr and Mrs Randall, washed, dusted off their clothes as best they could and wolfed down the sandwiches that the innkeeper sent up.

When they had finished, Sarah collapsed into bed. However, Blake went out and walked about in the twilight until he found a taxi stand where there were two cars parked.

'I have to leave tonight,' he said to one of the drivers. 'For Eilat. Can you be in front of the news kiosk at three o'clock in the morning?'

The man, an Ethiopian Falasha, agreed and Blake returned to the inn. No one was on the streets but, every now and then, he saw military patrols passing in their vehicles.

He found Sarah fast asleep with the light on. She hadn't even had the strength to turn it off. He set the alarm on his watch, turned out the light and sank into oblivion.

In the darkness, he felt Sarah's hand reaching for him and he kissed her before falling back to sleep again.

At 2.45 a.m. he was awoken by the shrill buzz of the watch going off and, still dead tired and groggy from lack of sleep, he roused Sarah, who sat up in alarm.

'What is it? What's happening?'

'We're leaving. I don't trust anyone here. And I don't think

255

the innkeeper trusts us either. We don't want to have a nasty surprise at dawn. There's a taxi coming to get us in quarter of an hour. Get ready.'

Blake left a fifty-dollar bill in the room and went down the fire escape, followed by Sarah. They crept along slowly, trying to make as little noise as possible. The wind was still strong and the city was wrapped in a haze.

Blake and Sarah slipped behind the inn and headed for the main street, which was lined with acacia and mimosa trees.

They saw the news kiosk at the first crossing and, shortly after, the lights of an approaching car.

'The taxi,' said Blake. 'We're OK.'

The Falasha had them get in, with Blake in front and the girl behind, and set off. They passed Shamar, Elipaz, Beer Ora and reached Eilat when it was still dark. Blake told the driver to go to the Egyptian border.

'I just need you to get us across the border,' he told him. 'Then we can manage on our own.'

The Falasha nodded and drove to the passport control at the border with Egypt.

'Have you got an Egyptian visa?' Blake asked Sarah.

'No.'

'It doesn't matter. You can get one here. I tore the page with *"persona non grata"* out of my passport. I hope they don't start counting the pages and that they haven't got me on their wanted list.'

'And if they have?'

'The worst thing that can happen is they won't let us in. Then we'll have to get a ship to the Emirates.'

Sarah got out and went to the automatic booth to get three passport photos which were so awful she didn't even recognize herself. She started to fill in the forms. Blake showed his visa to a sleepy border guard with a yellow, nicotine-stained moustache. He stamped the passport without asking any questions.

Blake breathed a deep sigh of relief, got in and waited for Sarah, then asked the Falasha to take them to the bus station. The place was still deserted and the wind was raising litter and sheets of newspaper that were strewn all over the dusty ground. He took the agreed fifty dollars out of his wallet and shook the man's hand.

'Goodbye, my friend, and thanks. I'd give you more but I still have a long way to go and it's likely to be difficult. *Shalom.*'

'*Shalom*,' answered the Falasha, looking at him for a moment with his big, liquid, African eyes. Then he got back into his car and disappeared in a cloud of dust.

The ticket office opened after a while and Blake bought two tickets for Cairo, then got two coffees and some sesame-seed cookies and went to sit beside Sarah.

'We're nearly home,' he said. 'If we make it to Cairo, we can go to the embassy. There'll be someone there who can help us.'

'If we make it to the embassy, that'll be the end of our troubles,' said Sarah. 'And someone had better give me an explanation of what happened at Ras Udash. Who the hell thought they could play a practical joke like that and get away with it?'

'You're right,' said Blake. 'I can't explain it.'

He dug into his pocket and pulled out a somewhat squashed packet of Marlboros. The cigarettes were all broken except one. He put it in his mouth and lit it, breathing in luxuriously.

'Don't you have enough crap in your lungs without that?' asked Sarah.

'It helps me relax,' said Blake. 'I feel like the hero in an action movie who's lost his stunt man. I ache all over. Even my nails and hair ache.'

Sarah looked at him. His face was all twisted up into what was trying to be a smile, but his expression couldn't disguise an anxiety that wasn't due to fatigue or physical pain. Just when safety was in sight, William Blake felt that it might have been better for all mankind if he and his companion had suffocated to death in the dust of the Paran desert.

'What're we going to do with this secret?' asked Sarah, reading his thoughts.

'I don't know,' said Blake. 'At the moment, I can't believe that what happened was real. It seems like I dreamed it all.'

'But when you wake up . . .'

'Then I'll decide. If I were sure I could stop this war by revealing what I've seen, by revealing that there are no "Chosen People" anywhere, I'd do it in a flash.'

'Maybe you should do it anyway. Truth must out, don't you think?'

Blake shook his head. 'The truth isn't always believed. When it comes down to it, silence may be the only possible option.'

He was interrupted by the sound of the bus stopping under the shelter. They were first on and went to sit at the rear. Shortly after, they were followed by other small groups of people who boarded the bus in dribs and drabs: women carrying heavy bags and men with cartons of American cigarettes that they had probably bought in Aqaba.

At last, the engine started with a jolt and the bus set off, gradually building speed. Rocked by the movement and the noise of the engine, and weary beyond words, Sarah leaned her head on his shoulder and fell into a deep sleep. Blake tried to stay awake, but he too gradually gave in to fatigue and the warmth of Sarah's body.

He woke up when the bus stopped unexpectedly and thought that the driver must be picking up a few things. He was about to go back to sleep when he felt something hard poking into his shoulder. Suddenly fully awake, he saw a man standing in front of him, pointing a machine gun.

13

WILLIAM BLAKE WOKE SARAH, who was still fast asleep. He pretended not to understand the two Egyptian soldiers who were ordering them to get out.

Extremely agitated, the higher-ranking of the two yelled something in Arabic, forcing them to get up, while his companion shoved them with the butt of his machine gun down the aisle of the bus, as the rest of the passengers looked on in amazement.

Once outside, Blake could see that the bus had been stopped by an army Jeep parked sideways across the middle of the road.

The soldiers searched them, lingering longer than necessary when it came to frisking Sarah, then had them get into the back of the Jeep and took off on a road heading towards the interior. In the meantime, the bus had started up with a faltering wheeze and began proceeding west, soon disappearing from sight.

'I can't believe it . . . None of this makes sense,' Sarah started to say, but Blake shushed her, because their escorts were speaking to each other and he didn't want to miss what was being said.

Sarah noticed that Blake's face darkened as he listened to the soldiers' voices, their words interspersed with sinister bouts of giggling.

'Can you understand what they're saying?'

Blake nodded yes.

'Bad news?'

Blake nodded again, whispering, 'They've got orders to take us to a military prison, where we will be interrogated and tried –

no doubt a summary trial. But first they intend to have a little fun with you, both of them, the officer first, naturally.'

Sarah turned pale with impotent anger.

Blake held her hand tightly. 'I'm sorry, but it's best that we're prepared.'

The soldier ordered them to be quiet, but Blake kept on talking, pretending not to have understood a word, at which point the bully backhanded him, splitting open his upper lip.

Blake recoiled in pain, fumbling in his jacket pockets for a handkerchief to stop the blood, which was oozing into his mouth. Exhausted and unarmed as he was, he was trying to think of something he could do to get them out of this jam. As he removed a package of Kleenex from the inside pocket, he felt two fountain pen caps sticking out beside it. In actuality, one of them, despite the resemblance, wasn't really a pen at all, but rather an archaeological scalpel. He slipped it out and put it into his outside pocket, removing the protective cap as soon as the soldier had turned around to say something to his superior.

The Jeep had been moving inland for about half an hour when they reached a hilly area. Once they were down on level land again, the Jeep stopped and the soldier opened the door and made to get out. Before he could, Blake leaned forward and thrust the scalpel straight into his liver. With his other hand, he snatched the pistol out of the limp and profusely bleeding man's holster, firing it at the officer at the wheel and then again at his first victim – the man had tumbled out of the car and was now writhing in the blood-soaked sand – putting an end to his misery.

The whole episode took only a few seconds. Sarah could hardly believe her eyes as she stared at him, reeling back against the seat, still gripping the bloody scalpel in his left hand and the smoking revolver in his right.

'Jesus, Blake, I'd have never thought that you—'

'Me neither,' he admitted, cutting her off.

He dropped his weapons and bent over to throw up what little he had in his stomach. When the violent spasms of gagging had ceased, he stood up, grey in the face, and cleaned his mouth as best he could with a tissue. Then, still woozy and teetering a bit, he stumbled to the back of the Jeep and pulled out a shovel.

'We've got to bury them,' he said, starting to dig.

When the hole was ready, they stripped off the dead soldiers' uniforms and threw the bodies into the hole, quickly covering them with sand. Blake threw away the soldier's blood-soaked shirt, but put on his jacket, trousers, hat and boots. Sarah did likewise, making allowances as best she could for the fact that the officer's clothing was much too big for her.

'I assume you know that if Egypt happens to be in a state of war, this could land us in front of a firing squad,' said Sarah as she donned her new garb.

Blake glanced over at the grave. 'That's a shooting offence too, but since they can't shoot us twice, we might as well take a chance and give it a try. We certainly can't go around in a military vehicle dressed in civvies. And without a car, we won't get anywhere. We'll figure out what to do when we get close to a town.'

He cleaned off his scalpel with a Kleenex, making it shine. 'It's English,' he said, putting its cap back on and sticking it into his jacket pocket next to the pen. 'The best they make.'

They walked up to the Jeep and began rummaging through it. Finally they found a military map of the Sinai.

'Great,' said Blake, 'with this we can stay off the beaten path. I recommend heading towards Ismailia rather than Cairo. It will be a lot easier to pass unnoticed that way. I think there should be enough gas.'

'Wait, look what else I've found,' said Sarah. She held up a plastic envelope that had been in one of the inside pockets of the jacket she was wearing. It contained two pieces of paper with Arabic writing, along with their photographs.

Blake read them. 'They say we are spies for Mossad who have been sent to prepare the way for the Israeli occupation of the Sinai.'

'That's absurd. Someone's playing a dirty trick on me for some fucking reason or another, but they don't know who they're dealing with. If I get out of this mess, someone is going to really be sorry.'

He started the engine and took off, but within a few minutes the radio began chattering hoarsely in Arabic. 'Abu Sharif calling Lion of the Desert, come in, over.'

Blake and Sarah looked at each other in bewildered dismay as the radio repeated its summons. Blake took the microphone. 'Lion of the Desert to Abu Sharif, we read you.'

There was a moment of hesitation at the other end, then the voice said, 'Any news, Lion of the Desert?'

'The lion has seized his prey. The gazelle and ibex are in his clutches. Mission accomplished. Over.'

'Very good, Lion of the Desert. Return to base. Over and out.'

Blake let out a deep sigh of relief. 'Thank goodness this radio has a lousy filter and there's a lot of static. I don't think they realized that it was my voice and not the officer's.'

'But where did you learn Arabic that way, with that florid style and all?'

'I've spent more time in Egypt than Chicago.'

'Is that why your wife left you?' asked Sarah.

'Maybe. Or perhaps there was someone else. I never wanted to admit it, but basically, why not?'

'Because you don't deserve it,' said Sarah. 'You are an extraordinary man.'

'Mild-mannered Clark Kent turns into Superman. Don't get carried away by your imagination. It's just a question of environment. Once I go back to Chicago, if we get out of this mess, I'll revert to Clark Kent, or worse.'

He rummaged instinctively through his pockets 'I wonder if this bastard smoked.' He found a packet of Egyptian cigarettes and a Zippo lighter. 'He smoked real crap, but better than nothing,' he said, lighting up.

They drove for several hours without running into anything other than a few military trucks, which greeted them with their horns. Late that afternoon, they finally reached the port of Ismailia. Looking for a place to conceal the vehicle, Blake parked it behind a low rise in the ground. He removed the licence plates and buried them, then they both changed back into their own clothing and began walking towards town.

The place was abuzz with a strange excitement. Howling sirens could be heard in the distance and steely flashes of blue light could be seen streaking across the warm crimson hues of the sunset.

'I've got a little Egyptian money,' said Blake, 'from the last time I was here. I brought it with me the night I left Chicago because I actually thought I would be coming to Egypt. We can take a taxi and look for a hotel.'

'Damn, that's tempting, but I think a bus would be better,' Sarah cautioned.

They bought the tickets and some bread rings topped with sesame seeds at a kiosk and proceeded to wait in the shade of the covered bus stop. The peaceful setting was interrupted when a squadron of low-flying fighter jets heading east roared overhead, creating such a din that the surrounding buildings looked like they might almost shake loose from their very foundations.

A column of Jeeps full of soldiers appeared from a side road, followed by a line of armoured personnel carriers.

'What the hell's going on here?' Sarah wondered out loud.

'Nothing good, I'm afraid. There are soldiers and armoured vehicles everywhere. There's been either a rebellion or a coup. We'll know as soon as I can get my hands on a newspaper.'

They got onto a bus which made its way down the city streets, but when they noticed that there were all sorts of roadblocks and check points, they decided to get off at the first stop and sneak into the bazaar district, where it would be easier to become lost in the crowd.

They got to the area around the mosque as the sky started to darken above the roofs in the old part of town and the chant of the muezzin began drowning out all the other sounds of the city. For a second it seemed that even the whine of the sirens and the thundering of the tanks subsided to allow the people to hear the call to prayer.

Blake stopped as well to listen to the mournful chant fluttering through the hazy, dense evening air. He was overcome by sadness at the thought that there had never been a God up in the heavens to listen, not the God of Israel, not Allah, not even the Christian God.

Once again they set out walking through the narrow winding streets of the centre of the old town, looking for a cheap place to stay.

'We don't have much time,' Blake said. 'By now they will have noticed that the Lion of the Desert hasn't returned to his den and will probably realize he has been put out of commission. They will start searching everywhere. If we go to a regular hotel, we'll be found immediately.'

They found a room in a small boarding house in the neighbourhood behind the mosque and arranged to stay for two nights.

The bathroom was in the hall and had a squat toilet. The stench of urine was so strong that their eyes watered, but there was an accommodating tap just high enough for washing one's private parts. The shower, located in a separate stall, was encrusted with soap as ancient as Egypt itself and the filthy walls were smeared with foul mildew.

Sarah decided to wash using a plastic basin in the room, bird-bath style with a sponge and soap. Blake, for his part, turned on the radio to try to hear some news. All the stations were playing religious music, so he stretched out on the bed to rest and watch Sarah, who was lost in her arduous ablutions. Shortly, the music faded out, to be replaced by a man's voice. It was then announced that the President had recognized the new government which had instituted Islamic law and rejected the peace treaty with Israel.

'Jesus,' Blake exclaimed when he'd heard the entire broadcast, 'there's been a coup and Egypt has gone to war. That means Israel is completely surrounded. Even Lebanon and Libya have declared war, and the Algerian government could fall at any time now. Why doesn't our government do something about it? What the hell's going on? Something really terrible must have happened while we were locked up at Ras Udash, Sarah, something that evidently triggered this whole bloody mess.'

Sarah began to towel her hair dry. 'What a disaster. And it doesn't help our situation one bit, either. Being wanted as spies for Mossad in the middle of a war means our goose is cooked if they catch us. We seem to have got ourselves into a much worse situation than the one we just got out of!'

'Our only hope is to somehow reach the American embassy. We have to get in touch with them to find out what we should do.'

'OK. I'll handle this one. I know someone important who works there. Just give me two more minutes so I can get dressed.'

'All right,' said Blake. 'In the meantime, I'll make a phone call myself. I know someone who can arrange for a hiding place and some help here in Egypt in case we have problems getting to the embassy. It's my assistant, Selim.'

He went out into the hall, where there was an old-fashioned wall telephone, equipped with a meter and connected to the outside world by means of a plug, and dialled Selim's number. The phone rang for a long time, but no one answered in the Chicago apartment. Blake had no choice but to impose upon another friend; he dialled Husseini's number and let it ring.

Husseini answered almost immediately. 'Hello,' he said.

'Omar, this is William Blake.'

'My God, where are you? I've tried everything to get in touch with you. Why are you not responding to emails any more?'

'My computer was bombed! I'm in Egypt, in the middle of a damned war. Listen, I desperately need to get in touch with Selim, my assistant. Do you know where he is? Can you help me set up a phone call?'

'Selim's in Egypt himself, at El Qurna. The papyrus is still there.'

'You've got to be kidding! I can't believe it—'

'Believe me, it's true,' Husseini insisted. 'Selim is trying to buy it.'

'And what's he using for money?'

'Don't ask me. That's something you'll have to ask him yourself. If everything has gone according to schedule, he should already have made contact. Try to get him at this number.' Blake jotted it down on the palm of his hand. 'Just before midnight, Egyptian time.'

At that moment one of the other guests came out of his room right across from where Blake was standing, so he stopped talking in order not to be overheard. When the man had disappeared down the stairs, he tried to resume his conversation, but he had been disconnected. He redialled the number but got a busy signal, and continued to get a busy signal every time he tried.

He wrote Selim's number onto a piece of paper and went back to his room. Sarah had got dressed and was going through her backpack.

'Did you get hold of the person you were looking for?' she asked.

'No, but I've got his number here in Egypt. I'll try again later. If you want to use the phone, go ahead. There's no one around just now.'

Sarah continued rummaging through her backpack. 'I've got something better in here, if it still works.'

'But they searched you at the border.'

'That's right ... but not here,' said Sarah, pulling out a package of sanitary napkins.

She opened one and pulled out a tiny bivalved electronic

jewel: on the right half was a cellular telephone and on the left, a computer. She turned it on and the tiny monitor lit up with a green glow.

'Hooray, it works!' exclaimed Sarah, before typing in her access number and holding the phone up to her ear.

'American embassy,' a man's voice said. 'Public Affairs.'

'My name is Forrestall. I'm here in Egypt with another person. We are in great danger and desperately need to reach the embassy. What should we do?'

'Where are you?' answered the voice after a moment's hesitation.

'In a boarding house in Ismailia, number 23, Shara al Idrisi, second floor, second door left.'

'Stay where you are. I'll send someone to pick you up. We'll use some of our Egyptian collaborators, but it may take some time.'

'Please hurry, for the love of God,' said Sarah.

'Just take it easy,' the voice answered reassuringly. 'We'll do everything we can.'

'Well?' asked Blake.

'They said to stay put. They'll send someone here to get us.'

'It's better that way. Listen, I'm going down to the bazaar to buy some Arab clothes. It's best not to attract any attention. I don't think there are many Westerners around here after what's happened. I'll get something to eat, too. I saw someone selling doner kebabs on the corner. Is that all right with you?'

'I hate mutton. If you can find some fish that would be better, but if that's all there is, I'll eat anything. I'm absolutely starved.'

'I'll see what I can find,' answered Blake as he left.

Sarah went back inside and checked her watch. It was nine. Outside the streets were almost completely empty. In the distance you could hear highly agitated voices speaking on loudspeakers. She figured that they were probably preparing for some sort of demonstration in the square and that this might work to their benefit.

267

She tried to imagine how Blake was progressing with his errands, worrying a little that he might have got lost in the bazaar. Naturally, the rescue operation would take a while. The embassy would have to notify agents who perhaps lived outside the city, who would probably have a tough time getting around what with the tangle of military vehicles blocking the streets. No use expecting anyone before midnight, or maybe even later.

As time went by, she began to wonder what had happened to Blake. How much time did someone need to buy a few clothes and a couple of kebabs? She moved the curtains aside a little so she could look down into the street. All she could see was a man selling pistachios and oranges standing on the corner of the half-deserted block.

Ten o'clock arrived and Sarah called her contact again.

'The operation is under way,' the same voice answered, 'but it will take some time. You two just stay put, though. They'll come and get you.'

Eleven o'clock rolled around and by this time Sarah was sure that something terrible must have happened to her companion. Perhaps they had arrested him and taken him to the police station for interrogation. Maybe they had recognized him and made the connection with the disappearance of a soldier and an officer of the Egyptian army in the Sinai desert.

She imagined how they might be interrogating him, torturing him, perhaps, and how he would attempt to resist in order to give her enough time to realize what was going on so she could escape. She felt a lump in her throat, a growing tightness.

She had to make up her mind. Blake could have called the boarding house from any phone booth; therefore, the fact that he hadn't meant he had been obstructed from doing so. She had to get out of there and try to reach the American embassy on her own. Surely that would be where he would go too, if he could still manage to get there.

She still had some money, which she could use to hire a taxi and get to Cairo.

Sarah realized that she had no choice. She wrote a note – 'I can't wait any longer. I'm going to try to get to the place we agreed on by myself. I'll be waiting for you. Be careful, Sarah' – and stuck it to the door. This way, either Blake or the embassy agents, whoever came by, would understand.

She picked up her backpack, hid Blake's in the wardrobe and, before going out, took one last look out at the street, which was dimly illuminated by a single street light. She was just in time to see a car stop and two men get out, Egyptians from their appearance, but wearing European clothes. They'd finally arrived! But Sarah's initial euphoria at seeing the men quickly faded; she was beset by all sorts of doubts and decided she'd prefer to sneak out and reach the American embassy in Cairo on her own. It was too late, though. She could already hear the men coming up the stairs and that was the only way out, unless she went via the window.

While she was weighing her limited options, someone knocked on the door. She tried to be calm, reassuring herself that there was nothing to be worried about; after all, they were the agents sent by the American embassy. As soon as she opened the door, however, and got a good look at her callers' faces, she realized she was in big trouble.

'I'm an officer of the Egyptian Military Police,' one of the men said in halting English. 'The owner of this boarding house told us that you hadn't left any identification at the reception desk. Can you show us your passport, please?'

The two agents couldn't see the note stuck to the back of the door yet, because it was opened towards the wall and, at this point, Sarah was still hoping that it was just a routine hotel check. Holding out her passport, she said: 'My name is Sarah Forrestall. I came to Egypt on a tourist visa and I'm stuck here now due to this silly war . . . It's a real shame. I didn't even have a chance to see Luxor or Abu Simbel, but . . .'

The man looked over her papers and then exchanged a quick knowing glance with his companion.

'Madam,' he said with a grimly stern voice, 'where is your friend?'

Sarah realized she no longer had any way out. 'I don't know,' she said. 'He left over two hours ago and hasn't come back. I have no idea where he is.'

'You will come along with us to the police station. You can tell us everything you know there. We'll take care of him later.'

'But I—'

She tried to say something, but she didn't have a chance. The man took her by the arm and dragged her out of the room, while his companion stayed inside to gather up the things lying on the bed and around the floor, then all three of them walked down the hall. They hadn't gone more than a few steps when they ran into two other people who had just popped up from the landing holding pistols with silencers.

Guessing what was about to happen, Sarah dived for the floor, covering her head with her arms, as the hallway lit up with flashes of fiery orange light and the air was permeated with dense, acrid smoke. There were two dull thuds as the Egyptian policemen collapsed on the floor next to her without so much as a whimper.

She raised her head and saw one of the two men holding his right hand over his wounded left arm, as the other fellow approached her with his gun still smoking. They were both Egyptians.

'Just in the nick of time, it seems,' he said as he walked up to her. 'Sorry about the delay, Miss Forrestall.' Then, half smiling, he added, 'But we ran into a little traffic. Where's your friend?' You could tell by his sense of humour that he was used to being around Americans, and this reassured her.

'I don't know,' answered Sarah. 'He left to buy some things around nine and still hasn't come back. I've waited this long for him, but I don't think he's coming back any more. We can't stay here any longer, though, and besides, your companion is injured—'

'It's just a graze, fortunately,' the other man said. 'I need to have my arm wrapped tightly. A handkerchief should do.'

He got some help in this elementary first-aid operation, then put his overcoat back on and headed down the stairs, followed by Sarah and his companion, who was still holding his pistol at the ready.

An old Arab gentleman who happened to be going up the stairs with the help of a cane murmured under his breath, '*Salaam alekum.*'

'*Alekum salaam,*' responded the man with the pistol.

Sarah couldn't help giving a start, immediately recognizing Blake's voice.

A moment later the same voice was heard again, this time more powerfully from behind: 'Drop your weapons and get back up here. Now.'

There was a pause.

'I said drop your weapons!' Blake repeated emphatically, pointing a pistol at the men.

Sarah looked closely: it was the pistol he'd taken off the Egyptian he'd killed in the Sinai with his scalpel.

The two men dropped their weapons, which Blake scooped up. Then they started obediently back up the stairs, followed by Sarah. They stepped over the bodies of the two policemen still lying on the floor in a widening puddle of blood, drenching the carpet.

'Inside!' said Blake, pointing to the open door of the room. He pulled off the keffiyeh that almost completely covered his face. 'I noticed some suspicious movement around the boarding house,' he said to Sarah. 'So I had to hide. That's why I wasn't able to come back up.'

'But why are you holding them prisoner?' said Sarah in disbelief. 'They came here to rescue us. One of them was wounded in the fight with the two Egyptian policemen, the ones you saw out in the hall.'

'Mr Blake,' the other man began, 'please, be sensible . . . We don't have any time to waste. We have to get out of here. Don't you understand?'

'How do you know my name?' asked Blake, still pointing the gun at them.

'Miss Forrestall told us—'

'That's not true! The young lady only said that there was another person here with her. How do you know my name?'

'Will, please,' Sarah implored.

'Sarah, don't interfere. I know what I'm doing. We can't trust anyone. The only place my name was listed was in the Warren Mining Corporation's files. How did it end up at the American embassy? And how did it wind up on the documents those two guys who pulled us off the bus had? Tie them up for now. Get some cord from the curtains and tie them up.'

Sarah did as he said and, once the two men had been immobilized, Blake went through their pockets. One of them had a mobile phone. He turned it on.

'What number do you report in on?'

The man just shook his head. 'You're nuts. The police could be here any time now.'

Blake raised the muzzle of his pistol. 'I want that number!'

Biting down on his lip, the man dialled the number with some difficulty and the phone began to ring.

'As soon as they answer, say that you have had a shoot-out with the Egyptian police and that the two of us are dead. Have you got that? Dead. And no funny business, if you don't want to end up like those two out in the hall.'

A voice answered and Blake put his ear up to the receiver so he could hear too. 'Office "M", state your business.'

'This is Yussuf. Something's gone wrong. The Egyptian police were waiting for us and there was a shoot-out. Our friends were caught in the middle of it and both of them were killed. Abdul was wounded, but it's nothing serious.'

There was silence at the other end.

'Did you understand what I just told you?' the man queried.

'I understood, Yussuf. Get out of there immediately. I'll send an ambulance to the place we agreed upon for the handover.'

Blake folded the phone back up.

'What are you going to do with us?' the man named Yussuf asked.

'We'll send someone to get you,' said Blake. Then he signalled Sarah to gather up their things and they left the room, locking the door behind them.

'Put this on,' he said to her, tossing her a dark jellaba. 'We've got to get away from here as soon as possible.'

They went down the stairs and walked past the elderly owner, who was standing behind the front desk, bewildered and alarmed by the mysterious goings-on.

'Call the police right away,' Blake told him in Arabic. 'There are dead and wounded people upstairs.'

He slipped out into the street, dragging behind him Sarah, who was wrapped in the jellaba, her head and face covered by a veil.

'What in hell possessed you—' she tried to ask him.

'Not yet. I'll explain everything later. Right now we've got to get out of here and fast. We only have a few minutes.'

Blake went down a narrow, dark side street, following it to the end, stopping at every intersection to make sure there were no unpleasant surprises waiting for them. There were still a fair amount of people in the bazaar area, sellers and porters for the most part, carrying in goods for the next day. Trade obviously continued, despite the holy war. Every once in a while, the still atmosphere was interrupted by the sound of helicopters or the roar of jets heading towards the battle front. Blake came to an abrupt halt beneath the sooty arch of an old blacksmith's forge and ducked into the shadows, pulling Sarah in behind him.

'What now?' the girl asked.

'Pick a god and start praying,' answered Blake, checking his watch. 'In just five minutes we'll know if he or she was listening or not.'

They stood in frozen silence, keeping their ears peeled for any sound. Five minutes went by, stretching into ten, then fifteen long minutes of agonizing tension. Discouraged, Blake sank to the ground, resting his head on his knees.

Sarah laid into him. 'Would you please explain to me what we're doing here? Why didn't we just go with those two men? By this time we could have been happily on our way to the American embassy, damn it!'

'By this time we could also have been dead for all I know. I got suspicious when those Egyptian soldiers arrested us on the bus and we found those papers on them. You felt just as uneasy, if I'm not mistaken. Then this guy pops up, and he knows my name as well. Where did he get that little piece of information?'

Sarah shook her head. 'I don't know. I'm not sure about anything any more . . . It could have even been me . . .'

She didn't have time to finish her sentence. An old black Peugeot 404 appeared from around a corner and pulled up right in front of them.

'Maybe this is him,' said Blake. 'I should have known that Egyptians are rarely on time. Quick, get in.'

He had Sarah sit in the back, while he got in the front, next to the driver: a young Nubian with dark skin who greeted him with a beautiful smile full of gleaming white teeth.

'Salaam alekum, el sidi.'

'Alekum salaam,' rejoined Blake. 'You must be Khaled.'

'That's right, I'm Khaled, el sidi. Selim told me I'd find you here and he told me to bring you back to his house in Cairo as quickly as possible. He will join you tomorrow from Luxor. We'll have to drive all night, because we're taking a very indirect route, sticking to the back roads so we won't run into any soldiers or policemen. There's some food for you in the plastic bag. You must be famished.'

'You said it,' answered Blake. 'It's been days since we've had a decent meal.'

He took out some Arab bread stuffed with vegetables and

minced lamb and handed it back to Sarah, who bit into it with relief and delight.

Khaled drove slowly and very carefully, taking secondary roads where there was practically no traffic.

'I'll be glad to keep you company as you drive,' said Blake, 'but my wife is dead tired and needs to sleep.'

He reached back to where Sarah was sitting and took her hand, holding it for a long time. He leaned back then against his seat, listening to the chugging of the old engine and watching the road as it was slowly devoured by the headlights.

Khaled almost immediately got off the tarmacked highway, taking a dusty dirt road full of bumps and holes, heading into the fertile delta plain. Now and then they would pass through a sleeping village with mud-brick houses topped by roofs made from bullrushes, just like in the days of the Exodus. Blake could smell manure and mud, the same smell that permeated the villages of Upper and Lower Egypt, Mesopotamia and the valley of the Indus. The scent of places forgotten by history.

The biblical city of Ramses, whence the great migration originated, couldn't be far away: they were crossing the land of Goshen.

At midnight, Khaled turned on the car's radio to listen to the news and Blake could hear the triumphant tone of the speaker as he described how Israel was surrounded on every side; a country whose fate was already sealed! Next they interviewed a politician who declared that after the Arab victory, the few surviving Jews who could prove they were born in Palestine would be allowed to remain by becoming Palestinian citizens and swearing loyalty to the new flag.

Blake fiddled with the dial in search of a European or Israeli station, but there was too much static, making listening impossible.

Around one o'clock they stopped along the bank of one of the Nile's many distributaries there in the delta and Khaled got out to urinate; Blake followed suit. The nearly full moon was lolling just above the horizon, leaving most of the heavenly vault to the teeming array of twinkling stars. A gentle gust of wind nudged the tufted manes of the papyrus plants, gleaming silvery in the pale moonlight, their shaggy crowns reflecting like jellyfish tentacles on the placid surface of the water.

The spell was broken by the dull thud of artillery against the eastern horizon, pulsating with terrible rhythmic flashes. A deafening roar pierced the profound peace of the night sky as four jet fighters flourishing the Star of David swooped low over the canebrakes, extruding long trails of ghostly white exhaust fumes: Israel was reacting angrily to the provocation. Blake couldn't help but recall the implacable law that had guided this long-memoried people for thirty centuries in dealing with its enemies: an eye for an eye.

Khaled dropped the hem of his jellaba, which he had raised to his belt, letting it float back to the toe of his shoe. After taking a quick look inside the parked car to make sure that Sarah was asleep, he took a letter out of his pocket and handed it to Blake.

'Selim wants you to read this alone,' he said. 'Stay out here. I'll turn on the side lights.'

Blake crouched down on his heels in front of the car and with each line he read he felt the blood boiling up in his veins as he broke out in a sweat. When he had finished, he fell forward onto his knees, covering his face with his hands.

He felt Khaled's hand on his shoulder. 'Let's go,' he said. 'We've still got a long road ahead of us.'

Khaled had him get into the car and then sat back down behind the wheel, ready to continue their journey, unruffled. The remotest outskirts of Cairo began to appear against the pearly grey sky around five in the morning, just in time to hear the eerie chant of the muezzin echoing stentoriously through the deserted city from the slender spires of the minarets, more like a call to arms than to prayer.

Khaled stuck to the more obscure winding streets of the sprawling metropolis's suburbs. After what seemed to be hours of pointless, labyrinthine meandering, they stopped at the end of a dusty little street lined with shabby buildings made from reinforced concrete and bricks without any stucco, unruly metal bars sticking out here and there menacingly. The pavement was a disaster, more rubble than pathway.

Electric wires were strung along the unfinished walls like bizarre garlands and some of the pylons were still lying in the middle of the street, eloquent testaments to the totally out-of-control expansion and impossible urban planning situation of the largest city on the African continent.

Khaled pulled a big bundle of keys out of his pocket and opened the main door to the building, escorting his companions to the second floor, where he opened a door off the landing and showed them into a modest, rather barren apartment, which was nevertheless surprisingly clean and tidy, free of the usual gaudy frills that tend to clutter Egyptian homes. There was a telephone, a little television and even a portable typewriter on a desk.

Blake checked all the windows, one by one, to assess how the building was situated. Upon opening the door leading to the little balcony at the back of the apartment, he was surprised to see the imposing silhouettes of Giza towering in the distance: the tip of the enormous pyramid and the head of the Sphinx rose majestically out of the squalid grey sea of wretched hovels.

A shiver went up his spine. The monuments which loomed so suddenly before him reminded him of the same shapes, fashioned by nature, on the desolate landscape of Ras Udash. The circle had closed and he, William Blake, was the fragile point of union in this magical, ill-omened ring.

Khaled heated up a little milk and made Turkish coffee for his guests, but Blake drank only a cup of milk.

'If you'd like to rest, there's a bed in there,' said Khaled. 'I'll wait up until it's time to get Selim.'

'I rested in the car,' said Sarah. 'I'll stay up with Khaled. Why don't you get some sleep?'

Blake would have liked to stay awake as well, but decided to surrender to the incredible drowsiness that had hit him after drinking the warm milk. He was out like a light as soon as he hit the mattress.

He was awakened much later by a ringing sound in the dark, deserted apartment.

GAD AVNER leaned over the stainless-steel railing and let out a sigh as he looked at the enormous illuminated topographic model at the centre of the underground bunker. A giant virtual screen displayed the movements of the armed forces deployed in the field like some harmless video game. The realistic three-dimensional design of both the territory depicted and the various moving objects gave the observer the impression of being right in the middle of the action.

You could see the towns and villages where prophets had once preached: the heights of Gelboe, where Saul and Jonathan had fallen in battle, Lake Genezareth and the River Jordan, where Jesus and John the Baptist had once spoken, and, further off, the inviolable fortress of Masada, surrounded by the ruins of ancient Roman siege ramps and traces of military fortifications and bulwarks, a monument to that horrible human sacrifice offered in the name of freedom.

You could also see the Dead Sea encased by its shimmering salty shoreline, burial ground of Sodom and Gomorrah, and further out, at the edge of the desert of the Exodus, Beersheba, the dome of Sheol and the cavern of Armageddon.

At the very centre, between the waves of the Mediterranean and the Judaean desert, was Jerusalem itself on its rock, with its golden dome, the Old City wall and towers.

A voice interrupted his reverie. 'Quite a toy, isn't it?'

Avner found himself face to face with the imposing figure and unusually grim countenance of General Yehudai.

'Look,' he continued, 'it's obvious that the enemy's efforts are directed at surrounding Jerusalem, as if they were trying to lay siege to it by cutting off every point of access.'

A young officer sat at the controls of an enormous computer, simulating, at the behest of his commander, the movements of armoured divisions and low-flying fighter bombers. The computer was able to elaborate any number of attack and defence scenarios for any area involved in a particular battle.

This was nothing like the Six Day War. The failure to make a pre-emptive strike on the enemies' air forces while they were still on the ground had resulted in an almost even match between the opposing forces, degenerating – with every hour and day that passed – into a dangerous stalemate, with destructive artillery battles and constant bombardment by rockets from mobile launchers.

The continuing infiltration of commando squads into Israeli territory was demoralizing the civilian population and playing real havoc with the country's communications system. The necessity of carrying out air attacks on all fronts was putting superhuman demands on the pilots due to their numerical inferiority and the lack of replacement personnel.

'We're in trouble,' said Yehudai, 'especially now that Egypt has joined the conflict. And things could get worse. We absolutely must deliver a devastating blow to our enemies now, before they are joined by new allies. If things start looking even vaguely hopeful for them, they'll be lining up to jump on the victory wagon.'

'You're right about that,' said Avner. 'So far, Iran is providing only indirect support, quite satisfied with its conquests in Saudi Arabia, where it wants control over the holy places of Islam, but more radical, extremist forces could gain the upper hand at any time and press for direct intervention, especially if the threat that has kept the Americans and Europeans out of the conflict continues to function. Let's not forget that the Iranians have sworn to take Jerusalem. Plus I've been getting reports that even the Islamic republics of the former Soviet Union are showing signs of unrest.'

He was silent for a while, as if lost in some disturbing thoughts and then went on to say, 'What chance is there that we'll have to resort to nuclear arms?'

'It's our last card,' said Yehudai, letting his eyes fall on Beersheba, 'but it could become inevitable. Here's how it stands. We are trying to counterattack wherever the enemy has penetrated deep into our territory in the direction of the capital. By tomorrow, we should know if this counteroffensive has worked or not.

'If we don't manage to push them back, it means that the situation could worsen drastically in the following twenty-four hours, turning everything in their favour, pushing us to the point of no return. At which time we would have no other choice.'

Avner lowered his head. 'Unfortunately, there's no news from Washington. The situation in the US is still the same. They can't locate the commando squadrons, they don't know where the bombs are, and there's no indication that anything's going to change much for the better in the next forty-eight hours.

'We have to rely on our own resources. The only person on our side seems to be the Pope, who has called for a cease-fire, but I don't see much hope in that particular solution.'

Just then, the pneumatically sealed door of the bunker opened and Ferrario came in, visibly excited. 'Gentlemen,' he announced, 'the satellite listening equipment has just located an enemy communications centre within our national borders. According to the American experts, it could be the main nerve centre coordinating the entire Operation Nebuchadnezzar. If we hook our main computer up with the satellite, the location will be shown on our virtual war theatre. Watch!'

They went up to the officer at the control panel and gave him the sequence of commands he needed to tune into the geostationary military satellite and, in less than a minute, there it was: a little blue light began blinking on the three-dimensional map.

'Why, it's between here and Bethlehem!' Yehudai exclaimed, dumbfounded. 'Practically right under our noses.'

'Between here and Bethlehem,' mumbled Avner, repeating the geographical coordinates, as if scrolling down a series of mental files. 'There's only one son of a bitch with enough balls and know-how to locate a hostile communications centre right in the middle of Israel . . . Abu Ahmid!'

'That's just not possible,' Yehudai snorted.

'I beg to disagree,' replied Avner. Then, turning to Ferrario, 'Where's Allon?'

Ferrario looked at his watch. 'He should still be in the tunnel.'

'Arrange for a meeting as soon as you can.'

'Who's Allon?' Yehudai asked.

'An archaeologist,' replied Avner, turning round and heading out behind his assistant. 'Someone who knows everything there is to know about Nebuchadnezzar.'

14

THE DOOR OPENED with a slight squeak and a dark shape stood in the doorway: a tall man carrying a briefcase.

'Selim? It's me,' he said. 'I just got here.'

'Why ask for the assistant when the professor's in his office, Olsen?' asked a voice from the darkness.

'Who is that? Who's in there?' asked the man, retreating.

'Don't you remember your old friend?' continued the voice from the dark room.

'My God. William Blake. Is that you, Will? Oh, Christ, you really surprised me, Will. What are you doing here, in the dark? Come on. Stop kidding around. Where are you?'

A light bulb came on unexpectedly and Bob Olsen found Blake right in front of him. He was sitting on a torn armchair with his hands on the armrests and a gun lying on the table next to him.

'Here I am, Bob. What are you doing in Egypt at such a bad time? Why here, in such an out-of-the-way place?'

'Will, I was in Luxor, and the reason that I came here is because Selim promised to help me contact the US ambassador. You know, Will, I've managed to do a lot, just like I said I would. I've been looking for witnesses, for someone to testify on your behalf. I was even trying to clear things up with the Egyptian authorities and I think I was getting through to them. I promised you that I would have them reopen your case at the department, and I'll convince them, believe me. If we can get out of this inferno, I swear you'll get your job back. Everyone will just have to recognize that they were wrong.'

'Bob, I can't get over how much you've done to help this unfortunate friend of yours.'

Olsen was trying not to look at the gun, as if to demonstrate that it was not there for him, but it glittered insistently in that dim light. He looked around with a bewildered expression and the surreal situation began to erode his show of calm.

'What do you mean by that? Why the sarcasm, Will? Listen, I don't know what you've been told, but I swear—'

'What I mean is that you betrayed my trust and my friendship in every way you could. You're even screwing my wife, Bob. How long has it been going on?'

'Oh, come on! You don't believe that slanderous gossip. They're only trying to—'

'How long, Bob?' repeated Blake.

Olsen backed away. 'Will, I . . .' A nervous tic caused his right eyelid to twitch convulsively as sweat trickled down his forehead.

'That's why you worked so hard to get me the financing. So you could have the run of the place while I was in Egypt.'

'No, you're wrong. I was sincere, I—'

'Oh, that I can believe. You knew I was on the right track. In fact, you had a couple of your friends from the Institute in Cairo keeping an eye on me, and when you found out I'd made an appointment to see the papyrus, you sent the Egyptian police after me. So I would be out of the game and you could get your hands on it yourself. But something went wrong, didn't it? They didn't have the papyrus with them. In the meantime, it was all over for me, wasn't it? Kicked out of the house, out of the Institute, out of your fucking way, right? The papyrus would pop up sooner or later, you thought, just a little patience and you could take the credit for the discovery. Just think. An Egyptian version of the biblical Exodus, the only non-Hebrew source for the most important event in the history of the East and the West. Not bad.

'You would have become the director of the Oriental Institute, the successor of James Henry Breasted. Glory, popularity, lucrative editorial contracts . . . and Judy's bed too.'

Olsen was stuttering. His mouth was dry and he kept licking his lips. 'Will, believe me, it's all a bunch of lies. Whoever told you those things is trying to set us against each other for some obscure reason of his own. Think about it, I've always been your friend—'

'Really? Fine, there's nothing I'd like better than to believe you. Right now, though, let me finish what I have to say. We have time; nobody knows we're here. Selim's on my side, obviously. You see, someone had his friend killed. Ali Mahmoudi, the man who had the Breasted papyrus. They murdered him before he could deliver it to Selim and then sent the police in. Doesn't that story sound familiar at all, Bob? But the problem is that Ali didn't die right away.

'Funny, isn't it? A man with three bullets in him. But see, Bob, these Egyptian peasants are from sturdy stock. They're descended from the race of the Pharaohs.

'So poor Ali, half dead from loss of blood, drags himself to the place where he'd agreed to meet Selim and, before he dies, tells his friend who shot him. A bald man with a red moustache. A man carrying a briefcase with silver buckles. Isn't that the one, Bob? Isn't that the briefcase you have in your hand?'

'This is totally, absolutely crazy,' mumbled Olsen. 'You cannot seriously believe that—'

'Fine, I won't believe it. If you show me what's inside that briefcase.'

Olsen grasped it to his chest. 'Will, I can't do that. This briefcase contains reserved, confidential documents that I'm not authorized—'

Blake put his right hand on the gun. 'Open that briefcase, Bob.'

At that moment, an explosion rocked all the windows and chandeliers, and the room was illuminated for an instant by the stroboscopic reflection of the detonation, immediately followed by the roar of jet engines and the cadenced thunder of anti-aircraft guns. Israel still had the force to strike at the heart of Egypt. Neither of the two men blinked an eye.

Olsen lowered his head. 'Whatever you say, Will, but you are making a big mistake. There are documents in here that—'

The two silver buckles opened one by one with a metallic click and Olsen's hand plunged into the briefcase to pull out a gun, but before he could raise it to aim, Blake shot him. Once, through the heart.

There was the clatter of footsteps outside on the stairs, and Sarah and Selim appeared at the door.

'Oh, Christ!' gasped Sarah, practically stumbling over Olsen's body stretched across the threshold. 'Don't tell me this is—'

Selim shot Blake a knowing look. 'Olsen. Sorry I didn't get here in time. I tried to warn you what he was up to in my letter.'

'He had a gun, as you can see. And he tried to use it. I didn't have a choice.'

Sarah looked at him, aghast.

'We have to get him out of here,' said Selim. 'The noise of the bombing and the anti-aircraft fire may have covered the sound of the shot, but we can't keep him in here.'

Blake seemed not to hear him. He knelt on the ground as the flares from more explosions outside cast wild shadows on the walls of the room, and opened Olsen's briefcase, feeling around inside with his hand. He pulled out a metallic box, set it down on the table next to the armchair, under the lamp, and opened it. Another round of explosions, even closer this time, shook the entire building and the blinding flashes bounced off the walls and the ceiling. Blake's pupils reflected something else: ancient symbols, the enigmatic ideograms he had sought for so long.

'Oh, my God,' he breathed. 'My God. The Breasted papyrus!'

And he would have sat there in total absorption, unaware of anything around him, deciphering those words. Unravelling that centuries-old message which had finally emerged from the darkness. At that moment he seemed even to have forgotten that he had just killed a man.

Sarah shook him. 'Will, we have to get rid of the corpse.'

'At the end of the hallway there's still some scaffolding that was erected by the construction company with a service elevator they were using to send up materials. We can use that,' Selim said. 'But I'll need your help.'

He took his car keys from his pocket and handed them to Sarah. 'Miss Forrestall, kindly go down and take Khaled's Peugeot, which is parked out in front, drive it around the block and stop in front of the scaffolding. We'll be down in a minute with Professor Olsen's corpse.'

Sarah nodded, rather bewildered by the young man's macabre formality, and went down the stairs in the dark, while Selim and Blake, after checking the hall, dragged Olsen's body, which they had wrapped in a blanket, over to the window at the end of the hall. Selim opened the window, climbed out and into the service elevator. He began to pull Olsen's body in, helped by Blake, who was busy pushing him out.

When they had loaded the corpse, Selim cut the connections on the elevator's control board so he could hot-wire them and power up the motor. The platform began moving with a slight buzz; Selim gave Blake a thumbs-up gesture and disappeared beneath the sill with the body.

Blake tiptoed down the stairs, exited onto the road and walked around the block to the base of the scaffolding. All the lights in the neighbourhood, and as far as the eye could see, were out. A curfew was obviously in effect.

Sarah had already opened the hatchback on the Peugeot and Selim was dragging the body out of the service elevator. It took all three of them to lift the heavy burden and get it into the boot.

'I'll stop by Khaled's and get him to help me dump him into the Nile. You two wait for me at home and don't move for any reason.'

'Selim, thank you,' said Blake. 'I'll never forget this.'

'Everything's OK, Professor Blake. Don't answer the phone before the tenth ring,' added Selim, and drove off.

Sarah and Blake went back up to the apartment and locked the door behind them.

'We'd better not turn on the light,' said Sarah. 'The curtains don't close well and the light will filter through. We don't want it to look like anyone's in here. You can work on your papyrus when we get back.'

Blake embraced her in the dark and they stayed in each other's arms, listening to the sounds of war in the sky above the city. Eventually Sarah broke the silence.

'How can we get out of this country?'

'I don't know. We'll have to rely on Selim. He's been great so far.'

Husseini suddenly came to mind. He had high-ranking friends in Egypt. Maybe he could help them.

'Sarah, your mobile phone. There's a person I trust who may be able to save us. Let me give him a try.'

Sarah passed the phone and lit it up with a tiny torch so he could dial the number. Husseini's phone began ringing but no one answered and the answering machine wasn't even on. Strange. He tried again and again, but without success.

Blake shut the phone, felt around in the dark for a chair and sat down, trying to organize his thoughts. He still had the phone in his hand and he had an idea.

'Sarah, this thing is also a computer, isn't it?'

'Yes,' said Sarah. 'And it's much more powerful than you'd think.'

'Perfect, then I can send him an email. He checks them every day.'

He opened the device and turned on the tiny computer, connecting it to the Internet. Sarah gave him her password and he typed in Husseini's address.

Blake watched the little fluorescent screen incredulously, imagining the signal bouncing off an artificial satellite and going via a switchboard on the other side of the Atlantic, through the phone and into the computer of Professor Omar al Husseini at 5,500 Ellis Avenue, Chicago, Illinois.

'This thing is incredible,' he exclaimed.

'Now you can write in your message,' instructed Sarah. 'But first type in ZQ to get the screen.'

Blake typed in the two letters, but before he could begin to write, another window appeared in place of the message window.

'Christ, what did I do?' he said.

Sarah came closer. 'I don't know. Let me see. You probably pressed the wrong keys and sent off a remote access code without meaning to. See? You're in your friend's file manager.'

'Well,' said Blake, 'get me out. I don't want to nose around in his files.'

'It's easy,' said Sarah. 'Just press "Alt" and "Tab" and that will get you out, then repeat the procedure for the email window.'

'Shine the light on it, will you?' said Blake. 'I don't want to get it wrong again.'

As Sarah tried to illuminate the tiny keypad, Blake's attention was drawn to one of the files in Egyptian hieroglyphics.

'What is that?' asked Sarah.

'It's our secret communication system. I sent and received messages under Maddox's nose at Ras Udash by telling him that I had to consult a colleague in Chicago about certain hieroglyphic symbols.'

'Interesting. Is that how you found out where you were?'

'Right. Want to see?'

'Why not? Khaled and Selim won't be back for a couple of hours at least.'

'OK. First we have to load the program for reading hieroglyphics. I can do that directly from Husseini's computer.'

He moved the cursor down the list and stopped on the program. He loaded it onto the tiny device and went back to the file name he had noticed at first, made up of five ideograms.

'What does that mean?' asked Sarah.

'Nothing, in this sequence. Maybe there's a password. Forget it. Let's go back to the email.'

'Wait,' said Sarah. 'Let me play with it a minute.'

She passed the torch to Blake and took the keypad. She highlighted each one of the symbols with the mouse in turn, then pressed a series of keys, and the ideograms began to rotate in sequence, stopping at each possible new composition for a couple of seconds.

'Can you see any meaning in any of this?' she asked Blake.

He shook his head.

'No problem. The computer will continue to look for alternative combinations. It's very fast.'

'Listen, Sarah, I don't think we have the right to—' He didn't finish his phrase. 'Stop right there,' he said suddenly.

Sarah hit a key and froze the sequence of ideograms as they appeared a second before.

'This means something?'

'Yes,' said Blake grimly.

'Well, what does it mean?'

'Armageddon.'

'Armageddon?' repeated Sarah.

'The battle of the last day: four kings of the Orient against Israel. The battle that will end with an apocalyptic catastrophe. It's what's happening now. Think about it. Israel is being threatened by her ancient enemies: by the peoples of the Nile, the Tigris and the Euphrates.'

'We have to open that file,' said Sarah. 'There's something I don't like about this.'

'Come on. That has to be impossible. The password must be in hieroglyphics, or in Arabic.'

He tried to open the file. 'See? It won't open. It wants a password.'

But Sarah was in no mood to give up. 'No, wait. It's not as hard as it seems. Usually the password is something really obvious, like his phone number.'

Blake gave it to her, unconvinced.

'Or his date of birth. Do you know what it is?'

'No, I don't. Leave it alone, Sarah. Come on. Husseini is a good guy, a friend, you know, and I don't want—'

'Or his wife's name. Has he got a wife?'

'He has a girlfriend. Sally, I think her name is.'

'Sally, huh? Nope, doesn't work. Try it in Arabic. You know Arabic. I've got a program.'

Blake surrendered and tried to cooperate. 'Sally in Arabic. Come on, Sarah. Anyway, no. See, it doesn't work.'

'A son, a daughter . . .'

'No, he doesn't have children.'

Sarah shrugged. 'OK, you win. It's not nice to stick your nose in other people's business, right? But basically, that's what I do for a living—'

'Hold on,' Blake interrupted her. The photograph of a little boy on the table in Husseini's apartment flashed through his mind. The dedication, in Arabic: *In memory of Said. Dad.*

'He has a son. Or did.'

He typed 'Said' in Arabic. And the file opened.

'Oh, Christ!' exclaimed Sarah. 'What the hell is this?'

Blake looked closer and couldn't see anything more than a cluster of dense ASCII characters.

'Doesn't look like anything to me,' said Blake. 'Why are you so alarmed?'

'Because this program is very complex and difficult to use, and it's also very rare. As far as I know, just a few intelligence services use it. What kind of people does your friend hang out with anyway?'

'No, no, you've got to be wrong . . . He's just a professor of Coptic studies. I've known him for years. He's the quietest, most habit-bound person you can imagine. I don't know anything about computer systems, but I'll bet you anything it's something harmless. A spell check for Aramaic or something.'

'Unfortunately, I'd say not. Damn this tiny screen. If I could just print it out ... Wait, let's see if I can feed it through my decoder.' She continued to press keys frenetically and the tips of her nails sounded strange, like the ticking of a clock. As the decoder succeeded in interpreting the cluster of computer symbols on the screen, Sarah's expression became more and more apprehensive.

'Can you figure it out?' asked Blake again.

'It's an automatic system of sorts, divided into three sectors. The cluster system that you see here automatically controls the rotation of three objects, or people, on different objectives, like targets, I'd say.'

'Can you identify them?'

'I have to try to enlarge a single sector and then identify the topographic support. Let me give it a try. OK, baby, here we go ... Good. Come on, keep it up ... OK, yes, it's just as I thought. Here's our topographic support and here's one of the objectives. All right, let's take a look at the other one now ... Perfect, OK, and now the third ... Oh, Christ, what the hell—'

'Do you mind letting me in on this?' insisted Blake.

'Listen,' said Sarah. 'If I'm not mistaken, the system controls the continuous rotation, once every twenty-four hours, of three objects that are identified with this word ... What is it, Arabic?'

'Yes,' said Blake, putting on his glasses and peering at the screen. 'It's Arabic and it means "donkey". Actually, the full expression is "the three donkeys of Samarkand". Lord only knows what that might mean.'

'Donkeys? You're the expert. Anyway, these three "donkeys" are trained on a different objective every twenty-four hours, in rotation. The system includes six rotations, four of which have already been completed,' she explained, pointing to a tangle of symbols in a corner of the screen. 'At the sixth rotation, another program is activated. The final program is another automatic system, like a computer virus this time, that culminates in an irreversible consequence. That might be the destruction of the computer memory, or the loss of the files, or even something else.'

'Like what?' asked Blake.

'What was the name of the file?'

Blake suddenly remembered.

'Armageddon.'

'The battle of the last day, right? Doesn't that bring anything to mind?'

'Oh, my God. That's why our government, and our allies, haven't acted in defence of Israel,' said Blake in shock. 'The country is being threatened by some kind of catastrophic time bomb, and this is it.'

'You know, I think you may be on to something,' said Sarah. 'Say that those "donkeys" are tanks of nerve gas, or deadly bacteria, or tactical nuclear bombs. At the sixth order of rotation, they will be aimed at their final targets and the program will be ready to go. Triggered. And boom.

'Will, we've got to warn the embassy. Do you think they'd believe us? Or just send over another couple of henchmen to get rid of us?'

'Improbable,' said Blake. 'They don't know where we are and would have no way of locating us. They'll have to listen. Close that file and call the embassy. Immediately.'

'All right,' said Sarah. 'I just hope they will listen to us. You know, I'm not completely sure about this. I might have analysed the program for a video game.'

'Maybe,' replied Blake. 'But a false alarm is better than no alarm. It can't cost them anything to check. If the worst comes to the worst, I'll explain to Husseini that it was my fault. Call them.'

Sarah closed the file, disconnected from the Internet and turned off the computer. Then she dialled the number for the embassy that she had already called.

'It's busy,' she said.

'That's funny. It's ten o'clock at night. Try it again.'

'I'll put it on automatic. It'll keep trying until the line is free.'

Blake switched off the torch and they listened in silence as the little mobile phone tried the number again every two minutes, and every two minutes got a busy signal.

'This is impossible,' said Blake after a while. 'It's been half an hour. All the lines can't be busy.'

'Well, there is an emergency going on. Lots of people are probably calling for help.'

'Even on the reserve line that you've been dialling? Yesterday they answered you, didn't they? What if the line is completely out? Or maybe the embassy has been evacuated.'

Sarah grimaced in the dark.

'Listen, call someone in the States. You've worked for the government, haven't you? You must know someone important who can get the ball rolling. Christ, we can't just sit here waiting until the damn telephone line is free.'

'I've never had direct contact with anyone in the US administration. I always went through Maddox. But he's dead, along with everyone else.'

'Telephone anyone!' said Blake. 'A police station, the FBI. The Salvation Army! They'll have to listen to us.'

'It won't be easy to explain what we're talking about, and even if they listened to us, how could they possibly figure out how to block the program or identify the three rotating terminals?'

'All they have to do is pull the plug on Husseini's computer.'

'I doubt it. There's got to be a reserve circuit. It's impossible that such a wide-scale operation is exclusively dependent on a personal computer sitting on the desk of a professor in Chicago. Unplugging the computer could be catastrophic. What's more, first they have to find it, and there's no saying it's just sitting on his desk anyway.'

'They'll arrest Husseini and make him talk,' insisted Blake, feeling a bit ashamed and still unwilling to implicate his friend in this affair.

'Talk about what? Is he some kind of computer whiz?'

'Well, as far as I know he's good at deciphering ancient texts, but he probably doesn't know a thing about programs.'

'See? I wouldn't be surprised if the whole thing were planted in his computer somehow without him knowing.'

'You may be right,' admitted Blake. 'But there's no way we can get through to him. He's not answering the phone. He may not even be still living in that apartment.'

The phone started to beep repeatedly and Sarah shook her head. 'What's more, the battery is out and we've got no power. No way to recharge.'

'Let's use Selim's phone,' suggested Blake.

Just then they heard footsteps on the stairs, followed by Selim's voice. 'Professor Blake, Miss Forrestall, it's me. Open the door.'

Blake switched the tiny torch back on, but its batteries were nearly flat as well, and the faint glow was of no help. He felt his way across the room, stumbling and swearing under his breath.

Selim entered, holding a torch. 'We have to get out of here,' he said. 'They're rounding up foreigners everywhere, especially Europeans and Americans. People are being searched on the street. The radio is continuously exhorting all citizens to report any suspicious persons or movements. And that's not all.'

'Not all?' asked Blake.

'Your mug shots are up everywhere. We have to leave Cairo while it's still dark.'

They took their backpacks and Olsen's briefcase and got into Khaled's Peugeot, which was parked out on the street. He took off in the direction of the desert.

'Where are you thinking of taking us?' asked Blake.

'I have friends in a Bedouin tribe that moves between Ismailia

PHARAOH

and the Gaza Strip. They'll take care of you until things calm down.'

'Until things calm down? Are you kidding, Selim? We have got to get out of Egypt and find an airport. We're running out of time. We may have only forty-eight hours until—'

'Until what, Professor Blake?'

'Nothing, Selim . . . It's hard to explain. But it's an emergency.'

'Professor Blake, you're asking for a miracle. There's no airport you could get to within that amount of time.'

'Oh, yes, there is!' said Sarah suddenly, snapping her fingers.

Blake turned towards her in surprise. 'What are you talking about, Sarah?'

'The Falcon! The Falcon is still in the hangar, inside the mountain five miles from Ras Udash. And I can fly it to the US.'

Blake shook his head. 'It's still impossible. How can we cross a war zone and get to Ras Udash, with this car, at night?'

Sarah had no answer and they sat for at least half an hour in gloomy silence. They were now surrounded by the steppe-like landscape that preceded the desert. Wide, flat boulders, their surfaces rounded by the wind, emerged here and there, surrounded by sparse bushes and dried grasses, looking like the bald heads of old giants under the wavering light of the moon.

Khaled was now driving very slowly over a dirt road, navigating by the light of the moon and trying not to raise any dust. Selim began talking with him in a low voice, using the El Qurna dialect so Blake couldn't make out a word of what they were saying.

'Maybe I know what we can do,' said Selim more loudly.

'Really?'

'Khaled knows a Bedouin tribe that lives near the border. They're used to sneaking across to rob the old vehicles that the Israelis leave on their shooting ranges so the American fighter planes can use them as targets. They take them to pieces to sell the spare parts, or sometimes they get them running again. They can take you to Ras Udash, at night, in the dark. It doesn't matter to them as long as they're well paid. And we've got the money.'

'Well, then, let's get moving, Selim,' said Blake, putting his hand on the other's shoulder. 'In the name of Allah, let's get moving!'

Khaled speeded up until they turned off onto a secondary road that led into the Sinai peninsula and drove fast for at least four hours. Suddenly, quite unexpectedly, the voice of war began to make itself heard. First a suffocated thundering that pounded the ground, resounding dully, then long, shrill whistles followed by deafening explosions, closer and closer, erupting into apocalyptic flames on the horizon. Flashes of blinding light whitened the sky and set fire to the earth.

A group of fighter bombers burst out of the blanket of clouds advancing from the south in a nosedive, sweeping the ground with furious volleys. Other planes shot up towards them, as if springing from the bowels of the earth, instantly engaging the others in fierce combat. The sky was scored by a multitude of tracers in every imaginable colour, rent by the angry screaming of the engines that urged the fighters past the sound barrier in a crazed tangle of impossible acrobatics.

One of the planes plunged to the ground: a globe of vermilion light and a roar that made the earth tremble. Another, hit by enemy fire, spiralled off, vomiting a long trail of black smoke, to crash in the distance like a brief flash of summer lightning. A third released a small white umbrella into the air which swung down through the liquid light of dawn like a jellyfish in a transparent sea before being blown apart by an explosion, dismembered into a cascade of incandescent pieces.

Selim pointed north. 'Ras Udash is that way,' he said. 'In a few minutes we'll be at El Mura, where we'll meet our friends. Don't worry about paying them. I've got some cash with me, from the money I brought to buy the papyrus . . . which ended up not costing anything,' he added wryly.

'You still haven't told me how you found that money,' said Blake.

'I was asked not to tell you.'

'Selim, it's important. I have to know where that money came from. I swear I won't mention it to anybody.'

'Professor Husseini gave it to me. He was very concerned for you and when he heard that the Breasted papyrus had turned up again, he found the money.'

'How much?'

'Two hundred thousand dollars, in cash. I have 10,000 with me, that's more than enough. The rest is in a safe place.'

They got out of the car and Selim walked into the camp without so much as glancing at a group of women who were going to draw water from the well, the jugs perched on small cushions on their heads. The men asked Sarah, still wrapped in her jellaba, to walk behind them, at a respectful distance.

Selim called out at the entrance of the tent and a man in a black burnoose came out and greeted him. Selim and Khaled bowed again, touching their fingertips to their chests, mouths and foreheads. The man looked back and, seeing Blake as well, gestured for the three of them to enter his tent. Sarah was told to sit outside on the ground next to a palm tree.

The fact that Blake could speak Arabic made things much easier. Selim provided no explanations; he knew that what would take most time was negotiating the price. Blake abstained from telling Selim to accept their first request, knowing full well that instead of solving the problem, such an attitude would only complicate matters.

In the silence that reigned throughout the camp, Blake heard the rhythmic pounding of a pestle and mortar: someone was preparing coffee for the guests who had come from so far away. Blake was reminded of that freezing night in Chicago and of the hospitality that had warmed his heart. How could Husseini possibly be such a monster, involved in a plot to destroy so many innocent people?

The coffee soon filled the tent with its aroma and Blake, accepting a steaming cup, thought that he would give a good number of the dollars in Selim's pocket for a measure of bourbon to pour into the coffee. He imagined how humiliated Sarah must be feeling outside and was sorry he couldn't do anything to change the situation.

The negotiations proceeded as the women brought them goat's milk, yoghurt, ayran and dates. Blake asked them if they could take some to his wife as well, so weary from their long journey and hungry. The women nodded and, when they had finished serving the men, went out to Sarah.

Selim and the sheikh shook on 4,800 dollars, half of which was to be paid immediately and the other half at the end of the mission. They then began to discuss the itinerary on an up-to-date American 1:500,000-scale military map that their host pulled out of a chest.

They would approach by day on camel so as to avoid attracting the attention of the armed forces from either side. They would continue travelling in this way until they got to Abu Agheila, just a few miles from the border. There they would find a four-wheel drive with masked headlights which would take them by night to Ras Udash. Eighty miles of territory in all, at very high risk. The whole first stretch was practically up against the front line.

Selim counted out the money and they were soon taken, with Sarah, beyond the oasis where the camels were waiting for them. They said goodbye to Khaled, who had decided to wait for Selim to return to the camp so they could drive back together in his Peugeot.

'Thank you, Khaled. I'll be back one day,' Blake promised, 'and we'll have a nice cold beer together at the Winter Palace in Luxor.'

'*Inshallah*,' said Khaled with a smile.

'*Inshallah*,' replied Blake. 'If God so wills.'

He reached his companions who were already on their camels.

'How will they know at Abu Agheila that we're coming?' he asked Selim, as he hoisted himself up into the saddle.

Selim gestured with his head and Blake turned. The sheikh pulled an ultra-modern mobile phone out of the band of fabric he wore at his waist and began talking in an animated voice with an unknown speaker.

They travelled all day, stopping for just half an hour at the well of Beer Hadat, a pool of yellowish water covered with swarms of dragonflies and water fleas. Their path was often crossed by columns of trucks, tanks and self-propelled howitzers going towards the front. Evidently the battle was still raging furiously.

They reached Abu Agheila shortly before dusk and the caravan leader brought them to a small caravanserai packed full of donkeys, camels and mules with their drivers, saturating the air with every imaginable sort of odour and shriek.

The animals were watered and tended. Selim began talking and then arguing with the owner, and Blake realized that the man wanted the other half of the sum immediately, before they left.

He approached Selim and said in English, 'If he'll take half of the remaining sum, tell him that we agree. Otherwise tell him we're turning back. I don't want him to think we can't do without his help.'

Selim referred Blake's offer, and to be more convincing, took out twelve hundred-dollar bills and placed them in the man's hand. He seemed to refuse at first, then, having thought about it, called over a boy who opened an unhinged wooden door, revealing an old Unimog, freshly painted with camouflage colours.

'Finally,' sighed Blake, and looked at his watch: eight o'clock.

Husseini's computer was starting up the fifth cycle. Just thirty-six hours to the conclusion of the program.

The price they paid included a hunk of bread with lamb stew and a bottle of mineral water; the sheik had thought of everything. Sarah played her part as a Muslim woman to the hilt, eating separately from the men without removing the veil that covered her head and most of her face, but Blake tried to meet her eyes every so often to show he was thinking of her.

They got into the Unimog at eight thirty. The boy who had opened the shed sat at the wheel, with Selim at his side and Sarah and Blake in back. The vehicle was roughly covered by a camouflaged canvas roof stretched over a frame made up of iron poles.

About an hour into the trip, it was clear why the man at the caravanserai had wanted to be paid before they left: the explosions were frighteningly close.

Selim, guessing at the state of mind of his travel companions, turned to reassure them. 'The boy says not to worry. The front is towards Gaza, and we'll be turning off to the south-east soon, where we'll use the Udash wadi. After a few miles it narrows between the rocks. It'll give us all the protection we need to get to our destination.'

'How soon?' asked Blake.

Selim exchanged words with the driver, then said, 'If all goes well – if we're not hit by the machine-gun fire of some passing aeroplane and if this truck doesn't break down – at about two o'clock in the morning . . . *inshallah.*'

'*Inshallah,*' repeated Blake mechanically.

The boy drove calmly and very carefully, briefly switching on the headlights only when it became difficult to follow the track.

They got to the border some time before midnight and stopped behind a rise in the terrain. About 200 metres away they could see a fence with barbed wire and an asphalt road on the other side, in Israeli territory.

The driver and Selim got out and cautiously approached the border on foot, looking to the left and right. They snipped the wire with a pair of cutters, and crept back over to the Unimog.

'We've been incredibly lucky,' said Selim while the heavy vehicle climbed up the bank on the side of the road, clambering over to the other side in the direction of Wadi Udash, which glowed palely, completely dry, about a quarter of a mile ahead of them.

'Selim, I have to ask you something,' said Blake in Arabic.

'What, Professor Blake?'

'Do you know why the Americans and their European allies have not taken sides in this war?'

'The radio and newspapers say it's because they're afraid, but not many believe that.'

'What do you think?'

'Well, I tuned into a station in Malta. They were reporting a news leak that America is being immobilized by an immense terrorist threat. That seems like a plausible explanation to me.'

'Yeah, it seems plausible to me too,' said Blake. 'Selim, what do you think of Professor Husseini? I mean, did you ever notice anything strange about the way he acted?'

Selim's look was one of complete surprise, as if he'd never imagined Blake would ask him such a question. 'Professor Husseini is a very good person,' he said. 'He really cares about you. He went out on a limb for you, Professor Blake, let me tell you.'

'I believe it,' answered Blake, and bowed his head in silence.

Sarah seemed lost in her own thoughts.

'What are you thinking about?' asked Blake.

'The hangar will presumably be locked, and only Gordon and Maddox have keys. How are we going to get the Falcon out?'

'I don't know,' answered Blake. 'But we have overcome so many obstacles this far that I don't think any door, no matter how sturdy, will be able to stop us.'

They had been travelling for some time over the clean gravel and coarse sand of the dry Wadi Udash river bed. The banks were never less than a couple of metres high, often shaded by thorny acacia trees that sheltered them in critical moments, if they saw a plane or a helicopter passing through the sky or heard the engines of a column of tanks on the move.

At about one in the morning, Sarah, who had seemed to be dozing, pointed suddenly to the east. 'Look over there,' she said to Blake. 'The Ras Udash pyramid. We have to leave the wadi. The runway and the hangar are about four miles over that way.'

Selim, who had heard her, put his hand on the driver's shoulder and gestured for him to stop and to turn off the engine.

'Four miles over completely exposed terrain,' he said in English. 'Here's where it gets tough. If any plane or tank, on any side, sees us, we'll be incinerated immediately.'

'Selim, listen,' said Blake. 'We've absolutely got to get to that hangar, we can't give up now. And we need your help. We can use the Unimog to tow the plane, if we need to, or to force the doors if they're locked. You see, we have reliable evidence that the terrorist threat we were talking about is already in motion and that it will come to a head in –' he looked at his watch – 'just about thirty hours or so.'

'What kind of a head?' asked Selim.

'We don't know. We may even be completely wrong about this, but we can't run such a huge risk. What's most probable is that a group of terrorists has managed to plant devastatingly powerful bombs of some sort in several cities of the United States, three we think, paralysing the American system of armed response.'

'I understand.'

'So listen. I'll go ahead on foot and as I check the way, I'll signal to you with the torch and you move forward with your lights off, until we've reached the runway. One flash is "OK, the coast is clear"; two flashes mean "Watch out, danger."'

'I'm coming with you,' said Sarah.

'OK,' said Blake, getting out and taking his backpack and Olsen's briefcase with him.

Sarah ripped the veil off her head and stripped off the jellaba, shaking her head and freeing her blonde hair. 'Finally!' she exclaimed, jumping to the ground in her khaki clothing. 'I couldn't take that outfit for another minute. Now, let's get going.'

They waved goodbye to Selim, who answered with a thumbs-up sign, and they ran off.

They reached a hill that rose seven or eight metres over the surrounding territory and closely scanned the vast desert plain. Blake shone the little torch on and off once.

Selim turned to his companion. 'Get out,' he said, 'and wait for me here. I'll come back for you.'

The boy protested.

'I could be blown apart by a mine. You want to keep me company?'

He took the rest of the sum they'd agreed upon and handed it to him, saying, 'This is better, believe me.'

The boy got out without breathing a word and crouched down on the bottom of the wadi. Selim took the driver's seat, started up the engine and put it into gear. When he arrived at the hill, Blake and Sarah were already half a mile ahead.

He waited with the engine running for another signal. When he saw one short flash in the dark, he stepped on the accelerator and crossed the second stretch of desert. By the time he stopped at the third point, the mileage counter read almost two miles. They were halfway there.

Sarah and Blake proceeded, sometimes walking and sometimes running. To their left, the pyramid of Ras Udash rose higher and higher over the surrounding hills, and as their perspective changed it seemed progressively bigger and more imposing. Blake felt a chill run down his spine, although he was soaked with sweat, as he noticed other familiar elements in the landscape.

The runway was not much more than a mile away now. He signalled again to Selim that the coast was clear and they proceeded towards a rise topped by a pile of crumbling rocks which had partially tumbled down the sides.

'That's the hill with the hangar,' said Sarah. 'We've made it. I don't see anything around. Let's not waste any more time. We can tell Selim to come all the way.'

Blake flashed the light and the Unimog drew up next to them in the middle of the huge silent plain. They heard the distant echoes of cannon fire and saw flashes of explosions to the east and the north, as well as traces of aerial duels in the direction of Gaza and over the Dead Sea.

They climbed onto the running board while Selim accelerated, crossing the desert that separated them from the runway in just a few minutes.

Blake checked for damage to the runway and found only that the soil cover was uneven, probably as a result of the sandstorm. Sarah, followed by Selim, went straight to the door of the hangar, in front of which a considerable heap of sand and dust had accumulated. They took the two small shovels that were in the Unimog tool box and began to clear it away, with Blake giving them a hand as well.

It took them about ten minutes to free the doorway and Sarah grabbed onto the big steel handles at the entry.

'It's locked!' she said, swearing.

'To be expected,' said Blake. 'There's a twenty-million-dollar toy in there.'

He turned to Selim. 'Back it up and we'll try to pull the door off its hinges with the tow line.'

Sarah suddenly shushed him and gestured for Selim to turn off the engine.

'What is it?' asked Blake.

'A noise. Hear it?'

Blake listened. 'I don't hear anything.'

'Engines,' said Selim. 'A column approaching.' He jumped out of the Unimog and ran to the top of the hangar hill. Just three miles away, he could see the lights of three tracked vehicles, at a distance of about a mile from each other, closing in.

'A patrol of tanks on a reconnaissance mission!' he shouted. 'At least three. The first is headed straight this way.'

He ran down the slope to the hangar door.

'How far away are they?' asked Blake.

'No more than three miles. The closest one will be here at the runway in seven or eight minutes. As soon as they spot us, they'll start shooting. We've got to attempt it right away. We have to pull the door off.'

He hooked up the chain and sat down at the driver's wheel, set the four-wheel drive and blocked both differentials.

'Rev it up when the line is taut!' shouted Blake.

Selim nodded, put it into gear and pulled the chain taut, then accelerated. Sarah in the meantime had climbed to the top of the hill to keep her eye on the tanks. They were troop transport vehicles, probably Egyptian, and they were approaching at a slow but steady speed. She looked down. The Unimog was sinking into the ground, but the door was not budging.

'Accelerate! Accelerate! It's moving!' shouted Blake, noticing that the door had started to buckle at the centre, where the pull was strongest.

The vehicle's tyres were smoking, overheated by the friction, and the odour of burnt rubber was very powerful. Selim took his foot off the accelerator. 'I'm afraid the tyres will burst,' he said. 'I have to back up and make it a clean break.'

'No!' shouted Blake. 'If the chain snaps, the whiplash will kill you.'

'One mile!' yelled Sarah from above.

'We have no choice,' shouted Selim, starting to reverse.

But as he was about to accelerate, Blake stopped him. 'Wait,' he said. 'Just a minute. Help me to take off the tailgate.'

Selim got out and helped Blake to take the tailgate off its hinges, then he wedged it behind the front seat.

'This will protect us,' he said, getting in next to the driver's seat.

'No, Professor Blake! Get away from here!'

'Accelerate, I said! Someone has to hold this in place, other-wise it will fall over at the first bump. Move this thing, damn it, accelerate. Now or never!'

Selim stepped on the accelerator, the engine roared and the

vehicle skidded on the hammada ground, leaping ahead. He switched into second and third gear in just a few metres, accelerating at full capacity while Blake held the gate steady with both hands. In a fraction of a second, the line pulled taut and three tons of inertia at forty miles an hour snapped the chain like a string. The stump flew through the air, cracking like a whip and hit the iron shield with enormous violence. Blake screamed in pain, letting go of the gate, and twisted in his seat in agony. The tailgate fell onto the back of the truck with a crash.

Selim twisted around and waited a moment for the wind to clear away the dust and the smoke from the burning tyres, then said, 'It's open, Professor Blake.'

Blake tried to pull himself up, overcoming the atrocious pain in his arms and hands, and saw that Sarah was running down the hill towards the hangar entrance, shouting, 'Hurry! Hurry! They're here! Run, Will, run for God's sake!'

Blake got out and dragged himself as quickly as he could to the hangar. Sarah was already sitting in the Falcon cockpit and was starting up the engines.

'My wrists are fractured!'

He yelled to be heard over the roar of the jet engines and showed her his bloodied arms. Sarah understood and, abandoning the controls, opened the door and dragged him up, as he clenched his teeth to stop from screaming. Blake managed to get into the seat and Sarah was already back in the pilot's place. She grabbed the control column and opened the throttle, taking off down the runway.

'Stop!' shouted Blake. 'Stop, Sarah! We can't leave Selim behind! Olsen's briefcase, the papyrus! I left them with Selim.'

'You are crazy,' shouted back Sarah. 'There's no more time!'

But as the plane started to roll down the runway, he saw the Unimog approaching the plane at full speed. Selim had the briefcase in his hand! In the distance, a tank appeared from behind a dune, spraying the area with machine-gun fire.

'Open up!' shouted Blake. 'Open the door or I'll kill you!'

Sarah obeyed, shocked by his threat, and the cockpit was invaded by a gust of wind. Sarah started in pain, but bit her lip and continued to grip the plane's controls. Blake leaned forward until he nearly fell and Selim, leaving the driver's seat and standing on the running board for a second, threw him the briefcase.

Blake caught it more with his forearms than with his hands, and fell backwards onto the floor. He forced himself up again and held his arms out towards Selim. 'Grab on to my forearms! Hurry!'

The tank was now at the top of the dune and was aiming a machine gun in the direction of the runway.

'There's no time,' shouted Selim as he turned towards the approaching tank. 'Close the door now. Go!'

'No, Selim,' Blake shouted back. 'No!'

At that moment, the rattle of machine-gun fire sounded again, and Blake could see flames sparking off the tank's armour. Selim was shooting back, with a machine gun perched on the hood of the Unimog. The tank, heedless of the attack, advanced towards the runway to block the Falcon's take-off but Selim veered so sharply to the left that his vehicle nearly tipped over and raced at top speed towards the tank, which was forced to wheel round on its tracks to confront him.

As the Falcon was lifting its wheels off the ground, Blake and Sarah heard a powerful explosion and saw a globe of flame and smoke rising from the spot where the Unimog had collided with the tank.

Sarah pushed the jet engines to the max, flying as close as possible to the ground to avoid radar controls. She flew over an inferno of flames and smoke, of vehicles devoured by fire, of the carbonized remains of weaponry and human beings. She passed through a swarm of anti-aircraft shells and multicoloured tracers, without thinking of anything, without hearing anything, gritting her teeth and looking straight ahead until the vast peaceful blue expanse of the sea opened before her.

It was only then that she released a long sigh and turned to look at her companion. And Blake looked back at her, with tears in his eyes.

15

After crossing the entire city, which was in a state of black-out due to the strict curfew, Gad Avner finally reached the square in front of the Wailing Wall and headed towards the arch of the Antonian Fortress. The square was dark and deserted, but the sky was illuminated by flashes to the north, south and east: the front lines were getting closer and closer to the walls of Jerusalem.

The army was beginning to run low on munitions and fuel, while the enemy enjoyed abundant supplies, with more pouring in from every direction. Yehudai had decided to activate the launch procedure for the Beersheba nuclear warheads before General Taksoun's missiles could get within range of Israel's nuclear defences. And this scenario was very likely to become a reality within the next twenty-four hours, unless the army's present counteroffensive could turn the tide of battle.

Avner spotted Ferrario, who had been waiting for him. They walked past the two guards together, advancing inside the tunnel up to the place where he had seen the half-buried steps in the southern wall of the cave the last time he was there. Allon suddenly appeared out of nowhere, as if he had materialized from the wall.

'Are there any new developments?' Avner asked.

'We've excavated these stairs,' said Allon. 'They lead to an underground chamber that extends under the Al Aqsa Mosque all the way to the atrium of the Mosque of Omar. It may have been the crypt of the Temple or maybe an old cistern.'

Avner felt a shiver run up his spine. 'Have you spoken to anyone about this?'

'Why do you ask?'

'Because if anyone finds out that you can get under the Al-Aqsa Mosque from here, we'll have to contend with our own fundamentalist elements. They'd like nothing better than to be able to eliminate all the competition from the area around the Temple.'

'We have taken all the usual precautions,' answered Allon, 'but there's always the chance of some information leaking out.'

Avner changed the subject. 'What did you find in the crypt?'

'Not much yet, but it is a fairly large area. All we did was make a brief preliminary survey. We felt it was more important to continue with the tunnel.'

'Is it over this way?' asked Avner, pointing to the opening that led into the mountain.

'Just follow me,' said Allon. 'This tunnel is incredible. We've already explored about half a mile of its length.'

Allon lit a flare, which bathed a long stretch of the tunnel in brilliant light, and set off at an easy pace so his companions would have no trouble keeping up. The walls were rough but regular and you could actually count the grooves left by the ancient picks.

'I have the impression that work on this tunnel was done in separate stages during different historical periods. The central part is a mine shaft that was probably dug out by the Babylonians during the first siege in an attempt to collapse the city walls. Later on, the initial section we are presently walking through was connected to it, probably as part of a countermining operation on the part of the besieged city dwellers.

'The final section was probably excavated later to open up a secret escape route, leading out beyond the enemy lines in case of a siege. That graffiti we saw at the start probably indicated a section that led out to the Kidron Valley.

'At any rate, as far as we can tell, this route was known only to the Temple priests. We know that in 586 BC, King Zedekiah had a breach made in the wall by the pool of Siloah so he could escape with his family and the royal guards, so he must not have been aware of this passageway. But the sacred vessels of the Temple were almost certainly carried to safety through this tunnel.'

'Listen,' said Avner, almost reluctantly, 'is it also possible that the Ark of the Covenant was carried through this passage?'

Allon smiled. 'My dear friend, I'm afraid the Ark has been no more than a legend for many, many centuries. But I can't exclude anything. If you want to know what I think, though,' he continued, 'I hope it never turns up, assuming that it does exist. Can you imagine what an explosion of fanaticism something like that would stir up?'

'I know,' sighed Avner, 'but a miracle is exactly what we need right now . . .'

Allon didn't respond; he just continued walking, bending down when he came to a low place in the ceiling. After about half an hour, they stopped at a spot that had recently been widened by the archaeologists and led up to what appeared to be the base of a ramp.

'Just where are we, exactly?' asked Avner.

Allon took a map out of his inside jacket pocket and pointed to a spot in the direction of Bethlehem. 'Right here.'

Avner took out a military goniometric relief map. It too showed a spot that had been marked with a little circle.

'The two points are only about 300 metres apart, at the most,' commented Ferrario.

'That's right,' said Avner.

'What are you guys talking about?' asked Allon.

'Look,' said Avner, raising his eyes to the roof of the tunnel. 'How far is it from here to the surface?'

'Not very. I'd say three or maybe five metres at the most. That's almost certainly the ramp that leads to the surface,' he explained, pointing to the base of the wall. Then he added, 'Here, on this enlarged detail we have marked the place where the ramp probably ends. It should be directly under the floor of one of the houses in this neighbourhood.'

Avner, pretending to take notes on a pad, passed a slip of paper to Ferrario. It said, 'Get a commando squad ready for action immediately. In plain clothes. They mustn't be noticed by anyone. Have them ready to go into action in the next couple of hours.'

Ferrario nodded his head in affirmation, saying, 'If you have no further need of me, Mr Cohen, I have some urgent business to take care of. I'll see you later.' He turned around and retraced his steps towards the mouth of the tunnel.

Avner continued behind Allon. 'I have another question,' he said.

'Fire away.'

'Where was Nebuchadnezzar's camp during the siege of 586?'

'Well, there are two schools of thought regarding that particular point,' the archaeologist began, assuming a rather annoyingly pedantic tone.

'What's your opinion, Allon?'

'More or less, right here,' he said, indicating a point on the map.

'Just as I thought,' exclaimed Avner, almost shouting. 'What a God-damned megalomaniac!'

'I beg your pardon!'

'Oh, I didn't mean you. I was just thinking about someone I know.'

The place Allon had pointed to happened to be exceedingly near the spot on the military relief map that they had looked at a few moments before. It marked the location of the suspicious radio signal that had been discovered by Ferrario and his men.

'Look, Professor,' Avner began again, 'I have to ask an enormous favour of you, even though I realize how tired you must be. I'll send you more men to work under your supervision.

I need you to clear this ramp by tomorrow evening. I can't tell you why, because I too am acting on orders from my superiors, but at times like this we have to explore all our options.'

'I understand perfectly,' said Allon. 'I'll do what is humanly possible.'

Avner came back out of the tunnel and went back to headquarters, where General Yehudai was keeping track of all new developments in the field in real time on his three-dimensional model. The American satellite had just located a suspicious installation about 150 miles east of the River Jordan.

'What could it be?' asked Avner.

'It looks like a radio transmitter to me and the source we have located between here and Bethlehem could be a relay station.'

'Well, what's the sense of all that?'

'These guys don't have any satellite access, so they have to rely on ground-based relay stations. We noticed it during the advance of the sandstorm. These two points form a perfect equilateral triangle with our nuclear base at Beersheba. They are probably getting ready to attack it.'

'Destroy the transmitter on the other side of the Jordan. It could be a missile launching pad, as well.'

'We did destroy it. But it's reappeared. It's probably a mobile unit that can slip back into an underground bunker. And the radio source near Bethlehem is probably capable of directing a missile attack on the capital.'

'Jerusalem? They wouldn't dare. It's a holy city for them as well.'

'They wouldn't dare, you say? Remember how Nebuchadnezzar emptied the city of its inhabitants. These guys could do the same thing using different means . . . Gas, for instance.'

Avner nodded glumly.

'What did you find out from your archaeologist?' asked Yehudai.

'Something very interesting. How to get within metres of the Bethlehem transmitter without crossing a mile of high-risk area infested by thousands of Hamas snipers.'

'That's very good news.'

'Maybe I'll be able to report something even better in a few hours, if I'm right, but I'd rather not discuss it for now. How's our offensive coming along?'

Yehudai pointed to the zones on the three-dimensional model in which his divisions were engaged in battle. 'The initial thrust is beginning to flag, I'm afraid. We're already having to ration fuel and will soon be forced to ration munitions, as well. In a few more hours I'll know if it's time to order Beersheba to initiate launch procedures on our Gabriel missiles, arming them with nuclear warheads before it's too late.'

Avner lowered his head. 'I'll also be putting my plan into action by tonight. I'll keep you posted.'

He left general headquarters and had the driver take him to the King David Hotel to have a drink and sort out his thoughts before returning home. He was served a beer and lit up a cigarette. Just a few more hours and then he would know if his hunch was right, if his detective's nose was still any good. He stayed at the hotel a long time, lost in thought, considering every angle. When he raised his head he found Ferrario standing in front of him: he was in combat gear, flourishing the stars designating the rank of second lieutenant and a holstered pistol at his hip.

'I have taken care of everything, sir. The commando squad is ready and waiting for further orders.'

'And just where do you think you're going in that get-up?' Avner asked.

'With your permission, sir, to the front. I have submitted a request to be transferred to a fighting unit.'

'No more Armani for you?'

'No, sir. I'm afraid the army quartermaster doesn't shop in the same places as me.'

'And just when did you make this request to leave my unit?'

'I'm asking you now, sir. Lots of men are dying on the front, even as we speak, to keep the enemy away from the gates of Jerusalem. I just want to be able to do my part.'

'You're already doing precisely that, Ferrario. And very well, I might add.'

'Thank you, sir, but it's not enough for me any more. By now, you can manage perfectly well without me. Please, grant me this transfer, sir.'

'You're mad. You could have gone home after getting your degree, but instead you wanted to experience the thrill of this job, and now you want to go to the front of all places! It will certainly be more exciting. I only hope you realize that it's going to be very dangerous too.'

'I realize that, sir.'

'Don't you miss Italy?'

'I miss it a lot. It's the most beautiful place in the world and it's where I was born.'

'Well, then . . .'

'Israel is my spiritual homeland and Jerusalem is a heavenly star, sir.'

Avner thought about Ras Udash and of the secret that he had buried beneath a mountain of bodies and would have liked to scream, 'None of it's true, none of it!' Instead, he replied, 'I'll be sorry to lose you, but if that's your decision I won't stand in your way. Good luck, son. Just take care of your arse out there. If something happens to you, a lot of pretty girls back there in Italy are going to be awfully upset with me.'

'I'll do what I can, sir. And, by the way, you should stop smoking if you can. It's bad for your health.' Then, snapping to attention, he gave his superior a smart salute, adding, 'It's been an honour serving with you, Mr Avner.' Finally, executing a swift about-turn, he took his leave.

Observing him as he moved away, his gait slightly encumbered by the heavy army boots, Avner couldn't help but think what an elegant figure Italians always managed to cut, even if dressed in tatters. He dropped his head to watch the ash of his cigarette as it slowly burned away.

BLAKE'S VACANT STARE seemed to be watching the waves rippling under the cockpit.

'I'm sorry,' said Sarah. 'I never could have imagined that he would—'

'It was his choice. He decided to sacrifice himself to save us. But . . . the papyrus was the first thing I thought of, not Selim. I'm no better than Olsen, Sarah. I'm a goddamned egotistical bastard.'

'There are times when instinct prevails over everything else. Maybe one day we'll know why things were meant to happen this way.'

Blake dropped the subject and the roar of the engines was the only sound to be heard for a long while.

'Would you have really done it?' asked Sarah suddenly, to break that unbearable silence.

'Done what?'

'Killed me if I hadn't opened the door.'

'I doubt it. Besides, both of my wrists are broken: I would have had to bite you to death.'

'But there was definitely murder in your eyes.'

'Well, that's what made you open the door. So I guess it served its purpose.'

'How do you feel now?'

'The painkillers are starting to take effect. Not too bad. But you look pale. What's the matter?'

'Nothing. I'm just exhausted, that's all . . . Will?'

'Yes.'

'What did the last part of the inscription on the sarcophagus at Ras Udash say?'

'It said, "Whoever profanes this tomb shall have his bones

crushed and see the earth run red with the blood of his loved ones." '

'Why wouldn't you tell me before?'

'Because I didn't want to upset you. You see, it's precisely what's happening to me. I've already broken some bones and—'

'I'm not upset, William Blake. It's just a coincidence.'

'That's right. That's the way I look at it too.'

They remained silent for a while, then Sarah continued, 'Is that all?'

'No,' said Blake. 'It said, "And may this occur until the sun sets in the East." '

Sarah looked at him with an uneasy glimmer in her eye. 'In other words, forever. As far as curses go, this one is truly unrelenting. The sun never sets in the east.'

'Don't think about it,' said Blake. 'It's just a lot of ancient hocus-pocus.'

Then he fell silent, overcome by an oppressive drowsiness, but as he nodded off he noticed how the dawn light reflected in the Plexiglas dome began to darken. He turned around and saw the sun disappear slowly behind the eastern horizon. The Falcon hadn't yet reached its cruising altitude, but it was still faster than the reverse motion of the earth.

He looked at Sarah with a complacent smile and said, 'Sometimes anything can happen.' Then, leaning back, he dozed off.

An hour later he was jolted out of his slumber as the aeroplane encountered some turbulence. Turning towards his companion, he asked, 'How's it going?'

She looked deathly pale and was dripping with sweat. He noticed a pool of blood on the floor of the cabin.

'My God . . .' he exclaimed. 'What happened? Why did you let me sleep?'

'It happened when I opened the door . . . A piece of shrapnel hit me in the left shoulder.'

'Oh, Jesus!' Blake exclaimed. 'This is terrible . . . But why didn't you wake me? Come here,' he coaxed, helping her to her feet. 'Sit down in my seat. I need some room to work on your arm.' Blake couldn't stop fretting as he fussed with her wound and continued to mutter mechanically, 'What a mess . . . Damn, damn, damn . . .'

He found some bandages and wrapped his own wrists as well as he could. Then he took the scalpel out of his pocket and opened the sleeve of her shirt, slowly loosening the tourniquet she'd applied herself, restoring a bit of blood flow to the swollen, livid arm. He disinfected the wound and then applied a gauze dressing and wrapped it with strips of adhesive bandage. Drying her forehead, he insisted she drink as much water as she could.

They continued flying in the dark for hours on automatic pilot. Every once in a while, Blake towelled off her forehead and face, wetting her lips with a little orange juice he found in the galley.

Sarah looked up at him with shiny, fever-weary eyes. 'I might pass out at any time,' she murmured. 'I want to teach you the procedure for sending a mayday signal and for jumping out of the plane with a parachute. I don't think I've got enough time, though, to teach you how to land this contraption.'

'What about you?'

'If you're smart, buster, you'll forget about me. If you try to jump dragging all my dead weight along with you, you'll ruin your chances as well.'

'Negative, Commander,' said Blake. 'I just don't have any fun without you, sweetheart. It's either both of us or forget it.'

'You damned stubborn fool. So you're going to blow it after all, after everything we've done to make it this far.' From somewhere she found the energy to crack a joke. 'Do you realize this could be considered mutiny?'

'I'll gladly let them court-martial me as soon as we get this thing landed. Until then, I'm not budging, not an inch.'

He insisted that she drink some more water and somehow managed to keep her awake until the instruments had finally locked in on the control tower at La Guardia airport in New York.

'Well, maybe we've made it, after all,' Sarah managed to whisper. 'Now listen carefully. You've got to convince the tower to let us land and transmit your message to the proper authorities. I've done all I could, now it's up to you. You have to give it all you've got.'

CAPTAIN McBAIN of the United States Marine Corps stopped his car in front of the Pentagon and had a guard escort him to the office of General Hooker. 'General, sir,' he said, a bit out of breath, 'tower control at La Guardia in New York has put us in radio contact with an unknown aircraft that has wounded aboard, but insists on transmitting an absolute top priority message to us. I think it has something to do with the war and the threat of terrorism we are currently dealing with.' He handed him a file he had been carrying under his arm.

Hooker took the dossier and began thumbing through it. 'Another visionary or clairvoyant, I assume?'

'Actually, sir, these guys are aware of the threat we are facing, even though they don't know the details. Evidently they happened to get into the memory of some computer while surfing the Internet and, noticing a suspicious file, they managed to open it.

'They realized that they were dealing with some sort of very sophisticated military program and figured it might have something to do with the situation that has been paralysing our entire system of military response.'

Hooker raised his head from the text. 'Are you telling me these people have managed to do something our combined military intelligence agencies have failed to do? Don't you smell something just a tad fishy about all this, Captain? If what they say is true, how did they manage to break through the security system of such a powerful program and how did they figure out the access code? If they are on our side, we'd know who they are. But if they're not on our side, then who in the hell's side are they on?'

'General, sir, if you don't mind, I would like you to follow me into the operations room, where I have already sent the program to have it projected onto the giant screen. Just remember, if they're right, there are only sixteen hours left before the final procedure begins.'

Hooker closed the dossier, got up from his chair and followed Captain McBain through the labyrinth of halls leading to the operations room.

'Who does this computer belong to?'

'Some guy named Omar al Husseini—'

'An Arab?' Hooker asked with a start.

'An American of Lebanese origin, a professor of Coptic studies at the Oriental Institute in Chicago.'

'Where is he now?'

'He's nowhere to be found. Very discreetly, I had his house checked.'

'Did you say discreetly, McBain? If what you are telling me is true, you should have broken down the bloody door with a battleaxe and seized that goddamned computer if it's the one that's been fucking with us all this time.'

'Our experts say that it could be a very tricky business. Tampering with that computer could be like messing around with a bomb, or in this case three.'

'Well, then, let's get inside the damn thing, like those guys in the aeroplane did!'

'It's not that easy, General, sir. There are words in Coptic, files in Egyptian hieroglyphics and Arabic. It's like playing blind-man's bluff in a minefield. We're working on it together with the people who provided the original lead.'

'Have you at least managed to find out who they are?'

'No.'

'And why the hell not, might I enquire?'

'Because they don't trust us.'

McBain opened the door and ushered his superior officer into the operations room. The technicians were projecting the program onto the big screen, guided by the instructions of a man's voice broadcast over a loudspeaker, with the sound of a jet engine in the background.

Hooker glanced at the radar screen. 'Can you tell where they are?'

'We redirected them to the military airport at Fort Riggs,' said another officer. 'In any case, I've sent them a helicopter with a couple of military doctors.'

'Wait a minute,' said Hooker. 'What guarantee do we have that this program itself doesn't constitute a danger to us? Or even the aeroplane, for that matter?'

'I've had some checks run, General,' said McBain, 'and I can categorically and absolutely exclude that possibility, sir. Just step over this way, if you don't mind. '

He brought him in front of a monitor connected to a VCR and a computer. 'I had the FBI send me the cassettes they confiscated from the security camera installed at the lobby of the *Chicago Tribune*. This footage relates to the day the video with the nuclear threat was delivered. Watch.'

He had them start the video and then stop it at the point where the front of a FedEx delivery van appeared just outside the lobby of the *Tribune*. You could see a delivery man getting out with a package.

'That package contains the video cassette,' McBain explained. 'Now, watch carefully.' He typed in a stop-image command on the computer and then went on to enlarge a detail in the background, focusing on a car parked at the kerb and a man fussing around with a jack and spare tyre. The zoom lens further enlarged the man and then his face, obtaining a very blurry but still quite recognizable image. McBain typed in a few more commands and right next to the blurry face there appeared another, clear picture of a face. 'This, gentlemen, is a photo of Professor Omar al Husseini which we had sent to us by the faculty office of the Oriental Institute. As you can see, there's no doubt about it. It's one and the same person. The only question is, could Husseini have just happened to be passing by the *Tribune* at that precise moment? I doubt it seriously.'

'Gentlemen,' one of the computer technicians interrupted, 'we have just decoded the program.'

Hooker followed him to the central screen, at the top of which, in giant letters, was written:

The

A R M A G E D D O N

program

'It is designed to make three objects called "donkeys" rotate in six successive twenty-four-hour cycles,' explained the technician, 'trained on three objectives that are always different. After the sixth cycle, the final procedure is activated. If there is any interference, the final procedure is instantly activated, or perhaps a reserve circuit is activated. We have decoded the symbols for the objectives: they represent major American cities. The sixth cycle settles on New York, Los Angeles and Chicago. I don't think it's necessary to mention that the objects in motion are the mobile nuclear bombs we are looking for. Constantly moving them around makes it very difficult for us to get a fix on them.'

'Strange,' muttered Hooker, staring at the screen, 'why haven't they targeted Washington?'

'It's a question of the Middle-Eastern mentality,' said McBain. 'For them it's much more painful for a man to have his honour wounded, the things he holds dear, than simply to be destroyed physically. Their plan calls for the President to survive unharmed so he can witness the destruction of the nation.'

'Sir,' chimed in one of the communications sergeants, 'we have an answer from Jerusalem.'

'We sent the photos of Husseini to Mossad,' explained McBain, moving up to the monitor of the computer that was just starting to display a series of mug shots showing a young man with a thick moustache wearing a keffiyeh on his head.

Putting on his glasses, Hooker approached the screen, observing the images intently as a technician ran them through a morphing program. He removed the moustache and keffiyeh, thinned the hair, coloured it grey and deepened the wrinkles.

'My God,' he exclaimed. 'Husseini is . . . Abu Ghaj!'

'At this point, I don't think there's any doubt about it,' said McBain. 'Husseini is the key to it all. We need to get our hands on him and we don't have much more than sixteen hours to do it in.'

Hooker called in the entire staff. 'Listen up, gentlemen, this is what we've got to do. First of all, find a damned computer genius who can stop that program without blowing us all to smithereens. And second, run a thorough check on this Husseini guy, find out everything there is to know about him, anything that can identify him and trace his movements: his automobile licence plates, credit cards, social security number, ATM cards, everything. Then all he has to do is buy gas, get a prescription for sleeping pills or buy a pair of damn boxer shorts in a department store and we'll nail him. Third, find the three commandos who have the bombs and eliminate them on the spot, before proceeding to defuse the bombs if you can. Now get hopping, men!'

The non-commissioned officer in charge of communications came up to the general with an anxious expression. 'Bad news, sir. General Yehudai's offensive in Israel is failing. They are getting ready to start the launch procedure for the nuclear warheads at Beersheba.'

Hooker fell into a chair, covering his face with his hands. McBain walked over to him.

'I've got the aeroplane back on the line, sir. Do you want to say something?'

'Yes,' answered Hooker, 'let me speak to them.'

He moved up to the microphone. 'This is General Hooker at the Pentagon calling the unidentified aircraft, do you read me?'

'I read you, General, loud and clear.'

'You were right. Everything turned out just like you said. The three "donkeys" that appear in the file are actually three mobile nuclear warheads that could explode in exactly fifteen hours and . . . fourteen minutes in three major American cities.

'Professor Husseini was a notorious terrorist active around the middle of the 1980s, operating under the name of Abu Ghaj. So now, if you wish, you can identify yourselves. We are no longer concerned that you might pose a security threat.'

There was silence for an interminable minute in the operations room, then the voice of the man in the aeroplane said, 'My name is William Blake and I'm a colleague of Professor Husseini's at the Oriental Institute of Chicago. I'm on board a Falcon 900EX. It is being flown by Sarah Forrestall of the Warren Mining Corporation, but she has been seriously injured. We are the only survivors of the incident at the Ras Udash camp in the Negev desert.'

Hooker leaned his back up against the wall, as if struck by a bolt of lightning.

'Hello, come in? Do you read me, General?'

'I'm reading you, Mr Blake. Loud and clear.'

'Listen, General. I don't believe that Professor Husseini wants those bombs to explode. He may very well have been a terrorist in the past, but you have to look at the time and place he was operating in. I'm sure he's no longer one and he'd never willingly massacre innocent civilians. That program was probably operating without him even being aware of it. Didn't you notice how it resembles a computer virus? Perhaps he's just a victim as well. Perhaps he's being blackmailed himself. Do you understand what I'm driving at?'

'I do, Mr Blake.'

'Don't kill him, General.'

'We have no intentions of killing anyone. We are trying to save lives, those of millions of innocent human beings. Now I'm going to hand you over to the control tower.'

'We're just about out of fuel. Tell them to let us land as soon as possible. And good luck to you guys too.'

Hooker turned to McBain. 'I want to talk to Jerusalem. Get me Code Absalom.'

'Code Absalom is on the line, sir,' reported McBain, just a moment later. 'Go ahead and speak.'

Hooker moved up to the microphone. 'This is Hooker.'

'This is Avner. What's on your mind, General?'

'Is it true that you have started the nuclear launch procedure?'

'We have no choice.'

'Just give me six hours, Avner. There've been some new developments.'

'That was what you said last time. Where did waiting get us then?'

'Avner, we've cracked the control code for the explosives and our technicians are working on arresting it.'

'How did you manage that?'

'We received a message.'

'From whom?'

'I'd rather tell you all about it when this whole thing is over.'

'That's a risk you've already taken and, let me remind you, the results were hardly inspiring.'

Hooker managed to hold back his anger, mulling things over for a few moments.

'William Blake and Sarah Forrestall are still alive and about to arrive here aboard a Warren Mining Corporation Falcon. They were the ones who sent us the message.'

'It's just a pretext for getting onto American territory. Shoot them down. It's a trick and you're falling for it.'

Hooker thought about how Blake had said 'He may very well have been a terrorist in the past, but you have to look at the time and place he was operating in . . .' Was Blake justifying the actions of a terrorist?

Avner continued to plead his case. 'What do you have to lose, Hooker? If the system they gave you works, then you'll have sacrificed two lives to save a million. If it's a trick, and it obviously is, you're risking an even larger-scale disaster. Those two renegades had everyone at the Ras Udash camp murdered by Taksoun's helicopters, including ten of your Marines. Don't forget that. And how do you know what's onboard that aircraft? Believe me, Hooker, when this is all over, you'll realize just how right I am. Shoot them down, before it's too late! It's clear to me that the program you think is going to solve all your problems was given to them by Taksoun's agents to throw you off track and waste time, if not worse. Just think for a minute, Hooker. How could they have got out of Egypt in the middle of a war, and in an aeroplane of all things?'

Hooker wiped his forehead, which was drenched in sweat.

'Just do it,' urged Avner, 'and I promise that I'll stop the nuclear launch procedure at Beersheba. I'll convince General Yehudai, I promise, but for only five hours, not a minute longer. After that, regardless of what happens, we're going to let all hell break loose. Do you remember that passage in the Book of Judges, Hooker? Where Samson says, "Let me die, together with all the Philistines!"'

Hooker closed his eyes in an effort to calm his inner turmoil, trying desperately to evaluate all the evidence he had been presented with in a cool, logical manner. Finally, he announced, 'All right, Avner. You've convinced me.'

He then turned to McBain. 'I want my jet on the runway in five minutes. I'm going to Chicago.'

BLAKE WENT into the cockpit with some gauze and alcohol, changed the dressing on Sarah's arm and tried to medicate the wound, as she stiffened with pain.

'I'm a lousy medic and I'd make an even worse pilot,' he joked, 'but you're in no shape to be flying. Let me take over the controls and you can give me instructions. We can still do this.'

Sarah interrupted him. 'Shit. Look, we've got company.'

'What's going on?'

'A fighter at ten o'clock, twelve miles away. They're going to shoot us down, Will. It looks like they didn't buy our story.'

Blake watched the outline of the aircraft that was approaching them. 'Damn it!' he swore. 'He talked me into identifying myself. He seemed so sincere . . .'

Sarah was studying the expanse of partly snow-covered countryside stretching out below, interrupted by the red roofs of a small town. 'We've got only one chance,' she informed Blake. 'I'm going to drop this thing down over that town where they won't dare shoot at me and then I want you to jump out with a parachute. I'll lead the fighter a merry dance. Will, let me do this. I know I can.' She pushed the control stick forward and the nose of the plane descended sharply. 'Quick, put on the parachute. We've got less than two minutes.'

'Not on your life,' Blake began protesting, but he didn't have time to finish, because a voice coming in over the radio interrupted their altercation.

'This is Captain Campbell of the United States Air Force. Welcome home. I have instructions to escort you to a place where you can land. Please follow me.'

'We're right behind you, Captain,' replied Sarah, 'and quite honoured, to say the least, by the reception.'

Running on fumes alone, they landed ten minutes later at a military base near Fort Riggs, where a helicopter was waiting for them on the runway. Two stretcher bearers immediately began attending to Sarah's wound, but when they started getting her ready to be loaded into an ambulance, the still-feisty girl wouldn't hear of it.

'I'm going with you,' she said to Blake. 'I want to see this thing through to the end.'

There was no chance of changing her mind and so the attendants handed her over to the doctors on board the helicopter. One of them put her arm in a sling and the other started giving her a transfusion. She was then given a sedative so she could get some precious sleep.

Two hours later they landed at Meigs Field in Chicago in the driving rain. An ambulance was waiting for them at the side of the runway with the motor running. General Hooker was standing next to it, wrapped in a raincoat.

Sarah was loaded right away into the ambulance. Blake kissed her goodbye. 'Forgive me,' he said. 'It was all my fault.'

'It was just a piece of rotten luck,' said Sarah with a tired smile. 'Next time don't forget your fucking briefcase.'

'Sarah! You were great!' Blake yelled as they carried her away.

Hooker reached out to shake Blake's hand, but withdrew it as soon as he noticed the very conspicuous splints and bandages on both his left and right wrists. 'Welcome home,' he said. 'I see that our medics have done their best. Do you feel up to another helicopter ride?'

'You won't believe this, General, but for a minute, when I first saw that fighter, I was sure it was going to shoot us down,' said Blake, following the general.

'Shoot you down? You must be joking. What would we do that for?' asked Hooker, eyes wide.

They got on board and the helicopter, which had never stopped its engines, slowly lifted off into the leaden sky.

'I don't know,' answered Blake, 'it's just that we haven't been receiving very cordial greetings lately ... How are things progressing at this point?'

'We're fighting against the clock,' said Hooker. 'There are only twelve hours left until the final launch signal. Our technicians are deactivating the system, but we're not sure it's the only one around. There could be a back-up system we're not aware of. Plus Husseini is still at large. He must have noticed something fishy because he hasn't been to his flat in days.

'Four hours ago the President was forced to make an announcement to the nation, but he hasn't revealed the whole story. The population living in the central areas of the three cities at risk are being moved into underground shelters and subway tunnels and out of the city where possible.

'It's all we've been able to do. The metropolitan areas of New York, Chicago and Los Angeles alone contain almost forty million people. If panic were to break out, the situation would spiral completely out of control. A full evacuation would require at least a week and we have only a few hours. At this point, finding Husseini is a top priority. Obviously, he knows that we know, otherwise he would have touched base. Maybe he has noticed our surveillance activities, or else someone could have tipped him off.'

'I think you're right. But it's also true that he hasn't transmitted any orders to activate the bombs, assuming that it's in his power to do so.'

'All our efforts to locate him have been in vain. He hasn't used his credit cards, hasn't purchased any gas and hasn't even withdrawn any money from an ATM. There hasn't been a sign of him. It's as though he's disappeared into thin air.'

'Husseini used to be Abu Ghaj, General. I'm sure he still knows how to survive for days without eating, drinking or washing, hiding wherever necessary, even in the sewers. Our rules of the game simply don't apply to him.'

'Unfortunately, unless we find him, we can't locate the three commando units. The Armageddon program doesn't include specific locations.'

'Even if he knows that he's been made the intermediary in a blackmail scheme – holding the US government hostage with this terrorist threat – he may well believe that it will come to an end when Islam is victorious over Israel, with the fall of Jerusalem. We can't assume he knows the bombs are programmed to go off no matter what. I am certain that Husseini is unable to read that program and properly understand it.'

'Well, then, how do you suggest we proceed?'

'Where are we going now?'

'To our operational headquarters here in Chicago. I had myself transferred here because this is where Husseini is and he's obviously the key to everything.'

They flew along in silence for a while, giving Blake an opportunity to observe the thousands of lights twinkling throughout his city, its streets and highways, as it took a dreadful pounding from the torrential rainstorm. He could see the nightmarish snarl of traffic caused by an insane evacuation. Nevertheless, he realized that he had missed the city terribly and had to do whatever he could to stop anything terrible from happening to it.

He suddenly thought of something. Turning towards the general, he said, 'There's one thing he'll be doing for sure: listening to the radio. I want you to get me a wooden Bedouin pestle and mortar right away.'

Hooker's eyes opened wide in stunned disbelief. 'Get you what?'

'You understood me: a wooden pestle and mortar like the ones the Bedouins on the Arabian peninsula use.'

'But you're talking about Stone Age implements. Where am I going to find anything like that in Chicago?'

'I haven't the foggiest idea. Have your men scour the museums, the anthropological and ethnographic institutes. Just find me these things, please ... And one more thing: find me a drummer.'

'A drummer?'

'My wrists are broken, General. Surely you don't expect me to pound the pestle in the mortar!'

Hooker shook his head in bewilderment, but he called the Chicago operations room and gave the appropriate orders. 'And I'm warning you: don't waste your time making wise cracks. We'll be landing in about ten minutes. Don't let me down on this, boys.'

The bizarre objects arrived by Pony Express from the Field Museum within half an hour and a drummer was brought in by taxi, a young black jazz musician named Kevin, who was performing downtown at the Cotton Club.

'Listen carefully, Kevin,' said Blake. 'I'm going to drum out a rhythm with my fingers on the table and I want you to imitate it by pounding the pestle inside the mortar, while these gentlemen record it on a cassette. So let's try to do a good job. Think you can handle that?'

'No problem. Piece of cake,' replied Kevin. 'I'm ready whenever you are.'

Blake began drumming with his fingers on the table as an incredulous General Hooker and the other officers looked on in utter disbelief. Kevin followed him with instinctive mastery, making his unlikely, improvised instrument come to life with a brusque yet resonant rhythm, a more than convincing rendition of the simple, evocative beat Blake had heard for the first time at Omar al Husseini's home one Christmas Eve and then again two days ago in the sheikh's tent at El Mura.

When they had finished, Blake turned to Hooker. 'Have this tape played by all the radio stations every ten minutes until I tell you to stop. We'll just have to put our faith in God.

'Right now, gentlemen, I need to go to the bathroom,' he announced, picking up his briefcase. 'I have to adjust my bandages.'

He went out into the hall and towards the door they had pointed out to him, but instead of going in, he went straight for the elevator and down to the garage level. The place was full of cars, both civilian and olive-drab military versions. He got into the first one he found with the keys in the ignition and took off, squealing his tyres, to the consternation of the approaching guard who wanted to ask to see his pass.

He drove through the torrential rain, gritting his teeth, dealing as best he could with the pain in his wrists, which was increasing now that the effect of the painkiller the doctor had given him was starting to wear off.

The main arteries were gridlocked, reduced to a tangle of

collisions, accompanied by the wild cacophony of angry horns and shouting, brawling drivers. As soon as he could, Blake slipped off the main road and found himself driving through a series of more peaceful, out-of-the-way neighbourhoods, where the people were so badly off they didn't appear to be overly concerned about the prospect of an atomic explosion.

He had turned on the radio and before he had reached his shabby old apartment, he was able to confirm that the regular programming was being interrupted to broadcast a strange, rhythmic pounding, a monotonous beat that periodically built to a crescendo of dramatically intense, hammering percussive effects. No doubt about it: that Kevin was quite the artist.

He left the car in a parking lot and ran through the driving rain all the way to his door. He pulled his keys out of his pocket and with a hefty nudge was in.

The tiny apartment was dark and cold; it looked just like he had left it two months ago. Thieves knew better than to look for valuables in a place like this.

He turned on the lights and the heat. In a cupboard crammed with canned goods, he found a package of coffee that was still sealed. He opened it, found a filter, put water into the pot and set it on the stove. He tried to tidy the place up a bit and, as he was busy putting away shoes and dusty clothes, he turned on the radio. At that particular moment it was broadcasting classical music: Haydn.

He sat down and lit a cigarette.

An hour slipped by and he could no longer hear even the slightest noise from the surrounding neighbourhood. Maybe they had all left, or perhaps they had decided to await God's judgement in reverent silence.

Once again, to no avail, the radio broadcast the haunting rhythm of the Bedouin mortar and Blake began thinking the whole scheme was totally nuts, that certain things only happened in fairy tales. He turned it off with an annoyed flick of his sore wrist and turned on the gas under the coffee. He seemed to sense the souls of Gordon and Sullivan hovering about in the tight space of his little studio, may their souls rest in peace. He wondered whose turn it would be next. His? Sarah's? How many countless other people would have to pay?

Somebody was knocking at his door.

16

'I'VE BEEN WAITING for you,' said Blake. 'Come in. Please, sit down.'

Omar al Husseini was soaking wet from the rain and could barely stand up. His hair was unkempt and his beard scraggly.

The deep circles around his bloodshot eyes revealed his sleep-deprived state.

'How did you get back here?' he asked, collapsing onto a chair. 'And what have you done to your hands?'

He was deathly pale and shivering from the cold. Blake had him take off his wet coat and he put it on a radiator. He then placed an old blanket over his shoulders and handed him a cup of steaming black coffee.

'It's fresh,' he said. 'I just made it.'

'I heard the sound of the mortar,' said Husseini with a weak smile, 'and I thought, someone around here is making coffee, and I . . .'

He didn't finish his sentence. He brought the cup to his lips and took a few sips. 'It's funny,' he said. 'Both of us are the repositories of devastating secrets . . . and just a couple of months ago we were a couple of untroubled college professors. Isn't life strange? Tell, what is the tomb of the great leader like? Did you see his face?'

Blake drew close. 'Omar, listen to me. It's your secret that can do the most damage now. We've discovered an automatic system in your computer which in six hours will trigger off three nuclear bombs in three different cities in the United States.'

PHARAOH

Husseini did not bat an eye. 'No . . . no, you're wrong. None of that will happen,' he said. 'Jerusalem is about to surrender and it will all be over. They'll stipulate some sort of a treaty and this will all just be history soon. You know as well as I do that there's no place in the world where an individual could override the safeguards that stop a nuclear weapon from actually being set off. There won't be any bombs exploding.'

'And you think we can afford to run this risk just on the basis that you hope it won't happen? You know that's crazy, Omar. Or shall I call you . . . Abu Ghaj?' This time Husseini raised his head suddenly and met Blake's eyes as he continued relentlessly, 'My God, how could you have agreed to help plan the deaths of millions of innocent people?'

'That's not true! I fought when it was time, and I thought I'd done my part. I thought it was all over . . . but sometimes your past catches up with you. Even when you think you've buried it forever. They came asking me to hold this threat over the heads of the Americans until the rights of our people were restored . . . That's all. And that's what I've done. What I had to do. But I'm no executioner. There won't be any slaughter of the innocents.'

'Six hours, Omar, and millions of people will die unless we can manage to stop this implacable mechanism. Only you can help. I've given Pentagon technicians the password to the file you've called Armageddon. Do you believe me now?'

Husseini widened his fatigue-reddened eyes. 'But how—'

'There's no time to explain it now. There's one thing I have to know. If the computer is cut out while the program is being executed, what happens?'

'I don't know.'

'Where are the "donkeys" bought at the Samarkand market?'

Husseini reacted with even greater surprise at the realization that Blake was familiar with the language in the most protected files of his computer.

'I can't talk about that.'

'You have to.'

335

'If I do . . . I have a son, Blake. A son I thought was dead, a son to whose memory I dedicated every action, every assault, every gunfight, over all those years that the fame of the exterminator Abu Ghaj spread across the globe. I thought I had buried him in a squalid cemetery in the Bekaa Valley, but they've given me proof that he's alive and he's in their hands. If I talk there's no limit to the suffering they could inflict on him. You wouldn't understand . . . You can't begin to imagine . . . There's a world in which poverty, hunger and endless war kill off any form of compassion, make any horror possible . . .'

'But even Abraham was ready to sacrifice his only son because God asked him to. You're being asked by thousands of innocent men, women and children who would be burned alive, or contaminated by radiation and condemned to living their lives in agony. Omar, I can prove that they've lied to you. The bombs will explode even if Jerusalem surrenders and falls to its knees, begging for mercy. Hold on, let me prove it to you.'

He picked up the phone and dialled a number. 'This is William Blake,' he said. 'Pass me over to General Hooker.'

'Blake!' cried Hooker as he picked up the line. 'What have you done? Where the hell are you? We need you here to—'

Blake cut him off. 'General, please tell me what's happening with the Armageddon program.' He gestured for Husseini to get closer so he could listen in on the conversation.

'We're working on Husseini's computer, but it's just as we feared. Our technicians have figured out how to block the detonation procedure but, if they do so, an auxiliary command will be given for a second system. If they turn that one off the same thing will happen again. The bombs are timed to explode at half-hourly intervals. The first one will explode in four hours and forty minutes, and the others will follow. We've asked the Russians to help us to defuse them, but there's nothing they can do unless we can tell them what type of bombs they are.'

'General,' he said, looking straight into Husseini's eyes, 'I hope to have some important information to give you soon.

Don't move from there for any reason and . . . tell Miss Forrestall that I'm thinking of her, if you should see her.'

'Blake! Damn it, tell me where—'

Blake hung up and said to Husseini with an expressionless voice: 'More coffee, Omar?'

Husseini fell back in his chair and lowered his eyes, closing himself into a silence that seemed endless in the little bare room. When he raised his eyes they were full of tears.

He put his hand into his inside jacket pocket and took out a little black box. 'This device contains a copy of the program that's in the computer. They told me to carry it with me whenever I had to leave the main computer. That's all I know.'

'Can it be connected to the phone?'

Husseini nodded. 'The hook-up's inside. There's also a little plastic card that contains the password.'

Blake opened the box and found the card. It contained a word in cuneiform characters that spelled out Nebuchadnezzar.

He said, 'Thank you, Omar, you've done the right thing. And now let's hope that luck is on our side.'

He called the switchboard again and had them pass him to General Hooker.

'General, I have the back-up system. Press the voice button on your phone. I want your computer technician to hear this. OK, the unit I'm holding in my hand looks like a very powerful, sophisticated portable computer. I'm hooking it up to my phone now. You can connect this line to your main computer and download it. As soon as you're asked for a password, type in "Home" and a sequence of cuneiform letters will appear. Click on that word and the program will open. General, you can have them stop with the radio broadcast. We don't need it any more. Good luck.'

He sat and watched the LEDs lighting up on the little display, signalling the flow of information through the telephone lines.

'Is there any coffee left?' asked Husseini.

'Certainly,' said Blake. 'How about a smoke?'

He poured the coffee and lit a cigarette for him.

They sat in silence opposite each other as the room got warmer, listening to the tapping rain on the foggy windowpanes. Blake checked his watch: 200 minutes to the start of the apocalypse.

Husseini sat shivering. Neither the blanket on his shoulders, nor the hot coffee could overcome the chill inside him.

Abruptly the little LEDs blinked off: the data transmission was complete. Blake unplugged the computer and hung up the receiver.

He waited a few minutes before calling them back. 'It's Blake. Any news? Yes ... I understand, the abandoned factory at the intersection of the Stevenson and Dan Ryan expressways. No, it's not too far from here. We can meet in the parking lot at Wells and 37th in half an hour. Fine, General. See you there.'

He hung up and turned to Husseini.

'They've found the bombs. The one here in Chicago is at the intersection of the Stevenson and the Dan Ryan, in the abandoned Hoover Bearings factory. It's being guarded by at least three armed terrorists. One of them, the only one who isn't wearing a face mask, is stationed in the control booth of a crane, thirty metres up from the ground. He's armed with a machine gun. Thousands of people are on those expressways, trying to get out of the city. The subway tunnel is right there; the train lines are close by as well. If the bomb explodes, the consequences couldn't be more disastrous. Don't go anywhere. I'll come back here to get you.'

Husseini didn't answer, although he had had a sudden flash of understanding. Abu Ahmid had never stopped considering him a deserter and he realized now, with absolute clarity, what punishment had been prepared for him.

Blake walked down the rain- and wind-racked street to his car and set off towards the site. Police cars were reversing crazily in every direction and sirens on the street corners sounded an alarm every few minutes, like in an old war film.

He had just reached the parking lot when he saw Hooker's car turn off at 37th Street. He sounded his horn repeatedly.

'The special assault teams are already in place, Blake. What are you planning to do?' shouted Hooker from his car window.

'I'm coming with you!' yelled Blake.

He got out of his car and into the general's and they took off at top speed. Sitting next to the driver in front was Captain McBain.

'Do you know how to stop the priming sequence?' asked Blake as soon as he sat down.

'No, we don't,' admitted Hooker. 'But I've sent the best men we have. Let's hope we can do it. We're still on line with the Russians. As soon as we see the bombs and can describe them, they'll try to figure out the model and send us the defusing procedure.'

'How much time have we got?'

'The special assault team left fifteen minutes ago in a helicopter and should be at the site already. They have sixty minutes. It could be enough.'

'They've run into problems, sir,' interrupted McBain.

'What's happening?'

'The resistance is worse than anticipated. The terrorists are holed up inside the old factory. There are at least three men armed with rocket launchers and machine guns. One of our helicopters has been downed.'

'Damn, that's all we need,' grumbled Hooker.

'They're trying to buy time,' added Blake. 'Weren't there any specifics in Husseini's files?'

'No, nothing at all,' said Hooker. 'Except that word – donkeys. But donkeys are donkeys.'

'Yeah, but . . . wait a minute.'

'What?'

'You could ask your friends in Moscow the Russian word for "donkey". Maybe it means something. Maybe military slang,' mused Blake, thinking out loud.

'Wait, hold on a second, Blake. McBain, have them pass you the line with Captain Orloff in Moscow. Ask him how they say "donkey" in Russian and if the word means anything else to him.'

McBain connected to his Russian colleague and put the question to him. Astonishment evident on his face, he was soon repeating, 'O-s-jo-l.'

'Oblonsky . . . sistema . . . jomkostnogo . . . limita.'

'Oblonsky limited capacity system. Bingo! *Spasibo, spasibo, Kapitan!*' he shouted enthusiastically to the Russian officer, and then turned to his superior. 'The initials do mean something, General Hooker!'

McBain, still listening to his Russian colleague through his earphones, used the other line to communicate with the special assault team. 'This is Golf Bravo One, do you read me, Sky Riders?'

'This is Sky Riders. We've got the situation under control. The two commandos inside the factory are dead but the third is still up on the crane. We have one dead and three wounded. And we have the bomb.'

'Attention, Sky Riders, we have the detonation override code. It must be transmitted to the other teams in Los Angeles and New York. Attention, this requires your full attention. I will be giving you the instructions directly from Moscow, who is on the other line. Repeat, Sky Riders, any error can be fatal. Don't let the third terrorist out of your sight. He could be very dangerous.'

'We've got a team looking to take him out. Proceed with instructions. We're ready to roll, Golf Bravo One,' said the voice on the other end of the line.

Their car arrived at its destination ten minutes later, and while McBain remained on board to continue transmitting the instructions from Moscow, General Hooker and Blake got out and ran towards the building. They instantly found themselves under machine-gun and rifle fire. The entire area was powerfully illuminated by photoelectric cells, but many of the bulbs had been destroyed in the shoot-out.

The captain leading the special assault team immediately dragged them behind cover. The storm continued to rage on and the lot in front of the factory was invaded by angry gusts of wind and freezing rain.

'Foul weather, isn't it, sir?' The officer had to shout to be heard over the noise of the storm and the gunshots.

'Where's the bomb?' asked Hooker.

'Up there, General,' replied the officer, pointing to the top floor of the old factory. 'But the third terrorist is barricaded in the crane booth and he's got us in his sights.'

Blake tried to shield his eyes from the squalling rain with his hands as he looked up towards the enormous trestle on which the long crane jib swung, pushed by the wind.

The barrel of a machine gun protruded from the booth, spurting fire against the assault team stationed around the building, who immediately responded by attacking the steel girders and walls with their guns. Each burst of fire set off a sort of prolonged, sinister pealing in the entire structure, sending sparks cascading like tiny bolts of lightning in the raging storm.

The gigantic structure started to vibrate and revolve on its axis.

'Oh, Christ!' said Blake. 'He's rotating the jib. If he positions it crosswise to the wind, he'll cause the entire structure to come crashing down onto the expressway. Captain, send someone to disengage the clutch, for God's sake.'

The officer signalled to one of his men, who hurried forward under a rain of bullets to the base of the tower and began to climb up the iron ladder.

At that moment, a window in the crane cabin opened and a man crawled out onto the boom as the jib continued to rotate. He was about twenty-five years old and his face was uncovered. Amazingly agile, he was somehow managing to avoid the bullets that whistled past him. For a moment he looked down and it seemed that he would fall. And suddenly Blake heard a desperate cry behind him. It was Husseini.

He was standing stock still in the pouring rain and yelling, 'Said! Said!' He ran across the big lot in front of the building to the tower of steel. He was shouting as loudly as he could, his face streaked with tears and rain. He was shouting at the youth who continued to advance towards the tip of the crane's jib.

Blake whispered excitedly into Hooker's ear and the general raised his arm to order a cease-fire, while the leader of the assault team relayed the order to his men as well.

Even the storm seemed to obey that order and the downpour subsided, while the force of the wind lessened.

Husseini's voice rang out even louder: *'Said! Said! Ana wali-duka! Ana waliduka!'*

'What is he saying?' asked Hooker.

Blake looked back wide-eyed. 'He's saying, "Said! Said! I'm your father! I'm your father!"'

Hooker watched the rain-drenched man in the middle of the lot and the youth who continued to crawl towards the outer tip of the jig. His weight on the long arm, almost completely crosswise to the force of the wind, made the whole structure shake precariously.

'Oh, my God,' muttered Hooker.

The youth on the jib was rising to his feet and the officer who was watching his every move with a pair of binoculars shouted, 'Watch out! He's full of explosives! Take him out! Fire! Fire!'

A shot hit him in the leg and the young man staggered.

Husseini swung around, gripping a gun. 'Stop!' he yelled, out of his mind. 'Don't shoot! Stop or I'll kill you!'

The officer gestured to his men and, just as Husseini was about to pull the trigger, a shot brought him to his knees. As he fell, he raised his eyes to the sky and saw his son dragging himself to the very tip of the jib, from where he dived into the void, an angel of death making for the river of cars on the highway below. But as soon as he had taken wing a furious fusillade was heard.

The boy was caught in mid-air by the special operations snipers and his body simply disintegrated.

His blood fell along with the rain onto the face and shoulders of his dying father.

Blake leapt forward running towards Husseini through the deserted lot, shouting, 'Omar! Omar!' A rivulet of blood dyed the water streaming under his body pink. Blake took him into his arms; he was still breathing. 'Omar . . .'

Husseini opened eyes already dulled by death. He said, 'You went east. Did you see . . . did you see the columns of Apamea? Did you . . . see them?'

'Yes,' said Blake, his eyes glassy. 'Yes, I did see them, Omar. They were pale in the light of dawn, like virgins awaiting their husbands, and red at dusk, like pillars of fire, my friend . . .' And he held him close as he died.

THE CRANE groaned and creaked in the wind, which was picking up again, but the special force operator managed to reach the cabin at the top and disengaged the transmission. The jib, now swinging free, rotated slowly on its platform until it came to rest, immobile, in the direction of the wind.

The assault team captain approached General Hooker. 'The bomb has been disabled, sir, and so have the other two. The operation is concluded.'

'Thank you, Captain,' said Hooker. 'Thank you for a job well done.' He crossed the lot on foot to where Blake was still kneeling. He put a hand on his shoulder and said, 'It's over, son. Come on, let's take you to a hospital. Someone has to take care of those arms of yours or you'll lose them.'

Blake got into Hooker's car and said, 'Take me to Sarah, please.'

He found her sleeping, sedated and receiving a blood transfusion. He asked if he could sit in the waiting room until she woke up and the doctor on duty agreed to let him do so.

343

The room was empty. There were sofas along the wall and a TV, turned off, in a corner. On one side, near the window, were a table and lamp.

He sat down, opened his briefcase and began reading. The first human being to read the Breasted papyrus in three thousand and two hundred years.

A nurse came up to him in the middle of the night and said, 'Mr Blake, she's awake now. You can talk to her, but you will have to be very brief, as she's still in a critical condition.'

Blake closed the briefcase and followed her.

Sarah's left shoulder was bandaged and she had a drip in her right arm.

'Hello, darling,' he said. 'We did it. You were incredible.'

'I can't see myself,' said Sarah, 'but I'll bet you look worse than I do.'

'Yeah, well, it was a long day. I'm lucky to look like anything.'

Sarah fell silent for a moment, turning her face towards the pillow and then back towards him. She looked straight into his eyes. 'We're the only ones left who know the secret of Ras Udash,' she said. 'Maybe it would have been better if I had been blown up with everyone else.'

Blake caressed her forehead. 'Don't say that, darling,' he said. 'You're wrong.'

GAD AVNER put on his old combat uniform, buckling up the belt, slipped his Remington calibre thirty-eight into the holster and took the elevator down to the basement, where about a dozen men from the special forces were waiting in a couple of Jeeps. Armed to the hilt, they were dressed in black and their faces were covered by ski masks.

Their commander introduced himself. 'Lieutenant Nahal, at your command, sir.'

They got into Jeeps with special darkened windows and drove down the deserted streets of the city until they had reached the Antonian Fortress archway.

Ygael Allon was waiting at the entrance to the tunnel and did not seem terribly surprised to see the civil engineer in combat fatigues. He guided the men through the passage to the start of the second section. At the point where the stairs leading under the base of the Temple began, the wall appeared completely solid.

'The men who did the work were brought here blindfolded after long walks through the city to disorient them,' said Lieutenant Nahal into Avner's ear. 'Once the job was completed, they were brought back to their quarters using the same procedure. As you can see, there's not the slightest trace on the wall. Besides us, only the Prime Minister himself knows about this passage.'

'Good work,' said Avner, 'and now let's get on with it. We don't want to be late for our appointment.'

Fifteen minutes later, they reached the end of the tunnel, where the ramp had been completely cleared.

'In ancient times, the tunnel led out into the open countryside at this point, behind the siege lines,' said Allon. 'Nebuchadnezzar's camp couldn't have been far from here, in that direction. Good luck, Mr Cohen.' And he turned back alone.

The men ascended the ramp until they reached a kind of trapdoor. They opened it and found themselves inside a house already guarded by their fellow soldiers.

Avner, accompanied by a couple of his men, went upstairs, where his technicians had set up a listening post.

'Their Silkworms are scheduled to be launched in the direction of Beersheba at ten tonight. They're using mobile launching ramps, sir, and the report of a ramp aimed at Jerusalem has been confirmed. Probably gas. The countdown begins in half an hour,' said Nahal.

Avner looked at the stopwatch on his wrist. 'Get the helicopters out and occupy points four, six and eight of the operation plan. We'll move in exactly seven minutes' time.'

The men grouped around the exits and Nahal drew closer to Avner. 'Please allow me to insist, sir. There's no reason for you to take part in combat. We can handle it. If Abu Ahmid is hiding out in that house, we'll bring him back here, tied hand and foot.'

'No,' said Avner. 'It's an old story that has to be settled between the two of us. He was the one who led the ambush in which my son was killed in Lebanon. I want to do this personally, if I may.'

'But sir, there's no saying that Abu Ahmid is down there. You could be risking your life in vain at this critical moment.'

'I'm sure he's there. The bastard wants to be the first to enter the city deserted by her inhabitants, just like Nebuchadnezzar. He's there, I can smell him. And you leave him to me, Nahal. Do you understand?'

'Yes, sir.'

The officer looked at his watch, then raised and lowered his arm. His men sprang silently out of all the exits, sliding along the walls towards their objective.

On the other side of the city, about half a mile from where they were, the sound of helicopters and machine guns could be heard. Their diversionary manoeuvre had commenced with perfect timing.

Nahal's commando unit was just a few metres from its objective now, a little whitewashed building surrounded on every side by taller buildings which hid it from sight. On the rooftop a powerful radio antenna was being raised as they watched, masked by laundry and rugs hung out all around.

'Just like you predicted, sir,' said Nahal. 'We're ready for the assault.'

'Proceed,' ordered Avner.

Nahal signalled to his men. Four of them slipped up on the guards posted at the front and rear entrances of the house, taking them out with daggers, swiftly and silently.

Avner advanced with Lieutenant Nahal to the windows. Nahal nodded and his men threw a cluster of flash grenades and rushed in, shooting everything in sight with deadly precision.

Nahal moved into the next room and took out a man sitting in front of a radar screen. He saw the mobile ramp reference signals, which were beginning to become stronger.

'Here they are,' he shouted. 'They're coming out into the open!' He called headquarters. 'This is Barak calling Melech Israel. Ramps identified. Launch the fighters. Grid 264 788. I say again, grid 264 788, over.'

'We read you, Barak. Is the Fox with you?'

Nahal wheeled around and just caught sight of Avner as he disappeared down a hallway. He came to a stop and fired three or four times in quick succession. Nahal shouted to his men, 'Cover him!' Into the microphone he reported, 'The Fox is hunting his prey.' With that, he took off after his men.

Avner was heading down a second hallway, with a trapdoor at its end. He lunged forward, opened the hatch and descended the small staircase on the other side.

'No!' shouted Nahal. 'Wait!'

But Avner had already disappeared underground. Nahal followed with his men.

Avner stopped for a moment, heard the footsteps of a man escaping and shot in that direction. He ran forward and found himself in an underground chamber, its ceiling supported by a dozen brick columns. There were cases and cases of weapons and ammunition everywhere. At the centre of the room was the base of the large retractable radio antenna.

'Secure the entire area!' he ordered and, as the men were combing the room, he ran towards a staircase that led up to the surface. He lifted another trapdoor and found himself outside. Helicopters were hovering low, tasked to eliminate any snipers in the area.

Avner saw a figure running along the wall and he shouted, 'Stop or I'll shoot!'

The man turned, a fraction of a second, and Avner recognized his flashing eyes under the keffiyeh. He took the shot, but the man had already vanished around the corner.

Nahal and his men pulled up short, stopped by a group of women and children, who were milling about in the road.

'He's in there someplace, damn it! Surround the block and search the houses one by one!'

The men obeyed but there was no trace of Abu Ahmid.

Lieutenant Nahal turned back to Avner, who was leaning against the corner of the house where – for a single moment – he had seen his enemy face to face.

'I'm sorry, sir, we haven't found him anywhere. Are you sure you got a good look? Sure it was him?'

'Sure as sin. And I wounded him,' he added, pointing to a spray of blood on the edge of the wall. 'He's got my bullet in him. Just a little advance payment, but I'll settle the account before these things kill me off,' he said, lighting a cigarette. 'Have this shack razed to the ground and let's go home.'

As they gathered at the helicopter pick-up point, Nahal got a call from headquarters. 'This is Melech Israel here,' said the easily recognizable voice of General Yehudai. 'Are you reading me, Barak?'

'Operation concluded, Melech Israel. Objective destroyed.'

'Ditto here,' said the General. 'The ramps were blown up three minutes ago. Pass me your boss.'

Lieutenant Nahal handed the earphones to Avner. 'It's for you, sir.'

'Avner.'

'Yehudai here. It's all over, Avner. The "Gabriel" launch procedure has been suspended. The Americans have defused the bombs. Reinforcement fighters are taking off from five aircraft carriers in the Mediterranean.'

'Five, you said? Which are they?'

'Two are American: the *Nimitz* and the *Enterprise*. Three of them are European: the *Aragòn*, *Clemenceau* and *Garibaldi*.'

'The *Garibaldi* too? Won't Ferrario be pleased. Over and out, Melech Israel. I hope you'll buy me a beer before we call it a night.'

They boarded the helicopter, which rose up over the city. In the west, a hollow roar soon turned into a thunderous explosion and a thousand ribbons of fire streaked across the sky.

Avner turned to Lieutenant Nahal, who was just taking off his ski mask. 'Any news of Lieutenant Ferrario?'

Nahal hesitated a moment, then said, 'Lieutenant Ferrario has been reported missing in action, sir.'

'He'll make it through,' replied Avner. 'He's too quick for them,' he added, his gaze wandering off towards the Judaean desert and the barren Moab hills.

EPILOGUE

GAD AVNER finished his beer at the bar of the King David Hotel, but when he pulled out his wallet, a voice behind him said, 'Let me get it, sir, if I may.'

Avner turned around and found himself facing Fabrizio Ferrario. He was wearing a finely tailored light blue linen suit and had a beautiful tan.

'I'm glad you made it through, Ferrario. Leaving for somewhere?'

'Yes, sir, and I wanted to say goodbye before I left.'

'Did you remember to bring home those things I told you about?'

Ferrario glanced down at the crotch of his trousers. 'They were there last time I looked, sir.'

'Magnificent. Well, then, have a good trip.'

'Will you come and visit me in Venice?'

'I'd like that. Who knows. Maybe, one day, once I've retired from this damn job.'

'Otherwise here, in Jerusalem, whenever you need me. *Shalom*, Mr Avner.'

'*Shalom*, my boy. Say hello to your lovely city for me.'

Avner watched him walk off. He thought of all those beautiful girls who were surely waiting for him in Italy and sighed.

He threw his overcoat round his shoulders and left the bar, walking through the streets of the old city until he found himself in front of his house. He went in and took the stairs all the way up, slowly, as he did whenever he'd managed not to overdo the cigarettes. When he got to his landing and paused to catch his breath, a voice he had not heard for some time sounded from a dark corner.

'Good evening, sir.'

Avner was slightly startled but did not turn. He said, as he was turning the key in the lock, 'Hello, night porter. Frankly, I never thought we'd meet again.'

'I believe you. It wasn't easy to outlive all those cut-throats you sent out after me. From land and sky.'

Avner opened the door and gestured for his unexpected guest to enter. 'Come in, Professor Blake. I imagine you have something to say to me.'

Blake walked in. Avner switched on a light and indicated a chair, then sat down himself. He brought his hands to his face. 'You have a gun in that briefcase, don't you? You've come to kill me,' he said. 'Go ahead, if you want. For me there's no difference between living and dying.'

'We had a pact,' said Blake.

'That's true. I had you released from fifteen years of prison in Egypt. You, in return, were to continue researching the Breasted papyrus, for us this time, providing us with any useful information you found in the course of your research.'

'And that's what I did. Taking considerable risks. So why . . .'

Avner cracked a mocking smile. 'The unexpected, Blake. Unforeseen circumstances are those that determine the course of events. When my agents went to Chicago to bring you the documents you'd need to establish a new identity and a new cover that would get you back into Egypt, you weren't there any more. You'd disappeared. At first I thought that the shock of being kicked out of your university had proved too much for you, but then I heard your voice.'

Blake widened his eyes. 'That's impossible. But then . . . Gordon and Sullivan—'

'They never worked for me. I didn't even know their names before you started talking about them. Now, if you had violated the rule that you were given – never speak of the organization or refer to the true identity of another agent, not even with the person himself – you would have realized the truth right away.'

'I always respect the terms of an agreement.'

'So do I. When I can. The first time you called, I realized immediately that something was wrong. But what you were discovering was even more interesting. And so I let you continue, as if it had all been prearranged. It was extraordinary how you reported in without ever referring to yourself in the first person, not even when you were talking about your own dig. Extraordinary! A natural talent.'

'I was following the security measures you had given me. You can never be sure that someone isn't listening in.'

'That's right.'

'And yet you ordered the massacre at Ras Udash! Pointless slaughter! Then you unleashed everyone you could on me: the Israelis, the Egyptians, the Americans—'

'Pointless?' Avner jumped out of his chair, incensed. 'You stupid, naïve American. Do you realize what consequences your discovery would have had if the world had found out about it? Blake, you would have deprived most of humanity of their faith in eternity! You would have wiped out what remains of the spirit, the soul, of Western civilization. And you would have destroyed the identity of my people. Isn't that enough for you? I would have done what I did for much less.'

'So, if I don't kill you now, I'll never leave this country alive.'

'No, you won't,' said Avner. 'You should never have come here.'

'You're wrong. You'd just be committing another senseless murder.'

'So you still don't understand,' said Avner as he watched Blake's hand slip into his briefcase. His thoughts wandered, and he knew that he didn't care about anything any more and that he had absolutely no desire to fight back. He turned his gaze to a photograph on the tabletop, of a young man of about twenty, and said, 'Hurry up if you're going to do it. I can't stand indecision.'

Blake didn't say anything, but placed a white folder on the table.

'What's that?' asked Avner, suddenly perturbed.

'The Breasted papyrus. I always live up to my word. My translation is alongside. If you trust me.'

Avner opened the folder. The colours and the ideograms of the papyrus shone under a sheet of protective plastic. He began to read the translation, his expression filling, line by line, with increasing amazement and consternation:

> *From Pepitamon, scribe and overseer of the sacred palaces of the Royal Harem, humble servant of your Majesty,*
> *to the princess Bastet Nefrere, light of Upper and Lower Egypt. Greetings.*
>
> *I followed the Habiru from Pi-Ramses through the Sea of Reeds as you commanded me, and then into the desert of the east, where they wandered for years living on locusts and roots. I lived like them and spoke like them. I ate what they ate and drank the bitter water of the wells and only in secret did I pray to the great Gods of Egypt.*
>
> *On the day that the Habiru went back to worshipping Apis the sacred bull, melting their golden earrings to build an image, I rejoiced, hoping that even the heart of your beloved son Moses would be won over. But Moses destroyed the Bull, committing a sacrilege, and built an altar to the God of the Habiru and a wretched sanctuary made of goat skins.*
>
> *When his time came and Moses became ill and died, the Habiru buried him in a hole in the sand, like the carcass of a dog or a jackal, without even a marker that remembered his name.*
>
> *Since I could not bring him back to Egypt, His Majesty having forbidden the return of the exile, I waited until his people had gone, and then I did your will. I had our quarrymen and stone-*

cutters come all the way to the heart of the desert, where they excavated a tomb worthy of a prince. The place I chose was the same where Moses had raised his sanctuary of goat skins, so that it might be purified.

I embalmed his body and I laid a finely fashioned mask on his face. I added the images of the gods and everything that a great prince could need for his journey to the Immortal Place and the fields of Yaru. And I have ensured that the secret will never be violated. No one left that place alive, except your humble servant.

May Osiris, Isis and Horus protect Your Majesty and your humble servant Pepitamon, who prostrates himself in the dust before you.

'You killed them for nothing,' said Blake when Avner had finished reading. 'It's true that Moses was buried according to Egyptian ritual, in the tomb of Ras Udash. But he was already dead, and it was done against his last wish.'

'I . . . I could never have imagined . . . and neither could you, Blake. No one could have imagined this. Where is the tomb, Blake? Where is he buried?'

'I won't tell you, Avner. Because where he was buried is also the site of the tent sanctuary, the place where the Ark was hidden during the siege of Jerusalem. I saw it, Avner. The Ark. I saw it shining through the dense dust. I saw the golden wings of the cherubs. But you have the nuclear bombs of Beersheba, Avner. You don't need the Ark of the Covenant.

'Oh, I was forgetting,' he added. He reached into his jacket pocket, extracted a small transmitter shaped like a fountain pen and laid it on the table. 'I can only use this to communicate with you, and, frankly, I have nothing more to say.' He left and closed the door behind him.

When he was at the bottom of the stairs, he heard a pistol shot, dampened by a silencer. He turned on the landing and looked up.

'Goodbye, Mr Avner,' he said. '*Shalom.*'

And he left, losing himself in the crowd.

AUTHOR'S NOTE

The idea for this novel emerged during my four excavation campaigns at Har Karkom in the Negev desert of Israel, several kilometres south of the Mitzpe Ramon crater. The place was apparently insignificant, a windswept landscape carved by erosion, but the mountain hid a secret. All around its base were traces of dozens of semi-nomadic settlements, with altars, shrines and necropolises testifying to human presence there from Palaeolithic times to the Hellenistic age. At the peak of the mountain we found signs of a sanctuary; on the plateau surrounding it I excavated a large mound of flint blocks that contained a single artefact: a piece of white limestone carved into a half-moon shape. I hypothesized that the mountain had been consecrated to the moon-god *Sin*. Along with other finds, this led the director of the mission, Professor E. Anati, to believe that Har Karkom might be the true Mount *Sin-ai* of the Bible. Over thirty thousand stone carvings have been identified and catalogued on the mountain's slopes, but on the land surrounding it there is no trace of human activity for kilometres and kilometres, not a single scratch or symbol. Some of the carvings on the mountain are very striking because they reproduce biblical symbols, such as the staff and the serpent, a man praying before a fire or a burning bush, two tablets divided into ten sections and an oft-repeated eye, hinting at an invisible but ubiquitous presence. On Mount Karkom proper there are no traces of human presence after the early Bronze Age (in fact, the beds of the Palaeolithic huts are still perfectly conserved), possibly indicating that it had become taboo to set foot on the mountain itself.

The events that lead up to the story told in the first chapter are inspired by the Book of Kings as well as the Book of Baruch, which reveals that the prophet Jeremiah hid the Ark of the Covenant at Mount Horeb (Sinai) and returned to Jerusalem two weeks later, coincidentally the exact amount of time it would take for a man on foot to reach Mount Karkom from Jerusalem and make his return. Not too far from Har Karkom there is another mountain topped by enigmatic stone platforms which may be altars, on which traces of extremely high-temperature fires have been found. I excavated one of these platforms, but was unable to find a single element that could help me to understand its significance.

The rest of the story is pure imagination, but the reader will soon notice that the plot embodies the threat of a monstrous terrorist assault on US soil, although using different means and methods than the attack of September 11th, 2001. The novel was first published three years before 9/11 and could not have foreseen the actual turn of events, but I was certainly influenced by the premonition of an imminent act of extreme violence, made inevitable, to my mind, by the clash of civilizations. The novel also hypothesizes that in a time of great political tension, such as that engendered by the situation in Israel and Palestine, a chance discovery might rock consolidated religious 'certainties' and seriously destabilize the balance of international power.

The story is told in the fashion of a classic international thriller, but it contains many well-founded – and quite chilling – suggestions and hypotheses, which I hope will not pass unnoticed.

Valerio Massimo Manfredi
Christmas 2007